Blood Moon

PAINTING THE MISTS, BOOK 2

PATRICK G. LAPLANTE

Published by:

Patrick G. Laplante

Third Edition, 2019

ISBN: 978-1-989578-07-0

Dedication

To all the good people in the world.
May they be blessed for all the sacrifices they willingly make.

Author's Note

Thank you all for your support as I continue to write the story of my dreams. As I write this note, I'm a half dozen chapters into Book 3, which will be roughly the same length as this book. I wrote all of Book 2 with Book 3 on my mind. As such, this second book has been written with special care, and it is crucial in the development of all my key characters.

As the title suggests, *Blood Moon* is a key turning point in all the point-of-view characters' otherwise peaceful lives. Violence and heinous deeds take their toll on the victims, the perpetrators, and the heroes who fight against them. It isn't easy being good. Many choices and sacrifices must be made to help others, and it is rarely as simple as lending a cup of sugar to a neighbor in need.

As you read this book, I would like you to focus on a key question. What is choice? And what is destiny? Most people simply go with the flow, and they don't truly *choose* anything. Choice entails freedom, and every choice has a consequence. Cha Ming and his friends have been living sheltered lives all this time.

And now, the gloves come off.

Prologue

A black-robed stranger urged his horse forward along a clay trail. The clay was dried and cracked, likely due to the lack of rain in recent months. It was winter, though winter in this part of the continent did not necessarily mean snow. Instead of snow, the trees and yellow-green grass were all covered in frost every morning, which would dissipate once the sun came out. While the scenery was beautiful, it went by unappreciated. The black-robed stranger didn't bother to look anywhere but forward as he continued urging his horse toward the village.

Of course, he had enjoyed sightseeing at some point in his life. In fact, he had once traveled throughout the four neighboring kingdoms with great gusto, sampling the various delicacies and painting the beautiful sceneries. There was no greater joy in life than perfectly capturing a moment on a canvas.

Unfortunately, that was all in the past. His greatest joy now was surviving yet another day and seeing his daughter once a month. And that didn't happen unless he stayed focused on his work. Therefore, the beautiful scenery went by unnoticed by this man who would have loved to appreciate it.

As the man traveled, he took note of bleating sheep, which were somewhat agitated at being gathered. They were pasture animals, used to wandering around and eating grass all year round. Such a large gathering only happened twice per year—during shearing and during culling. It was currently only midway through winter, therefore it was not yet time for shearing.

The man quickly put such things out of his thoughts and focused instead on the road ahead. Those who didn't focus on the road ahead made mistakes, like urging their horse to step into a deep puddle and thereby breaking their ankle. That would lead to costly delays and could ultimately cost him his job. Without his job, how would he and his daughter survive?

Soon the man arrived at a small town. He passed by many people, and while it was not as bustling as a larger city, everyone here was in a hurry. Not a single person could be seen walking slowly. As if to emphasize his thoughts, an agitated clerk ran out of the building he had halted in front of. He quickly collected the purse of gold the man passed him, as well as the ledger which accompanied the bag. The clerk exchanged these with another ledger containing the man's next mission. They didn't greet each other, since it was a waste of time. Their business completed, the man proceeded to a small inn. Tomorrow was the day that he had custody of his daughter, so he wanted to be fully refreshed for their meeting.

The town never used to be so busy. That was, until the Merchant came. He brought with him great opportunity and great hardship. The rider was an example of a man whose family had been torn apart by the Merchant's arrival. The clerk, on the other hand, was one of the few examples of those who saw great success with the Merchant's coming.

The Merchant had always been a calculating man. Back when he was a store owner in the capital, he had always been exact and fair. Further, he had always been rigorous in his accounting. Whenever his customers tried to cheat him, he supressed them. Whenever thieves stole his goods, he always demanded the maximum punishment allowed by the law, even if the price of prosecuting the thief exceeded the damage to his property.

Likewise, he had always been particularly strict with his employees. The many checks and audits he had incorporated over the years had kept embezzlements to a limit. His rates of embezzlement were the lowest in the entire country for the volume of business he dealt with.

Occasionally, he caught a schemer who tried to line his pockets with his rightly earned gold. He was always sure to make the strictest examples of these people. It was a matter of principle, after all, the cost be damned.

This was all in the past, however. He spotted several examples of corruption as he pored over a paper copy of his current accounts. They were blatant and unhidden, as though they were advertising their "good" behavior. All that mattered to him now was the ever-increasing amount of gold that filled his vast pockets. Consequences be damned! He was especially delighted whenever one of his minions managed to cheat one of his many customers.

After confirming that his accounts were still aggressively growing, he walked downstairs and grabbed a bite to eat from a nearby employee's lunch. The pitiful employee didn't dare protest, lest the Merchant take more from the meager fare he had prepared for the day. In fact, he was currently worried that the food might displease the skinny man, propelling him into a fit of uncontrollable rage. The Merchant never bought food, relying on his fearful subordinates to fill his stomach. Even then, he ate very little, as though frugality was part of his very being.

After finishing his brief meal, the Merchant walked outside onto a poorly maintained street in the small town he currently occupied. All those who saw him gave him a wide berth, granting him a twenty-foot kill zone in every direction.

His current destination was the pleasure house, where they trained some of their more profitable merchandise. The door was quickly opened for him as soon as he arrived. The doorman sweated profusely as he chastised himself for almost being late in opening the door. He was paid handsomely for his services, as the owner of the establishment knew that the Merchant especially valued his time. Time was money, after all.

After walking through a few more promptly opened doors, the Merchant arrived in front of the latest group of fresh "recruits." The selection process was quite simple. Every time they took a village, they first separated the men and the women. The women would then be separated into two categories: the chaste and the beautiful. Those who were both chaste and beautiful were especially prized. The ugly were not even considered, and their fate could only be imagined.

Innocence was of primary importance to the process. Virtues like kindness, purity, and humility would be transformed in unimaginable ways, until a final product was produced. Slaves produced in this fashion possessed many advantages, undying loyalty being only one of them. To the Merchant, their resulting depravity was only a meaningless consequence of his end goal: profit.

After completing his business in the pleasure house, the Merchant continued his daily inspection. A small group of skinny monks and boys were chained to a wall. For the next month, they were to be fed increasingly large amounts of food, building the appetite of these formerly small eaters. The remainder of the process was a secret, but the result was not. Those who survived would be trained as the toughest slave warriors.

Finally, the Merchant arrived at the last training house, the house of choice. The training program in the house of choice was different from the others. The facility was also much larger than the other training houses, since many "assistants" were required for every candidate.

There was no age limitation for a candidate; the only requirement was that the candidate be patient and kind. Each candidate was accompanied by all their friends, family members, and loved ones. The more loved ones they had, the better. Every day, the trainees were presented with a choice.

The choices would become increasingly difficult, and suffice to say, not many people survived the process. Ultimately, the experience culminated in vengeance, resulting in a slave warrior full of viciousness and rage. They were the fiercest killers and yielded the highest profit.

The Merchant chuckled as he checked the rosters: fifty kind men, and eight hundred friends and family members. With so many helpers, it would be easy to generate many fine slaves. This training camp would be his most profitable one yet.

Far away in a distant place, a fisherman was slowly pushing his boat forward with a long pole, propelling himself against a vicious current. The river was the largest he'd seen in a long time. When King Yama said "a long time," no one dared refute him.

After pushing himself along the river for many centuries, he finally stopped, anchoring himself to the river bottom with a small tethered anchor. Centuries meant nothing, and time flowed differently in Diyu than in the material planes. Yama creased his brow as he observed the raging Yellow River. His black eyes glazed over as he recalled events from countless eons ago. A wave of sadness overwhelmed him as he recalled the events he had buried in the recesses of his memory. He was destined to be an observer for all eternity.

A fierce wave buffeted his small boat, threatening to capsize it should he be the least bit negligent. The flow of souls was strong and overwhelming, over ten times its previous rate. Such a fierce tide of souls could only be the result of countless deaths throughout millions of mortal realms in the cosmos.

The fierce torrent was also much lighter than normal, indicating that many innocents had died, and that many people had died prematurely. Yama sweated as he pondered the implications of such a flood. It seemed that the Ten Courts of Hell would have to do the unthinkable, something no one would ever dare to suggest to him ever since he'd implemented his foolproof system: They would need to hire contractors.

Contractors made the worst employees and were very bad for morale. If his business had been profit oriented, he would have questioned whether hiring contractors was even worth the effort. Unfortunately, his business affected the very underpinnings of the universe. Despite being immortal, his staff was physically incapable of working more than triple overtime. He gnashed his teeth once again. He *would* have to hire contractors!

Worse yet, to hire so many contractors on such short notice made it necessary to involve the various recruitment companies throughout the Underworld. These companies hired the worst scum, and as soon as they managed to find someone half decent for you, that recruit would soon find a better-paying job with another employer. All the efforts made in training their recruits would be wasted, leaving him with a rabble of inefficient trash that performed at forty percent or less efficiency. This fact alone was infuriating to Yama. The Yellow River System had long been performing at 98.5% efficiency for billions of Underworld years.

He sighed as he pulled up his anchor, letting the raging river entrain his little boat all the way down the river. The river flowed five times as fast as it had during his previous, fruitless excursion. He quickly arrived at his office near the Bridge of Forgetfulness. The office was located on premium real estate, but his time was very valuable.

Over the next year, he placed orders for vast amounts of ingredients to shore up his stock of Aunty Meng's tea. Meanwhile, his research and development team were hard at work, searching for ways to optimize the usage of their precious tea stores. Perhaps they could produce an additive that increased the contacting efficiency between the tea and the souls… Or perhaps they could design a better mixing system than passing them underneath a bridge? As he pondered the possibilities, he regretted his decision of not hiring more engineers during his tenure in Diyu.

A soft knocking sound interrupted his train of thought. It was his assistant. The pretty lass was very tired, as she had hardly gotten a wink of sleep over the last decade. Nothing but sheer resolve and willpower saw her through these trying times. He was very impressed with her performance. Perhaps he should give her a raise soon. It was outside of the regular performance review cycle, but exceptions could be made for trying circumstances.

"Sir, Potential Vendor 1008796 is waiting in the lobby for his scheduled appointment. He's due in ten minutes." She placed a stack of papers in front of him, which contained information on the prospect. The information included the vendor's response to the request for qualifications (RFQ), complete with a resume of the CEO and a company audit. "I've included the necessary company evaluation sheet for when he gives his presentation. Please let me know if you need anything else. I need to go pick up my son from his spiritball practice. I'll be back shortly after."

Yama gave her a smile of appreciation. "My dear, you should take the rest of the day off. This past decade has been very trying, and you need to take care of yourself."

In response, the pretty assistant shot him a coy smile. "We're in this together, boss. I'll come back after I drop my son off. I can't slack off, after all. How about a raise instead?"

Yama choked on his hot cup of tea. He'd been trapped! After assuring her that she was indeed due for a raise soon, he stressed the need for strict adherence to the performance evaluations. He then quickly skimmed the tea-contaminated vendor application, careful to avoid tearing the wet pages.

Thank Pangu I requested a soft copy on a jade slip, he thought.

A short while later, a man with a fashionable hairstyle and a prominent beard confidently walked into his office. The man wore dark-bordered glasses and a very professional suit. Yama was a collector of suits, and he noticed that this man was wearing a limited-edition suit crafted by the most popular tailor in the Underworld, Hades. The crimson suit accented his dark, handcrafted leather shoes. The man gave him a very good impression.

"Sir Yama, my name is Usama the Lion, and I'm the CEO of Spiritas Staffing Solutions. I'll be very brief today, as I'm sure your time is very valuable." The man was charming but reserved. Yama motioned for him to continue.

"The soul industry, as you know, has been booming of late. Everyone has been scrambling to snatch talents everywhere, unfortunately leaving nothing but the chaff from otherwise full fields of wheat," Usama said with a grave voice.

Yama's heart palpitated slightly. None of the previous staffing agencies had mentioned this! Was this really true?

Observing the slight reaction, Usama continued. "Regrettably, the Yellow River is flowing at record speeds, and the industry has been flooded with various natural resources— like soul fragments, excess spiritual force, and spirit floss. Many industries that might not otherwise be possible have been flourishing! Premium talents have been requesting outrageous salaries. In turn, the entire consumer goods and services sector has experienced a huge influx in demand, propagating an ever-increasing shortage of competent labor.

"The consequences of such a shortage are quite clear.

If you aren't able to incorporate competent labor into your organization quickly, the entire system that you've worked hard for, and for countless billions of years, will collapse, leaving you to pick up the broken pieces. Conversely, if you can grasp this opportunity, you will be able to bring your organization to new heights!"

Yama was intrigued. How was this an opportunity? Worse yet, his friend was the CEO of Soul Power Ltd., and he knew for a fact that the great dam was operating at excess capacity, producing soul stones like they'd been going out of style. This required vast amounts of experienced personnel.

As if reading his thoughts, Usama projected an image on the wall, which reinforced his carefully chosen words. He showed an example of several successful companies that had collapsed over a few short nights. Finally, he showed several examples of recent successful staffing events, in which crunch labor was required. These companies, instead of collapsing, acquired several high performing talents over the course of their stay in the company.

When it came time to lay off these excess employees, several key talents were integrated into the company. The new blood stimulated change, challenged the status quo, and finally, the efficiency of the company soared from 95% to 111%. In other words, the introduction of new blood revolutionized the industry and enhanced the output of each employee to the point that the previous efficiency metric was rendered obsolete.

The gentleman in the red suit finished with a call to action. "Here at Spiritas, we turn nobodies into somebodies. At the end of this ordeal, we guarantee key talents that you will be begging to recruit into your organization. All we ask is a generous finder's fee. If we can't boost your efficiency by at least five points, we'll give you your money back!"

A few minutes later, Yama was filling out the rest of the evaluation form on his desk. This young man was quite the talent. To think that he had only been in the Underworld for a few millennia. Previously, he had been a mortal on a small world called "Earth" on one of the many material planes. He frowned as he recalled his last adventure up the Yellow River. Wasn't that small trickle he had been observing for many years from Earth as well?

Shaking his head self-deprecatingly, he continued poring through the large amount of paperwork on his desk. Even in the Underworld, there was no rest for the weary.

Chapter 1: Full Recovery

A young man currently occupied a fourth-grade chamber in the cultivation pavilion. The dull glow of his Green Leaf jade was shining softly on the outside of the chamber, both locking the door and indicating that he should not be disturbed.

It had been a full week since Cha Ming returned from the spirit woods, and the fatigue accumulated during the journey had long since faded away, leaving him with a healthy complexion. Huxian was also in the chamber. Regrettably, he couldn't do much in these cramped conditions. The practice dummies were far too fragile, and they had already gotten three replaced. The latest replacement was accompanied with a firm warning, threatening to ban them from the cultivation pavilion if it happened again.

As a result, all Huxian could do was lounge, sleep, and eat. He showed no interest in reading, leaving only one other activity available: bothering Cha Ming. Unfortunately, Cha Ming was hard at work and couldn't be disturbed. Sighing, the small fox withdrew a large haunch of roasted meat from his collar. In addition to concealing his identity, the collar conveniently included a hundred-cubic-meter storage space.

Huxian's storage space also contained a useful feature: a large refrigerator that encompassed half the space. Any food preserved in the refrigerator would maintain its freshness for ten times as long as storage in a normal refrigerator. Huxian speculated that the powerful Mr. Mao Mao also had a ravenous appetite and carried all sorts of delicacies with him whenever he traveled.

After finishing his delicious supper, Huxian decided to eat another one of the tasty ore rocks, the ones containing the interesting crunchy gray chunks. Whenever he ate one, he would always fall fast asleep for at least a day. With every one he ate, he felt his beast crystal growing steadily. The rapid growth would always be followed by a cycle of compression, increasing the density of his beast crystal.

The small crunchy chunks were very delicious, like a dessert at the end of a large meal. He always needed to chew them down to a sandy grit, lest he be left with a stomachache that lasted for days. In addition to the taste, he always felt his fur grow smoother and his skin grow tougher. Lady foxes liked smooth fur and thick skin, right?

Meanwhile, Cha Ming was carefully drawing out a new talisman. This talisman was a defensive talisman called Iron Skin. After using the talisman, the user's defense would increase drastically, as though he were wearing iron armor on his whole body. Surprisingly, this did not come with any weight impediments and lasted one minute per level of qi condensation of the maker.

To draw the talisman, he was using the Clear Sky Brush.

He was also utilizing a higher quality parchment paper, which was waterproof and fireproof and increased the lifespan of the talisman significantly. He intended to sell a good portion of these if he was successful, and there was no poorer marketing strategy than making a product with an inferior appearance. The paper he used was thick and tinged with yellow, like the material used to print hardcover books.

The ink he was using this time was much different from before. The liquid silver ink was heavy like mercury, and it was an all-purpose ink used for pure metal element talismans. The ink was called liquified metal essence. Cha Ming's talisman crafting skills had reached a point where he could use this kind of high-quality ink freely. In addition, his Clear Sky Brush would never waste any ink, making this slightly more expensive crafting medium a hassle-free choice.

Elemental essence could be obtained at half the price of liquified elemental essence. Besides, he didn't want to use the liquified elemental essence stored in the Clear Sky Brush. He didn't even know how much elemental essence he had left, or if there would be any surplus. This essence was crucial in Painting the Skies, an essential component to the Seventy-Two Earthly Transformations Technique.

A large amount of sweat was beading on Cha Ming's forehead, proving that the complexity of this talisman was much greater than the others he had tried previously. Of course, this didn't include painting the three-dimensional wood-element rune. After a few more breaths, he finally completed the final stroke of the Iron Skin talisman, after which he collapsed with a smile on his face in exhaustion. The experiment was a success!

Iron Skin was a fifth-grade talisman, a mid-grade talisman one level higher than his current cultivation base. He had previously been unsure if it was possible to complete this grade of talisman, but after departing the forest, he noticed that his level of crafting had once again improved. He had evaluated his level of crafting, using success rates for the various grades of talismans as a benchmark.

He speculated that the increase in skill had something to do with experiencing various lifetimes in his game with Huxian's mother. The experience had strengthened his soul by a full level, which now exceeded his qi condensation level. He also speculated that the wood body-refining talisman was in essence a fifth-grade talisman as well.

After recovering for some time, Cha Ming exhaled a breath of turbid air. He was now fully recovered, thanks to his strenuous efforts in talisman crafting over the past week. All that remained now was breaking through to the next level.

Cha Ming quickly entered a meditative state, entering his sea of consciousness while observing his dantian from afar. His dantian contained five small lakes of qi, each constrained by thin, invisible membranes. This membrane was a natural restriction that prevented the lake from expanding past its pre-defined borders. A cultivator would need to break past it to increase his level of qi condensation.

Connecting the different lakes together in a circle was a narrow white river. It flowed in a clockwise motion, maintaining the balance between the five lakes. Conversely, five interconnecting black rivers linked the five small lakes from the center. Oddly enough, one of the five rivers was always dry, as though they were taking turns.

Taking a deep breath, he pulled out the crystal essence conversion formation he had bought from Wang Jun, in which he placed a refined crystal essence gem. The gem contained far greater and far purer energy than even mid-grade spirit stones could provide. He drew energy through the formation, which suddenly flooded his dantian with newly created qi. The qi divided itself naturally into five different streams and jointly impacted against the invisible membranes in all five lakes. They did not budge, not even a little.

He wasn't dejected and continued the process, impacting the five membranes over and over. He knew this restriction was due to his poor talent. Each subsequent breakthrough required more and more effort to materialize. This restriction would continue past qi condensation—establishing his foundation would be a monumental undertaking, and he would have no choice other than to resort to pills to aid him in the future.

Cha Ming continued this process for a full week, finally succeeding on the seventh day. As soon as the five membranes were breached, the room available to fill each lake doubled. They didn't instantly fill up—that would take some time. Cha Ming also noticed that the room available in both the black and white rivers also doubled, steadily growing along with the five qi pools in his dantian.

Elated with his success, Cha Ming stood up and exhaled a turbid breath full of impurities. He then proceeded to find a new cultivation room, since he had finally reached the fifth level of qi condensation. The living and cultivation conditions in each chamber were not substantially different. However, there were vast differences in the durability of training mannequins. In addition, the cultivation rooms at the fifth level had a strength-recording pillar, which the students could use to test their improvement in the techniques they trained.

Cha Ming spent the remainder of the day testing various techniques on the mannequin to stabilize his cultivation. If he neglected this, his body may not grow fully used to his increase in cultivation, causing infrequently used meridians to get damaged with the sudden introduction of vigorous qi.

Finally, after he was satisfied with the results, he continued practicing fifth-grade talismans for a week and proceeded to sixth-level talismans. All this practice was in preparation for his next goal, the second part of the Seventy-Two Earthly Transformations Technique: Fire Body Refining!

Hong Xin was in a very good mood. Tonight, she was going to see a famous play with Elder Brother Jun, *The Prince's Shadow*. The play had been around for two weeks and had received rave reviews. Normally such a play was reserved for the nobility. She had just mentioned the play yesterday in a casual conversation, but the next thing she knew, Elder Brother Jun had procured a pair of tickets!

As such, it was only natural that she spend a whole half day getting ready for their date. She took a scented bath around noon to give enough time for her long black hair to dry. While she could easily dry it with flames, she had heard somewhere that this could damage her hair in the long term. Women valued their appearance immensely, and so she didn't want to take a chance.

After taking her bath, she went through her dresses and tried to pick something suitable for the occasion. She only had a half dozen pretty dresses, and she was afraid of making Elder Brother Jun lose face. Finally, she settled on a slim green dress covered in vines and beautiful mauve blossoms. The dress was soon matched with a mauve hair clip and earrings.

Naturally, Hong Xin lost track of time. She didn't notice the soft knocking from downstairs signifying Wang Jun's arrival.

The door was answered by a smiling Madame Xu. While her daughter had never told her anything, she had long since observed her daughter's strange behavior: her long absences, her increased attention to her looks, and the light blushing every time she lied to her father when asked why she had gotten home so late.

Today Xin Er had locked herself up in her room for a good half day. Was she possibly getting ready for a formal date? Her mother wondered which young man had taken a fancy to her precious daughter. The names of the various sons around the same age flashed through her mind.

Was it perhaps the master tailor's son, Ling Tai? No, his temperament didn't suit her; he wasn't patient enough to handle her moody daughter. Perhaps Cha Ming? No, she had long seen that they only saw each other as brother and sister. One of his friends would be fine, of course. He was a good boy, and she refused to believe that he would tolerate any bad people in his company.

If this boy Xin Er was interested in ended up being a bad egg, perhaps she could ask Cha Ming to scare him off. Hadn't Xin Er mentioned that he had gotten very strong since his return from their last trip?

She opened the door quickly and found a handsome young man waiting respectfully at the door with a pleasant smile on his face. Unlike most people in Green Leaf City, the young man had long blond hair with a thin streak of white dangling down from his temple. He was dressed in a simple green robe. A foreigner, perhaps?

He also seems modest, she thought.

"Greetings, you must be Xin Er's mother, Madame Xu," said Wang Jun, clasping his hands together and bowing lightly in respect. "My name is Wang Jun, and I'm pleased to make your acquaintance. Is Xin Er ready? We'd agreed to head out at this time."

Madame Xu smiled at the naïve young boy. He would learn in time.

"She isn't ready yet," Madame Xu replied sweetly. "Would you like to come in for a cup of tea while you wait?"

"I would be happy to. Thank you for taking care of me," Wang Jun replied, following her into the house.

Wang Jun was sitting patiently in front of a small table in the living room. Madame Xu, who was currently pouring tea for herself and the young man, began inquiring about his background.

"So, your name is Wang Jun. I can't recall there being a Wang family in Green Leaf City. Did you come from abroad?"

"Yes," said Wang Jun, "I was born in Gold Leaf City, but for business and family reasons I needed to move to Green

Leaf City. I consider myself very fortunate, since winter in Green Leaf City is ranked as the seventh most beautiful tourist destination by the Jade Bamboo Conglomerate." He then took a sip of the tea Madame Xu had poured for him.

"Good tea!" Wang Jun said with a surprised and pleased expression. "This is Pu'er tea from the Jade Magnolia Kingdom. From what I know, it is in very short supply in this city. It warms my heart that you've picked out such a precious tea just for me."

Madame Xu, who had been listening to Wang Jun speaking, suddenly blushed at the compliment. "You're very knowledgeable about such things despite your young age. Does your family deal in tea trade?"

Wang Jun laughed. "You flatter me. Tea is a hobby of mine, and I take it very seriously. But yes, my family does deal in tea trade, among other things." He didn't take the initiative to refill their cups, instead waiting for Madame Xu to do so as the host.

Suddenly, loud footsteps could be heard coming from outside the door. The door was flung open unceremoniously, and a large man in full guard uniform entered the house. He rapidly closed the door behind him, preventing the warm air from leaving the fire-warmed living room.

"Husband, you're early! Why don't you have a seat while I serve tea? This young man is taking Xin Er out tonight, and he's waiting for her to get ready."

A surprised expression flashed across Hong Jin's face as his gaze focused on the handsome man in green robes. It was then followed by a look of understanding.

"Give me ten minutes. I'll go change out of this sweaty uniform." Hong Jin quickly climbed upstairs and returned quickly. He was wearing maroon robes, and his shoulder-length hair had even been washed and dried. Wang Jun took note that he was either a fire- or water-element cultivator. Judging by Xin Er's proficiencies, he was likely the former.

Wang Jun, who had only been planning on picking up Xin Er to go to a play, was now sitting in front of both her parents and drinking tea with them. Such a cross examination was a nightmare for any man.

"So, you look young," Hong Jin said a bit aggressively. "Are you a student?"

"Yes, I am a student at Green Leaf Academy," Wang Jun replied dutifully. "I also work part-time at the Jade Bamboo Auction House. However, my focus is still on my cultivation and studies."

"Oh, the Jade Bamboo Auction House? Our eldest son, Hong Ling, works there. Perhaps you know him?" Hong Jin asked.

He's likely thinking how he can use his son to get more information about me, Wang Jun thought. Hong Ling was becoming increasingly influential in the auction house. He was currently an assistant to one of the managers and was being groomed to take over his position as manager once his boss was promoted.

"Oh, Hong Ling? Yes, I work with him quite frequently. He's hardworking and very easy to work with," Wang Jun replied. Meanwhile, like Hong Jin, he was also formulating a strategy. *This is the best news I've heard all night!* he thought. *All I need to do is treat Hong Ling very well, and he'll naturally put in a good word for me. I just need to make sure I get in touch with him before he gives away my position in the company.* It wouldn't do to show off too much; he needed to be modest and introduce himself a bit at a time.

Madame Xu felt very helpless, as she sensed sparks flying

between the two clashing individuals. They continued their discussion in a civil manner while repeatedly probing each other for more information.

Suddenly, the front door opened once more, letting in the subject of their current discussion, Hong Ling. He had a smile plastered on his face, as though an event worthy of celebration had occurred.

As he took off his coat, he noticed an unusual and tense atmosphere in the living room. His father was currently beaming at him, while Young Master Wang was looking at him with a warning gaze. Wait, what was Young Master Wang doing in his house? Panicking, he looked to his mother, who had an imploring look.

After taking off his coat, Hong Ling bowed. "Father, Mother, I'm back from work! Young Ma—Manager, what might you be doing here?" Wang Jun relaxed at the introduction. It looked like his insistence on low-key addresses at work was paying off.

"Manager? Didn't you say you only worked part-time?" asked Hong Jin, taking the opportunity to dig a little deeper.

"My father is a little influential in the company, and I was given a strict business education in my youth. Therefore, I have been taking on managerial duties for the past two years. My coworkers endearingly call me Young Manager," Wang Jun said, scrambling to make up an excuse on the spot. This information was mostly correct.

"Young Manager is too humble," Hong Ling chimed in. "Father, Young Manager is very talented and has been at the forefront of many large business deals."

"No need to exaggerate," Wang Jun said humbly. "Most of these decisions come from the upper echelons of the company, and I'm only implementing the decisions." He shot a warning glance at Hong Ling, who seemed like he was going to spurt blood at his shamelessness. After all, he was technically correct. It was just that as the one representing the upper echelons of the company, he was both making decisions *and* implementing them. He was confident that Hong Ling knew that saying anything right now would be a career-limiting move.

Just as Hong Jin was about to probe deeper, they all heard frantic steps running down the wooden stairs. Both Wang Jun and the rest of the family almost dropped their teacups as they saw the stunning Hong Xin. Her green dress with mauve flowers was accented by her green slippers, mauve earrings, and the mauve hair clip fastening her lustrous black hair behind her head.

She had put a great deal effort into her makeup; her white skin was highlighted with light rouge on her pretty cheeks, and her phoenix eyes were accented with black paint. She was now the spitting image of a beautiful immortal fairy.

"We're late, we're late, let's go!" She quickly rushed up and pulled Wang Jun toward the door, and he didn't resist. "Father, Mother, I'll be back later tonight. I love you both!"

Not giving them a chance to reply, she pulled Elder Brother Jun out the door while blushing furiously.

"I'm sorry about that, Elder Brother Jun. This is the first time I've ever brought a man home. They are just curious." Her face was beet red.

Wang Jun chuckled amicably. "No worries. It went all right. I didn't know Hong Ling was your brother. Fortunately, he put in a good word for me."

Hearing Wang Jun's assurances, Hong Xin sighed with relief. Wang Jun smiled. They could finally focus on enjoying a wonderful evening together.

Chapter 2:
Fire Body Refining

A faint red light was flickering in a dark chamber. Cha Ming was hard at work, attempting to draw the "fire" character while painting the skies. Over the past few days, he had relentlessly drawn the character, one stroke at a time. With every failed attempt, his spirit strengthened ever so slightly, ensuring that his next attempt would progress a tiny bit further.

The fire（火）character was just as complicated as the wood（木） character he had drawn previously. It was shaped like dancing flames. Groups of five flames were joined together at twelve major points, which would eventually be connected to form the two-dimensional fire（火）character upon completion.

The process of drawing this character made him sweat. The character, while not complete, released small amounts of heat to the surrounding air. Regrettably, Cha Ming was working in an enclosed room. The temperature had slowly built up over time, until the room was finally as hot as a steam bath.

The red runes floating in the air rapidly drew back to the

Clear Sky Brush as Cha Ming failed one more time. Without pausing to rest, he quickly got up and opened the door to his cultivation chamber. The hot air was quickly replaced with a fresh, cool draft, which Cha Ming breathed in greedily. Once the exchange was completed, he sat down again in the chamber, replenishing his qi and spiritual force.

He was almost there. In his latest attempt, he had drawn everything but the last two strokes. With luck, he would be successful in his next one to ten attempts. Taking in a deep breath, he raised the white brush to start once more. The black brush tip glowed with a vivid red color.

Huxian had been sleeping in a corner of the room, recuperating from his lazy cultivation method. He was now wide awake, hoping that Cha Ming would complete his training soon. He longed to exit the training room and find a decent meal. He was almost out of his rationed roast meat, which he now ate sparingly.

Cha Ming didn't notice Huxian's gaze and focused on painting with smooth and efficient brush strokes. He no longer needed to draw the details in his carefully drawn flames. Every two strokes would draw a small candlelike flame, complete with the tiny chaotic whips inherent to a naturally lit fire.

Finally, the twelve groups of five flames were joined together in twelve main points. Only four strokes remained! Taking a deep breath, he drew the two larger strokes first, squeezing ninety percent of the remaining energy from his exhausted mind. After resting for five breaths, he drew the second to the last stroke, bringing him to the brink of failure. Instead of resting, he continued with the final stroke, which completed the three-dimensional character. Its completion brought about a fierce wave of heat, which surprised the attentive Huxian. The roaring character writhed in the darkness, flickering with red, yellow, and white light.

"Ohm!"

The Clear Sky Brush let out a commanding hum. Cha Ming was prepared this time; he had put away anything Huxian could use to create trouble. The newly formed character quickly rushed to his chest, imprinting itself like a red brand. This time, pain flooded every part of Cha Ming's body as the fiery energy rampaged.

Unfortunately, the soothing wood energy could do nothing to help him; whenever it traveled to soothe the pain, it provided fuel for the fire and intensified the burning. Cha Ming could do nothing but grit his teeth as he struggled to remain conscious. His attempts were futile, however, and the world was soon covered in darkness. The fire continued burning as he slept, transforming his physique one cell at a time.

Paff! Paff!

Cha Ming's robes made crisp snapping sounds as he practiced his fist techniques in the air. He had measured his fist strength just prior to leaving the cultivation chamber. His powerful physical body now boasted a fist strength of 648 jin!

Once he was comfortable with his control over simple punches, he spent time familiarizing himself with his Ghost Steps Technique. As he practiced the steps, he noticed a drastic increase in speed. This caused his Ghost Steps to be clumsy; he would need some time to accommodate the increase. After practicing his staff arts, he confirmed his guess: the Fire Body Refining had increased his speed.

This increase in speed did not affect his overall strength delivery. He guessed that his current speed was a full level higher than other body cultivators at the sixth level.

"All right, Huxian, come at me, bro!" They were in a secluded training courtyard. The courtyard was built for sparring and could be reserved for two hours at a time.

All right, I'm coming! Don't worry, I'm much stronger than you, so I'll only use sixty percent of my strength. Huxian's sharp teeth were revealed as he shot Cha Ming a condescending grin. The duo sparred for the next two hours without using any qi or special abilities. Naturally, Cha Ming was trounced thoroughly. Nevertheless, he had achieved his goal of familiarizing himself with his full strength.

Looking at a flashing lamp near the entrance, he realized that his time was up, and another group was waiting to enter. He and Huxian quickly gathered up wood and metal splinters from the ground—all that remained of his staff. His strength had surpassed the limitations of what the staff could handle.

He wasn't too upset, however. Their trip to the underground caves had provided him with the perfect material for forging a new weapon. He only needed to find a spiritual blacksmith willing to accept the work. Money wasn't an issue—he now had a small stockpile of crystalized elemental essence and refined soul alloy just begging to be used. Strengthening himself was also a priority. Who knew when Zhou Xian would show up for revenge?

Cha Ming and Huxian quickly exited the training room and were quickly replaced by an impatient pair of students.

"Boy, your fighting skills are garbage," a rough voice

sounded out from inside his mind. Cha Ming slapped his forehead. He had forgotten about the red-bearded man inside the Clear Sky Brush, who had been quiet for a long time.

"Aren't I pretty good for my age?" Cha Ming exclaimed defensively.

"Sure, you're so-so. You're okay. In my language, that means you're garbage. I've seen a five-year-old chimpanzee fight better than you," the man said dryly. Knowing that arguing wouldn't get him anywhere, he decided to go for Plan B: boot licking.

"Of course, your perspective is a lot higher than mine. I haven't yet received your guidance on this. As my teacher, you should have a solution to this problem since you brought it up, correct?"

Silence ensued. Cha Ming didn't press the issue and went out to a decent restaurant. He and Huxian were famished. They ordered several tasty dishes. Cha Ming slowly ate his vegetable dishes while Huxian ate a variety of barbecued meat.

"There is a way to fix up your fighting," the man said eventually. "I'll be honest with you, I've never taught anyone at such a pitifully low level before, so I don't have any garbage techniques to teach you. Here's what we *can* do: if you go to your school library, we could browse through a variety of techniques, and I can pick some that I think are suitable. Then we can make you a whole new fighting style, which you can come practice with me at any time. How about it?"

Cha Ming was surprised at the red-bearded man's solution. That was very practical!

"All right, we'll do what you say. We'll finish eating first, though. By the way, can I bring food into the brush? Can you eat?" Cha Ming felt very guilty about eating in front of the bearded man.

"You've got to be kidding me! I'm trying to help you, and here you go attacking my sorest spot? Of course I can't eat! The Clear Sky Brush can't take in any food, and further, I'm just a spiritual body! I'd need to somehow get a new body before being able to eat anything." His aggressive, berating voice now sounded extremely sad. Little did Cha Ming know that the red-bearded man appreciated his concern.

"If I get strong enough, can I free you and make you a new body?" Cha Ming inquired. He felt very sorry for the bearded man, who had been a prisoner for countless years. The man gave no reply, and so they finished eating.

Soft sounds of booted feet and the pitter-pattering of clawed paws could be heard as Cha Ming walked toward campus from the merchant district. It was late in the afternoon, and he had made trips to both the Jade Bamboo Auction House and Elder Ling's house. He had spent two days making talismans, yielding a total of twenty-two sixth-grade talismans. These talismans were the ever-popular fireball talismans, which had the power to decimate many foes at the fifth level of qi condensation and lower. Of course, this was quite literally burning money, so most people kept these as insurance.

The economics of crafting talismans had changed drastically for Cha Ming. There were three reasons for the change. The first most important change was that he no longer wasted ink thanks to the Clear Sky Brush. Even while using the more expensive inks like fire elemental essence, it was most economical to craft the highest level of talismans available. This was because although the crafting rate would drop by half for every level, the price would quadruple for every level.

In addition, the Clear Sky Brush had increased his success rate by a full level, and his soul force was a full level higher than his cultivation base at the fifth level of qi condensation. Setting aside ten talismans to replenish his materials, he was left with a tidy profit of about 60,000 spirit stones. He used 50,000 of these to exchange with Elder Ling for 250,000 contribution points. Elder Ling was very pleased about the progress of his student and encouraged him to work hard.

Cha Ming's ability to create wealth was now much greater than before his trip to the spirit woods. He was now beginning to realize that he was much like a frog in a well. With every hop, he could barely catch a glimmer of the clear sky above. He used the remaining 10,000 spirit stones with confidence, purchasing a heavy but durable staff as a replacement for the one he had just broken. Tragically, he had a load of quality materials that could be used to craft a much better staff, but Wang Jun had informed him that he would need to travel to another city to have it made. The new staff weighed thirty jin, which was the limit of what he could wield comfortably.

Coupled with the thick and heavy staff on his back, Cha Ming cut an imposing figure. Every step he took was bold and powerful. Many female students shot him curious glances as approached the bright red library with his bronze medallion engraved with a large "five." The medallion had automatically updated his cultivation level the moment he broke through. He suspected that the academy used these medallions to track and monitor the students on campus.

After a short half-hour wait, Cha Ming was greeted at the

entrance of the library by the short Elder Xiao. "Cha Ming, my young friend, you've finally come to visit me again! Don't tell me you're here for business again? It really breaks my heart, you know." Elder Xiao's face was plastered with toothy grin, making it apparent that he wasn't sad in the slightest.

"Elder Xiao, you know that I'd come here to visit you more often. Alas, I was out of town for a month, and I've been recuperating for two weeks. You can hardly hold that against me, right?" A hurt look appeared on the younger man's face. It was mirrored by a similar expression on Huxian's face.

"Sure, sure, I believe you. With weak muscles like these, I can see how it would take you a while to recover." Elder Xiao pinched his thigh hard. A stinging pain ran throughout Cha Ming's entire body.

What the hell! He's a body refiner? Cha Ming vowed never to underestimate any of the elders or instructors ever again.

Elder Xiao gave him a meaningful look. "I had expected that your thin frame would be physically weak. It looks like you've started cultivating your body, just like I did. You might not know this, but the Xiao clan's small bodies are tailor-made for body cultivation.

"Speaking of which, who even gave you that body cultivation technique? We don't have all that many on campus." He then glanced at the bronze medallion on Cha Ming's chest. "Are you sure you're just a third-grade talent, you monster?"

Cha Ming shrugged shyly. The truth was that since practicing the Seventy-Two Transformations Technique, his talent had begun to improve. A second yin and a second yang organ had been strengthened. When combined with his two previously strengthened organs, he now possessed a rough talent rating of three and four tenths.

"I'm going to start calling you little monster from now on," said Elder Xiao, shaking his head. "By the way, little monster, since you've practiced body refining to the sixth grade, you can go to the administration building and have your medallion changed manually to reflect your actual strength. While the school doesn't discriminate against body refiners, the medallions aren't programmed to measure anything other than qi condensation level."

"Is there an advantage to being a sixth-grade student?" Cha Ming inquired.

"Sure, there are a few. The most important benefit is that you can enter the Alchemists Association and commission work. Students below your level are assumed to be too poor, and those below your level that are rich enough definitely have other connections. In addition, using pills to propel your cultivation at lower grades, while possible, is quite harmful to your foundation.

"The second benefit is that each grade six and higher student obtains a personal courtyard, which possesses a cultivation array, a training mannequin, and a sparring chamber in the backyard. Of course, all these functions require spirit stones, which you will need to provide. That's why you never see anyone at that level in the cultivation pavilion. Students who are too strong get fined whenever they break a mannequin. Cultivating without an array is also very inefficient. The cultivation pavilion is really for beginners and untalented students."

As Elder Xiao concluded his explanation, the three of them proceeded up to an observation room on the second floor. He walked over to a stone on the side of the wall and pressed a button. With a helpless expression, he explained to Cha Ming, "Computer needed to be shut down for maintenance just yesterday. It will take a good ten minutes until it's active again. Meanwhile, you can explain to me what you need."

"It's like this, Elder Xiao: I'm looking for a movement technique and a staff technique that are well suited for me to use. I practice five-element qi refining and five-element body refining. Do you happen to have anything that suits me? I have 250,000 contribution points to spend," Cha Ming said sheepishly.

"Five-element body cultivation! Are you nuts? First you decide to practice five-element qi refining, the hardest of all of them, and now you try five-element body refining? You're a monster! A little monster!" Elder Xiao wracked his brain for fifteen minutes. The computer had long since activated and was awaiting Elder Xiao's instructions.

"Sorry, I can't help you this time. I've got nothing like that. I suggest that you pick a silver staff art and a silver movement technique and make do with what you have," Elder Xiao advised, looking up location codes for various techniques.

Cha Ming frowned slightly, but he had anticipated this problem before arriving. "Would it be possible to see an abridged version of all the bronze and silver staff techniques and movement techniques? I can't make up my mind just by looking at the title."

"Way ahead of you!" The small elder quickly stepped out of the room and motioned with his hand. Two hundred scrolls flew out from the various shelves and piled up on the small table in the room. "Knock yourself out. You have until sunset to read through these. You can come back tomorrow and continue if you aren't done by then."

Chapter 3:
An Ambitious Goal

Cha Ming stared at the pile of scrolls. Looking through these hundreds of scrolls was a daunting task. Thankfully, he could rely on the red-bearded elder to provide him guidance. Otherwise, he would be here for days before deciding on a rudimentary plan.

Each bronze and silver scroll could be opened one to two feet, which contained an abridged version of the technique. Accessing the full techniques could only be done via an illusory scroll. Each scroll was affixed with a seal to prevent tampering.

First technique: Guardian Staff. Earth-attribute staff technique, requires small amounts of qi for support but relies on physical body strength. This technique is heavy and emphasizes brute force and reach to repel enemies. The technique was created by Tu Yan, a personal guard of the late King Song Liufeng.

Second technique: Shearing Staff Art. Wind-attribute staff technique. Used to repel foes as well as attack foes from a distance with shearing blades of wind. Formidable for group battles. The technique is rumored to have been developed by a monk, emphasizing the importance being merciful to the weak but fierce against evildoers.

Cha Ming tossed the second scroll into a reject pile after reading the introduction. He did not practice the wind element.

"Dummy, pick that one up, it's not total garbage." Unable to refute the bearded man, he dutifully picked up the technique with a puzzled expression.

"Exalted Teacher, I don't understand. How can I use this technique if I don't cultivate wind?" It made no sense to Cha Ming.

"Let your teacher worry about that. For now, keep reading these techniques, and I'll tell you what to keep and what to throw away."

Cha Ming continued sifting through the pile of scrolls.

Overbearing Staff Art—Trash

Lotus Staff Art—Trash

He barely opened a scroll called Spring Leaf Staff Art before it was deemed as trash. To his surprise, the least expensive scroll available, the Foundation Staff Art, made it into the keep pile after barely any consideration at all.

The same rigorous selection process was implemented for all the movement arts. In the end, Cha Ming was instructed to purchase twelve scrolls:

Shearing Staff Art—Bronze Level, Wind Element Staff Art

Foundation Staff Art—Bronze Level, Unattributed Staff Art

Flaming Wheel Defense—Silver Level, Fire Element Staff Art

Wading Through the Reeds—Silver Level, Water Element Staff Art

Quake Staff—Silver Level, Earth Element Staff Art

Sword Staff—Bronze Level, Metal Element Staff Art (very rare, disproportionately expensive)

Trapping Staff—Bronze Level, Wood Element Staff Art

Seven Cloud Steps—Silver Level, Wind Movement Art

White Willow Shade—Silver Level, Wood Element Movement Art

Three-Layered Burst Step—Bronze Level, Fire Element Movement Art

Mountain Stance—Silver Level, Earth Element Movement Art

Skating in Paradise—Bronze Level, Water Element Movement Art

The last item on the list made Cha Ming especially confused and frustrated. The introductory scroll indicated that it was made for fun by a core formation cultivator in the northern provinces. It had been made specifically for his female disciples to show off at parties on arenas made of ice! Despite his reservations, he accepted it without complaint. Prior experience indicated that it was no use fighting the bearded man.

It was nearing sunset now, and Elder Xiao was patiently waiting at the library checkout for Cha Ming to come down. If he needed an hour or two more, Elder Xiao didn't mind. He was the guardian of the library, in charge of making sure that no one broke in and stole any techniques. As such, he was required to stay on the library premises for long periods of time.

Cha Ming approached the checkout desk and put down the twelve scrolls. "Elder Xiao, if you'd be so kind, I'd like to purchase these twelve scrolls."

Elder Xiao almost fell to the floor in anger. "Little Monster,

I know you're confused about what you want to practice, but please be a little more reasonable. It's not too late to come back after you've tried one of them…" By this point, the short man was massaging his brow with one hand.

"No need. I want to practice all of them and decide which one is best after successfully cultivating them."

"I see, I see…" Elder Xiao nodded. An enraged look suddenly appeared on his face. "Practice all of them? Are you a pig? Do you think these techniques are all snacks that you can eat casually? I should report you for such behavior!"

Cha Ming spent some time reassuring Elder Xiao, and finally, his rage subsided. There was no rule on how many techniques could be taken out, after all. Depressed, Elder Xiao produced illusory scrolls for each of the twelve techniques and sent the young man on his way.

"Gah!"

A maid flinched as her young master woke up suddenly in the middle of the night. He looked confused and exhausted. Eventually, he was doused with a cold shower of realization, and his gaze instantly became cold and aloof. He stared at the wall, brooding as he recalled the events that had led up to his incapacitation.

He had been chasing a prey out in the woods for his younger brother. At the last minute, the small fox had released a large amount of power, which forced him to take a forbidden medicine to temporarily raise his cultivation.

Just as he was about to succeed, the young whelp from the Wang family and his chaperone had interfered, and he was forced to flee for his life with a teleportation talisman gifted to him by his brother. It would have been fine if he had either taken the medicine or used the talisman, but the combination had caused great damage to his body. Shortly after arriving back at the Zhou family mansion, he passed out and was transported to his bedchambers. One of the best spirit doctors in the city had presided over his recuperation, ensuring that no substantial damage had been done to his foundation.

"How long have I been sleeping?" he asked the maid.

"Young Master, you've been sleeping for two months," she replied meekly, her voice laced with fear. The Young Master was notorious for mistreating his servants and shooting the messenger. It was her lucky day, though; Zhou Xian was too focused on his recovery and immediately ordered her to fetch food and pour him a hot bath.

At the crack of dawn, the fully recovered Zhou Xian walked to the other end of their massive mansion. The guard on duty swiftly opened a door and let him into a cozy office. His father, Zhou Tian, was a strict man. He always started his work at dawn. This was when his mood was at its best; naturally, this was why Zhou Xian chose to visit him at this hour.

Upon entering, he did not bow or seat himself, but instead stood just inside the door, awaiting further instruction. His balding father continued poring over documents, signing them as required. After a half hour, he finally looked up at his son.

"So, I see that you managed to wake up after your miserable failure?"

Zhou Xian kneeled in apology. "Father, I have failed you. Please punish me."

His father didn't pay any attention to the gesture and turned his attention back to the documents on his desk.

"I don't have time to punish you. Please report what happened."

"Father, I entered the woods with twelve friends from school. We journeyed quickly toward the location provided by Brother Li, where we encountered a strange force field. We were unable to penetrate it. Further, soon after we reached the force field, a large group of hounds, including two ninth-level spirit beasts, surrounded us. I was lucky to escape and awaited further instruction from Brother Li. My twelve friends all perished.

"After two weeks of waiting, I was instructed to pose as a wounded student for help at certain coordinates. I lured a snow leopard to the location at the appropriate time, baiting a man and a fox into saving me. The man was Du Cha Ming, who had recently disappeared in the spirit woods. A hefty bounty of 50,000 spirit stones had been offered for his retrieval. The fox was black and white in color.

"We returned to the campsite where they treated me. Since I had told Du Cha Ming of the ransom, it was going to be difficult to ambush him at any other time. Further, if we met any other groups in the forest, he would have quickly been alerted and suspicious. He would also have been suspicious if we avoided everyone. In the middle of the night, at the time that he should have been the most sound asleep, I attempted to stab the fox, which I perceived as the greater threat.

"The fox was expecting me, however, and so was the youngster. While I managed to kill the fox with a poisonous strike near his heart, it displayed extraordinary racial abilities, splitting into two clones. One of his clones was pure white and emanated a terrifying purifying power. The other was pure black and could hide in shadows. The black clone had terrifying devouring powers and could attack my shadow directly, which inflicted wounds on my physical body.

"Having been pushed into a desperate situation, I quickly took a forbidden medicine to forcibly raise my cultivation level, lest the target escape. I quickly overcame the fox, but before I could do anything, Wang Jun and Elder Bai from the Jade Bamboo Conglomerate interfered. They were unimpressed by any threats, and Elder Bai quickly attacked me with his mid-foundation establishment cultivation.

"In desperation, I used the teleportation talisman provided by Brother Li to escape. Unfortunately, I was not in the best shape, and the rigors of teleportation forced me to severely deplete my strength while still under the effects of the forbidden medicine. As a result, I passed out, and I am currently reporting to you two months later." Zhou Xian stood silently while his father digested the report.

"You made three mistakes," he replied after pondering.

"Your humble son begs for instruction."

"The first mistake was the choice of a snow leopard. Not only was it very foreign to the area, but it was too weak to injure you. A peak ninth-level dire wolf would have been a much more appropriate and less obvious opponent. There was also a chance that your targets could have expended some energy or exposed their strength when saving you.

"The second mistake was when you threatened the Wang family. They would never have given in to your petty threats, since their influence in the continent is far reaching. You should have immediately retreated when they gave you the chance and informed myself and your younger brother.

"The third mistake: Du Cha Ming isn't dead."

"Impossible! I hit him with my poisonous sword at point blank range right beside his heart! How could he possibly survive?" Zhou Xian was livid. How was this twerp so lucky?

"He is in very good health," his father replied. "He was treated by the best spirit doctor in town and was observed walking around the streets in the city one week after your arrival. He is also accompanied by a small ordinary-looking fox. You should never assume your opponent is dead until you cut off his head. Dismissed."

An angry Zhou Xian walked out of his father's office. Just as he was exiting, he passed by a beautiful lady, his older sister. She was nineteen years old this year and was currently betrothed to the crown prince.

"You got beat up again, I see," she said, ridiculing him. "Why don't you ever measure up to our little brother? At least he can get things done properly."

"At least I can do something other than whoring around. How's that working out for you, seducing men for a living?"

"Oh, it's going very well! Seduction is an art that requires a lot of practice and a lot of... innate talent." She leaned forward coquettishly while exposing her cleavage. "Would you like a lesson, dear Eldest Brother? You might not be the most attractive man I've ever seen, but a little makeup can *definitely* make you more successful than you currently are. After all, there are a lot of plump noble ladies that need loving, too."

Zhou Xian pushed her away and started walking toward his room. "I'll show you what success is, and when I do, I'll have you indecently moaning underneath me, begging me to please you."

Zhou Jia shrugged and proceeded to the door to their father's study. Meanwhile, a slightly less enraged Zhou Xian went back to his room. The verbal jousting had let him forget his bitter hatred for Cha Ming for a few moments.

Upon returning to his room, he sat down in front of his brightly lit desk. He then removed a small black book from his bag of holding and prepared to write a message. Just as he was about to write, a message appeared.

"Are you awake now?"

Zhou Xian shifted his pen down to reply.

"Yes, I'm up and about, and I've just reported to Father."

Zhou Xian then reported what had happened in detail. Shortly after, a message appeared.

"Thanks for the hard work. I'll tell Father that the information you obtained was worth the price paid. I now know what type of spirit beast the fox is. I also speculate that they formed a life-and-death contract, which allowed this Du Cha Ming to survive the initial poison, in conjunction with his strong mortal body."

"How is this good news?"

"My dear elder brother, it's good news because we now have access to potential leverage for the fox. If we capture Cha Ming as a slave, the fox will have no choice but to obey our commands, lest he and his owner die."

"I see. You're smart as ever, brother."

He was tired and wanted to continue resting. His fully hale appearance in front of his father was just for show.

"Do you want revenge?"

Zhou Xian's heart palpitated. His hand trembled as he wrote out a reply.

"I would die for revenge, what do I need to do?"

"I'll coordinate with you, Father, and Sister for a three-pronged approach. What I need your help with will raise your power by a large margin, giving you the opportunity to defeat Cha Ming. Remember, I say defeat because we can't have him die. However, that doesn't mean that he can't suffer a fate worse than death."

Wang Jun was busy looking over documents in his courtyard on campus. It was much easier to work in the courtyard, where he was able to have Elder Bai and two other assistants aid him while removing himself from everyday business. His presence at the school was partial ruse and partial utility. Since a young age, he had been a perfectionist and obsessed with getting involved in everything, from management to day-to-day tasks.

On campus, he was not directly confronted with business-related activities and could dedicate more time to cultivation. A dull bronze badge was affixed to his chest. However, no one would accuse him of being untalented. He had been attending the school for less than six months and was already a seventh-grade student.

His desk and fireplace had been moved to this new courtyard, of course. He had also replaced the cultivation array with a much higher class array. The crumbling walls surrounding his cottage had also been reinforced with a defensive array, ensuring that no one below core formation would be able to force their way in or eavesdrop.

While Wang Jun was in the middle of signing an important document, Elder Bai swiftly entered and delivered a report.

"What's this?" Wang Jun inquired.

"The Alchemists Association in Green Leaf City has officially informed us that they are terminating the existing pill supply contract, effective thirty days from now," replied Elder Bai.

"Have they indicated that they are open to negotiations?"

"Yes, they also supplied this letter that states that the current contract price of seventy-five percent of market value is too low, that their alchemists are overworked and require two weeks to supply any orders instead of the current three days, and that they need to be paid on delivery." Elder Bai was not new to these business dealings. He understood that the proposed conditions were not only unfair but completely counter to what Wang Jun had been attempting to accomplish.

"Elder Bai, let's pause for tea." The news was not unexpected to Wang Jun, but he had not been expecting it so soon. The duo sat down in front of the cinnamon-scented fireplace, listening to the merry crackling of slow-burning cedar logs.

"Elder Bai, it seems like Zhou Xian has woken up. We should both get used to sleepless nights—the Zhou family's revenge has finally begun."

Chapter 4: The Arena

In a nearby city called Clearwood, a loud cheer erupted in a large, crowded room. Officially, this place was a bar. They served drinks and hired entertainment from all around the Song Kingdom. In truth, the bar was just a front for a much larger industry: an underground gambling arena.

The arena was built below ground. The excavation was an impressive feat, and many powerful geomancers had been hired to ensure its stability. Geomancers combined their earth affinity with spirit power. Their understanding of the earth and its composition was much deeper than a normal earth-element cultivator, and they were highly sought after in any kingdom.

"Blood Queen, Blood Queen! Victory! I bet everything on the Blood Queen!"

Drunk patrons were throwing money around like it was out of style. The Blood Queen had been there for the past two months. That was a long time for a prize fighter, especially someone like her, who only accepted death matches.

In the caged arena, a lithe young lady dressed in tight-fitting red leather wielded two vicious sabers. The sabers were also red; despite having been forged from iron, these sabers had been soaked in the blood of countless men and beasts alike.

Her opponent this time was an extremely large man, who was confident in his strength. He wielded a huge sledgehammer. A single strike from that hammer would definitely kill the young lady on contact.

"Does anyone want to make any other bets? The betting will close in one minute, assuming one of the contestants isn't defeated first!" A glamorously dressed lady was the head bookie for the gambling arena.

"Fifty mid-grade spirit stones on the Blood Queen."

An expected customer in a dark cloak arrived, as expected. He was the main reason why she'd lowered the odds in the first place. She had proactively reduced the odds for the Blood Queen, ensuring that they still earned money from every fight. Call it women's intuition.

"Sir Gong, your business is truly eating us out of house and home. Won't you consider betting on the other side?" the head bookkeeper suggested.

"Stop looking so innocent. You lowered the odds so much only three days after she showed up! There's no way you're not swimming in spirit stones after these past two months," Sir Gong replied.

"But it's not the same," she replied softly. "I want to swim in *your* spirit stones. I want them all over me. You'd like that, wouldn't you?" As she leaned forward, her ample cleavage became partially uncovered in the process.

"Let me get that for you," Sir Gong said, leaning in and fixing her problem. The woman blushed. She wasn't there for touching, but he was a rich man. She had no choice but to smile at his cheeky grin.

"You know, Yi Bing, we did compromise this time. Her current opponent is at the sixth level of qi condensation, a whole level higher! I'm sure a lot more people will bet on him this time. And if they don't, you'll be *swimming* in my spirit stones. You'd like that, wouldn't you?"

After their teasing exchange, Sir Gong went to take his seat near the front of the cage arena. A few high rollers were there as well. They had personal boxes, and topless women sat on their laps as they spectated, satisfying their every need.

He disliked places like the arena. Especially the smoky, unventilated air. He was used to it, of course. Back when he fought here, he was known as the Blood King. It was where he made a name for himself and where he'd built up enough funds to bankroll his mercenary group in Green Leaf City.

The reason he had returned was for his sister's sake. She had finally grown up and had a desire to get stronger. Her original half-hearted, squeamish attitude was why he'd previously been reluctant to include her in the mercenary business. The last two months had completely obliterated his previous assumptions. She would do just fine out in the real world now.

The two fighters in the cage were currently walking in circles, occasionally making probing moves. Of course, the Blood Queen did most of the probing. She was nimble and could quickly recover from any mistakes. The large hammer-wielding brute did not have that luxury. While he was a whole level stronger than her, he had personally witnessed her vicious techniques and strong killing intent.

After probing for a hundred breaths, the Blood Queen finally started her dance, quickly building momentum with her twin blood-red sabers. She spun in rapid circles like a dervish, striking with a steady rhythm that contained very few gaps. As her dance intensified, so did her strikes.

The brute's defenses were very hard, however. He was what they called a "buffer". In addition to some level of body refining, the brute utilized his qi to cover himself in an iron skin. He didn't use any qi at all for attacks. As a result, he was able to avoid taking damage from the attacks that snuck through.

Every once in a while, when he saw an opening, he would lash out with all his power, swinging out in large arcs at the agile demoness. Every time he lashed out, however, she would leap over each strike, taking advantage of his momentum to land some heavy blows. While she hadn't injured him yet, his qi was rapidly depleting. If things continued this way, his iron skin would be as effective as wet paper and he'd truly be in trouble.

There were only two ways out of this death match—winners got to live, and the losers would die. No mercy was allowed. The rewards for these fights were very steep, and the admission fees were correspondingly high. The arena guaranteed at least three of these battles. If no fighters were available, they kept a large stock of demonic beasts that could take the place of human contestants. Of course, the arena preferred people fighting—people didn't cost them anything.

The Blood Queen's attacking frequency had now reached its peak, putting the brute in a tricky position. It was now or never! He had kept a trump card this whole time, but he was experienced and had patiently waited for the time to strike.

Clank, clank, clank, clank, clank, clank.

After six strikes, the brute stepped in quickly, using his hammer to deflect the blows. The blow occurred at a moment where there was a very slight pause in her movements. The pause only lasted for a fraction of a second, but for the experienced brute, it was enough.

The charge surprised the Blood Queen, who couldn't help but interrupt her rhythm and step back. She had lost the initiative, which was very dangerous due to the large gap in cultivation level. As she twisted to attack at the large man's waist and regain the initiative, she shivered slightly as a tremor traveled up her leg through her foot.

Shit, she thought, *he's not a pure buffer!* The brute had used a stomping battle technique, which utilized earth qi to create tremors and paralyze his opponents. Unfortunately, this was the Blood Queen's Achilles heel. If her dance was interrupted, she would be nothing but a sitting duck.

A feeling of pure dread invaded her subconscious as she eyed the large hammer, which swung downward toward her exposed shoulder. That single strike would surely kill her if it landed.

I can't let my brother down! I can't let him down like I did Cha Ming!

These thoughts instantly converted to courage. To survive, she would have to break her limits. With a roar, her dantian trembled, and she angrily slashed at an invisible membrane using her qi pool. She channeled her anger—at the situation that led to Cha Ming's death; at her brother for getting her into this cage match; and most importantly, at herself for failing them both.

Her righteous anger made her qi lake shudder, but to no avail.

Again! Another fierce impact on her dantian had her coughing out blood.

Again! Finally, the third attempt managed to crash the invisible membrane that had caused her to be caught in a bottleneck. Instantly, qi at the sixth level of qi condensation rushed toward her and cleared her mind.

She quickly exercised her movement technique, which had improved after her breakthrough. The tremors in her legs were quickly neutralized by the surging qi. Having shaken off the tremor, she quickly danced forward toward the brute, using one of her sabers to slightly shift the smashing hammer. The hammer barely avoided her, but she took advantage of her closed-in position to swing both sabers upward toward the brute's neck.

Blood Saber Art—Twin Decapitation!

The vicious blow, powered by her increased cultivation, smashed through the remainder of the brute's iron skin. His previous attacks had exhausted most of his remaining qi, leaving him open to an attack. The crowd cheered as the underdog of the fight, the reigning champion, Blood Queen, lifted both of her blood-red sabers above her head to announce her victory.

Blood dripped from the sabers onto her sexy, slender figure.

As the reigning champion, the Blood Queen had her own changing room. The changing room was filled with three baths. The first bath was to rinse her swords and leather outfit. She unceremoniously dumped them into the tub and jumped into the second one, the pre-bath wash. The water instantly turned crimson as the dried blood was rinsed off her perfect slender frame. She also gave her hair a quick wash, as it had been doused with a couple cups of hot blood as she decapitated her opponent.

After the initial rinse was completed, she dunked herself into a scented bath. It had been treated with various perfumes ideal for countering the bloody smell. Initially, the smell had disgusted her. The more she fought, however, the more she yearned for that smell. Was she perhaps changing too much?

As she relaxed in the bath, a familiar figure walked in.

"Elder Brother, you know it's inappropriate to enter a girl's room while she's taking a bath, right?"

The man shrugged as he heard the comment.

"It's not like I haven't seen it all. Plus, you're my younger sister. I used to give you baths when you were little, and I've already seen you naked countless times."

"That's different!" she said, blushing and sinking deeper into the bath, ensuring that the foaming soap properly covered anything inappropriate. He took the hint and sat down, facing away from the bathtub.

"Congratulations on your breakthrough. It's been a hard two months, but you've already broken through two whole levels. If I didn't know any better, I would have guessed that you were a fourth-grade talent!" He was truly happy at her sister's progress. This was much faster than his initial training.

Perhaps she was better to suited to the Blood World Scripture than he was?

"It's all thanks to the Blood World Scripture. What an amazing cultivation method! It channels killing intent into offensive power, killing intent into cultivation, and life-and-death struggles into breakthrough opportunities. There's also no chance of having an unstable foundation, since the user's qi is constantly stabilized through combat."

"Lan Er, I think it's more to do with your compatibility with the technique," Sir Gong said blandly. "If I didn't know any better, I would think you were a sadist."

"Wuling, you know better than I do that that's not the case. I'm just much too disappointed in myself. Cha Ming died because of me, and I never want the same situation to repeat itself."

She wore a cold expression. The sweet Gong Lan no longer existed. Only by being cold to herself would she never let down anyone ever again. This saddened her brother greatly.

"Speaking of which, a messenger from the Jade Bamboo Conglomerate came by this afternoon. I didn't want to interrupt your focus before the match. Do you want me to read the message to you now, or do you want to wait until after your bath?"

Gong Lan perked up when she heard the words Jade Bamboo. What could Brother Jun possibly need?

"Open it now and read it to me!" Gong Lan instructed.

Gong Wuling chuckled as he ripped open the letter. After opening it, he read it out loud using a sensual voice.

"My Dearest Lan Er, I can't hold it in any longer. I've decided that it's now or never, and that I need to confess my love for you. I—"

"The hell? Read the real letter!" she shouted, lashing out furiously, throwing a bar of soap at her brother's head.

"If you keep throwing things, I'll have to turn around and teach you a lesson," he teased. "Ahem, where was I? Gong Lan, I'm happy to inform you that one month ago, Cha Ming returned from the spirit woods safe and sound. I'm sorry I didn't inform you earlier, however, it took a while for our intelligence agency to track you down. The underground gambling arena is not strictly legal, so information on it is quite hard to come by. I hope you're well, and that you'll come for a visit soon. Xin Er misses you dearly, and Cha Ming inquires about your whereabouts every few days. Sincerely, Your Dearest Brother Wang."

Wuling lifted his eyebrows as he recalled the tragic story of the young man falling off Greatwood Bridge after an explosion destroyed it. Their portion of the group had only survived since it was close to the edge. They had managed to keep hold of the bridge because the portion supporting them slammed against the cliff wall.

This guy Cha Ming has some dogshit good luck, he thought.

"Elder Brother, you're not joking, are you?"

He looked back at his teary-eyed sister and handed her the letter. The paper quickly started falling apart as she held it in her soapy wet hands.

"Let's go back to Green Leaf City, brother. We'll keep training after I go for a visit, okay?"

Wuling chuckled as he stood up and ruffled her wet hair. "Anything for you, little sister. You know that."

Chapter 5: Murder Most Fowl

In a courtyard within Green Leaf Academy, the constant sound of metal on wood echoed throughout the entire residential district. Birds avoided this courtyard like the plague. There were two reasons for this, the first one being the constant hammering noises that started at dawn and ended at sunset. At least the person who caused the disturbance had a minimum level of decency, the nearby residents said. This was reassuring small talk, of course. These were trying times, and they wanted nothing more than to rip the perpetrator apart limb by limb.

The second reason caused the birds to shiver in fear. Noise they could deal with; death they could not. A vicious predator had appeared near the student courtyards. A strange demonic fox now lurked between the stone houses. It took great pleasure in capturing the birds that wandered around the premises.

In a courtyard ten rows away from Cha Ming's, a cultivator was indulging in his favorite hobby: feeding his chickens and collecting their eggs. The cultivator had previously been a commoner, one who had expected to spend the rest of his life raising farm animals. Little did he know that he would have talent in cultivation. As a fourth-grade talent, his rate of growth was very rapid. After a mere three years, he was now an eighth-level student.

Despite being a cultivator, he was still very fond of his farming lifestyle. In his courtyard, he had several plots of land, which he used to grow various medicinal herbs. In addition, he also had a chicken coop and a few milk cows. This young man was very particular about the quality of his milk and eggs. As such, he always fed the chickens and cows special spirit grain, which he also cultivated within his courtyard.

While he might have been indulging in his favorite hobby, his demeanor was not in the least bit relaxed. He had a dreadful problem he needed to resolve—the looming threat of the chicken thief. At present, he only had fifteen chickens, two less than the original number. Another kindred spirit within Green Leaf Academy had reported a similar matter. In this case, the poor student had lost one of his geese, two of his ducks, and three of his carrier pigeons!

In addition, they had both noticed a peculiar lack of wild birds in the surrounding area. The only logical conclusion was that a voracious predator had started living in the area. Despite their suspicions, they had no hard evidence or eye-witness testimony on the matter. Even if they wanted to find the thief, they didn't know what it looked like.

Sighing heavily, the cultivator continued feeding his chickens spirit grain and collected their eggs. He then started installing various upgrades to fortify the chicken coop. The first thing he did was replace the wire around the chicken coop; the old wire did not provide adequate protection against predators and had only been useful in preventing the chickens themselves from escaping. The predator had changed everything. In addition to replacing the wire, he also ensured that it completely enclosed the pen. This rendered it impossible for a predator to approach from above.

Protecting the coop from an underground assault was also a tricky task. What if the thief was a ferret or a fox? He dug up all the soil inside the chicken coop to install a deep brick foundation, which connected to the fence wire. He covered up the foundation with soil, something the chickens enjoyed while they walked outdoors.

Following this major renovation, he then focused on the building itself. The windows were potential points of entry, so he installed iron bars on each one. He also installed locks on all the doors for good measure. Perhaps this chicken thief was a student?

This massive project took three days. Fortunately, he finished the project before any of his chickens were stolen. Despite the greatly strengthened chicken coop, he was still a little nervous. During the entire construction, he experienced a tingling in the back of his neck, the kind that only happened when one was being watched. As a martial cultivator, he had developed a sixth sense for things like these. It was hardly ever wrong. Or perhaps the hammering noises from the nearby courtyard had unnerved him, causing him to imagine enemies that didn't exist.

It was now late at night. The consistent pounding of metal

on metal had stopped, as it always did at sunset. This granted the occupants of nearby courtyards a temporary reprieve and ideally a good night's sleep. Despite the absence of the rhythmic clanking, some of the residents were still profoundly affected. They now heard these sounds in their dreams. Hammering aside, the night was very quiet, almost too quiet. If one observed carefully, they might have noticed a large absence of birds or other small animals near a specific courtyard.

The owner of the courtyard was fast asleep, and so were his chickens. Huxian had been observing them for the past few days. Despite his ability to steal the chickens over the past three days, the actions of the cultivator in this courtyard had intrigued him. It was as though the cultivator thought he could prevent Huxian from taking the chickens that rightfully belonged to him!

His curiosity piqued, Huxian's observations had continued for three days. When the cultivator finally finished, the renovated chicken coop emanated a special aura, an aura of challenge toward the chicken thief.

Challenge accepted, Huxian decided.

His small and agile figure vanished as he jumped over the courtyard wall, careful not to make any noises that might alert the cultivator or the chickens. Once inside the courtyard, Huxian merged with the shadows near the edge of the wall. While the entire courtyard was well lit, it was impossible for there to be a complete absence of shadows. The shadows were his home.

After observing the front of the chicken coop for a short while, Huxian decided to give up on sneaking through the metal wires or digging through the brick. While this was a simple task for the baby fox demon, it didn't suit his style; he wanted the cultivator to be completely baffled by the theft!

Since accessing through the front of the coop was physically impossible, he opted for the next option—the back. The back of the coop was now only twelve inches away from the courtyard wall, enough to allow air circulation through the tightly barred window. Huxian ignored the small gap and also ignored the bars for good measure. He blended into the shadows and immediately found himself inside the chicken coop.

The chickens were sleeping soundly and hadn't noticed his approach. The juvenile fox sneakily approached a chicken's bed, but just before approaching, his instincts told him something was off. After observing carefully, he noticed that there were several snares set up. He quickly bypassed these snares and approached the sleeping chicken from the side. He made short work of it.

After dispatching his unfortunate victim, he decided to make his exit and call it quits. Stealing a single chicken without leaving a trace or clue was much more fun than outright plundering. After licking his lips, he vaulted himself outside the coop through the shadows. He didn't notice the fluorescent trail he left behind, his little pawprints lighting up his journey from the chicken coop to the top of the wall and finally to Cha Ming's courtyard.

The next morning, Cha Ming was forced to host a guest in his courtyard. The guest was an angry-looking cultivator, evidently the man who took great care in raising his chickens. Cha Ming massaged his brow as he listened intently and wracked his brain for a solution.

"What were you thinking, keeping a fox as a pet?" the man said, livid. "Don't you know that they're vile creatures that eat every bird in sight?" Like all angry people, it was best to first let them vent while showing sympathy.

"I understand sir," Cha Ming replied.

"No, you don't understand. These are my prize chickens, and I've spent many months raising them and feeding them expensive spirit grain. Heck, I wouldn't even eat any of them myself! I keep them around, I care for them, and in return they lay the most delicious eggs available in the country. These chickens are the culmination of my life's work," the man explained. His anger had lessened somewhat, and he now looked distraught and sad.

"So you're saying that these chickens are very expensive to raise, almost priceless?" Cha Ming inquired.

"Yes, exactly. In fact, I often deprive myself of cultivation resources to nourish them adequately. I grow the spirit grain myself, at the expense of raising less medicinal herbs. Raising medicinal herbs is my main source of income!"

"So if I reimbursed you a sufficient amount, you would forgive me? Huxian's behavior is, of course, unacceptable. However, he is a little difficult to control sometimes. I humbly apologize on his behalf. What sort of compensation would make up for your loss?" Cha Ming started to relax, as they were finally getting somewhere. It was impossible to reason with an angry man.

The chicken farmer was at a loss. He had mostly come to yell at the new, irresponsible owner. Unfortunately, there was really nothing he could do. It was difficult to prove the value of his chickens, and making a formal complaint would have been very difficult. Therefore, the best he was able to do was attempt to intimidate the fox's owner.

"This… well, it's really difficult to estimate the total cost. To make a rough estimate, it could be anywhere between three hundred and five hundred spirit stones to raise a single chicken. However, this doesn't factor in the amount of labor required, the three months where I don't have a chicken…" The farmer really didn't have a good case to make, and so he left the specifics ambiguous. In fact, he didn't expect to get anything at all in compensation.

"Unfortunately, I'm really short on cash right now," Cha Ming said apologetically.

The chicken farmer was livid again. Just as the chicken farmer was about to speak up, Cha Ming withdrew a silver talisman from his bag of holding.

"I have this Iron Skin talisman that I crafted not too long ago. The retail value for one of these talismans is 1,280 spirit stones. Is this sufficient to cover your losses?"

Cha Ming's question fell onto deaf ears, as the man was now observing the exquisite penmanship used to craft the talisman.

"My apologies," the man asked nervously. "What did you say? Are you offering this to me as compensation?"

"Of course. Even if I don't have spirit stones on me, this talisman should have a certain amount of resale value if you don't want it. If it's useful to you, however, you've even made yourself a hefty profit! What do you say?"

Cha Ming was hoping the man would accept; he really didn't have anything else on his person right now. Perhaps it was time to craft a few more to fill his pockets, especially with the gluttonous Huxian around.

"Of course it's sufficient! More than sufficient! You said you made this?" The man's expression subtly changed. The man now seemed *grateful* that Huxian had eaten his chickens.

"Might I ask, what kind of talismans are you able to craft? I have a need for them, from time to time. There are also many residents in the courtyard who would be very interested in purchasing them." The man was no longer livid. In fact, he was now quite polite.

"There is demand within the residences? Well, I can craft most readily available fifth- and sixth-grade talismans, in each of the five elements. I'm not better in any one of the elements, so I can accommodate a large variety of requests. If anyone has any specific requests that I am not familiar with, and the talisman is within my artistic capabilities, I can also give it a try. Since we are all fellow students here, I can also craft them at ninety-five percent of the list price," Cha Ming explained while musing to himself, *How did getting scolded suddenly turn into a business relationship?*

"Sixth-grade talismans! You can craft sixth-grade talismans? At ninety-five percent of list price? Whatever element we want?" The chicken farmer was now very excited. There were very few people in the city who were willing to craft sixth-grade talismans. Most of the people that were able to do so economically were at the ninth level of qi condensation, or even foundation-establishment elders!

"Yes, I do have a knack for crafting them. I can at least break even at ninety-five percent of the list price, and it will be good to practice my crafting skills."

Technically, none of what Cha Ming said was a lie, but he didn't want to reveal the secret of the Clear Sky Brush. Crafting talismans for practice to break even, however, was something a student would consider doing.

"It's been a pleasure meeting with you, sir! If you don't mind, I would like to place an order. It's fine if you finish them whenever is convenient. Do you have a pen?"

Somehow, Cha Ming had now become a "sir." He had also secured some orders at profits higher than he could normally accomplish. Little did he know that many orders would soon come his way from the surrounding courtyards, and the goodwill he earned would far outstrip the amount of annoyance caused by Huxian or Cha Ming's incessant beating of his mannequin.

The chicken farmer was in a very pleasant mood on his way out of the courtyard. Just as he was about to leave, he remembered that he had forgotten to do something important.

"Sir, what's your name?"

"It's Cha Ming. You're welcome anytime!"

Cha Ming retreated into his courtyard after the surprisingly profitable scolding he'd received. He took a seat cross-legged in front of Huxian. Huxian's eyes were downcast. He knew he had messed up.

How can I stay mad at you? Cha Ming thought while massaging his brow.

"Can you not eat other cultivators' pets? It's very troublesome to deal with them. I know you eat meat, but you need to show some restraint," Cha Ming scolded.

But, big brother, they are so tasty! I didn't eat a lot of them... Huxian had ditched the dejected look and opted for showing puppy dog eyes.

"Come on, there's no way they can be tastier than the roast spirit beast meat you get from the restaurant every few days. Also, you wouldn't be having this problem if you hadn't hunted down a hundred wild birds as soon as we arrived in this courtyard. You need to show moderation." Cha Ming didn't give in to Huxian's cute act. If he wasn't firm with him as a baby, who knew what kind of trouble he would cause once he got older.

"Fine, fine. I will be good," Huxian said. He slowly walked over to Cha Ming and rubbed his head against Cha Ming's thigh. "Can I have pets?"

Cha Ming shook his head and scolded Huxian once more. "Only good foxes get pets. Maybe tomorrow if you behave."

Soon after Huxian left the room to go outside, Cha Ming got up and grabbed his heavy staff to continue his practice. Before he could go out to practice, however, he heard a familiar voice calling out to him.

"Kid, that's as far as you're going to get by whacking that mannequin. Come inside the brush and I'll teach you how to fight!"

It was the bearded man, of course. Cha Ming hadn't heard from him for a while. The last time they had spoken, he had been instructed to practice his footwork and staff techniques against the mannequin. The constant beating had destroyed the mannequin countless times, and Cha Ming had been forced to supplement its energy with spirit stones.

Cha Ming's excitement at the prospect of practicing in a way that didn't involve beating a piece of living metal was evident. He even used his newly learned movement techniques as he retreated to his bedroom and sat down cross-legged. His body stood still, but his soul did not.

His soul had now entered the space inside the Clear Sky Brush.

Chapter 6:
The Power of Creation

The scenery inside the Clear Sky Brush was the same as before: a misty white color. There was no up or down, but he could walk up or down as he willed it. He enjoyed this sensation, the sensation of pure control over his surroundings. In this space, physics meant nothing. Imagination was everything.

A literal bucket of cold water was poured over his head as he realized that he was falling out of control. He tried to imagine various solutions, like flight, a parachute, or even falling on a soft memory-foam surface. His control over the environment had been obliterated by someone else. That person was the bearded man.

As he continued falling, he started to notice some changes in the surrounding environment. Some plumes of mist shaped themselves into large trees, the likes of which he had never seen before. Each tree was over two hundred feet tall, and he could see large bunches of fruit on each tree. He quickly identified these fruits as a sort of giant red banana.

Farther off into the distance, he could see four large stone monkeys. The first monkey statue covered his eyes, the second covered his ears, and the third covered his mouth. This was a common arrangement, signifying see no evil, hear no evil, and speak no evil. The third statue, however, made him raise an eyebrow. The monkey held its large stone hands guardingly over its large stone crotch.

Do no evil, perhaps? Cha Ming chuckled inwardly at the bearded man's sense of humor.

Finally, his descent slowed, and he landed softly on a grassy field. The grassy field was adorned with various unique terrains, such as a small desert, some wooded areas, and even a large lake. Everything was enclosed in an impressive ring wall filled with circular stands. The building was very reminiscent of the Coliseum in ancient Rome.

"So you think you've had it hard for the past month, eh? Whacking that mannequin over and over? Well, the hell training is about to begin!"

The bearded man now wore a set of crimson combat robes, and the gray staff he typically wielded was now as large as Cha Ming's. He could only hope that it also weighed the same, lest he be blown to bits in a single strike.

If you die in a dream, do you die for real? he pondered.

"All right, first things first. You've learned six staff arts so far: Foundation Staff Art, Flaming Wheel Defense, Wading Through the Reeds, Quake Staff, Sword Staff, and Trapping Staff. The Foundation Staff Art is very solid, giving you something firm to build on. It covers the basic staff moves: blocks, strikes, sweeps, and entrapments. As you learned, there are many variations of these moves.

"Flaming Wheel Defense taught you a very superficial defense, which involves spinning the staff in circles and using flame qi to create a flaming shield. It's very effective against projectiles and qi attacks, but very weak against direct strikes. Despite being very superficial, it has its place in your staff martial art.

"Wading Through the Reeds is a staff art where the defensive capabilities of the staff are maximized. While the movements themselves are very effective at redirecting an opponent's physical strikes, adding an extra layer of water qi maximizes the effectiveness of the technique. Mastering this technique in turn provides the user with a very good defense against physical attacks. It does nothing at all against special attacks like a burst of flame or frost.

"Quake Staff is the most offensive move of the bunch and is my personal favorite. It concentrates brute physical strength with localized vibrations formed with earth qi. However, to execute these techniques, one needs to grasp the staff near its end and sacrifice mobility, technique, and defense. Nevertheless, any sweep, downward strike, or spear strike will achieve devastating levels of power."

The bearded man suddenly grabbed his stone staff and lifted it over his head. To Cha Ming's surprise, as he struck downward toward the arena floor, the staff extended by several hundred feet and came crashing down with devastating impact. The staff had been swung down so hard that it had curved into a half-moon shape before slapping down onto the ground.

As the dust settled, Cha Ming could see a large trench had been carved along the length of the staff. The trench was very narrow at the starting point but fifty feet wide where the strike ended. The strike ended even further than the staff physically reached. Cha Ming had no choice but to confess himself impressed.

"That, my boy, is why you need to get yourself a soul-alloy staff as soon as possible. As part of my strike, I not only extended the strike zone by extending the staff, but I also increased the weight of the staff by a hundred times. This let me do two things: First, I was able to start swinging quickly while the staff was still short and light. Next, the longer staff can achieve a much higher velocity closer to the tip. You'll notice that the trench is much, much larger near the end of the strike. In this case, the tip of my staff reached a speed a hundred times greater than its original length was capable of.

"Additionally, just before the impact, I greatly increased the weight of the staff. Combined with the increased speed, my strike was over ten thousand times more powerful than it could have been originally." The bearded man gave Cha Ming a hundred breaths or so to have the lesson sink in.

"Continuing with your remaining staff arts, the Sword Staff Art is very nice. It increases the striking power of your staff by sharpening it with metal qi. While not strictly a blade, this gives the staff a much smaller area over which to apply force whenever you strike. Combined with the staff's heavy characteristics, it's akin to fighting with a dull heavy sword. Like sword techniques, the Sword Staff makes it easy to parry blows and attack swiftly. The creator of the technique really didn't hesitate to go against the grain on this one.

"Last but not least, you have the Trapping Staff Art. This art is unique because it emphasizes jamming techniques, tripping techniques, disarming, and all sorts of underhanded moves. In addition, the wood qi used can add sticky properties to your staff or to the ground it immediately touches, making it possible to jam your opponent's footwork.

"Overall, combining these various staff arts with your

Foundation Staff Art is very beneficial because it allows you to easily amplify and better use its specific abilities. In addition, these abilities can be strengthened by using a very small amount of elemental qi. This allows you to keep your qi to operate your soul pearls while concentrating on fighting physically.

"Do you have any questions so far?" the bearded man asked. After thinking for a while, Cha Ming shook his head and continued to listen to the lecture.

"All right kid, the next part of the plan is to properly teach you the remaining movement arts. White Willow Shade, Three-Layered Burst Step, and Skating in Paradise are all mediocre movement arts on their own. They each have their benefits, however. White Willow Shade is very good for concealed and sneaky movements, like your atrocious Ghost Steps. It combines best with the Trapping Staff Art, Wading Through the Reeds, and the Sword Staff. Three-Layered Burst Steps is useful for instantaneous movements, and it is good with the Sword Staff and the Quake Staff. It is also good for evasive maneuvers in combination with the Flame Wheel Defense.

"Mountain Stance is best combined with Sword Staff and Quake Staff as well, as its purpose is to increase your weight and root you to the ground. Otherwise, wielding a heavy staff would throw you away or take away your center of gravity. Finally, Skating in Paradise is very beautiful and exquisite. I can't wait to see you practice it while wearing the little dress I prepared for you."

A cold look appeared on Cha Ming's face when he heard this, and he prepared to leave the white brush immediately. Who would have known that the bearded man had such a weird fetish? Before he was able to leave, however, he saw that the bearded man had fallen on the floor, laughing while clutching his gut.

"You should have seen that look on your face! Seriously, it's like you thought I was a sexual predator or something!" After continuing his laughter for several breaths, he finally calmed down. "In all seriousness, this technique is very useful when combined with Wading Through the Reeds, and it's also very useful in pinch situations. Sometimes you get hit so hard that you're sliding around. This movement art lets you control those situations instead of getting beaten around like a ball. In addition, if you ever need to impress the nobles, you'll be able to show off your perfect figure skating technique!"

Cha Ming rolled is eyes at the continuous prodding. The bearded man would likely never let it go.

"Teacher, what about the two wind-element techniques, the Shearing Staff Art and the Seven Cloud Steps? I presume you have a workaround for my lack of wind qi?"

"Right, the wind-element techniques! The Shearing Staff Art, on its own, is not very powerful. It's necessary to combine it with a corresponding movement art. Both techniques place heavy emphasis on a single thing: speed. Seven Cloud Steps was designed to emphasize instantaneous acceleration and speed above all else, utilizing a film of wind qi to cut through the viscous air. The Shearing Staff Art, on the other hand, has three main techniques: Wind Wheel Repulsion, which is similar to the Flaming Wheel Defense; Cyclone Strike, which is used to sweep away all surrounding enemies; and Wind Cutting Strike, which uses pure speed and wind qi to create an extremely sharp blade of wind.

"With respect to using wind qi, I have a special technique you will need to practice in the outside world. Here, take this!"

The bearded man passed him a white and translucent ball.

Cha Ming pressed it to his head without hesitation, and his mind was flooded with new information. The technique was called the Creation Qi Manipulation technique. It was not a cultivation technique, but a technique for manipulating existing creation qi.

Cha Ming was very familiar with the circulation of qi pathways. Due to his use of the five elements, he had needed circulate to qi along five separate existing pathways to keep the elements separate. The Creation Qi Manipulation technique, however, was extremely shocking! To cultivate it, one would have to create a new qi circulation pathway from the dantian out to each part of the body. The pathway would be created little by little and would require large amounts of mental strength, tolerance to pain, and of course, creation qi.

For his five elements, he had not been required to create separate pathways. The pathways he had used were inherently present in the human body. They just required cleaning and strengthening the pathways, which was done as part of regular cultivation. Not only did cultivation absorb qi into the dantian, it also circulated it throughout the body to facilitate the execution of martial techniques.

"Teacher, I don't understand. How can I cultivate this without creation qi? I only have five-element qi inside my dantian..." Cha Ming was hesitant to ask because he knew he would be scolded.

"You dolt! You have as much creation qi as your other qi! You see that circular white river connecting your qi lakes? That's creation qi! Your cultivation technique is very good, and it gives birth to both creation qi and destruction qi in your dantian to maintain the equilibrium between the five elements.

"However, you didn't even know about this and have been wasting the technique's potential! Therefore, what you'll need to do for the next long while is forcibly carve out and create a qi pathway that will enable you to use your creation qi. Once this step is complete, you can practice transforming the qi into wind-element qi. Creation qi is the most flexible qi in the world, and it can be used to replace any qi except for space, time, and destruction." The bearded man had a very satisfied look on his face. He liked nothing more than belittling juniors while teaching them.

"Can I do the same thing with the black qi in my dantian?" Cha Ming asked.

"Sure, sure, if you think your weak body and meridians can handle the purest form of destructive energy in the universe, we can give it a shot!" The bearded man's sarcasm was an unequivocal no.

"All right, I can definitely cultivate this technique once I exit the Clear Sky Brush. What is the next step in the training?" the young man asked nervously.

"Next? Next, you dance!"

Huxian had returned to the courtyard after a busy day of chasing birds and chickens. Chasing, mind you; he didn't hurt any. Hurting them would make him a bad fox, and bad foxes didn't get pets. After arriving inside the courtyard, he noticed that Cha Ming was still sitting cross-legged in meditation. Boring.

Huxian had a quick snack, which he withdrew from his collar. It was a whole side of roasted spirit deer. After finishing the side of deer, he let out a large burp and curled himself up into a ball on Cha Ming's lap, where he fell asleep. A few hours later, he woke up to the sensation of a hand gently rubbing behind his ears. He quickly adjusted his head in order to maximize the effectiveness of the petting and scratching.

"Were you a good Huxian today?" Cha Ming asked gently.

Yes, yes! Huxian replied. I *chased birds and chickens all day, but I didn't eat any of them. I promise!* Huxian was quite proud of his self control.

Cha Ming paused for a moment, as though deciding whether to continue petting or not. The petting turned into a belly rub.

A half hour later, Huxian was sleeping soundly and comfortably on the bed they shared. Cha Ming didn't mind. He thought it was nice to have a furry companion to hug as he fell asleep. After putting Huxian to sleep, he sat cross-legged once more, this time in the courtyard garden. The mental exhaustion that had accumulated during his training session inside the brush slowly but surely faded away. Surprisingly, he noticed that his muscles were sore. It seemed that his body was also stimulated while he trained inside the brush.

Thinking of his training, he shuddered at the inhumanity of it. The first step of his training had been a game of hide and seek, where he had to run quickly through the woods without making noise. Meanwhile, he was chased through the woods by strange creatures. Once they found him, Cha Ming had to escape their detection within ten seconds, otherwise he was subjected to a fear beating. There was no limitation on which movement arts he could use, but White Willow Shade was the most appropriate. He could use defensive staff arts to deflect and entrap his opponents as well as to defend against incoming attacks.

The second drill had been extremely scary for Cha Ming. He was forced to jump between many stone platforms floating in the skies. The stone platforms would randomly shift, sink, crumble, and reassemble. They were so small and far apart that he had no choice but to use his Three-Layered Burst Step Technique to instantaneously accelerate prior to jumping. Every time he fell off the platforms, he was beaten once again.

The last drill seemed impractical at first, but Cha Ming eventually saw the value in it after a few rounds of practice. During this drill, he had to keep a thin layer of water qi below his feet, which he shaped like a blade. Effectively, the last drill was just like ice skating. While "skating" on a stone arena, various fans would send a strong or soft burst of wind his way, which would push him in one direction after another. He quickly realized that he needed to first skate in the direction of the wind, after which he could use his skates to curve and change directions before being blown off the ring. Lo and behold, Cha Ming was somehow a natural-born figure skater. He didn't get any beatings, and the only judge at the performance gave him an eight out of ten.

After meditating for a quarter hour, he was finally able to forget the day's training, focusing instead on the Creation Qi Manipulation Technique. The technique, which had been imprinted directly into his mind, was said to be very painful and exhausting. The first step was to establish a connection between his dantian and his yin and yang organs, which would then be used to direct flow toward his four limbs. Each limb had three major connection points along the qi pathways. For an arm, it was the shoulder, the elbow, and the palm. For a leg, it was the hip, the knee, and the sole of the foot. All twelve points connected to the center of the body, where the organs and the dantian were located.

Cha Ming braced himself as he proceeded to practice the technique. The first connection Cha Ming chose to establish was the lungs. The lungs and the heart needed to be connected before anything else, and the heart would be the most painful. Therefore, he chose the lungs without any hesitation.

As his consciousness descended into his dantian, he became aware of the gentle white creation qi and the fierce destruction qi. He avoided the black qi and instead proceeded toward the white qi. Just as he would with his other five qi pools, he used a thread of consciousness to will the qi to flow out of the river. It flowed out in a single lazy thread, reluctant to go anywhere, as no qi circulation pathway had been established.

With Cha Ming's gentle coaxing, the white thread moved toward the edge of his dantian, the edge closest to his lungs. There were nine connection points for each organ, for a total of one hundred and eight connection points.

Gritting his teeth, Cha Ming willed the creation qi to pierce the dantian and form an initial connection point. The process was unbearably painful. After what seemed like an eternity, a small seal formed on the surface of the dantian. The seal allowed creation qi to enter and exit. No other qi was allowed through.

Once the seal was established, Cha Ming proceeded to the next step. He urged the creation qi to painfully bore a path through his flesh toward the first lung connector. This was done with great care. He was especially careful to avoid the natural meridians in his body that accommodated the other five types of qi. Under normal circumstances, the maximum number of elements that could be cultivated in a human body was five. This was also only possible for the five basic elements that Cha Ming cultivated, due to the peculiar construction of the human body and its affinity for these elements.

Boring out each qi pathway was extremely painful, despite the constant replenishing properties of the creation qi. The process continued for a very long time, constantly exhausting the creation qi connecting the five qi pools. While the creation qi was constantly being replenished, it couldn't keep up with the massive consumption. Just when Cha Ming thought he would have to continue the process after resting, he was finally successful in establishing a seal on the first connection point in his lungs. Success!

Following his success, he continued to cultivate for two hours until his creation qi was fully replenished. As he ended his meditation and opened his eyes, he realized that it was finally dawn. The whole process of connecting a single point on an organ had taken him four hours! Practicing this technique would take him about a month. Meanwhile, he had to continue training his techniques, crafting talismans, and cultivating.

After considering many solutions, he finally came to a grave conclusion: from now on, he was allowed to sleep once per week.

Chapter 7: War on the Horizon

An eerie quiet presided over a valley near the town of Crystal Meadows. The trees here were different than those near Green Leaf City. While both cities were situated in the Song Kingdom, they were separated by several hundred li. Here, the trees were conifers. Their thin green needles were frosted despite the absence of snow on the ground. The morning frost would last for another two months, until the end of winter.

Crystal Meadows had two main industries. The first main industry was livestock. Specifically, they raised sheep for wool and meat, since eighty percent of the surrounding land was only suitable for grazing. The remaining twenty percent near the river was used to grow vegetables and potatoes. Any grain required by the residents was imported.

The second industry was the crystal glass industry. While the town was not very large, it had a deep artistic tradition that produced many famous crystal glass artisans. They produced a variety of decorative objects such as cups, vases, and stained-glass windows. These goods were sold across the continent for considerable prices.

Within the valley, a squad of lightly armored men was traveling by horse along the main road. The road was made of clay. It weaved through the grazing pastures, which the local farmers would use as feed for the sheep. It was also more or less dry, since there wasn't much rain in the winter.

Every so often, a crackling sound broke out, indicating that one of the men had guided his horse to break one of the few shallow puddles that froze over every morning. Every time this happened, the guilty soldier was chastised by a fierce gaze from the squad leader. He was a short, well-built man, the graying hair at his temples a testament to his experience in battle. Being a forty-year-old army veteran, Captain Chou Tai was strict and did not allow for carelessness.

After traveling on this road for a few hours, the captain held up a closed fist. The well-disciplined squad instantly came to a halt. Once everyone had stopped, he lowered his hand closer to the ground, indicating that everyone should quiet their horses. The older man frowned; something didn't feel right, but he couldn't put his finger on it.

"Sergeant," he said to the young beside him, "what do you make of the situation?"

The young man was his second in command, and while he rode beside the captain, he always made sure to stay a foot or two behind to indicate their difference in rank.

Unsurprisingly, the young man was also concerned. "Captain, it doesn't feel right. No birds are flying or chirping, and I've seen no squirrels, mice, or foxes. There's only an eerie quiet. Also, isn't Crystal Meadows known to have many sheep? Where are the sheep?"

The older man nodded. "Yes, Sergeant Feng, you are correct. The lack of sheep is concerning. While they could easily be pastured elsewhere, how could the grass get so tall?"

The grass by the road had grown to a foot in height, which was abnormal for any pasture. The farmers should have relocated the flock to take advantage of the surplus grass, which was always in short supply on these infertile plains.

Feng Ming nodded. "Captain, perhaps we should inquire with the villagers? They might be able to clarify this strange situation. In addition, they may have also have first-hand news regarding the rebels."

"Yes," the captain replied. "However, we must be quick about it. We are a scouting squad, and this intelligence is of utmost importance to the kingdom. It is always best for a scouting squad to return safely, even without new information, so that the commander can have confirmation either way. Even a single missing squad can jeopardize the fate of the entire army."

"Yes, sir!" Feng Ming saluted. He deeply admired the captain's strict disposition and his dedication to his duty.

"Move out!" the captain instructed. The six dozen men followed behind him as he led the way. Eventually, they arrived at a small town. The village was surrounded by short stone walls. It didn't even have a main gate at the entrance, nor did it have guards monitoring entry into the village. Surprisingly, they discovered a small flock of sheep just outside the city gate. They were locked in a pen, their fearful bleating mixing in with the sounds of the frigid wind.

Strange, the captain thought. *Are they locked up in this pen for slaughter? How wasteful.* Normally this would not happen until after shearing season.

The squad proceeded into the small village through a gap in the stone wall. The clay road continued through the village. Clearly the traffic did not warrant stone or gravel roads. As they continued, they observed that the streets were not very busy. This was expected; it was winter, after all. A plume of smoke could be observed coming from each chimney. Some select buildings, supposedly the crystal glass shops, had much larger plumes. This was due to the intensity of fire required to produce the crystal glass. This normal occurrence reassured the captain.

"Sirs, are you perhaps from the army?" A pleasant voice sounded out from behind them, revealing a beautiful lady and one of the town's guards. It was not a festival day, but nonetheless, the lady was well dressed and dolled up.

"Yes, madam. Who might you be?" The captain's voice had softened considerably. He was harsh to his men but was impeccably polite to the fairer sex. The woman smiled at his polite response.

"My name is Li Piao[1]. I am the owner of the Clearglass Inn, and I double up as the mayor in town. Our town is so small that a normal lord wouldn't be bothered with it. Nevertheless, the revenue here is plentiful thanks to the crystal glass industry. Therefore I manage the town while reporting directly to the Fairweather County lord," she explained dutifully.

This was surprising, as the captain had expected to be escorted to the local mayor or lord's house. Female leaders were extremely rare.

"Then you're just the person we're looking for. Do you

---

[1] Piao can be used in many situations. Piao Liang is beautiful. Piaozi is a banknote, but another tone can be used to describe a prostitute's fee for service.

have an office where we can discuss some official business in private?" While the captain didn't think the conversation would lead anywhere, due diligence saved lives.

"Yes, of course. I'll lead you back to the inn where we can discuss things in my office. I assume you'll want to stay the night?"

"Let's go back to the inn and discuss first. We'll make a decision on staying the night once we're done there." Although the captain hadn't stayed in a decent inn in days, he didn't want to waste time staying in this small town. However, it would have been rude to decline directly, even though Li Piao did not seem to care either way.

The squad followed the beautiful lady and her guard back to the inn. They saw many cheerful faces along the way, all of whom waved at the squad and Li Piao. It seemed she was quite popular in town. These were not the faces of rebels, and these people certainly didn't look mistreated. If anyone in the squad had turned around and looked back, however, they would have come to a different conclusion. As soon as each villager passed the guard squad, their cheerful expressions instantly disappeared. They had been replaced with expressions of suspicion, caution, and fear.

Chou Tai and Feng Ming were seated at a small wooden tea table just outside Li Piao's office. Li Piao was at the host's seat, pouring herself and Chou Tai a cup of tea. Feng Ming had refused a cup. Ever since he was young, he had despised hot drinks, only drinking them when formalities required it. Of course, he still had an inkling that something wasn't quite right about this town, further cementing his refusal.

After taking a few sips, Li Piao started off the conversation. "Captain Chou, you mentioned that you wanted to discuss official business. Is anything the matter?"

"There may or there may not be, Madame Li," he said. "Have there been any major problems around here lately? Any *unusual* circumstances?"

"This... well, there was one unusual thing that happened recently." Chou Tai and Feng Ming edged forward to listen. "You see, two weeks ago, there were a few reports of missing sheep. Originally, we didn't make a big deal of the matter, thinking that it was just hungry wolves in the middle of winter." Madame Li took a sip of her tea and refilled the captain's cup and her own.

"Unfortunately, we were wrong. We soon discovered that they had been stolen by a new bandit group, ten strong in total. They are based a half day's ride toward the west, where they have established a small camp. Unfortunately, the county lord has been unresponsive to our request to drive away these bandits. We have been forced to bow our heads down in fear, lest they attack our small town. We only have five guards here, and we are very reliant on the county lord's guards for our security." She appeared demoralized, and her fatigue was evident despite her best efforts to cover the bags under her eyes.

Chou Tai frowned. This was indeed strange. While they shouldn't go investigate directly, perhaps they should go pay a visit to the Fairweather County lord prior to reporting in.

"Is there anything we can do to help?" he involuntarily blurted out.

That's strange, he thought. *Why would I try to help them so easily? We're on duty and can't get sidetracked.* But she seemed very helpless and alone, as if there was no one else in the world she could rely on. How could he abandon her in her time of need?

Madame Li's expression lit up when she heard this. "How generous of you, Captain. However, I'm sure you have important work to attend to," she said, reluctantly declining. Nevertheless, she continued pouring tea for herself and the captain. Her expression indicated that she had accepted their fate.

The captain felt guilty now. If he declined to help, wouldn't that make him heartless? "It's decided," he said. "We'll go in the morning and investigate. However, I can make no promises. If they are normal rabble, we can take care of them. However, if the group is larger or well armed, we can't jeopardize our mission. We can, however, confirm our findings with the county lord and instruct him to dispatch guards. I do have a certain amount of authority in the army."

Despite his words, the captain was confused. *Why do I care so much about this? And why am I trying to impress her? This isn't like me.*

"Thank you ever so much," Madame Li said while standing up. She was glowing with joy, to the point where she seemed like she could cry at any moment. "I'll go arrange for a feast tonight to celebrate! Please make yourselves comfortable for a quarter hour while I make the necessary arrangements." She left the two of them alone in the tea room and began to run around, busily giving out orders.

"Captain Chou, why did you agree to help her?" Feng Ming asked. "This isn't like you. You always say that it's best to be cautious, lest we endanger the mission. Any delay in providing information can lead to the loss of many lives."

"You're right. I understand your concern. However, I've already agreed, and she is already preparing a feast. It would be a little awkward to refuse now, wouldn't it? I don't want to tarnish the Royal Army's reputation." Chou Tai knew he had made a mistake. Feng Ming sighed as well.

"Besides, these bandits could be affiliated with the rebels. Even if we don't fight them, we can at least confirm their location and attempt to extract information from them. Failing that, we could possibly obtain information on rebel banners." While the older man justified himself calmly, he knew that he was only making excuses.

"What's done is done. However, we need to agree that there can be no drinking at the feast, and no overeating. We're on duty, and it's best to be cautious," Feng Ming warned the captain once more.

"Right, right," the captain said tiredly. "Tell the men. We need to make sure everyone stays sober and is ready to leave first thing in the morning."

"And they need to stay away from pretty girls. Something doesn't feel right." Feng Ming insisted on this. Chou Tai's reaction to the innkeeper seemed unnatural.

Chou Tai hesitated for a bit, then nodded. "Yes, please let the squad know on my behalf. Your caution is admirable, Sergeant." He didn't notice his own hesitation.

The feast began four hours later. It was already dark outside, as the winter days were much shorter than in the summer. Feng Ming looked around the inn, admiring the decorations that had been hastily set up. If he didn't know any better, he would have sworn that they had spent days preparing. Not only was the place impeccably clean, rare pieces of art were prominently displayed on the walls. The chairs were all covered in bright, decorative fabric. Unsurprisingly, the plates, bowls, and utensils were all crafted out of beautiful pieces of crystal glass. The crystal glass had been shaped and carved to resemble mythical creatures, like dragons and phoenixes. Not a single piece was the same.

The captain sat at the seat of honor, while Li Piao sat in the host's seat. She had changed for the occasion. Her beautiful, lithe figure was showcased by a form-fitting, low-cut red[2] dress. Her curves were accentuated by carefully placed slits along her legs, back, and upper chest. Although Feng Ming would have thought it impossible, she was even more dolled up than previously. Among other things, she had painted her eyelids with a light coat of red glitter, which matched her cherry-red lips and her red dress. A passerby would think they were attending a traditional wedding ceremony.

The only other guests called to the feast were three of the town's five guards. Due to their large frames, they looked quite menacing. They did, however, express their gratefulness to

---

[2] Traditional Chinese wedding attire is red, not white. White is used more for funeral attire in China, and quite frankly, most of eastern Asia. That being said, the West's influence in China is very large, and as a result, two or more costumes are now used. These costumes include the white Western wedding dress (the man wears a suit), the red Phoenix dress (the man wears the dragon outfit), and usually a red cocktail dress, mostly because wedding dresses are a real pain to walk around in.

the captain for helping them deal with the bandits. Clearly the presence of the bandits had placed a significant amount of pressure on these guards.

Once all the guests were seated, Li Piao stood up and lifted her cup, which was filled with tea. The captain had insisted that tea be served instead of liquor to maintain compliance with military regulations.

"Thank you all for attending this feast that we've prepared for you. You'll have to forgive me for the meager fare, but all of this was prepared on very short notice. Now, I would like to join our guards in a toast to these brave soldiers who will go out to investigate the bandits tomorrow." She quickly downed her cup of tea, regretting that it was not wine. The guards and soldiers joined in as well. "Let the feast begin!" she yelled. This was followed by a cheer from the soldiers and guards.

Immediately after her announcement, a half dozen maids flooded into the room bearing large dishes and serving tea. There were several vegetable dishes, most of them involving local produce that could last the winter, such as onions, carrots, potatoes, taro, and the like. The meat dishes mostly featured sheep and goat meat, likely obtained from the pen outside. Given only four hours of preparation, such a grand spread was very impressive.

The soldiers and guards chatted and ate, and while they didn't drink, they became intoxicated with the atmosphere. The cautious Feng Ming sniffed at his tea cup. He also lightly rolled some of the liquid around his tongue. It didn't seem poisoned, which reassured him. The guards had cultivations no higher than the fourth level of qi condensation, which reassured him as well. What *didn't* reassure him was how friendly Captain Chou was getting with Li Piao, and how forward she was being with him. Neither was he reassured with the half dozen maids' overly friendly behavior, and their too-perfect appearances. How could so many pretty maids appear in such a small town? Why hadn't they been snatched up by some local lord? Heck, with so much local talent, the town could support a professional matchmaking agency.

He also didn't like the way the guards looked. He occasionally spotted vicious glints in their eyes, which leaked through their friendly façade. Some looked hungry while others looked angry, but invariably these emotions were quickly suppressed by another before they continued chatting and joking. Was it… fear? Unfortunately, it was difficult to come to any conclusions, as guards were fighting men and could easily have their own traumas.

The feast continued for two hours. At some point, one of the maids took out a guqin, a pleasant stringed instrument. She was quite skilled, and she immediately became popular with the men and guards alike.

"I didn't know she knew how to play! What a surprise!" one of the taller, lanky guards said.

Before long, the soldiers and guards were singing along. Even the captain couldn't help himself. Eventually, one of the guards brought out a flute, which he used to accompany the maid. Seeing the joy in the room, Feng Ming had second thoughts. Perhaps he had been overthinking things.

Chapter 8:
A Clue

Feng Ming was sitting in a corner of the banquet room, looking sullen. One of the maids came by to take a seat beside him.

"Why are you sitting here looking all grumpy while everyone else is out there having fun?" she asked. Feng Ming massaged himself between his eyes with one hand.

"I'm just tired," he lied. "It's been a long trip, and I've never been one to celebrate."

Anyone who knew Feng Ming would know that this couldn't be any further from the truth. Fortunately, they weren't acquainted.

"I know what you mean," the maid said, sighing. "There's always so much noise at events like these. I would never stay in a small town like this if my family didn't live here."

"Your father?" asked Feng Ming.

"Yes, my father is a famous crystal glass artisan. It's the same with the rest of these maids. My father used to live in a large city in the north of the continent. He met my mother there. After living in the north for twenty years, he reached the peak of glass artisanship in his kingdom, making a great name for himself. Unfortunately, he felt that he had reached a bottleneck of sorts in his art. Crystal Meadows is well known in the world of glass artisans, so he brought our family here to live a peaceful life while he learned to better his craft.

"Honestly, none of us daughters need to work a day in our lives. We wouldn't even need to get married—the fortune that our fathers have earned is more than enough for us to live a pleasant life in a large city. There used to be more of us, granted. Those of us that remain are here to take care of our aging fathers."

It was truly a touching story, and it addressed his previous concerns. Was he being too cautious?

After another two hours, they finally stopped the celebration. The captain instructed the men to get to bed. Military protocol dictated that they must be ready for departure at dawn. Feng Ming was glad to see that the captain had delivered on his promise.

A half hour after the feast, Captain Chou was busy writing his log. It was a habit that he'd maintained in his childhood, and it had accompanied him throughout his military career. He attributed much of his success as a military captain to this simple habit.

He heard a soft knock on the door and sighed. He knew what Li Piao was up to, but duty dictated that he'd have to turn her down. He opened the door softly, only to find the beautifully dressed woman with red eyes full of tears. Her makeup, which had been impeccable earlier, was now smudged. Seeing the distraught lady, the captain invited her in and sat her down on the bed.

"What's wrong, my dear? What happened?"

She took a while to calm down. Seeing her red eyes and blotched makeup, the caring captain brought out a handkerchief, which she used to wipe her eyes and blow her nose.

"I'm sorry. I shouldn't have come here." Just as she was getting up to leave, a large hand pressed down on her shoulder.

"Come now, something is clearly bothering you. How about you tell your story?"

Li Piao hesitated slightly and nodded. "I didn't tell you the whole truth this afternoon. It's not just bandits that are troubling us. There are rumors that they are backed by a rebel army, which is why the lord of Fairweather has been reluctant to interfere in our affairs. I've been hesitant to share this because… I am afraid that you'll do the same." As she began crying again, he hugged her close.

"There, there now." The older man stroked her beautiful black hair. "You don't need to worry. In fact, this makes it a lot easier. The goal of our squad is to retrieve information about the rebel army, so now that we know, we can't leave without verifying."

The small figure stopped shivering. "Really?" she said, looking up with her tear-stained face.

"Yes, really. You don't need to worry about it anymore."

"But… I don't know how to thank you for this…" she said shyly.

The older man chuckled and shook his head. "It's all a part of my duty. You don't need to worry about a thin—"

He was interrupted by a fiery sensation invading his entire body as her tongue wandered into his mouth. For a moment, he lost his ability to think. A few minutes later, he regained his clear mind, only to realize that he was lying on his bed, and she was straddled on top of him. Somehow they had shed their outer garments, leaving them both with few remaining clothes.

Just as he was about to say that they should stop, a soft, slender finger pressed against his lips.

"Please don't say anything. I just want this so much..." She began shifting her hips back and forth, and although they still had their undergarments on, he knew that it wouldn't last much longer. It felt like pure heavenly torture.

As she continued her sensual movements, her loose hair fell across her bountiful bare chest. Her hair tickled Chou Tai's face as she leaned forward to kiss him gently. It was an electrifying sensation. He hardly noticed her devious smile, as the world suddenly went blank. Her silver hairpin, which she had carefully removed earlier, was now lodged deep inside his neck. His shocked expression seemed to ask her, *Why?*

She didn't answer as she quietly observed his body spasming as the last of his life left him.

Feng Ming was nervous. He wasn't sure why. The men had returned to their beds without drinking, as he had planned. He had seen the pretty ladies exit the inn, as planned. The vixen

Li Piao didn't even accompany the captain to his room, as he'd thought she would. He sat down on his bed for a half hour in silence. The heavy silence that pervaded the inn unsettled him.

In his nervousness, he had decided to don his armor, his boots, and his sword for good measure. While it might be overkill, the cured leather and cold steel reassured his restless feelings.

Perhaps I should check with the captain again, he thought. He hoped he was being overly imaginative. He couldn't be reprimanded for visiting his captain in full uniform, could he?

After mustering his courage, he walked out of his room into the hallway. It was far from quiet, as the sounds of moaning men and women filled the inn.

So much for no women tonight.

Ignoring the other men, he stepped up to the captain's doorway, which was silent.

He knocked softly on the door and waited for a response. The captain was normally very aware of his surroundings, and even a quiet knock would immediately wake him up. The door opened a few seconds later. To his surprise, the person answering the door wasn't the captain. It was Li Piao.

"The captain is sleeping now. Can't it wait until morning?" Her ample figure was partially covered with hastily gathered clothes.

Feng Ming frowned. *The captain seemed like he had a lot of self control near the end of the night. How did it turn out like this?* He wouldn't waste his time on this vulgar woman, though. He would ask the captain himself.

"No, it can't wait. Open the door, I'm coming in." Without waiting for a response, he shoved the door inward. Li Piao was thrown to the ground, her naked figure fully revealed. Feng

Ming was overcome with an overwhelming urge to pounce on her, to violate her. He started walking toward her, and she tightened her hand around her silver hairpin, waiting for an opportunity to strike.

Without any warning, a war started raging inside the young man's mind.

Yes, I haven't had any action in ages! Maybe I can get some now!

But where is the captain? Isn't he asleep?

But she's right here, I could take her back to my room and the captain wouldn't notice!

Is he asleep? Why haven't I seen him?

Who cares? She must be telling the truth.

These questions bombarded his mind in the time it takes for a spark to fly off a piece of flint. During this exchange, his eyes finally managed to flicker to the captain, who was lying on his bed. His formerly white bedsheets were red.

Is that blood?

The sight of the blood jerked Feng Ming back to reality. He regained his lucidity just in time to notice the beautiful naked woman pouncing toward him. Instinctively, he drew out his sword using his quick-drawing sword technique. The draw and the strike were completed in a single, swift motion. The last of the bewitching presence quickly faded as Li Piao's body was cut in two and hit the floor. She was clearly not a cultivator. Yet she had almost killed him by beguiling him. Just like she had killed the captain.

The naked corpse's eyes flashed red and finally faded to white. A red mist quickly left her body, unbeknownst to Feng Ming. Even if he had seen the mist, he wouldn't have been able to stop it. As he stared down at the woman and the captain's corpse, the gravity of the situation dawned on him. What about the rest of the soldiers?

Feng Ming quickly grabbed the captain's bag of holding as he left the room. He rushed toward the next room, worried that he might be too late. He kicked open the first room, only to find a similar scene. The soldier in the room was lying on a bloody bed. Instead of looking at him, the woman in this room appeared to be crying, regretting what she had done. His eyes turned cold as he hacked the beautiful naked body in half before continuing. He continued knocking down door after door, until he finally reached the last door. Inside the last door, a soldier sat down on his bed, shaking. A beautiful naked body lay crumpled on the floor, devoid of life.

"Li Hao, wake up!" Feng Ming barked. The man finally awoke from his daze and immediately started throwing up.

"I didn't mean to, Sergeant!" he said, trying to explain.

"No need to explain. The captain and the others are dead, and it's only you and me! Gear up, soldier!"

Li Hao's eyes went wide as he digested what Feng Ming had said. He then immediately went about obeying his orders. The soldier dressed himself up for battle more quickly than he had ever thought possible. He and Feng Ming crawled out from the window. He knew it was only a matter of time until the guards wandered upstairs. Li Hao's hands were shaking, barely able to keep a grip on the sword.

The duo rushed behind the inn toward the stables. As Feng Ming quietly opened the stable door, he was overwhelmed with the stench of blood. He looked into the dimly lit stable— four of the six horses had been decapitated, and the ground was strewn with blood and gore. Two of the horses were still tied up, but instead of whinnying loudly, they were paralyzed with fear, the hay beneath them covered in excrement.

Just as they were about to bolt for the two horses, they were startled by a strange chewing sound. They looked downward, only to find a gruesome figure staring at them. It was one of the guards, the largest one. In his hands, he was holding a large piece of bloody horse flesh, which he had just carved out from a dead horse's stomach.

Enraged and horrified, Feng Ming and Li Hao charged forward with their swords. What used to be a guard yelled, his body swelling by thirty percent. His mouth was four times as large as what should normally be possible, and it could now barely be called a human.

Feng Ming, being at the fifth level of qi condensation, used his footwork technique, Three-Layered Burst Steps. He swung out with his sword, which glowed red like a brand, ready to slice through anything in its path. He swung the sword toward the monstrosity's head, attempting to decapitate it.

To his surprise, the monstrosity that used to be a guard quickly moved his head, interrupting the trajectory of the blade. The hideous creature bit down on it with all its power, causing Feng Ming's spirit weapon to crack.

What the hell? What kind of infernal beast is this?

The blade snapped. However, just as the beast prepared to pounce on Feng Ming and give him the same treatment, Li Hao snuck up behind it and decapitated it.

The creature fell to the ground, twitching. The duo didn't wait to confirm it was dead and quickly hopped on their horses, who gratefully led them out of the stable at a breakneck pace. As they passed the inn, they noticed two angry men charging out. One bore a large great sword, and the other held a large spear. They both burst forth with unreasonable speed. While

Feng Ming was able to dodge the great-sword-wielding fiend's blow, Li Hao wasn't so lucky. He was struck in the chest with a spear. The horse continued to run beside Feng Ming. Li Hao was gone.

As Feng Ming and the two horses ran toward the edge of the village on the main street, he spotted a glint of metal in the light of the moon. He quickly jumped off his horse, stumbling to the ground just in time to see a large figure with red eyes holding a great sword, swinging through the air above the horse. Judging by its uniform, it also used to be a guard.

"What are you?" he whispered. "Desert Sandstorm!" he roared as the monster charged forward, and a thirty-meter cyclone of heated sand surrounded him. The beast roared in rage, its sight blinded by the burning sand. Its agility was frightening, and the abilities it displayed far exceeded what was capable of a cultivator at the fourth level of qi condensation.

Feng Ming took advantage of its obscured vision to attack its side, his blade glowing red at the last second and cutting deeply into its thigh. Despite the vicious blow, the monster roared as it struck out with a palm. The palm, which was covered in a black energy, struck Feng Ming several meters away, breaking several ribs in the process.

Coughing up blood, Feng Ming got up as fast as he could. He noticed that his sword was still embedded in the monster's thigh. Hopefully its mobility had been affected.

Seeing that he had been disarmed, he pulled out a spare sword from his bag of holding. It wasn't magical, but it was better than nothing. He darted toward the monster, which was busy removing the sword from its thigh.

Just as he was about to reach the monster, he changed his direction, quickly darting toward another nearby monster, which was hacking about wildly in the sandstorm.

Three-Layered Burst Steps!

He took advantage of the large gaps in its swordsmanship, thrusting his glowing red sword into the creature's abdomen. He felt the sword slide into the strange humanoid creature. Having learned from his previous experience, he quickly let it go, darting off to the side toward the last remaining horse in the distance. The other horse had already been cleaved in two.

Darting away had been the right decision. Just as he left the space he had previously occupied, a great sword hacked down with tremendous force. Feng Ming's ability, Desert Sandstorm, finally expired. The two monsters noticed him running toward his horse, but the grievous wounds Feng Ming had inflicted were sufficient to slow down their otherwise swift movements.

Feng Ming didn't hesitate and quickly hopped onto the fearful horse, which darted toward the nearby woods. He didn't trust the roads anymore.

What were those creatures? he thought. Were they devils, the creatures that my nanny told me about to scare me into behaving?

While he didn't know the answer, he knew what he had to do next. He had to get back alive, and he couldn't go missing. Even the slightest delay in information could prove fatal to the king's army.

Clink. Clink. Clink.

One gold coin after another fell onto a heavily used desk,

joining the rest of its shining brethren in neatly piled stacks of ten. A pair of bony white hands inspected each of them carefully, evaluating their weight by touch alone. This was an impressive skill, one that had taken the Merchant many months to learn. At first he had weighed piles of fifty coins on a merchant's balance, verifying the gold content in batches. However, the cool feeling of gold on his hands brought warmth to his entire body. It was the only thing that could excite him.

Suddenly, a sound that only he could hear rang through his head. It sounded like a page tearing. Only important and urgent things would accompany this sound. Sighing, he carefully put away his gold coins. They vanished in his hands, leaving behind only a trace of gold gas, as though they had disappeared from the material plane into another dimension. The feeling was exquisite, second only to the aforementioned feeling he experienced when touching the gold.

Now that his previous earnings had been properly stored, he retrieved a black notebook from his bag of holding. It was vibrating intensely, threatening to break free of its bindings if it was not opened soon. This method of communication, while convenient, was extremely annoying to the Merchant. Whatever happened to the good old days? People used to take the time to see each other in person or via astral projection. Now everyone insisted on sending each other bits and pieces of text every few minutes.

Opening the black book, he saw a piece of writing in red. In the convention of the black notebook, this meant the message was extremely urgent. He started with the less urgent messages immediately before it and then proceeded to the urgent message. It contained troublesome news.

The skinny man pondered for a bit. He couldn't let the

man escape, but he also didn't want to endanger his assets. In addition, Crystal Meadows was short on manpower and would now have to evacuate the artisans. The profit they brought in with their crystal glass pieces was nothing to sneeze at, especially since he had increased their work hours to sixteen hours per day. After thinking up a solution, he sent a message with further instructions.

After this brief exchange, the Merchant put down his pen and proceeded downstairs. He was feeling a little faint, as he hadn't eaten all day. As he walked downstairs, he pondered what delicious meals his underlings had brought today.

After all, he never brought his own lunch.

Chapter 9: Guidance

Meanwhile, in Green Leaf City, Cha Ming was oblivious to the dangers befalling his friend Feng Ming. He continued to train hard. During the day, he crafted talismans, kept Huxian company, and cultivated. At night, he alternated between sparring with the red-bearded man in the Clear Sky Brush and carving out his qi pathways. After a whole month had passed, he finally completed the full qi pathway, which fully connected his limbs, organs, and dantian.

Once this was completed, he redoubled his efforts in sparring to master the final two techniques: Shearing Staff and Seven Cloud Steps. Eventually, they were integrated into his fighting style as much as humanly possible—that is, without going through life-and-death battles. Only an epiphany would enable him to further comprehend these techniques.

"Tsk. Huxian, it seems like we'll have to go on another adventure soon. Are you getting bored yet?" Cha Ming asked the fox that was currently resting on the sunlit grass in his courtyard.

These long breaks are unbearable, Elder Brother. Plus, all of this restaurant meat is getting really boring. I want to eat spirit beasts. High-level spirit beasts!

Huxian got up lazily and stretched before running up to his brother's leg. A hand gently reached down to scratch around his ears.

Cha Ming's cultivation had once again reached a bottleneck. And if previous experience was any indicator, he would require a full month to push through the bottleneck this time. The young man's head ached as he struggled to determine exactly how he would find an adventure, a proper weapon, and medicinal pills.

Two of these three things required a large amounts of spirit stones. Therefore, he began to fully pursue talisman crafting, churning out one sixth-grade talisman after another. This trend continued for a full month, until he was left with a full 206 talismans after trading for materials. Their face value was 105 mid-grade spirit stones and change. He wasn't sure if this was enough, but it was a start, at least. With Huxian in tow, he walked across many courtyards on his way to Wang Jun's new abode.

What he needed now was advice.

Wang Jun was currently seated at his desk, reviewing pile after pile of documents. Unfortunately, his work hadn't progressed as quickly as he would have liked. He was distracted, and he knew the reason. The cause of his confusion was the pretty girl named Hong Xin. In just a few short weeks, the new couple had grown much closer. He enjoyed spending time with her, and he enjoyed making her happy. But was there any way this blissful situation would last?

Every time he asked himself this question, the clear image of a bloody-faced little girl appeared in his mind. His sister had been very beautiful but very naïve. Talent without wisdom eventually led her to an early grave.

He had never envied her talent. Quite the opposite—he had always encouraged her and played with her. He had fought for her interests in the family countless times. This caused his older brother to feel insecure with his position in the family. To further his own ambitions, his brother had schemed and arranged an "accident." While Wang Jun knew the cause of his sister's death, his elder brother had meticulously planned everything, leaving not a single shred of evidence behind.

Thus his dilemma. Hong Xin tugged at his heart strings. She was beautiful, kind, and passionate. And she reminded him of his little sister, the one he hadn't been able to protect. He wanted to spend time with her and take care of her. Was it for love or for atonement? Wang Xia had been his only ray of hope in a dark, cruel world.

He knew that his indulgence with Hong Xin was extremely irresponsible. The ongoing dispute with the Zhou family was bound to be violent and treacherous. Hong Xin was one of his weaknesses, a weakness that grew greater with each passing day. Ignoring the damage this might cause him, it would place Hong Xin in a great deal of danger.

Even without *external* enemies, the Wang family's internal politics were cruel and unforgiving. Hong Xin herself was not a major threat to family interests, but their relationship would prevent potential marriage alliances. His family had often utilized marriages to secure new allies and to appease existing ones. In theory, his influence in the family was considerable. But there was always room for treachery, either through threats, coercion, or outright elimination.

Wang Jun sighed. He put down his pen and walked over to his small cultivation room. He sat down cross-legged on a large and brilliant array formation. Several light-blue stones littered the floor beside the formation. A few of them had crumbled into piles of gray dust—their power had been completely sapped by the large array and converted to qi for his cultivation.

As he cultivated, he regained his calm and focus. His determination was best expressed by the maxim shared by countless cultivators: Fate blesses the strong.

Cha Ming and Huxian's journey to Wang Jun's courtyard took much longer than expected. On the way, Cha Ming was stopped and greeted by every cultivator he met on the streets. His status as a talisman artist had cemented his position in the community, as his goods were welcomed by all. Even the pretentious junior alchemists treated him politely. They were not afraid of his status, but the goods talismans artists produced were always in high demand and commanded an exaggerated premium. A high price for service was the telltale sign of a prestigious occupation.

While Cha Ming proceeded at a snail's pace, Huxian entertained himself by running around and chasing birds.

His reputation was less than stellar, and his current actions provoked many glares from the nearby cultivators. Although they wouldn't assault Huxian in front of his master, all options were on the table if they happened to encounter each other in a dark alley. Which, to Huxian, was just fine.

Two hours passed by quickly and they soon found themselves in front of another student's courtyard. On the surface, it looked identical to any other courtyard in the neighborhood. Only Cha Ming and a few others were aware of the truth. He braced himself as he and Huxian forced their way through an invisible defensive barrier. They were greeted at the door by Wang Jun's assistant, who led them to a cozy living room much larger than the external appearance of the courtyard. Wang Jun's cinnamon-scented fireplace had been brought to this new residence.

They did not wait long.[3] After an incense time , Wang Jun walked out from a small door looking refreshed. Cha Ming's eyes narrowed as he was overwhelmed with a dense cloud of qi, which wafted over from Wang Jun's cultivation room.

"I see that you have quite an energy-gathering formation in there. What grade?" Cha Ming was very curious—his portable energy-gathering formation was only a second-grade formation plate, a mortal-grade treasure.

Wang Jun laughed. "Nothing too fancy. It's only a mid-grade magic treasure."

Once again, Wang Jun's wealth and connections never ceased to amaze Cha Ming. Magic treasures were goods created by professionals in the Foundation Establishment realm. Even a low-grade magic sword was many times more expensive than

---

[3] The time it takes for an incense stick to burn is about five minutes. From now on, it will be stated as an "incense time."

a ninth-grade sword—that is, if you could find someone to make it for you.

According to what Cha Ming had read, mortal-grade treasures were classified by grades one through nine, while magic treasures were ranked as low grade, mid grade, high grade, and top grade. Most magic treasures could not be activated without the use of foundation qi. It was likely the case that this mid-grade magic formation—which was useable in the Qi Condensation realm—was worth as much as a top-grade magic treasure.

"Then how about your current cultivation? I refuse to believe it's only at the sixth rank, despite your identity medallion." After all, Wang Jun had nearly unlimited wealth at his disposal.

"Oh, I'm not doing too badly. I'm at the eighth level of qi condensation. If everything goes properly, I'll be able to break through to foundation establishment within the year."

Wang Jun carefully sat down and started pouring tea for the three of them, ignoring the duo's shocked expression. He only noticed their slack-jawed expression once he finished serving them.

"Don't look at me that way. It's not like this medallion means anything." He removed his bronze identity medallion and flicked it through his fingers. "I worked hard to mask my talent, you know. It's often best to remain unnoticed until an opportune moment. Besides, as a fifth-grade talent from a rich family, this level of growth is rather mediocre."

This information caused Cha Ming to question his will to live. The difference was too extreme, and he needed to work extra hard for every breakthrough. Huxian, on the other hand, simply expressed his sympathy. As a god-beast, his talent far eclipsed these so-called geniuses.

Seeing his friend's dour expression, Wang Jun cleared his throat and spoke first. "To what do I owe the pleasure today, Brother Cha Ming?"

Hearing his name, Cha Ming snapped back to reality and scolded himself for moping.

"Brother Jun, I've come to a bottleneck in my training, and I've realized there are a few things I need to do. After all, I can't just stay cooped up in my cottage and train all the time. I've decided I need to do three things. First, I need to purchase some medicinal pills to aid me in breaking through bottlenecks in my cultivation. This latest breakthrough has made me realize that it takes me four times as long to break through each cultivation level than it takes to fill my qi lakes!"

"Right," confirmed Wang Jun. "This is normal. While you require increasing amounts of energy to break through, your cultivation speed can be increased using an energy-gathering formation and qi supplements. However, the amount of time required for you to break through will increase exponentially with each level of qi condensation.

"Fortunately, your talent grade is at the third grade. For every talent grade increase, the time to break through typically doubles. You're still not doing too bad on average.

"There are two main ways to remedy the problem: the first way is to take medicinal pills that weaken the barrier in your qi lakes, making it much easier to charge through. The second way is to take medicines that increase your natural talent. Medicines that increase natural talent are extremely rare, to the point that they can't be purchased. The only way our Wang family can even obtain a few of these medicines is by finding them ourselves or through our subsidiary families.

"Therefore, only the first option remains. You must hire an alchemist to concoct pills for you."

Cha Ming nodded. He had managed to gather this much information by rummaging through the library, but it was helpful to have this knowledge confirmed by a trusted and well-informed source.

"Yes, I gathered as much. The second issue I need to resolve is the issue of my weapon. I have all the necessary materials to construct a spirit alloy weapon, however, I don't have any way of forging it myself. Lastly, I'll need to go around and adventure. I have been training my staff and movement arts, and the only way I can make any progress is to experience some hardships," Cha Ming concluded.

"So you're asking if I have any advice on where you should go next?" Wang Jun smiled as he poured them another round of tea. He then took out two objects from his bag of holding. He rolled out one of these items onto a small side table. It was an aged leather map of the surrounding area. He then withdrew a couple dozen oddly shaped coins from a used leather pouch. They were irregularly shaped but resembled rectangles more than anything else.

Wang Jun swept all two dozen coins into the air above the map, where they floated as though unaffected by gravity. Each individual coin spun around in a haphazard manner.

"All right," Wang Jun exclaimed. "Wishful Coins, what are the best places for Cha Ming to forge a soul-alloy staff?" He quickly followed up by forming over a hundred hand seals. These movements were completed in less than thirty breaths.

As soon as he completed the last hand seal, the coins stopped twirling and fell onto the map. They tumbled around in a random fashion, but to Cha Ming's surprise, they were all oriented toward three separate points. Wang Jun quickly touched each of these points, leaving behind a glowing yellow light.

After marking each point, Wang Jun swept the coins up once more. He formed another hundred or so hand seals, instructing the coins to find locations where Cha Ming could obtain medicinal pills. The coins fell, and he marked five cities with glowing red marks.

Finally, Wang Jun swept up the two dozen coins and added another seven dozen. These coins were not plain like the original ones but were covered in strange runic characters. Some were colored, and others were marked in white. Many seemed plain, but Cha Ming could vaguely make out obsidian marks that slightly contrasted the other shade of black.

Wang Jun inhaled deeply and formed another set of hand seals. He continued forming them until he completed a total of 1,080 hand seals. This time, the coins fell down on the map violently. The results left the three of them deeply shocked. Instead of spreading all over the map like the last two times, the coins had somehow bounced around and piled up just north of Fairweather City, near a small mountain range. Every single one of the 108 coins had landed deeply in that pile. Many obscure characters could be seen on the mountain of Wishful Coins.

Wang Jun frowned. "My friend, this is something they call fate. While we don't know the reason, destiny requires you in Fairweather City. The runes on the outside of the mountain reveal a few clues. For one, this adventure is extremely dangerous. Further, it involves the fate of many suffering innocents. I also see an old acquaintance… and a bloody moon.

"Destiny?" Cha Ming wasn't convinced. Previously, Wang

Jun had told him that he was unable to foretell his destiny. Why had this changed suddenly? He voiced his concern to his friend, who laughed.

"Cha Ming, there is a big difference between reading your personal story and performing minor divinations. I'll give you an example to explain. Let's say that I ask an information agency two questions. The first question is: Can you please give me a book compiling Cha Ming's past, present, and future actions in exact detail? The agency would answer no, we cannot. Not for any price. It is because either your future or your past is too difficult to decipher. The same thing would happen with me—such a book would be impossible to compile as my fate is obscured.

"Now say you ask them another question: Where was Du Cha Ming, a student of Green Leaf Academy, last spotted? The intelligence agency could likely be able to find this information in a few hours. The information has a timeframe, and it is *definite* and *specific*.

"The same applies to divinations. I simply ask which direction you should go in immediately, and for a definite purpose. Granted, your result is a little unusual. A typical result would indicate many *choices*. In this case, the stones are dictating that you don't have a choice in the matter. Simply put, if you don't go, destiny will find a way to make it happen. Perhaps you could be framed for a crime, for which you need to go to Fairweather City for trial. Or you could get kidnapped and sent there as a slave. Worse yet, a close friend could die a tragic death there, forcing you to travel there for vengeance. This kind of result.... I hate to say it, but you can't fight it."

This greatly displeased Cha Ming. Since coming to Green Leaf City, he felt that his ability to chose had become restricted.

Every time, it seemed like his decisions were made for him. Wasn't he supposed to have free will? One thing was certain, however: whatever hand was guiding him, he would work his hardest to stop it. He didn't want to be controlled by destiny, even if it was for his own benefit.

Unfortunately, Cha Ming was extremely weak. The weak didn't get to make choices.

"The good news is that you can procure a staff and medicinal pills in this town. Give me a second to grab some information," Wang Jun said.

In a matter of minutes, he had his assistant bring a pile of documents labeled "Fairweather County." After flicking through a few pages, he withdrew two documents.

"For weapon crafting, I recommend seeking the services of Han Jinlong. He is one of the top three spiritual blacksmiths in the Song Kingdom. The only reason he stays in Fairweather County is because this city is the closest to his family. They currently live in a town called Crystal Meadows, which is famous for its crystal glass artisans. When you see him, make sure that he observes you sparring and unleashing your techniques. He will be able to implement what he observes in customizing your weapon. This is common practice, but people often forget.

"For medicinal pills, I recommend Zhang Yifeng. Coincidentally, he is also one of the top three alchemists in the Song Kingdom, and he also has family in Crystal Meadows. I recommend commissioning Zhang Yifeng to specially concoct pills using your blood and spiritual imprint as a medium. This will allow him to perfectly tailor the pills to your constitution. Alchemists are typically very proud and unapproachable, however, so your chances of meeting him are very low. You may have to settle for a lesser alchemist.

"Additionally, you should be aware of a famous custom for alchemists. They normally require the one requesting their services to supply medicinal ingredients, in addition to a fee. At least three sets of ingredients are required, depending on the difficulty of producing the pill in question. The fee is payable upon successful completion of a batch of pills, but the ingredients are non-refundable. This provides additional incentive for the alchemists to succeed, but it is often viewed as an avaricious custom by the masses as the alchemist is rarely responsible for failed ingredients.

"Therefore, the reputation of an alchemist is very important when commissioning pills. Alternatively, you can save yourself time and money by buying completed pills, but in this case, there is no ability to customize the pills to your constitution. Tailor-made pills are important because generic pills have reduced effectiveness and leave a greater amount of pill toxins in the user's body. These toxins greatly diminish the effectiveness of taking medicinal pills in the future and increase the difficulty in making breakthroughs." Wang Jun stopped, done with his impromptu lesson.

"Your information gathering ability is impeccable as always, Brother Jun. Would you happen to be free for this upcoming adventure?" Cha Ming had noticed large stacks of papers piled up on his desk. He had only asked to be polite.

"Alas, I can't separate myself from my work. Things will be very busy in the near future. Although I can't come, you might want to wait a while before leaving." Wang Jun picked up one of the black coins from the small mountain on Fairweather City. The black coin had a blood-red rune on it.

"A mutual friend of ours will be arriving soon. My

divination indicates that her presence will be very beneficial on this adventure."

Chapter 10: Gong Lan Returns

Cha Ming didn't need to wait very long. As he returned to his courtyard, he was welcomed by a pretty girl dressed in red leather armor. The dark red armor complemented her short black hair perfectly, and her exposed legs and midriff caused impure thoughts to surface in Cha Ming's mind.

He stopped ten feet away from the entrance to his courtyard, where Gong Lan was napping while leaning on the front door. His placid smile turned into an impish grin at the thought of scaring her awake. That thought quickly disappeared as he was instantly overwhelmed by a baleful aura.

"*Aiya!* Sorry about that Cha Ming!" Gong Lan got up and patted the dust from her armor and bare skin. The air in the student residence was quite dusty, and a light film of fine powder had accumulated on her red outfit during her nap. "You surprised me, so I lashed out instinctively."

Clearly, the baleful aura had emanated from the formerly gentle girl, Gong Lan. As he looked at her, he observed a stark change in her demeanor. Her previous kind and courageous aura had transformed. She now seemed *aggressive* and *incisive*. Wang Jun had told him that she'd taken the news of his disappearance very badly, but wasn't this a little *too* badly?

Cha Ming quickly regained his composure and invited her in for tea. He received an awkward look from her as he walked into the house. Only when he went to boil water did he realize that he was still maintaining a white-knuckled grip on his staff with both hands. Huxian, observing Cha Ming put away his weapon, relaxed his bristled fur and started prancing around to obtain pats from the pretty girl he'd met before.

A short while later, Cha Ming and Huxian were seated in a small living room. He didn't have much. He did, however, keep stock of a few good teas and some dried fruits, which he occasionally took out to serve guests. Gong Lan returned from a small guest room a short while later. She had used a small side room to wash off the dust and grime that had accumulated on her figure during her travels. Such a thing was child's play for a water cultivator, but it would have been improper to wash herself out in the open.

"So," said Cha Ming while pouring two cups and a bowl of tea, "it's been far too long. I heard that you've been traveling for the past couple of months?" He was very curious as to what could have changed her so much in a short period of time.

"Yes, I traveled with my brother to a city called Clearwood. I asked him to help me train, so he taught me a... *unique* cultivation technique that he was familiar with. He had used this cultivation technique in the past to make a name for himself over a decade ago," she replied.

"Oh? You changed your cultivation method? Such a thing is very risky, to say the least," Cha Ming said.

"Yes, normally it would be. However, the prerequisite for

this technique is an existing water-cultivation technique to use as a foundation. Therefore, there was no conflict," Gong Lan explained.

"What's the name of the technique?" asked Cha Ming curiously.

"Blood World Scripture," she replied in a soft whisper, sending shivers down Cha Ming's spine.

"Blood is mostly water," she continued. "As a result, there is a high compatibility with water-cultivation techniques. The technique is used to refine my control over my own—and my opponent's—blood. However, it can only be cultivated during life-and-death battles. As such, I went to Clearwood's underground arena to fight many matches. Because of this intense training regimen, I've now reached the sixth level of qi condensation. This is all without using any medicinal pills."

Cha Ming lifted an eyebrow in surprise. They were both third-grade talents. In truth, Cha Ming was a grade 3.4 talent. Why would there be such a huge disparity? His blood began to rush with excitement as he realized that she would be the perfect sparring partner for his new staff and movement arts. Then he remembered that he was also a body cultivator at the 6th level and let out a depressed sigh. Defeating her should be quite easy now that he thought about it.

"We should definitely take the time to spar sometime," Cha Ming said. "While I'm only at the fifth level of qi condensation, I've made quite a bit of progress. The only thing I'm missing is a test dummy."

Gong Lan's eyes instantly lit up. Her dormant fighting spirit was kindled, and Cha Ming could sense a disturbing amount of bloodlust seeping out from her. He shivered involuntarily while instantly regretting his decision.

"Let's go now!" she yelled. She literally dragged Cha Ming out of the courtyard. Huxian followed behind them dutifully, looking unconcerned.

A short while later, Cha Ming followed Gong Lan and Huxian into an empty arena. Huxian scampered off to the side as a spectator. Once the path was clear, Cha Ming turned and readied his heavy staff.

He laughed. "I haven't had a fight in days! It'll be nice to finally... blow off some steam." This was the wrong thing to say, because she immediately took out her blood-colored sabers and licked one of their edges.

Oh shit. Why does she keep giving me the willies? thought Cha Ming.

"All right, I'm ready!" he called out. She instantly charged toward him, launching out a surprise attack. One of her blades aggressively slashed toward his chest, forcing him to step back quickly with Burst Step. She continued to press the advantage and chased after him. Her movements were unusual and quick. Cha Ming suspected that she had a gold or silver movement technique. She closed the gap in an instant, threatening to decapitate him with a twin-bladed strike.

"*Tch.*" He chose to respond to her onslaught with a flawless defense. He instantly combined Wading Through the Reeds with White Willow Shade, deflecting her blades to the side and stepping around her with ease. This was just a warm-up, of course. Gong Lan quickly used the momentum from her missed strikes to spin in a half circle, jumping up to deliver a diagonal strike with both blades.

He continued to evade her, deflecting her increasingly aggressive attacks with his staff. He couldn't keep this up for long, though, as her rhythmic strikes were speeding up.

Fine, if you're going to play this way, I'll just have to jam you up! He quickly changed his strategy and quickly switched to using the Trapping Staff Art.

He immediately regretted his decision. The vicious strikes contained far more power than he originally expected, and they knocked him off balance. He took advantage of her fierce blows to slide backward. A thin ice blade had formed beneath his feet. He used them to redirect his backward momentum and swung around toward Gong Lan. Seven Cloud Steps! Shearing Staff Art! He quickly pushed himself forward, using the burst of speed to unleash a violent blade of wind.

Much to his surprise, she easily chopped the blade of wind in two with one of her sabers.

"Looks like I have to get serious!" he yelled.

Instantly, the white rosary on his wrist burst into pieces as sixty motes of light flew out to surround them. Unfortunately, he didn't have a wood-based manifestation with offensive capabilities. However, he knew that earth had a destructive interaction with water. Thirty-six of the pearls he unleashed formed a quaking circle, which he reinforced using both fire qi and wood qi thanks to his high-grade cultivation technique.

The quaking power rattled Gong Lan's rhythm, but she gritted her teeth and charged nonetheless. While charging, she cried out and unleashed six consecutive strikes with her blades. Six bloody blades of qi burst out from her swords and attacked Cha Ming from afar. He was forced to dodge these sharp qi-blades, granting her precious time to close in on his position. Her charge was perfectly timed, and she caught him in a precarious position.

Not wanting to be outdone, he quickly used his Shearing Staff Art to push down against the floor, launching himself fifty feet up into the air. While Gong Lan was surprised that he could use wind qi, she had seen the move before and remained unperturbed.

His maneuver didn't end there, however. As he reached the peak of his trajectory, he quickly jumped in midair using Seven Cloud Steps. He took advantage of gravity to gain momentum, which he was preparing to unleash in a single blow.

Gong Lan's expression turned grim. Seeing his vicious approach, she quickly stepped back to ruin his approach angle. In response to her movements, however, she noticed that the quaking pearls, which had constantly been hampering her movements, suddenly began glowing with a frosty light-blue color. To her horror, she was frozen to the floor by the element she was most comfortable with—water, in the shape of ice!

Normally such a crude ice field wouldn't pose a problem. However, she currently had less than half a second to react before his staff came crashing down. She gritted her teeth and decided to unleash her most powerful attack: Blood Saber Art—Twin Decapitation!

This was a technique that she would normally only unleash when she intended to kill her victim. However, the old her was no more. She was now relentless, unyielding. She braced herself as she poured blood-red qi and killing intent into her twin blades, accumulating her full power to unleash in a single strike.

Cha Ming, who was swiftly plunging down toward her, felt his blood run cold as a vicious killing intent swept through his flesh and blood, paralyzing him momentarily. This greatly reduced the momentum he had struggled to build for this single strike. Unfortunately, he was committed to the attack. Therefore, he gripped his staff on its end with both hands, sending the remaining five feet crashing down with unparalleled might.

Quake Staff!

His most powerful strike collided with hers, forcing them both back like kites with their strings cut. Both he and Gong Lan coughed up blood as they stared at each other, both of them weakly climbing up on one knee. Cha Ming was shocked by her ferocity and killing intent. Clearly she had not just fought normal battles over the last two months. No, she had been fighting death matches!

The thought overwhelmed him with sorrow. Why had such a pure and innocent girl transformed into a such a berserker for his sake? While it was her decision to make, he found it to be a huge shame. He had liked the gentle side of her, but it now seemed remote or nonexistent. It was like the old Gong Lan was dead.

No words were spoken as they sat down cross-legged to recover. Cha Ming revolved his Healing Circle manifestation, which quickly improved their rate of recovery.

Once they had completely recovered, Cha Ming let out a reluctant laugh. "You're pretty tough! At this fifth level of qi condensation, I have a ludicrously high soul force, and I've trained my body to the sixth level, yet we're evenly matched! I'm impressed!"

Her expression turned gloomy as she responded, "All I had to do was lose myself. That's the price I paid." She then averted her gaze as though ashamed of what she had become.

As Cha Ming wracked his brain to recover from the awkward conversation, their silence was interrupted by loud yipping noises from Huxian. Cha Ming also received a mental message. He laughed wryly as he lifted his staff over his shoulder. He sighed. "Huxian is so impressed that he wants to fight a two-on-one now."

"Oh, a two-on-one? I guess I can fight the both of you if you like," she replied. Her doting expression implied that she would go easy on him.

"You misunderstand. He'd like to fight *us*. Unfortunately, he's much stronger than me," Cha Ming said.

"How is this possible? He's only a three-month-old spirit beast!" Gong Lan asked in disbelief.

Cha Ming walked beside her and took out his staff.

"You'd better be ready, Gong Lan. Since it's two of us, he might actually take us seriously."

Cha Ming gulped as he manifested a metal-reinforced freezing circle targeting only Huxian, as well as two preemptive healing hands. After all, this was *really* going to hurt.

A while later, the three of them met Wang Jun and Hong Xin at a nearby restaurant. Hong Xin had not seen Gong Lan in ages, so they chatted about all sorts of things while Cha Ming and Wang Jun spoke for the second time that day.

"You really weren't kidding when you said a mutual friend would be coming by soon. She's seriously strong, so much so that we're evenly matched," Cha Ming said quietly.

Wang Jun lifted one eyebrow as he digested this piece of information. "So, she beat you up?"

"I said evenly matched! But then again, Huxian beat us in a two-on-one afterward. Still, she's seriously strong."

"Are you talking about this big sister?" Gong Lan interrupted with a proud air.

"Big sister, my ass! Huxian beat up the both of us, and I'm his older brother. You're definitely the little sister in the pecking order," Cha Ming snapped back.

As if wanting to confirm Cha Ming's words, Huxian dutifully jumped up on his lap and started licking his hand, causing the whole table to burst into a fit of laughter.

"So does this mean our dear little sister is going to accompany Cha Ming on his trip?" asked Wang Jun.

"What trip? Cha Ming never told me about a trip," Gong Lan said while shooting Cha Ming an evil glare.

In response, he coughed lightly before replying. "I never got a chance to bring it up. This bloodthirsty little sister dragged me to the arena five minutes into afternoon tea. Then she decided to try skewering me with her sabers. Finally, we fought Huxian, and we've been recovering from his 'beating of love' ever since.

"Anyhow, like Wang Jun was saying, Huxian and I are going to Fairweather County for an adventure. There's apparently some excitement there, and while I'm at it, I need to go commission some medicinal pills and get a staff forged.

Unfortunately, Wang Jun can't come along this time because he needs to take care of some family business."

He didn't mention Hong Xin. From what he could gather, she'd been so emotionally scarred by the event in the woods that she had given up all attempts at cultivation. Now she cultivated with minimum effort, barely driven by the fact that cultivating would help her maintain her youthful looks.

"How convenient!" Gong Lan exclaimed. "I heard that there's a lucrative mission happening in Fairweather. Many mercenaries in my brother's company will be traveling there in three days. We can just join their group to travel there."

It was *too* convenient, in fact. If Wang Jun hadn't explained how fate was basically begging him to travel there, he would have suspected a conspiracy. From the sounds of it, this "lucrative mission" was exactly why he had to travel there.

The matter was quickly settled. He spent the last three days visiting with friends and saying farewells. He made sure to visit the Hong family for supper one night, where he was pestered with questions about the mysterious Wang Jun that Hong Xin had started dating.

For some reason, Cha Ming couldn't help but feel he might never return to Green Leaf City again. This feeling was reinforced when he visited Elder Ling. Elder Ling essentially trapped him, forcing him to play several games of *Angels and Devils* while concurrently lecturing him on talisman crafting. Before parting, Elder Ling gave him a strange object. It was a glowing ball containing swirls of black and white. He was instructed to open it only once he reached foundation establishment.

When Cha Ming asked why he was giving him such a precious gift now, Elder Ling only replied that it was destiny, and that he would know the reason in the future. At this point, Cha Ming was fed up with destiny. However, he obediently accepted the gift and kowtowed three times to his teacher. Would they ever meet again?

The next morning, Cha Ming, Huxian, and Gong Lan walked out of Green Leaf City with ten Fierce Blood mercenaries. It was time for another dangerous adventure, one that would change their lives forever.

Chapter 11: Fairweather City

The pungent smell of iron and oil assaulted Cha Ming's senses as he waited at a table with Huxian for Gong Lan and the mercenaries to finish a pile of paperwork. They were seated at a small table in the corner of a larger hall, which was crowded with rowdy mercenaries. Many of them were waiting, carefully sharpening their swords. Others were oiling their armor, their knives, and various metal instruments susceptible to rust. After all, mortal-grade weapons were expensive, and not everyone could afford them.

The mercenary hall in Fairweather City doubled as a lounge. A few tables closer to the bar, six mercenaries were busy drinking their fill. It was noon, and it was clear that many people had revised their definition of "too early to start drinking." Drinking was an occupational hazard for most mercenaries.

The large hall was spacious enough to accommodate up to two hundred rowdy men. Certain missions had very large manpower requirements. The innkeepers, while relishing the mercenaries' business, were less than happy to have a few dozen of them scaring away their regular alcoholic customers. Therefore the large mess hall and bar was a necessity, even in this small city.

Located near the slums, the mercenary hall wasn't exactly built on prime real estate. Many places found mercenaries to be an unsavory bunch that should be kept away from the general population. The aged wooden bar tables reeked of ale. Cha Ming put up with the pungent smell, however. He was here on a mission. While they continued waiting for Gong Lan and her group to finish, a nearby mercenary began yelling loudly.

"Are you serious, Brother Hou? That sounds way too good to be true!"

This loud outburst was accompanied by the sound of a mug slamming down on a creaky wooden table. The burly man speaking was clearly drunk.

"Of course I'm serious. It's listed on the mission wall." The lanky mercenary pointed to the other side of the tavern, where various pieces of parchment and paper were nailed to a wall made of soft wood. "The two professionals in town are the ones funding this mission, after all. As such, they've decided to auction off a variety of premade goods in this restricted auction. This includes pills, spirit weapons, etc.

"In addition, everyone will be able to put any surplus goods up for auction prior to the main auction, so that everyone can liquidate their assets. Anything that isn't bought by others in the auction will be bought by the auction house for 70% of list price."

"This is great!" said another one of the mercenaries. "People rarely get the opportunity to buy Master Han's spirit weapons and Master Zhang's pills. They're very particular about picking their clients, and they usually refuse to mass produce lesser-grade goods. Why have they made an exception this time?"

He chuckled. "You might not know this, but it seems that Han Jinlong and Zhang Yifeng both have family in the surrounding towns. They have not received any news from these towns, and the county lord refuses to investigate. Therefore, they had a falling out and are currently recruiting us mercenaries. Better yet, aside from mass producing these lesser-grade spirit weapons, they're also auctioning out ten slots each. These slots are opportunities to have spirit weapons and medicinal pills custom-made prior to heading out. At cost!"

A fourth mercenary chimed in, scoffing. "At cost. It's not like they're *actually* supplying these services at cost. After all, they are auctioning out the slots! They're bound to make a killing, even if the auction is restricted to participants in this mercenary mission. I've also heard that they've sworn not to sell any weapons to anyone for the next year, with the exception of those who participate in the mission! This will surely drive up the price."

"Look, they're using both the carrot-and-stick approach. While they are going to make money at this auction, there's no way it will be enough to offset the bite of refusing business to non-participants for a full year. Besides which, auctioning these weapons out is a clever move on their part," the lanky man replied.

"Oh? How so?"

"Do I have to explain *everything*, you stupid fatty? Obviously, there are two types of people that can win in the auction. First, there are powerful and rich adventurers. Making these people even stronger before the outing is a perfect way to ensure better success for the mission.

"The only other people that can participate in such an auction are *influential* people. These people are most likely to bring followers along. In addition, to prevent people from participating just to buy things, they have restricted the auction for these custom slots to sixth level and higher cultivators. Any family who sends someone of that level will feel the bite if they lose him, therefore, they are more likely to send additional support."

"I see. That's very clever. But how will they control the qualifications for the auction?"

"Through a testing stone, of course. A qi testing stone will be used for qi condensation cultivators, and a strength testing pillar will be used to test body cultivators. Use your head."

The remainder of the conversation was no longer interesting, so Cha Ming and Huxian stopped listening. Gong Lan just happened to return from the mission desk at this point in time.

Most of the details were identical to what they had just heard. Apparently there had been many attacks on neighboring villages. The wealthy individuals in town, worried about the lack of news in the surrounding regions, posted an investigation and rescue mission.

The mission stated that they were disappointed with the support they received from the Fairweather County lord and had taken matters into their own hands. Over the next week, they would recruit a large force to investigate five nearby towns and escort the residents back to Fairweather City. If they found those responsible for the recent attacks on the neighboring villages, the mercenary force was to invade the attackers in the hopes of rescuing any prisoners taken.

The compensation was indeed very generous:

First Level Cultivators—100 spirit stones
Second Level Cultivators—500 spirit stones
Third Level Cultivators—1,000 spirit stones
Fourth Level Cultivators—5,000 spirit stones
Fifth Level Cultivators—10,000 spirit stones
Sixth Level Cultivators—50,000 spirit stones
Seventh Level Cultivators—100,000 spirit stones
… and so on.

The reward for foundation-establishment cultivators was a whopping 1,000 mid-grade spirit stones, in addition to a custom weapon forging slot with Han Jinlong. For every cultivator, a quarter of the reward was payable up front, and the remaining three quarters was payable upon completion of service.

The auction details were the same as explained previously, with one major difference: Instead of a large auction to liquidate assets, the auction house would allow cultivators to set up their own market stalls in a large hall the day before the auction. In addition, the auction house would purchase goods worth more than a certain amount at 75% of the list price. Cha Ming had had his doubts about the veracity of holding an auction for trinkets from various cultivators, but if the auction house truly decided to auction off these various trinkets, this auction alone would last weeks. By then, the mission would already be completed. Setting up an easy trade location was a pragmatic solution.

Yet a final piece of information shocked their small group thoroughly. The two leading craftsmen in the city, Han Jinlong and Zhang Yifeng, would be spearheading the search and rescue mission! Given this detail, Cha Ming concluded that the situation was very dire. He suspected that they had some sensitive information that indicated the need for *immediate* action. With or without the king's army.

Since the auction would take place on the next day, the three of them registered for the mission and found a nice inn to occupy. The ten mercenaries that had accompanied Gong Lan proceeded to a less savory establishment. Another "occupational hazard" in the mercenary world.

Later that evening, with nothing better to do, the group decided to wander around the merchant district. While Fairweather City was not a large city, it was still about the same size as Green Leaf City. Instead of being known to produce medicinal herbs, Fairweather City was known for its artisans.

Every street corner was graced with beautiful sculptures—a rare display of wealth in public areas. The various shops—at least, the ones lucky enough to own their own buildings—had hired master artisans to carve and paint the outside of their stores. The philosophy behind this was quite simple. Standing out from the crowd with a beautiful shop would undoubtedly lead to people heading inside out of sheer curiosity or appreciation. The competition in Fairweather was fierce, leading to a luxurious merchant quarter that overshadowed the entertainment district.

All sorts of craftsmen flourished in this city. Unlike in Green Leaf City, the craftsmen of Fairweather looked *beyond* function. For example, even the lowliest starting weapon on sale was a work of art. Anything less than beautiful was considered trash, something the weapon artisan wouldn't dare sign his name to.

Even something like medicinal pills were artistic creations, decorated with beautiful patterns or shaped like sparkling gems. Further, the bottles containing them were art products made of crystal. These decorations complemented the function of the medicinal pill. One that was meant to improve vitality, for example, would be decorated with patterns of vines or even be contained in a bottle shaped like a dragon. Some alchemists even housed their wares in stained-glass bottles, using color combinations to hint at their effect. In one shop, Cha Ming had seen a healing pill that was deep purple. It had been stored in an azure heart-shaped bottle.

These factors led to an amazing pricing phenomenon— huge price disparities could be seen for any and all goods. The same grade of spirit weapon, made of the same materials and supplying the same benefit in combat, could be worth anywhere between 80 and 150% of the usual list price.

Many thoughts went through Cha Ming's mind as he picked up an intricately carved soul-alloy dagger. The weapon was a third-grade spirit weapon, hardly worth any mention. Normally a weapon like it would be worth eight hundred spirit stones, more than double the amount of a dagger made with normal materials.

However, this weapon was worth fifteen hundred spirit stones. The abnormally inflated price was due to the high level of skill required to craft such unforgiving material. Each of the craftsmen qualified to forge such weapons were well known, and their prices were sky high. Even a blind man would be forced to admit that it was truly a beautiful dagger. It was clear as the purest ice, from tip to hilt. The handle had been engraved with a textured pattern. This decorative artwork, which featured beautiful leaves, vines, and flowers, rendered the handle non-slip.

On another shelf, Cha Ming spotted a beautiful spirit sword. The runes engraved on it were written in flowing script, much like an exercise in calligraphy. Strictly speaking, crafting weapon runes was akin to painting talismans. Runic characters had very specific shapes. Any deviations, while they could enhance the beauty of the resulting talisman or engraved weapon rune, ran the risk of ruining the character itself.

Cha Ming thanked his lucky stars that Elder Ling had been strict in this regard, forcing him to practice calligraphy while crafting his talismans. While the process of beautifying characters was initially risky, an artisan with sufficient skill would eventually learn that there were certain rules to beautifying a character, much like regular calligraphy. Only rules that didn't conflict with function could be used in runic calligraphy. Due to his various experiences, Cha Ming's talismans were much better looking than the average textbook talisman.

In the end, Cha Ming bought the dagger he had been admiring. He was currently lacking such a dagger, which was useful for things like gathering herbs and cutting ropes and bonds. Soul-alloy weapons were much sharper than their steel counterparts, albeit quite brittle. Such a dagger was useless in actual combat.

After purchasing the weapon, Cha Ming cheerfully walked over to the next stall, where Gong Lan was admiring a defensive brooch shaped like a blooming red lotus. The lotus was a full two inches in diameter and contained nine ruby-red petals. These petals were made from a glassy material. Each of the curved petals was engraved with a protective rune. It was the first time Cha Ming had ever seen such an item.

"Forty-five hundred spirit stones is way too much for such a trinket! Are you trying to rob me?" Gong Lan fumed, lashing out at the attendant with her incisive tongue.

"Miss," the attendant calmly replied, "this exquisite lotus brooch was crafted by Hong Lai, the nineteenth-ranked weapon artisan in this city. You would struggle to find something so beautiful given its form and function, and that's why it commands a fifty-percent premium above other lesser works.

"If you don't like this specific brooch, could I possibly interest you in this jade lily hairclip? It contains very similar enchanted properties compared to the lotus brooch. However, the price tag is only twenty percent higher than list price." The lady clearly had no intent to negotiate.

"May I take a look at that red lotus brooch?" Cha Ming said as he appeared behind Gong Lan. The attendant handed the brooch to him, and he observed it for a while before shaking his head. "I wouldn't buy this one, Gong Lan. While it seems very pretty, it's a flawed product. I would only pay 75% of the market price myself, but only because it truly is very beautiful."

The attendant seemed quite incensed, no doubt wondering how dare a country bumpkin besmirch her products. Cha Ming and Gong Lan moved to leave.

"Stop!" the attendant shouted, drawing the attention of nearby shoppers. This included some customers who had just looked over to the stall due to Cha Ming's comments about a flawed product. Reputation was everything in Fairweather.

"Young bumpkin, you can't besmirch Hong Lai's work at will. I demand either an explanation for your criticism of his work or an apology!"

The competition in Fairweather City was extremely fickle compared to that in other cities. Fashion was subjective, after all, and an unjust accusation might quickly lead to a ruined reputation and subsequent closure.

"Are you sure that you want to be having this conversation?" Cha Ming asked. "I really don't want to disparage such a beautiful work further. The reason that I haven't made a big deal about it is that, while it is a failed product, it still has much of its functionality intact."

Criticizing another's work was a very unprofessional practice and should only be conducted in extreme cases of negligence or willful misconduct. Judging by the artisan's current standing, it was likely a small, albeit noticeable, error.

"Hong Lai only crafts beautiful products of the highest quality," the attending lady insisted. "I'll have to ask you to either elaborate on your complaint or apologize." While it was a risky move, she might be fired if she didn't respond to the accusation.

"Very well." Cha Ming picked up the red lotus brooch, which glittered in his palm. "I am no expert on jewelry or weapon crafting, so I can't comment on the materials. Indeed, to my untrained eye, it seems like this decorative brooch was carefully shaped with soul alloy before being cut with glittering facets. Further, the vivid red color and sparkles make me think that this charming flower was infused with ruby dust during the molding process.

"Therefore, my complaint has nothing to do with the materials or forging of the brooch but rather the engravings. While this defensive spirit weapon is only a consumable, it is surely at least a fifth-grade spirit weapon. Therefore, it should be worth at least half as much as a non-consumable fifth-grade spirit weapon.

"The reason that I take issue with the engravings is that each engraving, while beautiful, does not follow convention for calligraphy when writing or engraving runic characters. This flaw diminishes the effectiveness of each runic character by one ninth. Unfortunately, this is only something that can be verified after the item is used, and it is difficult to spot. Only a sixth-grade or higher talisman artist could spot this mistake, and only if he was trained in proper runic calligraphy."

The attendant could not refute him, as she did not know that much about the occupations. Therefore, if he was qualified to make these comments, she had no choice but to accept the judgment.

"Might I ask if you are a sixth-grade talisman artist?" she asked begrudgingly.

"Yes, that is the case."

Everyone nearby was astonished that such a young man was such an accomplished talisman artist.

Chapter 12: An Introduction to Weapon Crafting

The jewelry shop's attendant was in an awkward position. If she could not protect the reputation of her goods, she needed to secure some official proof to present to the store's manager and avoid blame.

"Sir, if you'll please present your qualification jade, I will apologize and remove this product from our stock for inspection and verification."

This was standard practice in any city. The professions were self-regulated, therefore anyone making a complaint would need standing. Otherwise, someone who wanted to make a complaint had to seek the assistance of a qualified individual.

"I... don't have a qualification jade," Cha Ming replied shyly.

This response shocked the attendant. How could someone be so daring to make such an accusation without a qualifying document? This sort of behavior was extremely frowned upon by all professionals, who mandated the registration of each of their members. Someone like Cha Ming, who dared to disparage the work of a registered professional, could easily be sued for unqualified slander.

"Then I'm afraid that I will be requiring your apology or the backing of someone qualified to make such an accusation," the attendant replied coldly. Her expression had lost every ounce of respect that she had previously displayed when she was under the impression that Cha Ming was a qualified expert.

"That won't be necessary!" the voice of a young man sounded out from the crowd.

The crowd parted to reveal a well-dressed individual. His frame was small and skinny. However, the presence he exuded caused Cha Ming to shudder. He could feel it—this man was strong! Not just in terms of qi condensation; the man's presence was oppressive, both in terms of physical body strength and spiritual force.

Without explaining anything, the man picked up the brooch and briefly inspected it. He then nodded and dropped a pouch full of spirit stones on the attendant's booth. "My apologies, this pouch contains five thousand spirit stones. I'll be buying my failed product from your stall. Such things are unworthy of making it to market, and I'm ashamed to have put my name to it."

This man was clearly Hong Lai, the famous artisan who had crafted the brooch. He didn't seem flustered or angry at being exposed, however. If anything, he seemed genuinely *grateful*. The man turned to Cha Ming's group, smiling.

"Might I ask if you are both available for supper tonight? I would like to compensate you for your bad experience. In addition, I'll craft a complimentary custom gift for the both of you. How does that sound?"

This... is a little overboard, no? I basically slapped him in the

face, but now he wants to buy me supper and compensate me?
Seeing his befuddled expression, the young man laughed.

"My friend, judging by your clothes, you are new to the
city. This is an old tradition that has been around for hundreds
of years, so you'll need to indulge me. In return, since you were
able to spot the flaws in my work, you'll need to compensate
me in a different way. I'll be asking for your guidance on how
to improve the final design."

Now Cha Ming understood the man's intentions. He only
sought to improve his work! In fact, he could tell from this
brief interaction that this man did not pursue popularity but
perfection; his ranking was a mere consequence of this pursuit.

"Then I'll be asking you to take care of us," said Cha Ming
while clasping his hands and bowing. Gong Lan followed suit.

And so, three people and one fox traveled to a nearby
restaurant. This was, coincidentally, the most famous and
expensive restaurant in the city, Phoenix Cry Pavilion.

A short while later, Cha Ming, Gong Lan, and Hong Lai were
sitting at a medium-sized table. It was covered with a mauve
tablecloth carefully embroidered in green and red floral
patterns. A beautiful woman wearing a form-fitting black dress
came in through a sliding door, which was expertly carved with
depictions of various spirit beasts. The woman politely bowed
to Hong Lai.

"Master Hong, what will you and your guests be having
today?" she asked. Her red lipstick accentuated her beautiful

smile. The pay at such an establishment was based on commission, so the waitresses would do everything in their power to impress their guests and cause them to loosen their belt pouches.

"Do either of you drink?" Hong Lai asked both his guests. They shook their heads in response. "A pity. The Phoenix Cry Pavilion has an exquisite wine called Fireblood wine. It's not actually made with blood. It's a clever mixture of herbs and fruit, fermented to create a wine that makes your blood boil from its spicy flavor.

"Speaking of which," he said, turning to the waitress, "please bring me a bottle of wine for myself, and your best tea for these two guests. And, er…" He looked toward Huxian.

"He'll take water," said Cha Ming. "He likes to eat roast meat, but he's never developed an appetite for any kind of drink. With respect to meat, I'm afraid to say that he prefers quantity over quality and is effectively a bottomless pit. No need to worry about that, however. I'll get him a snack later."

"Nonsense! I insist that he eat his fill here. Now then, any dietary restrictions?" Hong Lai asked.

"I'm a vegetarian, but she seems to be carnivorous," said Cha Ming. Gong Lan scrunched her face together, pouting, but she didn't correct him.

"Right, if you would be so kind, miss, please bring us a feast as they've specified, and I'll just eat whatever they're having. And make sure that you bring out a roast pheasant!" Hong Lai said, sending off the beautiful waitress.

"Thankfully you youngsters aren't the only picky eaters in the city. It's become a hobby of sorts, especially amongst renowned artisans. This city is all about fashion, you see, and that involves standing out and being different in various aspects. Now, I know you are both foreigners, but where are you both from exactly?" Hong Lai asked curiously.

Gong Lan was the first to reply. "I live in Green Leaf City with my brother, but I was born in Clearwood."

"Clearwood, eh? Rough crowd over there. Quite the gambling industry. I haven't been there myself, but my esteemed master has been there in the past. How about yourself, young friend?" He sounded more curious about Cha Ming's background.

"I've lived in Green Leaf City for the past half year while attending Green Leaf Academy. That is where I learned to craft talismans. My teacher is Elder Ling."

"Elder Ling… I'm not in the field, so I can't say I've heard of him. Perhaps I should ask my cousin. He's also a talisman artist, though he's only a fifth-grade artist. Like any craft, the difficulty mounts exponentially."

"Right," Cha Ming replied. "It applies to all crafts and arts. A fifth-grade artist is quite something. Does he have a master in the city?"

"No, he doesn't. Unfortunately, there aren't many talisman artists in this city. My cousin is the highest-ranking talisman artist in the city. He travels to the capital city every year for instruction, and sometimes he'll make a lucky breakthrough. Still, his progress hasn't been very good compared to his cultivation. He's at the seventh level of qi condensation!"

"Oh? What is your rank as a spiritual blacksmith?" Cha Ming asked.

"Regrettably, I'm only seventh grade. It's very difficult to train as a spiritual blacksmith, you know. Not only do I need to train my qi, but I also need to train my soul and my body. Fortunately, the requirements for soul cultivation are not very harsh. Therefore, I'm at the seventh level of both qi condensation and body refinement," the man said proudly.

Cha Ming was impressed. Although the man was only in his midtwenties, he had pursued not only body cultivation, qi cultivation, and weaponsmithing, but he had also pursued the pinnacle of arts. Dividing one's attention was extremely taxing. The only reason that Cha Ming had found it easy was because he had obtained so many fortuitous encounters in the last six months in addition to his slightly elevated talent and peak soul force. Comprehension abilities were extremely dependent on soul force, so Cha Ming was particularly blessed in this aspect.

Their food arrived a short while later. Each dish was a work of art and extremely delicious. Cha Ming especially enjoyed the mushroom dish, which contained a combination of softer mushrooms and chewy mushrooms. With each bite he took, Cha Ming felt a warm sensation course through him that seemed to replenish his qi, body, and soul.

"I can tell from your expression that you've never had food like this before," said Hong Lai. Cha Ming shook his head, prompting Hong Lai to continue his explanation. "This type of food is called spirit food. Spirit food can only be prepared by spiritual chefs, which are very rare due to the requirements of their occupation. This is because they require triple affinity to water, wood, and fire. Most people would rather pursue alchemy or medicine. It takes someone who is truly in love with food to pursue this path.

"The chef at the Phoenix Cry Pavilion has pursued the culinary arts to the extreme, mixing in precious herbs, roots, and spirit-animal flesh to produce something both tasty and extremely nutritious. You likely felt like your cultivation was improving with every bite. That's because spirit food is much like a mild medicinal pill. Properly prepared spirit food comes from all-natural sources with minimal processing, and therefore their nutritional effect is weaker, but there is no chance of side effects. Plus, the taste is amazing. By the way, try this steamed taro dish," Hong Lai said, pointing to a white-and-purple dish. "It's amazing." Hong Lai helped himself to a generous portion, which was lightly sprinkled with what looked like onions and an unknown blue herb.

The food was so effective that Cha Ming felt the boundary holding back his qi lake weaken. Unfortunately, they were in the middle of a meal. It would be terrible etiquette to break through while eating dinner with someone.

After they finished their meal, Cha Ming and Hong Lai got to the heart of the matter—how to improve the runic engravings on the red lotus brooch. While Cha Ming was not familiar with the Shield Guard inscription, such a grouping of characters was well within his capabilities. He estimated that such an inscription could also be painted as a fourth-grade talisman. With Cha Ming's capabilities, his chances of success were one in two. He used gold elemental essence to paint the character two times. He didn't retract any spent ink, however. Only magic treasures could accomplish this, and revealing such an expensive treasure was tantamount to suicide in the cultivation world. No matter how genial Hong Lai seemed, he might be tempted by the appeal of a valuable treasure.

After two attempts, the base talisman succeeded. Hong Lai nodded approvingly.

"Yes, this is most definitely the basic form of the inscription rune. However, as I was carving the character, I naturally wanted to beautify it. That is why I carved it as it is now. I didn't notice anything wrong until you pointed it out, but now I can truly feel that the runes have each lost some of their functionality over the original I had carved into the prototype."

Cha Ming nodded. "Yes, your representation of the runic character is very beautiful, if judged by calligraphy's standards. However, there are certain conventions to runic calligraphy."

Cha Ming spent a good hour explaining a few standard conventions that would beautify characters yet not reduce their functionality. He also painted a much more beautiful representation of the runic character so that Hong Lai could use it for reference, which made him ecstatic. Having a simple diagram was very different from having an actual drawn character, where he could sense the thickness of the energy lines and essence.

During their conversation, Cha Ming learned many things about weaponsmithing. Spiritual blacksmiths were required to triple-cultivate body, qi, and soul. In addition, they needed to cultivate both fire and metal, a destructive combination. The combination was useful for their body cultivation, but more importantly, it facilitated the use of their primary crafting tools.

Blacksmiths needed to control fire to melt and purify the metals they used in their creation. Precise temperature control was necessary for melting, tempering, and quenching weapons. Fortunately, their creations could be reformed in the case of failure, unlike an alchemist's ingredients, where medicinal herbs could be burnt to ashes by excessive temperatures. This was why alchemy had such stringent requirements on innate soul force.

The control over metal was also a requirement, largely due to the need to condense their very own spiritual hammer. This spiritual hammer had to be imbued with rare metals and other materials, and a spiritual weapon could not be created without a hammer of the appropriate grade. This hammer was not restricted to a large smithing hammer; it could change shapes, becoming larger or smaller as required. In addition, it could be fashioned with a sharp end to inscribe runes onto weapons. These runes did not require any elemental essence while crafting but had to be energized with the appropriate elemental essence after the fact.

Weapon crafting, while expensive to practice, was not as prohibitive as Cha Ming had originally thought. Talisman crafting without high-level tools had extremely high rates of failure. Any ink used would be lost with a failed talisman. Spiritual blacksmiths, on the other hand, didn't need to worry about wasted material. Material could be recycled indefinitely, with some exceptions. Once a spiritual blacksmith failed an engraving, he had the option to melt down and reforge the item. Elemental essence would be used as a finishing touch to complete runes, and much less essence was required for a weapon than for a talisman.

Another key difference lay in the runes they used. Weaponsmithing runes were much simpler than talisman runes for the same grade of weapon. In addition, as they didn't have to handle liquid ink to paint the characters, they had no requirement to use qi as a guide for the inscriptions. As such, weaponsmiths were not restricted to crafting weapons of a particular element. This was an advantage in versatility over talisman artists.

The red lotus brooch, a fifth-grade weapon, only used a fourth-grade talisman rune. Cha Ming speculated that this was due to the materials used, which could support the runic inscription. Further, aside from some consumable items like the brooch, spirit weapons would be imbued with spirit-gathering inscriptions, enabling the weapon to borrow the qi of Heaven and Earth. For some reusable ignition-type inscriptions, the user's qi was often required to activate the rune and create a special effect.

While Gong Lan was bored, Cha Ming felt like he had discovered a whole new world. Gong Lan returned to the inn after the first hour, and Cha Ming and Hong Lai continued to discuss their respective crafts until four hours after sunset. If he had a chance in the future, Cha Ming decided he wouldn't mind settling down in a city like Fairweather.

The trio made their way to the auction hall the next morning. They were not accompanied by any of the ten mercenaries, as these men were technically one group of four and two groups of three. The mercenary company was a place to meet colleagues and obtain missions and news. Gong Lan's brother, the Blood King, took a small cut on every deal they were involved in.

Today's event, the trade meet, started early in the morning. The reason for the early start was because participants had to register their goods and verify their identities. Each participant had to be registered for the upcoming mission—no exceptions.

Cha Ming had full confidence that talismans would be in short supply. This was doubly so since his conversation with Hong Lai. He thanked his foresight for not selling them to the Jade Bamboo Conglomerate before leaving Green Leaf City.

After waiting their turn in line for a half hour, Cha Ming and Gong Lan proceeded to the registration counter with

Huxian at their heels. They were greeted by a cultivator in his twenties with short black hair. He wore simple clothes. The man looked studious more than anything, though Cha Ming felt a shiver run down his spine as he was looked over by the young man, who greeted them with a smile on his face.

"Will you both be participating in the primary auction, the secondary auction, or both?" Following his question, Cha Ming felt an intrusive scan of spiritual energy wash over the three of them. He furrowed his brow in response to the rude behavior.

The young man quickly noticed his expression. "My apologies, dear guest. Due to the nature of the auction, my employer has instructed me to verify every guest in attendance. My profession is that of an inquisitor. Of course, you are both qualified to attend the primary and secondary auction." He quickly gave them both a bidding paddle, which was affixed with a number. The paddle was fashioned out of simple wood but inscribed with silver ink.

The man also brought out two contracts for both Cha Ming and Gong Lan. "As part of registering for the auction, you must sign this employment contract for the mission. You will find that the contract is quite fair. I have already filled out your names and cultivation level," the man politely explained.

Cha Ming was extremely surprised at this revelation. How did the man know his name and cultivation level? More importantly, his cultivation level had been filled out correctly at the sixth level, his body refinement level. Noticing Gong Lan's unsurprised expression, however, he hid his shock and proceeded to review the contract.

The terms of the contract were straightforward. They simply stated that to participate in the auction, the cultivator would need to participate in the search and rescue mission. The duration of the contract was one month from the start of the mission, and the cultivators would be compensated in full regardless of the result of the mission. The cultivator need only participate to the best of his ability, without being obligated to utilize costly consumables, though the use of such items was encouraged, as they increased the survivability of the cultivator.

Should the cultivator encounter life-threatening danger beyond their capability, they could withdraw from the mission and cancel their contract with no penalty, only keeping the 25% advance for the mission.

The contract also specified compensation levels for each cultivation level at registration, in addition to basic indemnity language for both parties. Overall, the contract was indeed fair. The penalty for unlawful termination of the contract was a Heart Demon Enforcement, which would hamper the cultivator's ability to advance and break through.

Just as Cha Ming was about to sign his contract, he was interrupted by the young man. "Might I give you some advice? I am unable to evaluate the strength of your contract beast, which means it must be rather strong, among other things. With an appropriate subcontract, the contract beast can be included as part of your strength. Would you like to consider this?"

After pondering for a few moments, Cha Ming shook his head and signed the contract. He instantly became aware of a karmic obligation in the back of his mind.

What a mysterious contract, he thought.

"I prefer to register with my own strength for personal reasons," he replied.

The man shrugged and ushered him into the auction house.

Chapter 13: Trade Meet

Cha Ming and company proceeded into the auction house after their registration. Once they were out of earshot, Cha Ming asked Gong Lan about the young man at the entrance.

"Oh, him?" she said. "He is a professional inquisitor. They appear frequently in large cities, and their profession does not require any complicated materials or training. All inquisitors are required to cultivate light and have innate spiritual force.

"From what I understand, their profession allows them a few minor abilities that are quite useful. They can determine the strength of cultivators or demon beasts within about three levels of their own cultivation. In addition, they can determine the veracity or falsehood of spoken statements. It is rumored that they can manifest additional abilities, depending on their talents. I heard my brother say that some inquisitors can 'see' the merit or sin of a person, and that some legendary inquisitors can also identify disguises and break illusions.

"Overall, they are commonly employed as investigators, prosecutors in court, and police officers. They all have one thing in common—they abhor lies and deceit and are all morally upright. Deceit is the antithesis of their profession. In fact, excessive lying—even by omission—can lead to the deterioration of their profession and cultivation. As such, their statements are universally trusted."

"But why would an inquisitor need to verify entry into an auction house of all things?" Cha Ming asked as they headed toward a marble service desk.

"Beats me," she replied. "It's not unheard of, but it seems unnecessary. That is, unless there are hidden details pertaining to the mission that we are not aware of. In addition, the organizers of this event incurred great expense in hiring a scribe to create the contracts."

"A scribe?" asked Cha Ming.

"Yes, scribes are professionals that cultivate fate," Gong Lan explained. "They use spiritual force to create contracts that are binding through karma. The stronger the scribe, the stronger the contract they can enforce. I would imagine that they prepared many tiers of contracts, as the cost of a contract is proportionate to the strength of the enforcement. In fact, these contracts are very similar to talismans and could be considered a subset of the talisman artist profession."

At this point, Cha Ming felt overwhelmed by the massive amount of information he'd been exposed to since his arrival in the city. "There are too many professions. I naively thought there were only a dozen different occupations," Cha Ming thought out loud, sighing. Huxian nudged his leg in agreement, which reminded Cha Ming of a question that had been pushed to the back of his mind.

Huxian, why couldn't that man sense your strength? He should have been strong enough to detect your cultivation. I also don't remember you having strong spiritual force, Cha Ming asked mentally.

Oh. Well, at first, his spiritual force washed over me, and my bloodline power burnt it. Then he got a little aggressive and increased the strength of his probing. It was annoying, so I ate it, the little fox explained nonchalantly.

You... ate it? You mean, you ate *his spiritual force?* Cha Ming asked.

Yeah, it was tasty. I wanted to eat more, but he stopped. Huxian's mental voice was tinged with disappointment.

At the service desk, a beautiful female attendant in a red dress was stationed. Judging by her expression, she was tired of the less-than-savory company in attendance that morning. Cha Ming couldn't blame her. Mercenaries didn't know how to dress, they didn't wash or clean up frequently, and they often made crass and rude remarks. Seeing that she was distracted, he lightly cleared his throat. The attendant quickly snapped back to reality and shot them an overexaggerated smile.

"My dear guests, I assume you wish to set up a stall for the trade meet?" the beautiful woman asked politely. The phrase seemed well-rehearsed. It was likely a canned expression she'd been using to save energy and avoid much conversation.

"Yes, I would like to set up a talisman shop," Cha Ming replied. This seemed to pique the interest of the lady in red. She straightened up a little and pushed a loose lock of hair back before continuing.

"May I see the goods in question? Also, may I know what grade of talismans you will be selling? We are required to register the approximate value of goods, for tax purposes. Of course, the *hosts* will be covering the tax for this exchange, so you need not worry about paying a commission."

He neatly placed all the talismans he had produced on the desk. According to the Swiftwind Intelligence Agency, his talismans had a list price of 105 mid-grade spirit stones.

"Two hundred and five sixth-grade talismans," he declared.

The lady in red's face flushed as she heard his declaration. She then picked up one of the papers, which had been intricately decorated at the borders with ink matching the key character. While she had no idea what the talisman was used for, she couldn't help but admire the exquisite calligraphy. The elegance in the brushstrokes could easily match the exquisite runes she had seen on goods produced by top-tier weaponsmiths.

"Young master, may I ask if you absolutely insist on selling these at the trade meet?" Her form of address quickly adjusted itself to his perceived station; high-level artisans were practically worshiped in Fairweather.

"Oh? Should I be selling these elsewhere?" Cha Ming inquired after understanding her meaning.

"I believe there is the possibility of including your goods in the auction itself. Would you be available for a short meeting with my manager?" the lady asked in a hopeful tone. After all, there was *actual* commission at stake here.

A quarter hour later, they were seated in a luxurious office in front of a man with long black hair. Wisps of silver flowed down his head onto his shoulders, giving the impression that it was intentionally dyed this way for decorative purposes. He wore a silk cultivation robe, which was dark blue and decorated with silver runic patterns.

The office seemed more like a showroom than a place to fill out paperwork, due to the dozens of collectible items adorning the walls. Beautifully crafted weapons, armor, clothes, sculptures, and jewelry pieces had been carefully laid out, often inside clear glass cases. Not a speck of dust could be seen.

The man in question was the manager of the auction house. He was currently observing the talismans Cha Ming had crafted one by one, nodding his head in appreciation.

"Where did you learn your craft?" the man asked softly.

"In Green Leaf City, sir. I was taught by Elder Ling, the best talisman artist in the city," Cha Ming replied.

The man continued nodding his head. "I'll be honest, I've never heard of Elder Ling. However, I have frequented many auction houses and spoken to many craftsmen. Regrettably, calligraphy is seldom used by talisman artists, as it *substantially* increases the difficulty. There are maybe one or two talisman artists in the kingdom that would bother, and they are both foundation-establishment elders. They usually wouldn't bother themselves with mid-grade talismans like these.

"That being said, I'm not mocking your talismans. Quite the contrary, your attention to detail and exquisite penmanship is exactly what people look for around here, particularly in noble and craftsman families. Coincidentally, we expect at least half of the guests at this auction with higher-level cultivations to be in this demographic.

"Here is what I propose. I can give you a base price of twenty-five percent over list price. In addition, if this is insufficient, I offer to add these goods to tomorrow's auction. If they don't sell as I predict, I will buy them from you at said price, because

I can eventually sell them at a hefty profit. The starting price at the auction will be a twenty-five percent premium, and I am confident in our ability to fetch a thirty to fifty percent premium. These goods are in short supply, especially just before the rescue mission. Combined with their artistic value, I think this is a fair estimate.

"Normally, we would ask for a five percent commission on anything that we auction. In this case, I propose zero commission for the base price but a twenty-five percent commission on anything over and above the base price. This will give us plenty of incentive to fetch you the best price possible. What do you think of my proposal?"

"How about twenty percent?" he countered. "In addition, I want a letter of credit for 125% of their face value so that I can shop around during the trade meet and at earlier stages of the auction."

"Deal," the manager replied. They shook hands, and the trio walked out of the office with a stack of bills of credit. Each bill was redeemable for ten thousand spirit stones at the auction house.

Lively. That was the only way to describe the trade meet. A total of three hundred mercenaries consisting of foreign and local cultivators had chosen to participate in the mission. Truth be told, half of them were little more than cannon fodder. Alas, their situation was akin to the employees of pleasure houses. Mercenaries usually chose the profession out of desperation.

And just like their sister occupation, they did not live long.

Of course, that did not stop them from somehow accumulating odd treasures from time to time. Three quarters of the stalls dealt with low-quality goods or unknown goods. These rubbish treasures were of little or no use to these cultivators. That or they were saving up for something important like a life-saving treasure or a better spirit weapon. While everyone had heard that there would be plenty of spirit weapons at the auction, no one knew the exact number. Many of the warriors did not possess even the *lowest* grade of precious weapons, not to mention their upgraded versions.

Therefore, a young man, a young lady, and a baby fox decided to take advantage of the fire sale. Most of the goods were displayed on simple tables covered in black fabric, lest the tables draw attention from their glittering wares. What Cha Ming and company were doing now was akin to junk diving— sifting through the rubble in the hopes of finding a precious treasure.

A few hours passed, after which they stopped at an interesting stall, where a grizzled veteran's deep voice caught their attention. His hefty mane was draped across a set of burly shoulders. A suit of black armor covered his torso, his upper arms, and his thighs. Such a suit of armor was commonly used by cultivators since it did not restrict mobility. Cha Ming evaluated that it was a mid-grade spirit armor, given the runes that were inscribed. Spirit armor came with a substantially higher price tag than spirit weapons. The man had a dozen items laid out in front of him.

"This bottle of pills was obtained from an expert's tomb. I lost five brothers to obtain it, but alas, I am unsure of its contents. Breaking open the seal on this glass bottle will cause the medicine to quickly lose its efficacy. Therefore, I haven't had the heart to take the risk and open it."

Seeing Cha Ming was about to turn and leave, he tried again. "Young man, I'm quite desperate to obtain a mid-grade spirit weapon in this upcoming auction. Therefore I'm willing to part with this precious bottle for three mid-grade spirit stones." The man looked deeply aggrieved, as though he was selling his firstborn son. Given the man's professional-grade acting talent, Cha Ming would not have been surprised if he'd shed a tear.

Gong Lan, being the hot-tempered one, scolded him immediately. "How could anyone ever buy this bottle of pills from you for three mid-grade spirit stones? That's a small fortune! In addition, the pills in this bottle would need to be at least eighth or ninth grade for me to make a profit! Have you no shame?"

This was the third stall they had stopped at. Try as he might, Cha Ming had been unable to convince Gong Lan to stop buying things. Her demeanor made her easy prey for the various shady characters who had set up their stalls. This battle-hardened veteran was more cunning than the last two, however, and he immediately laid out some bait, which she bit into with gusto. It was only a matter of time until she obtained her "victory."

He sighed. "But how am I to afford a sixth-grade spirit weapon at this auction unless I sell these possessions of mine for a hefty profit? Without a good weapon, I might very well die!" the man replied in a saddened voice.

"That's not my problem! You can't rip people off just because you need more money. Five thousand spirit stones is a much more reasonable price." Unknowingly, Gong Lan had started to haggle with the grizzled veteran.

"Come on now, lass, that price is outrageous! Clearly fifteen thousand spirit stones is a much more reasonable price." The man looked quite heated now, but it was clearly all an act. Everyone but the young lady arguing with him saw it clearly.

"Well, you deserve it! You're the one who highballed us in the first place! Fine, since you're willing to be reasonable, lets settle this in the middle. One mid-grade spirit stone!"

Cha Ming coughed a couple of times to get her attention. "Are you sure you want to get this bottle of pills? You would have to go get them appraised later, and who knows exactly what's inside the bottle?"

In all fairness, the bottle seemed positively ancient. The seals placed on pill bottles had a convenient function that identified the date of sealing. Such a time-keeping function was difficult to tamper with, and the person who had established this specific seal was definitely an impressive elder. The bottle's seal was one hundred and six years old.

While the probability of there being at least a seventh-grade pill inside was very high, there was always a chance that the pills had been damaged despite the seal. In addition, the pills in the bottle might not be very useful for Gong Lan. Therefore, a price of ten thousand spirit stones was not unreasonable, given the potential risks and rewards.

The man was not one to give up, however. He immediately agreed to one mid-grade spirit stone in order to minimize the chance that Cha Ming would be able to convince her otherwise.

"Yeah! Here you go, sir! And remember to be more honest in the future!" Gong Lan laid down a mid-grade spirit stone and picked up the pill bottle, humming joyfully. Just as she was about to depart, she paused after noticing that Cha Ming was still observing an item on the table.

"Where did you get this?" Cha Ming asked the man, who was currently in a good mood. The object in question was an old and crumpled talisman. It had clearly been through many hardships. The edges were worn, and the paper was torn in many places. Despite its wretched appearance, Cha Ming could sense a mysterious power fluctuation.

Despite Cha Ming's proficiency in runic characters, he could not decipher the meaning behind the script. Not only was this script much longer than normal, but the characters were nonsensical. It was as though there was a mysterious veil that had been placed over them, making it impossible for him to clearly interpret their meaning.

Brother, that's space power! It's definitely a spatial transmission talisman, the usually silent Huxian chimed in.

Oh? How are you so sure? I've never sensed such power before, but I can tell that it's at least a magic-grade talisman, Cha Ming replied. The little fox was full of secrets, which he'd only discovered with the passage of time. Huxian had once called them inherited memories, and they only surfaced by chance or whenever they were useful.

My kind has a very strong affinity to space. I'll gain the ability to perform short-distance teleportation much earlier than most cultivators or spirit beasts. I can tell that this talisman is a damaged spatial transmission talisman. Unfortunately, the talisman is severely damaged. There is a ninety-eight percent chance that it will outright fail, while there is a one percent chance that it will work as intended and teleport the user and up to five people to a random destination within ten thousand li, the fox replied proudly.

What about the other one percent? Cha Ming asked.

I'm not too sure. Given the nature of spatial powers, my guess is that the user will get torn to pieces under the ravages of space and time, Huxian replied in a jovial tone.

That's... encouraging.

"Sir, did you hear me?" The man looked concerned, as Cha Ming had spaced out for a good sixty breaths.

Having regained his focus, Cha Ming looked a little embarrassed. "My apologies, could you repeat what you just said?"

"Yes, of course." The man was a little embarrassed but continued to explain. "This talisman was found in the same tomb as the bottle of pills. While it's clearly a high-level talisman, its ability to function is... *questionable* at best. I once sought out an expert, who took great interest in this talisman. In exchange for a few days time to study it, he reported that it was likely a minor teleportation talisman capable of traveling one thousand li in a chosen direction. In addition, the damage meant that there was less than a one-in-a-thousand chance of activation, but a ten percent chance of activating a less-than-pleasant function."

"I happen to find this trinket a little interesting. That and the eighth-level beast core on the table. Would five thousand spirit stones be sufficient?" Of course, the beast core had been identified by Huxian as a tasty morsel. Strictly speaking, the price of an eighth-level beast core was ten thousand spirit stones, but this was a fire sale, not an auction.

"The talisman is nothing. If you buy the beast core, I'll throw it in for free. However, the going rate for these is ten thousand spirit stones. But I can bring it down to nine thousand, since the auction is tomorrow..." the man said hesitantly.

"Eight thousand, take it or leave it," Cha Ming replied. After all, Huxian was easily capable of harvesting such items himself.

The trio soon left the merchant stall in a happy mood. They continued to peruse through the remainder of the stalls for the rest of the day, and Cha Ming made sure to pick up a few necessities at a cheap price. Fasting pills, while not particularly tasty, enabled one to continue for days without a meal. He also purchased low-level healing pills, which were useful in emergencies when his wood qi was depleted.

Their business finished, they spent the rest of the day in leisure at their new favorite restaurant, the Phoenix Cry Pavilion.

Chapter 14: The Auction

Cha Ming and company returned to the auction house after noon the next day. The street leading to the auction house was much busier than the previous day. Instead of trickling in to set up their stalls, everyone arrived together just before the start of the auction. Most people had been registered the previous day, and as a result the traffic flowed much more smoothly.

After a short wait, Cha Ming and company arrived at the entrance of the beautifully decorated auction house. He had failed to notice its beauty the first time he came, as he had been preoccupied with selling his wares. Unlike most buildings in town, which were made from carved stone, the auction hall was fabricated with expensive wood.

The wood had been carved with intricate patterns, both decorative and runic, and they meshed together seamlessly. While the wood was dark, the carved runes had been stained a bright purple to complement golden fixtures. The building could only be described as majestic.

To gain entrance this time, all Cha Ming did was flash his

bidding paddle, which identified him as a silver-level bidder in the upcoming auction. After entering, they proceeded to the seating area. It was entirely different than the cheap, undecorated hall in which the trade meet was held.

The rows up front were reserved for those with silver bidding paddles. Those with silver paddles had a proven level of strength, and their seating area was much less crowded than those used by the less powerful mercenaries. This was not their destination, however. They ignored the lower seating area and proceeded to the private booths. Given how well he and Hong Lai had hit it off, Cha Ming saw no reason to turn down his invitation.

After inquiring with one of the attendants, they soon arrived at a wooden door carved with a ferocious mastiff. There were only twelve booths in the auction house, one for each of the twelve guardian animals. Each year was named after one of the animals, and each one was featured five times in a sixty-year cycle. The five rotations had something to do with the five elements.

The attendant knocked on the large wooden door, and it was immediately opened by Hong Lai, who greeted them with a cheerful smile. "Cha Ming, Gong Lan, it's so good to see you!"

Cha Ming clasped his hands and bowed respectfully. "The pleasure is all ours. How could we refuse your gracious invitation?"

After exchanging pleasantries, Hong Lai quickly ushered them in and served them tea. They drank in silence for a quarter hour, then another soft knock sounded on the door. Two unfamiliar young men were ushered in by their host.

The duo clasped their hands in greeting to Hong Lai. "Greetings, Master Uncle Hong," they said in unison.

Hong Lai waved his hand in response. "No need for formalities. Let me introduce you to two new friends." He motioned toward Cha Ming and Gong Lan.

"This is Cha Ming and Gong Lan. They've come from Green Leaf City to join the rescue mission. We met when Cha Ming gave me some advice on calligraphy while crafting a fifth-grade protective treasure." He then motioned toward the two youngsters.

"Cha Ming, Gong Lan, these two are my apprentice-nephews. My master had five students, and although he has retired, his legacy lives on with me, my apprentice-brothers, and my apprentices and apprentice-nephews.

"The one on the left with the longer hair is Sima Qian, and the aggressive-looking one on the right is Wu Jin. They have both volunteered to participate in this expedition. As such, they are also your competitors in this auction."

The short-haired Wu Jin was expressionless. Sima Qian, however, laughed modestly and said, "Uncle Master, I would hardly call us competitors. Spiritual blacksmiths burn spirit stones to learn their craft. Truth be told, Wu Jin already has everything he needs and is participating out of curiosity. On the other hand, I only wish to participate and obtain a seventh-grade spirit weapon at less than market price."

The pair of apprentice-brothers seated themselves opposite Gong Lan and Cha Ming. The booth's seating was semicircular. This way, they would always be facing the auction stage. An ornate semicircular table was located in front of them. Hong Lai had already served tea on this table, and various snack dishes had been placed there for the booth's occupants. While Huxian had wanted to gorge himself as soon as they entered, he was scolded by Cha Ming and forced to withdraw rations from his collar.

Wu Jin, despite his simple-minded appearance, was extremely observant. "Your pet fox is quite extraordinary!" he said in admiration. "While I'm not very proficient at crafting artifacts, combat is my true passion. I can tell that I surely wouldn't last more than three rounds against it! Furthermore, it's just a baby!"

His comments prompted looks of admiration from Hong Lai, Sima Qian, and Wu Jin. The baby fox, unaware of what was happening, looked at them with a puzzled expression.

Cha Ming laughed. "I assure you, he's only a regular spirit fox. He did, however, experience a fortuitous encounter. While wandering the spirit woods near Green Leaf Academy, we happened to discover a demon blood ginseng. Huxian almost died after consuming it! He survived out of sheer luck. Afterward, he experienced a period of rapid growth. Perhaps he will be lucky enough to evolve into a demon beast when he grows up."

This lie had been rehearsed many times in the past. After all, not many baby spirit beasts were born with so much innate strength and potential. Revealing Huxian's identity might rouse jealousy in even the most honest cultivators.

Fortunately, before anyone had a chance to question his lie, the rowdy auction hall suddenly quieted down. They were silenced by an extremely beautiful woman wearing a red dress. The dress was tight-fitting, accentuating her generous proportions and well-toned figure. The woman's long black hair was fastened behind her head with a jade pin. Her cherry-red lips had been painted to match her dress.

After entering the stage, she spoke out in a magically amplified yet melodious voice.

"My fellow adventurers, welcome to today's special pre-mission auction. This auction has been sponsored jointly by our very own Han Jinlong and Zhang Yifeng, who will also be participating in the upcoming mission.

"As all of you may know, this auction has been launched by our leading artisans to rescue their dear family members, whom they have not heard from in many weeks. In order to increase the chances of success, they have spared no expense in hosting this auction. As such, except for the final two items in this auction, any weapons or pills that are sold will not be identified by their craftsmen. Unlike the shops in this city, these exquisitely crafted products will be auctioned off at a starting price of eighty-five percent of their list price.

"If this isn't enough, I have received a guarantee from our two hosts that within each grade, at least ten percent of the items have been crafted by them personally! After the expedition, they will be more than happy to identify these personally crafted weapons. Such a memorable item would be a priceless addition to anyone's collection!

"Regarding all other weapons, each of these are guaranteed to be crafted by one of the top twenty weapon craftsmen in the city. It is impossible to see these as normal weapons, however, because these limited-edition items, while beautiful, are also inscribed with a commemorative decoration. The resale value of these items cannot be doubted!

"The following items will be auctioned off in this special batch:

Third-grade medicinal pills—one hundred bottles

Fourth-grade medicinal pills—fifty bottles

Fifth-grade medicinal pills—ten bottles

Sixth-grade medicinal pills—five bottles

"Specialized pill-crafting session with Zhang Yifeng—ten units. Please note, this includes labor but does not include materials, which can either be supplied or bought at cost. One crafting session includes the creation of three cauldrons of medicinal pills.

Third-grade spirit weapon—one hundred units

Fourth-grade spirit weapon—fifty units

Fifth-grade spirit weapon—ten units

Sixth-grade spirit weapon—five units

"Specialized weapon crafting session with Han Jinlong—ten units. Please note, this includes labor but does not include materials, which can either be supplied by the cultivator or bought at cost.

"Without further ado, we'll begin this auction with the first item—one bottle of twenty lesser healing pills. These pills are ideal for treating injuries such as large lacerations and small fractures. They can effectively treat anything short of a severed limb, internal organ damage, or meridian trauma. Don't risk your life without sufficient insurance—buy some healing pills!"

With a wave of her hand, a small ornately crafted bottle was launched onto a pedestal. The mysterious device, sensing the presence of an item, projected an enlarged three-dimensional image of the bottle and its contents. The green pills were shaped like dodecahedrons. Decorative flower patterns were carved into the surface of each pill. These served no function, though. Unlike spirit weapons, spirit pills could not be reforged after their creation.

"Sixty-eight spirit stones!"

"Seventy spirit stones!"

"Seventy-five spirit stones!"

Multiple bids were made instantly. Unfortunately for the bidders, it was difficult to find cheaply-made medicinal pills in town. The stock of practically every shop had been completely exhausted due to the recent influx of mercenaries. After multiple rounds of bidding, the price finally settled at one hundred and five spirit stones, roughly thirty percent higher than the list price.

"It's not a bad way to make money. With so much excitement, these prices are going through the roof," Cha Ming commented. He was also regretting his prior purchases. The small amount of spirit stones he spent previously might have been enough to tip the scales for customized services in his favor.

"You can't say that. In reality, this auction won't even cover fifty percent of the costs," said Hong Lai.

"Oh? How so?" asked Cha Ming.

"Well, think about it this way," Hong Lai continued. "You're a sixth-grade talisman artist. If someone asked you to craft a bunch of first-grade talismans, would you do it? Perhaps for a friend or relative. However, your time is better spent crafting higher-level talismans. Even crafting items at a loss for practice is a better use of your time.

"In fact, my retired teacher has incurred a substantial loss for this auction. He crafted two of the sixth-grade spirit weapons, which might fetch two or three mid-grade spirit stones. The weapons he crafts normally sell for tens, even hundreds of mid-grade spirit stones. He only made these because the craftsmen in Fairweather consider themselves to be one big family. They made these weapons to encourage more participation."

"I see what you mean. Perhaps I would make low-level

talismans as a favor, nothing more." Cha Ming was solemn for the remainder of the pre-auction. The price of the sixth-grade spirit weapons reached thirty to forty thousand spirit stones. This made Cha Ming very nervous—would he need to liquidate some soul alloy or crystalized elemental essence to cover the price of his bid? After all, the amount in question didn't even include materials! Perhaps he had been too naïve in assuming he could successfully purchase one of the ten slots.

Once the pre-auction came to an end, there was a one-hour intermission. The regular guests were invited for a buffet-style meal in an event hall within the auction house. A special meal was served in each of the twelve VIP booths. Everyone enjoyed their meal with great gusto.

"Brother Lai, might you know where I can find an appraiser in this auction hall?" Cha Ming asked while retrieving a green bean with his chopsticks.

"Oh? What would you like appraised? I'm very curious, since most people would have registered goods they want to liquidate with the auction house," Hong Lai said while grabbing a piece of beef and stuffing it in his mouth.

"Well, I've been told by a friend of mine that an item I possess has a cash equivalent," Cha Ming said. "He's usually pretty good with these things, but he failed to mention the exchange rate." He was truly confused by Wang Jun's attitude toward his crystalized elemental essence. However, Cha Ming had never inquired about it because it was an ideal cultivation resource when used with an energy-gathering formation.

"Let's see it, then. There are no strangers here," Hong Lai said.

Cha Ming nodded and produced a light-blue stone. Hong Lai shot him a surprised look and shook his head.

"There is no need for an appraiser. This is a common cash currency," Hong Lai replied. "Crystalized elemental essence is worth roughly ten mid-grade spirit stones per refined stone that size. It's priced by weight, since there is no standard cut."

The hell? Why didn't Wang Jun tell me such an important detail? He would never have sold those talismans if he'd known he had such a large amount of cash! He would have also bought tons of pills at the auction. With no legitimate route to vent his anger, he had inadvertently yelled at Huxian via voice transmission. Huxian wasn't amused at the outburst and began to sulk.

"Are you okay there?" Hong Lai asked. "You spaced out all of a sudden."

"Nothing, nothing. I was just surprised. I have a few of them, and I didn't realize they were worth so much," Cha Ming replied. No one asked how many "a few" was, as prying into someone's wealth was considered rude.

Following the intermission, the second part of the auction began. This session featured a variety of rare treasures and higher-level wares.

Gong Lan, who wasn't looking for anything in particular, took a fancy to a pair of sabers called the Blood Drinking Blades. The auctioneer had introduced the weapons as a top-grade spirit weapon, which suffered from a serious drawback: amplified baleful aura. Many users of the blades had gone insane from bloodlust. For Gong Lan, however, it was a perfect fit. She purchased them for the very low price of eighty-eight mid-grade spirit stones.

Cha Ming's talismans were popular, as predicted. On average, they fetched 145% of list price, or 152 mid-grade spirit stones. While it pleased him that these goods were popular, his newfound fortune caused him to regret selling these life-saving treasures. Unfortunately, he had already commissioned their sale. As the seller, he was not qualified to buy back his item.

To his surprise, the stoic Wu Jin purchased three such talismans. When Cha Ming inquired about it, he sighed and shook his head before replying. "My younger sister is at the third level of qi condensation, but she insisted on participating in this rescue mission. I've been told that the mission is extremely dangerous. However, she says she won't stay close to me on the battlefield, as it will stunt her growth in the long term.

"Moreover, I've tried to give her protective treasures countless times in the past, but she is very picky. Perhaps only Master Uncle Hong Lai's goods stand a chance at passing her evaluation, but they are always expensive and in very short supply. In addition, too many single-use protective treasures start interfering with each other. I'm hoping that these talismans you made obtain her approval.

"At the very least, these wind-affinity talismans are very useful, and very rare. An instant increase in movement speed is very hard to come by. Where did you ever learn to craft these Cloud Step talismans?" Wu Jin inquired.

"They are something I made on a whim, based on a movement technique I practice. You praise me far too much," Cha Ming said while chuckling wryly. It had been an accidental creation from one of his practice sessions, and the Cloud Step runes he used to practice his calligraphy happened to produce a useful talisman.

"It looks like you lucked out, Wu Jin," Hong Lai chimed in. "If the auctioneers had known that this was an original and unique creation, the price would have doubled! Make sure you tell your sister this detail. She always loves purchasing my newest works."

They continued to discuss things in a relaxed manner for quite some time, and no longer paid attention to the ongoing auction. Suddenly, however, Cha Ming's attention was roused by the voice inside his head. It was the red-bearded man who lived inside the Clear Sky Brush.

"Cha Ming, make sure you get your hands on the treasure being auctioned in lot 76, no matter the price!" The excitement in the man's voice startled Cha Ming, as this was the first time he had ever heard him so agitated.

"No matter the price?" Cha Ming asked. "You mean that this treasure is more valuable than getting medicinal pills to aid my breakthrough or forging a soul-alloy staff?"

"Much more than that," he replied. "You might not know it, but you're currently a dead man walking. You've agreed to share tribulations with your fox friend, but you haven't made any plans on how to face it! He's already so much stronger than you. Has it ever occurred to you that by the time he faces his tribulation, Huxian will be a peak god-level spirit beast with the power of his second tail, while you might only be at the sixth or seventh level of qi condensation?

"Without sufficient preparation, you're going to get blown to bits! This treasure can help you through this first tribulation. Unfortunately, it can't do everything for you. It's a priority to get your cultivation up as fast as possible, in addition to the Seventy-Two Transformations Technique. The weapon can wait."

Cha Ming paled at the revelation. "Can Huxian not delay his breakthrough?"

"What do you mean, *delay*? That kid, even if all he does at this point is sleep and breathe, he'll naturally break through with ease. For a spirit beast at his level, there's no such thing as holding back. This is just a part of him naturally growing up. If you don't keep up, you'll both end up dead."

As if emphasizing his point, the auctioneer's melodious voice sounded out. "One hundred and ten mid-grade spirit stones going once. One hundred and ten mid-grade spirit stones going twice."

"One hundred and thirty mid-grade spirit stones!" Cha Ming shouted out in a hurry, to the surprise of everyone sharing his booth.

"Are you sure you want to buy this treasure?" asked Hong Lai. "It has been around the auction block a few times. Every time, someone 'borrows' the item for a few months only to return it in frustration. I dare say that I've personally seen it auctioned off twelve times!"

There was no use regretting, however. His sharp increase in price had dissuaded the single bidder, who was purely interested in seeing the famous item up close.

"Lot number seventy-six, sold to the man in the private booth!" the auctioneer announced. Just like that, Cha Ming's small fortune in mid-grade spirit stones had been viciously decimated. And he hadn't even seen the treasure that he bid on!

To succeed in any future auctions, Cha Ming would need to spend his crystalized elemental essence, which was extremely useful in his cultivation.

Chapter 15: Main Auction

During the next intermission, Cha Ming and Gong Lan went to the auction desk to pay their bills and collect the items they had purchased. In Cha Ming's case, he exchanged most of his remaining bills of credit for the mystery treasure in lot number 76.

To his surprise, the treasure appeared to be a bundle of metal stakes joined together by a long, thin chain. The stakes resembled throwing daggers decorated with elaborate runic patterns. He still had no idea how to use this treasure, but he was sure that his friend in the brush would explain everything when the time came. Given how important the treasure was to his survival, he carefully placed it in an empty corner of his bag of holding.

After storing the treasure, he turned around just in time to see a blood-red blade slash down toward his face. It stopped right on his nose before he even had a chance to scream. Satisfied with its performance, Gong Lan withdrew the other saber from its sheath and began admiring the pair. They looked very similar to a pair of oversized, black iron kukris[4]. The crude iron was rusted to the point that it was unfit for duty, yet the stench of blood permeating from the blades spoke volumes of its ability to perform its basic function.

As Gong Lan hefted the two cruel blades, her demeanor instantly changed. Her abnormal levels of bloodlust increased threefold in an instant, causing some nearby cultivators to wet themselves.

"Gong Lan!" Cha Ming yelled, calling his friend back to her senses.

"Perfect," she whispered softly, sending a chill down Cha Ming's spine. After a few moments, she came to and realized that she had caused a scene and shot everyone a bashful look as she sheathed the blades and fastened them to her back.

After returning to their private booth, Cha Ming performed some quick mental calculations. He estimated that he had 2,000 mid-grade spirit stones' worth of crystalized elemental essence to liquidate. That was the equivalent of twenty million low-grade spirit stones.

"Brother Hong," Cha Ming asked, "how much do you think those custom crafting slots will auction for?"

Hong Lai thought for a moment before replying. "Three million spirit stones."

"That much? Why would it be so high?" Cha Ming complained. His nouveau riche mentality quickly faded as he realized that he was only wealthy for a qi condensation cultivator.

"Well, it's because these famous artisans are foundation-

---

[4] Kukris are a type of curved dagger, commonly associated with the Nepalese Gurkhas. They are well suited to hacking and slashing but are inadequate for stabbing motions.

establishment elders," Hong Lai replied. "Their level in their craft enables them to make magic treasures. Many of the people participating in the auction will, in fact, be asking them to create their future weapons. These people are geniuses within their families, and their elders are willing to bet a significant fortune on their future, as it is closely tied to the destiny of their family."

Cha Ming sighed. "It looks like I'll have to go for a pill-crafting slot and ignore my weapon for now. Alas, Brother Hong, I'm still too poor."

"Oh? What kind of weapon were you looking to have crafted?" Hong Lai asked with interest. He was a spiritual blacksmith, after all.

"I'd like Han Jinlong to craft a soul-alloy staff. The staff must be six feet long and two inches wide. The problem is, I've heard that soul alloy is an extremely difficult material to craft, and I dare not trust anyone but Han Jinlong for this matter." Cha Ming's eyes were downcast. As the bearded man in the Clear Sky Brush had said, life before weapon.

"That… that is a huge amount of soul alloy. Are you sure you don't want it made with another material?" Hong Lai asked.

"Yes, and I understand that most soul-alloy weapons are small or thin. However, I really need the weight-increasing and length-manipulation properties intrinsic to soul alloy for my staff arts. I also practice five-element cultivation, and any other material will skew my fighting style. Besides, I already have enough soul alloy, and I only need to contract a spiritual blacksmith that can work with it."

"You already have such a huge amount of soul alloy?" Hong Lai asked, amazed. "Well, you're in luck. Don't bother with this auction. I'll simply ask for a favor from my master, Bei Ling.

While he is not the best spiritual blacksmith in the city, Han Jinlong himself would not dare say he is my master's match at crafting soul-alloy weapons!"

Cha Ming was elated. Hong Lai's offer was like receiving coal in the winter. He graciously accepted.

Now that his most pressing problem was solved, he waited leisurely for the auction to begin once more. This time, an old man with white hair walked confidently out on stage, and the noisy crowd quieted. Though he wore a set of plain blue robes and his appearance was unremarkable, the man's presence was stifling—the mark of a foundation-establishment elder.

"Ladies and gentlemen, my name is Li Taihou, the president of the Fairweather City auction house. The contents of this auction have already been explained, so without further ado, I will proceed to the main event." Even without a voice amplification device, Li Taihou's voice resonated throughout the entire auction house.

"I would like to remind you before continuing, however, that only those with silver voting paddles can participate. The rest of you may continue to watch at your leisure. The first item up for auction is the first custom pill-concoction slot. The winner will be entitled to three batches of custom pill concoction from Master Zhang Yifeng.

"Please note that while this price includes labor, it does not include the cost of materials. Success is guaranteed with three batches of materials, as long as the grade of pills requested does not exceed low-grade magic pills. Master Zhang has guaranteed that he will make an attempt to concoct pills with each batch of materials provided, to a maximum of three. Additionally, I would like to note that this is very unusual—alchemists will usually keep excess materials when they guarantee success.

"The starting price is one hundred mid-grade spirit stones. Each subsequent bid must raise the price by one mid-grade spirit stone. To place a bid, please yell out your offer and reveal your bidding paddle."

Despite his permission to begin, the people in the auction house were strangely quiet. A lone woman's voice broke the silence, yelling out, "One hundred spirit stones." This voice came from the sheep booth.

The voice was answered by that of a young man, who was seated in the ox booth. "I can't let you take a slot so cheaply. That would be an insult to Master Zhang's skill. One hundred and ten spirit stones."

A third voice rang out from the white tiger booth, that of a middle-aged man. "You youngsters think you can get everything for cheap. One hundred and twenty spirit stones!"

The trio continued bidding, and no one dared interrupt them. "Who are these three, and why does no one else bid?" Cha Ming inquired.

"Ah, they are from the younger generation from each of the three prominent families in Fairweather City," Hong Lai said. "While I wouldn't go so far as to say that no one dares offend them, I think that everyone here is grateful that they are participating in the mission. As a token of respect, they will naturally let these three fight over the first three slots. Even a foreign influence wouldn't haggle over these slots with them unless they are exceptionally arrogant. Conversely, they won't fight over the remaining slots as a reciprocation of their goodwill. The rest of the slots are fair game."

Cha Ming wasn't one to rock the boat unless someone greatly offended him. If this was the custom here, so be it. True to Hong Lai's words, they won the first three batches with no competition. Surprisingly, they did not pursue rock-bottom prices. Instead, they kept each other in check and ensured that the item did not go for below 210 spirit stones.

Hong Lai explained the phenomenon. "Cha Ming, you'll notice that the minimum bid was 210 mid-grade spirit stones. This serves as a signal to the other competitors. Two hundred ten mid-grade spirit stones is the minimum acceptable price in this auction, and they will snatch away slots if this minimum price isn't offered."

The auction was a lot tamer than Cha Ming imagined it would be.

Then the fourth auction started at a record price. "Two hundred forty spirit stones!" a man shouted out passionately from the general seating area. He was a fat, middle-aged man.

"Two hundred forty-five spirit stones!" a much younger man yelled out.

Cha Ming knew that the prices could only increase as the quantity decreased. "Two hundred eighty spirit stones!" he increased the price sharply to deter other bidders. The auction hall was quiet for a brief moment, until the fat man bid once more.

"Two hundred eighty-five spirit stones!" he yelled out nervously.

"Three hundred twenty!" Cha Ming yelled out immediately. Silence ensued. After thirty breaths had passed, the auctioneer yelled out.

"Three hundred twenty, going once! Three hundred twenty, going twice! Sold, to the man in the mastiff booth!" The elder proceeded with the remainder of the auction, but no one else in his booth participated.

The final prices ended up ranging between 280 spirit stones

and 380 spirit stones. While Cha Ming didn't get the lowest price, he also avoided competing at the tail end of the auction, when the prices were sky high.

With nothing better to do, their group stuck around for the final auction, the weapon auction. These slots fetched up to 400 mid-grade spirit stones, slightly higher than the pill-concoction slots. Instead of bidding, they enjoyed chatting about weaponsmithing, talisman crafting, and other things. At one point, Wu Jin recounted the story of how he had accidentally been betrothed to a fey creature.

"I was walking by myself in the Lonely Woods, a spirit wood not far from here. It was a lucrative mission, one where we had to search for a mobile target that had been terrorizing local adventurers. At one point, I desperately needed to relieve myself. Naturally, I found a nearby tree to 'water.'

"Little did I know, the tree I chose was a dryad! She mistook my urination for a courting ritual, after which she became completely infatuated with me. It was impossible to separate myself from her, and I could hardly go back to town with such an innocent, untamed fey. After much effort, I was able to convince her that it would be best if I meet her elders. They were very understanding of my plight, as this sort of thing had happened to younger fey many times. It took many days, but they finally convinced the young dryad that it was a misunderstanding, and I was finally able to return to town. I had trouble peeing for a week!" Wu Jin's story provoked a storm of laughter.

Two hours after the auction ended, Cha Ming proceeded to the auction desk and paid with thirty-two pieces of crystalized elemental essence. While the attendant was surprised at seeing this unusual currency, she had dealt with it before and didn't need to call the manager. Cha Ming was then led to a small room where the nine other winners of the pill-concoction slots were waiting.

Cha Ming was the fourth to be called in, and he was ushered into a quiet room, where an older man with white hair was seated. In addition to the usual pressure he felt from foundation-establishment experts, Cha Ming felt a little something extra, like a soft pressure on his spirit. Reflexively, he released his spiritual force to counteract this intrusion.

"Oh." The man raised an eyebrow. Simultaneously, Cha Ming felt the pressure undulate, and he was forced to constantly adjust the pressure he felt from the experienced alchemist. After thirty breaths, he was finally unable to endure the fierce wrestling match, and his spiritual force collapsed. The man's spiritual force did not continue its assault, however. Instead, the alchemist clapped and smiled.

"It's so rare to see someone with such a strong spiritual force for his cultivation level, and with such exquisite control. What profession do you practice, young man?" Zhang Yifeng asked.

Cha Ming clasped his hands together and gave him a short bow. "Master Zhang, I'm a mildly proficient talisman artist. My achievements aren't anything worth mentioning."

The old man laughed. "How modest. The talismans for the auction must have come from you, then. They are sixth-grade talismans, so it's very impressive that you were able to craft them at the fifth level of qi condensation. Were you assessed with very high innate soul force?"

"I was fortunate to be assessed with full innate soul force," Cha Ming replied.

Zhang Yifeng nodded. "Very good. I confess myself impressed. What can I help you with today? I owe you three instances of pill concoction, as stated by the auctioneers."

"Master Zhang, I would like to request one batch of a high-level spirit pill that can aid me in making cultivation breakthroughs in qi condensation. I also expect that establishing my foundation will be very challenging. As such, I would like to request two batches of foundation-establishment pills tailored to my qi method."

"Establishing your foundation will be challenging, as you say. As for the high-level spirit pill, it sounds like you are looking for Barrier Breaker pills. What is your talent grade, young man?" the alchemist asked.

"Alas, my talent is only third grade," Cha Ming answered. "I find myself taking more and more time to break through each level of qi condensation. If I can get the batch of Barrier Breaker pills tomorrow, I am confident I can break through to the sixth level of qi condensation prior to our departure. I am also fifty percent confident in breaking through to the seventh level of body cultivation."

"Interesting. Fifty percent success, you say?" Zhang Yifeng said. "Training the body is much more difficult than training qi. You must have a special method. Very well, what you are requesting will cost twelve hundred mid-grade spirit stones. Can you afford it?"

Cha Ming gritted his teeth and withdrew a small mountain

of crystalized elemental essence. "Will this be sufficient?" he asked.

The older man chuckled. "So rich at such a young age. Come, stand in front of me, and don't resist. I'm going to take an imprint of the qi in your dantian. I'll be using it to tailor the composition of your pills to your cultivation method."

Cha Ming nodded and immediately stood in front of the experienced alchemist.

Instead of forming some complicated hand seals, the older man took out a plain bronze mirror, which he held in front of Cha Ming's dantian. Of course, the mirror was anything but ordinary. As soon as the older man began pouring qi into it, the plate emitted a sucking sound and began consuming his qi. Cha Ming moved instinctively to resist it.

"Don't resist!" the man yelled, reminding him. Cha Ming relaxed as the plate slowly absorbed increasing amounts of qi. Engravings, which had previously been hidden on the mirror's surface, began to light up one by one. They lit up at five points in five different colors, and the points eventually expanded. After the five glowing engravings ceased their growth, a white circle and a black star had imprinted itself onto the bronze mirror.

"Done!" the man said, breathing quickly. The sweat on his brow indicated that this was no simple process, even for a foundation-establishment expert. "You can go on home now. I've decided to have your first batch of pills ready for tomorrow afternoon. Don't disappoint me, young man."

Cha Ming bowed and quickly exited the room.

Seeing the young man scamper off, Zhang Yifeng looked at the imprinted mirror once more. "Five-element cultivation?" he thought out loud. It had been many years since he'd prepared custom pills for someone who cultivated this method.

It seemed that things would be tricky for this batch of foundation-establishment pills, to the extent that he might even have to take a loss. Unfortunately, he'd already quoted a price. He quietly berated himself for this foolish mistake.

Fine, fine, he thought. *It's not every day that I get to help out such a promising youngster. If only the situation wasn't so dire... I don't want to throw so many talented youths to the wolves, but it seems I have no choice.*

Looking at the plate again, he finally noticed the white circle and the black star. *Is this creation qi and destruction qi? Shit.* He was *definitely* going to take a loss on this one. Who the hell even gave that boy that cultivation method? He'd never heard of a cultivation method that could generate seven types of qi in one body, much less creation qi and destruction qi!

Sighing, he called out to the next person on his list. This time, it was a young lady. Water and wood element cultivation. And a spirit doctor apprentice. Another good seedling who probably wouldn't get to see the next month.

But what choice did he have?

Chapter 16: Master Smith Bei Ling

A group of two youngsters, a young man, and a fox were walking along a shabby road in an otherwise resplendent city. In the merchant district, the philosophy of fashion over function had prevailed. Here, only function existed.

On the right, they observed a billowing forge out in the open air. A spiritual blacksmith pounded a piece of heated metal continuously, not stopping for a single breath. His apprentices were both channeling flames into the furnace, struggling to keep the metal at a consistently high temperature. Everyone was sweating profusely.

The smith used a spiritual hammer to forge the piece of metal. It was clear and fragile-looking yet harder than any metal Cha Ming had ever heard of. It shone with a bright white glow. Hong Lai had instructed Cha Ming on the subject previously. The clear hammer was condensed with pure spiritual force, which meant that it was also free from any material imperfections. It was the perfect instrument for forging an enchanted weapon.

Soon their group had passed the forge and stumbled upon an open-doored shop. Hong Lai motioned for the group to follow him inside, where they were greeted with a dazzling spectacle. To one side, a pile of roughly cut colored stones was stuffed in a corner. The odd loose stone had found its way to the path that ran through the middle of the store.

On the other side, there was a clear display case. Bright and colorful gems and intricate carvings had been mounted inside. One of the carvings, a life-sized statue of a fierce rabbit, had been carved out of pure emerald and covered in glittering runes. Its eyes were made of rubies, which appeared to be naturally embedded in the giant emerald gemstone. But could such a coincidence really occur in nature? The rubies glittered fiercely, and somehow Cha Ming could sense a baleful aura emanating from the carving.

In another corner of the workshop, a cluttered work desk was covered in glittering piles of dust. These were evidently precious gem shavings, which had been chipped off with specialized carving tools. Hong Lai explained that these tools were all composed of soul alloy and were inscribed with runes that increased hardness and sharpness. A middle-aged man was using one such carving tool to carve a small dragon out of a piece of purple jade. His motions were fluid and well practiced, a testament to the many years he had spent perfecting his craft.

Hong Lai was here for a few specific pieces. He paid an unknown amount of spirit stones to obtain eighteen uncut and unpolished red stones. They were covered in a familiar metallic sheen. Clearly Hong Lai was planning on crafting them each into a protective lotus brooch to fulfill his prior promise.

"Brother Hong," Cha Ming said, "with everything that you've done for us so far, there's really no need to compensate us for the brooch any longer." The recommendation he was about to receive was worth much more than these minor trinkets.

"Nonsense!" the man replied with full gusto. "It's not only to compensate you. Rather, I want to see the result of the final product after modifications. I also want you to evaluate the final product. It's something you owe me, after all."

Cha Ming was unable to deny the man's request. After the purchase was completed, they continued onward down the same ill-maintained street. As they walked, the buildings became more and more decrepit. There were even several abandoned buildings with for-sale signs attached to them.

Finally, at the end of the road, they saw a small wooden shack. It was covered in holes and seemed like it could barely stand up to the light morning breeze. Hong Lai didn't stand on ceremony and directly entered the building. Cha Ming and the others followed suit. The inside of the building was completely different than what they had imagined.

They were now standing in a warmly lit brick house draped in luxurious velvet carpets. Several pillars supported the ceiling on this single-floored abode. They were decorated with simple yet beautiful carvings, which infused the mansion with a lively and playful atmosphere.

A few loud footsteps were heard as a wiry old man of average height walked out of a room off to the side. A pair of goggles was hanging around his neck, and his toned body was covered in a layer of sweat. He had clearly been busy in his workshop until just a few moments ago. Retirement was obviously a relative term in the weaponsmithing world.

"Welcome to my humble abode," said the white-haired old man. "I hear one of you wants me to craft them an obscenely large weapon out of pure soul alloy." Not waiting for them to speak, the man grabbed a towel from a nearby shelf and wiped the grime from his face and arms. The blue towel was covered in a thin white powder.

Cha Ming stepped forward and greeted the elder. "Master Bei, Brother Hong has informed me you are the best spiritual blacksmith for forging soul-alloy weapons in the city. I'll be heading out on the rescue mission in one week, and I was hoping to have you craft me a new battle staff by the time I set out."

"All right," the man said. "Exactly how much soul alloy do you have on you? You might not know this, but looks can be very deceiving with this material. It's also surprisingly heavy. People just don't know about this little detail because they are used to dealing with small, thin objects like carving knives or herb-gathering knives."

Rather than explaining in words, Cha Ming dumped out a small pile of refined soul alloy onto the floor. There were 240 chunks in total. Without standing on ceremony, Master Bei walked up to the pile and brought up one of the soul chunks to his eye. He then took out a vicious-looking knife from his tool belt and chopped the ball in half. He observed the insides carefully and even licked the freshly cut surface.

"Not bad," Master Bei said, nodding. "This will be enough. How much do you weigh? And how long do you want the staff?"

"I weigh about 190 jin. Ideally, the staff would be seventy-two inches long and two inches thick," Cha Ming replied.

"Fair enough. The primary consideration for building the staff is its unmodified weight relative to yours and its length. The thickness can be adjusted accordingly. Let's step outside for a bit," the old man said. He led them to a brightly lit courtyard.

His "humble abode" was obviously a spatial treasure, as the shack they had seen previously most certainly could not accommodate such a large mansion. The man brought them to a small dueling pad, which the man stepped onto.

"Show me what you got, boy! Don't hold anything back!" the man yelled as a clear sledgehammer materialized in his hands. Though he was a foundation-establishment expert, he had restricted his cultivation to the sixth level of qi condensation. Unfortunately, there was nothing he could do to restrict his fleshly body strength; the pressure of a dual body and qi refiner flooded out from him like a breached dam.

Cha Ming didn't hesitate and took out his staff. Simultaneously, a group of seventy-two white soul pearls spread out to restrict the man's movements. They moved into a complex formation whose basic shape was akin to the simplest snowflake. As a result, the cold-based suppression on the man's movement reached an all-time high. As Cha Ming moved, the snowflake formation followed with Cha Ming as its center.

Since this was a demonstration and not an all-out battle to the death, Cha Ming displayed every movement he could. He zipped around with his Shearing Staff Art and Seven Cloud Steps, utilizing his advantage in movement speed. Despite his best attempts, Bei Ling's physical body was much too strong, and the slight cuts he managed to inflict on the older man's fierce body healed almost instantly.

Cha Ming attempted a different approach. If physical strikes didn't work, he would try energy attacks. Instantly, the snowflake formation surrounding him formed a vivid forest. The forest quickly burst into flames, surrounding the man in a blazing inferno.

"Hah!" the older man yelled, holding out his arms

arrogantly. "You dare to use fire against me, a person who plays with fire during his every waking hour?"

The smug look was replaced with a look of shock as the flaming power was quickly converted into a formation that looked like several overlapping circles. The wood-and-fire-fueled quaking formation concentrated all its powers of vibration on a single point, greatly weakening the man's defense and stability. Cha Ming took advantage of his surprise to increase his weight using Mountain Stance, and he smashed downward with a vicious Quake Staff.

For the first time, the older man was forced to block. Unsurprisingly, Cha Ming was forced backward due to the recoil of his technique. Yet he pressed forward quickly with Burst Steps and used Sword Staff to leave a few nicks on the man's torso.

"My turn!" the man exclaimed. He grabbed his war hammer with both hands, lunging forward with incredible speed. Cha Ming was forced to cancel his quake formation and rematerialize the frost formation. With Bei Ling's speed decreased, he managed to deflect a few fierce blows with his Wading Through the Reeds Staff Art, complementing it with his White Willow Shade movement technique. His deceptive movements were used to walk around the fierce man's relentless assault.

After a few breaths, the man's attack pattern changed. He was now anticipating Cha Ming's movements. He was clearly an experienced fighter. Accordingly, Cha Ming decided to prevent the man's assault with his Trapping Staff Art. Sometimes he interrupted the man's footwork for fractions of a second, buying himself time to outmaneuver him. Other times he proactively struck the man's hammer at the beginning of its movement arc, nullifying the attack entirely and disrupting his rhythm.

Frustrated, the man flung himself backward. "Let's see how you receive this technique!" Suddenly, the clear hammer he was holding started glowing with a metallic sheen. He then blew out a burst of roaring flames, which were also infused into the hammer. He raised the hammer up above his head and unleashed a fast and powerful strike. Seeing that he couldn't dodge this blow, Cha Ming could only block.

Cha Ming's heart palpitated as he reacted quickly. His pearls underwent three transformations. An inferno was infused into the quaking formation, which then infused itself into a peerless blade. The blade struck out, splitting apart the oncoming wave of power with pure sharpness.

The response was very effective, greatly diminishing the man's attack power. To confront the remaining power of the attack, Cha Ming held out his staff and executed the rarely used Flaming Wheel Defense Technique, which specialized in absorbing energy and projectile attacks. This managed to cancel out most of it, but the remaining power struck Cha Ming straight in the chest. Instead of taking it directly, however, he used the force to propel himself backward and skated into the direction of the force. The remainder was dissipated over a short amount of time, and Cha Ming finally came to a halt at the edge of the dueling platform.

A trickle of blood ran down Cha Ming's mouth, an indication of internal wounds. The original blow to his chest had still hit him, despite his best efforts at negating it. In response, he quickly formed a healing formation, completely restoring the damage he had just sustained.

"Now *that* was the best fight I've had in ages! I barely ever get to fight anyone nowadays, and my old bones can't stand traveling like they used to." Bei Ling's hammer dissipated, revealing his joyful expression. He wasn't even breathing hard.

With a wave of his hand, the man brought out a copper mirror. "Have you ever taken a qi imprint before?" Seeing Cha Ming nod, the man repeated the process that Cha Ming had undergone previously with Zhang Yifeng.

After retrieving the plate, the man walked off toward his workshop. "I've gotten some inspiration for your weapon, so I'm starting right now. I won't be seeing you off. Come back in six days to collect your staff, and I'll keep the rest of the soul alloy as my fee." With those words, he shut the door to his workshop. A click indicated that he locked the door from the inside.

"How was my teacher, Cha Ming?" Hong Lai asked when Cha Ming emerged. He had an expectant look laced with a slight bit of concern.

"Your teacher seems to be in excellent health, Hong Lai. If I were to describe his fighting style in any way, it would be: tyrannical, vigorous, and domineering!" Hearing Cha Ming's words, Hong Lai let out a sigh of relief.

"That's good," Hong Lai said. "Master is pushing one hundred and seventy years. You should know that foundation-establishment experts have a maximum lifespan of 200 years. However, that's in an ideal case. Every injury sustained can reduce this substantially, and my teacher is no stranger to battle and hardship."

Cha Ming, Gong Lan, and Huxian left Hong Lai at his master's abode. They left the shabby shack and the rundown street and made their way to the middle of town, where Zhang Yifeng resided. They were greeted at the door of an opulent house by a neatly dressed butler. He escorted them to a well-furnished lounging area, where they didn't wait long before the aged alchemist walked in.

Zhang Yifeng didn't betray Cha Ming's expectations. "You're in luck, young man. I succeeded in concocting two out of three stoves for these Barrier Breaker pills. The ingredients that I chose to complement your cultivation method also interacted beneficially with each other, creating pills of a higher quality than usual. Please use these pills to further strengthen yourself before we leave."

After Cha Ming bowed in thanks, the man quickly left to continue his pill concoction. Cha Ming imagined that preparing thirty stoves of high-quality pills was very taxing. Zhang Yifeng would likely get very little sleep in the upcoming week. And Cha Ming as well, as he immediately secluded himself to break through, with Huxian standing guard. Gong Lan went to the local arena to spar with the various mercenaries and nobles that were participating in the upcoming mission. It had been many days since she'd drawn blood.

Feng Ming urged his horse forward through a wide stream. He was careful not to guide it through any rocky areas for fear of the spraining the beast's ankle. The horse had accompanied him on their desperate week-long journey. The first few days had been uneventful, but the remaining days had brought rider after rider in hot pursuit.

He thanked the army's survival and anti-tracking training, which had enabled him to survive so long. Three quarters of the journey to Fairweather City was complete, but this last quarter would be the most challenging.

He had found it increasingly difficult to proceed. Not only had his wounds worsened, but they refused to heal despite the copious amounts of medicinal ointments he had applied or the pills he had taken. If that wasn't enough, he continued to stumble upon one misfortune after another.

For example, on the third day of his journey, the small lean-to he had erected for shelter from the rain was struck by lightning. The next day, he realized that the "grass" his horse was nibbling was actually an irritating weed that looked similar to grass. This caused the horse a significant amount of discomfort and diarrhea, which slowed their progress. Finally, they accidentally stumbled upon a small field of poisonous nettles, which covered them in a fierce rash from head to toe.

Despite these inconveniences, he and the horse carried on. If he didn't deliver the news, the whole army could suffer. He didn't want his carelessness to lead to the death of any more good men or innocent civilians.

Then yesterday, the riders had come. There were three in total, and their dogged pursuit left him no room to breathe and no room to sleep. They each had an extra horse, which meant that—at the very least—their horses were getting rest while his could not. The men were lightly armored but carried deadly weapons. Feng Ming didn't feel that he was a match for any of them, even if they *weren't* monsters. He still hadn't confirmed this fact.

Run around in circles to confuse your enemy, he recited his instructor's teachings mentally. *Use rivers as natural covers to mask your movements. Cover your tracks while exiting the river to ensure you maximize your enemy's lost time. Counter tracking isn't necessarily about completely evading your enemy's tracking method; rather, it's about rendering it cost-ineffective. In this way, even an injured man can buy himself time to escape multiple pursuers.*

He didn't dare slack off as they exited the stream several hundred feet away from where he had entered. He had covered their tracks as they entered, and now he hopped off his horse to cover their tracks while exiting. Once again, his bad luck resurfaced as he tripped in a well-concealed hole and twisted his ankle. Thankfully, it wasn't broken.

Ignoring the pain, he continued his meticulous work. The tracks were soon well covered, and he urged his exhausted horse to continue moving forward.

The brigand leader, Zi Shen, was carefully following concealed tracks in the woods. It was his third time going over this specific set, as he had been led in circles by deceptive movements two consecutive times. Thankfully only three circles overlapped this time, and he was eventually able to continue following the correct path.

Soon the tracks became increasingly obvious. He thanked his luck only for a short while—the tracks he had been following had split into three once more. He observed the three different paths for a long while before picking a path to follow at random. Just as he was about to head down that path, he noticed a trace of red a small distance down another path.

Oh? His wounds happened to reopen again? The last time

this had happened, Zi Shen had gotten lucky and found the correct path on the first try.

One hour later, he stumbled again upon his most hated obstacle—a stream. Shit. Finding tracks after an enemy crossed a stream was a daunting task. Sometimes his quarry had moved upstream for a thousand feet before finally heading out again. At other times, the victim darted back in the opposite direction. Therefore, it was vital to first check upstream and downstream on this side of the river before proceeding to the next. It turned out to be a phenomenal waste of time.

The river cost him several hours before he finally found the correct path. This time, the hidden tracks had been revealed by an overturned stone next to a small concealed hole. He hoped that his prey had twisted his ankle or something. While he enjoyed the hunt, this prey was too tricky for his liking.

He preferred easy prey, the type that he could toy around with for a while, like fish in a barrel.

Chapter 17: Planning

In the dark world, a white-robed figure was walking through the dusty, desolate woods. He had done this several times over the past few weeks, hoping to glean some insights on why things had gone so poorly. The Sight was never wrong, after all, but he himself was only human. Besides, he *had* been warned. Those sharp edges on the bagua coin had been a clear indication of the potential consequences.

The trees that adorned the twisted landscape were wreathed in white mist. They didn't obscure his vision but provided an accurate depiction of that day's events. The man in white briefly witnessed the appearance of a black dog's corpse. It disappeared momentarily. Just the same way, the corpse of a three-tailed fox also appeared briefly before disappearing. Strangely enough, the brief appearance of the fox's corpse felt like a hundred days. That surely meant *something*. The Sight was never wrong.

After the three-tailed fox disappeared, five figures fled away from the dangerous area. No wait, it was *six* figures. They were being pursued. Of course, they appeared differently than they would in the real world. One figure appeared as a pure, bloodied snowflake. Another was a gentle flame. Not the powerful type, but rather the kind that could kindle people's hearts in the darkest moments. The third figure appeared as armor made of silk and gilded with gold—hardly the most effective armor one could find.

Zhou Li had seen these figures before. They didn't concern him. He was here to see the last three figures, because they were familiar figures that he had seen in the mirror. One figure was coin-imprinted with a bagua. Its sharp edges were stained in blood. *Zhou Li's* blood. Another coin floated beside it. It was white-rimmed and imprinted with a black pentagram. It also glowed with five colors. There was now fate connecting these two coins, and the line was growing thicker and thicker with each passing moment.

The sixth figure was very mysterious. He had not seen this figure in the mirror per se, but its actions confirmed its presence. This figure could *evade* the Sight. Such cases were rare—even the most influential figures, whose fates could not be read, would still reveal some clues under the Sight's close scrutiny. Thinking back to the prior scene with the black hound, he had noticed long ago that it hadn't simply disappeared—rather, it had been whisked away by the mysterious figure.

Unfortunately for Zhou Li, this meant three figures whom he only had vague clues about. One figure who he couldn't see, one that would cut him if he drew near, and finally, a figure that was obscured with white mist. He wouldn't have known anything about these figures if it wasn't for his brother's timely report. He had used the first-hand information to deduct that one of them was a spirit beast, a fox. Also, this spirit beast was powerful enough to forge a contract of equals at a young age.

Regrettably, he had no access to information on its specific species.

The coin with the circle and the star, according to the ties of karma, was definitely its contractor. Du Cha Ming, according to the report, had suffered a lethal attack from his brother Zhou Xian and survived. This was also why Zhou Li concluded that the man and the fox had formed a contract of equals. From what he'd gathered, Cha Ming was a dual body and qi cultivator who was apprenticed under Elder Ling to learn to craft talismans. Yet why the white circle and the black star? And why did the white mist obscure his Sight? Despite ample information, he still had many questions.

The final figure was the obscured figure he couldn't see in the slightest. Such an unknown variable was far too dangerous. The web he had weaved over several months was spread very thin, and the slightest tug in the wrong place would cause it to unravel.

As this latest perusal in the bleak woods did not yield any benefits, the dejected Zhou Li moved his attention to matters he *could* affect, such as the ongoing plan in Fairweather County. There were some embarrassing failures there of late, a matter that he didn't want repeated. A tearing sound rang out as he grabbed the surrounding air, which ripped under his influence. This was *his* painting, one that he could create and tear at will. The rip gradually widened into a makeshift doorway, allowing him to step out into the darkness.

After a few quick steps, he arrived at a large table bathed in light. A large map was spread across it, and various miniatures indicated stationed forces—the empire's and his own, among others. The future was like a game of chess. As much as he could see the future, it was akin to looking several moves ahead.

Most people were pawns and were ultimately controlled by a "player." Only players could move pieces and make decisions.

On the map, he noticed his various forces, which had automatically adjusted due to a powerful Dao enchantment. There were forces spread out amongst various small villages, while others had been assigned to guard key areas.

One of the smaller groups on the map was chasing a soldier of the empire, who was clearly heading toward Fairweather City. Unfortunately, they had not seen him in a full day. It was likely that he would escape, though the advantage that this would provide Fairweather City's expeditionary force was negligible. For a moment, he cursed the Merchant. His greed had gotten the better of him, and he had made the wrong decision. The Merchant was the type of person that would choose wealth over security. It was his nature.

Since the soldier was escaping, he decided to cut his losses. The soldier was represented on the board by gilded iron armor. For a moment, Zhou Li remembered the gilded silk armor from his painting.

Is it the same armor? He rejected the thought, however. A person of that soldier's caliber could not change so profoundly in such a short time.

Sighing, Zhou Li removed a small crystal from the pouch at his waist. The stone glowed with an ominous red light, and a small film of black flames flickered on its surface. Any mortal who saw this crystal would find it repulsive. To Zhou Li, however, this crystal was incomparably precious. He would not use it under normal circumstances. However, it was his nature to choose security over wealth.

With but a thought, the crystal diminished in volume by fifty percent, producing a small quantity of pure black flames.

They danced about joyfully in Zhou Li's hand. After completing this simple yet exhausting task, Zhou Li focused his red pupils on the small figurine with the gilded armor. They were instantly connected with a small thread of karma. The thread was golden and inconspicuous. But not for long.

The black flame underwent some subtle changes as Zhou Li formed some complex hand seals. A thin thread separated from the main body of the flame and slowly imbued itself into the fragile karma thread. The thread slowly siphoned away the black flame over the next quarter hour, until it was finally depleted. The golden karma thread was now tainted with black and red spots that slowly migrated toward the suit of armor.

Satisfied, Zhou Li put away the half-consumed crystal. He then took out his notebook and quickly jotted down some instructions for his father and sister. Fortunately, *that* plan was proceeding quite nicely. After taking a moment to compose his thoughts, he moved on to the most important task of the day.

Brother, how are the preparations going in Fairweather County? he wrote.

Soon after, a reply appeared on the mostly filled page. *Elder Brother, everything is on schedule. Our allies are cooperating, and it seems that the "rescue mission" will be starting in one week's time. On another note, I've noticed the presence of two old friends, a man and his fox. Can I eliminate him yet?*

Negative, Zhou Li replied. *I guarantee your revenge, but only after the plan is completed. Moreover, your power will increase drastically, making revenge a walk in the park. After all, the blood moon draws near.*

Affirmative. I will update on progress in twelve hours, as usual, replied Zhou Xian.

After completing this portion of the conversation, he

wrote to the Merchant. The man was very enthusiastic about completing his portion of the plan. Zhou Li had used the simplest method to motivate the greedy individual—money.

More than he had ever earned in his short lifetime.

Tick... tick... tick...

The clock in Wang Jun's office repeatedly broke the silence as he read the latest report. It described the unrest near Fairweather City. There were also sections on recent trade disruptions, both within the country and outside the border. A rebellion in the kingdom to the east had caused a sharp increase in prices for food, metals, and medicinal herbs.

For a moment, he paused as he sensed a foreign presence. This had occurred thirty-seven times these past few weeks, much more often than usual. As was his common practice, he wrapped the thread of fate with obscurity. He knew who the intruder was, of course, and there was no way he would let that guy spy on him. It was a momentary distraction, a welcome respite from his intense workload. Wang Jun brought his attention back to the report and finished reading it.

A few minutes later, Wang Jun sipped a cup of tea and hummed in appreciation. "Delicious as usual, Elder Bai. Where is this tea from? I can't say I've tasted anything quite like it before."

"Right, this tea is rather special," Elder Bai replied. "It's from a small town in the Xia Empire. They grow this type of tea by splicing half the branches with a complementary tea. Not only does it provide the combined flavor of two different teas, but the fact that they grow together on one plant subtly changes the flavor of each component tea. It is a unique creation and always in short supply."

Nodding his head while licking his lips, Wang Jun proceeded to discuss the business at hand. "Elder Bai, did Elder Jin respond to our request for support these upcoming days?"

"Yes, Young Master. The family also supports your decision to establish the Wang family's economic dominance by any means possible. If the trifling Zhou family wants to push us around because they have the support of the Song Kingdom's royal family and advisor, they are in for a rude awakening. We'll teach them what it means to throw money at problems."

"Excellent. Then let's proceed to the next step of the plan. Please have our contacts begin importing medicines and placing orders from our preferred suppliers in both the Xia Empire and the Ming Empire. Use expedited shipping. I want the products at the border in three days.

"Further, please send word to Lijiang City's weaponsmithing guild that I will be making a trip there in three days for a one-day negotiation on a sole-source purchasing contract that includes the remaining thirty cities in the Song Kingdom. I want to completely crush the Zhou family in this market.

"Also, please begin spreading propaganda vilifying the Alchemists Association and their disdain for the poor. Go into detail about how their monopolistic tendencies are increasing costs for middle-class consumers.

"Finally, please proceed with triggering an election in the Song Kingdom Medical Association and run our candidate on a platform supporting affordable medical care and pharmaceutical reform. Simultaneously begin a conversation in the Song Kingdom Chamber of Commerce about the benefits of free trade and the limits of isolationism.

"Meanwhile, we will also move our agenda forward to standardize apprenticeships and institute craftsmanship standards for weaponsmithing—this will greatly increase the barrier for the Zhou family to enter in this field and increase our profitability. All in the name of consumer protection, of course."

Elder Bai nodded and took away a stack of papers from Wang Jun's desk. What had been said was simply a summary. The sheets of paper included detailed instructions and contingency plans.

Once Elder Bai left his office, Wang Jun took a deep breath and exhaled slowly to calm himself. His green robes were changed out for slightly more fashionable ones. He took a scented bath and put on cologne, something he rarely did.

After a half hour of preparation, he went to Hong Xin's residence and led her to the Jade Bamboo Restaurant, where they occupied a private room. After a sumptuous banquet, Wang Jun began *the conversation*.

"Xin Er," he started. He felt uncertain about how to proceed, despite rehearsing this moment many times. "I think that we should stop dating."

Hong Xin's pleasant smile suddenly disappeared. Tears began running down from her red eyes. "Didn't you say that you love me?" Her tears broke Wang Jun's heart. But this was something he had to do for her own good.

"Yes, I love you," he replied. "That's why I need to let you go. Even though you're the best thing that's ever happened to me, we're unsuited for each other. You need to move on and find someone else, someone better."

"But I don't want anyone else..." she said in a weak, quivering voice.

"I'm sorry. This is goodbye." With these words, he left the poor girl sitting by herself in the private dining room, her face covered in tears. As he shut the door to the room, he heard her uncontrolled sobbing. He shuddered slightly before continuing down the hallway. A drop of salty liquid traveled from his right eye to his mouth, which he quickly wiped away. This single tear was all he could afford.

Uncle Bai was right, he thought. *It was unfair for me to lead her along. Ending it now is for the best. One day she'll find someone much better than me. Someone who can care for her properly and keep her out of danger. Someone who won't let her die like I did my sister.*

He didn't return to his courtyard immediately. Instead he went for a walk to calm his nerves. Sadness was a luxury he couldn't afford yet a tax he couldn't avoid paying. It was snowing outside, a rare occurrence this time of year so far south. Hundreds of snowflakes pelted his face and wreathed his blond and white hair. While he could have made the snowflakes melt away, he chose to let them remain.

As the snow accumulated, he walked on the wooden floor of the entertainment district, leaving distinct footprints wherever he went. They would soon be filled in with fresh snow, leaving no trace of his passage. As he walked, he focused his attention on the snowflakes on his face. They had melted and subsequently soaked his green robes.

The melting snowflakes reminded him that he and Xin Er belonged to two different worlds. She was a precious snowflake, one that would surely melt into a liquid droplet if she touched him. The heat he emanated would change her into something she wasn't. It would sap away her innocence. And as much as he wanted to be with her, he could never forgive himself if he destroyed such a precious snowflake.

Chapter 18: Legacy Weapon

It was now dusk, and a slight chill pervaded the room where Cha Ming sat in meditation. He took a deep breath and circulated his cultivation for a full two hours before opening his eyes and withdrawing a sealed glass bottle from within his bag of holding.

After popping open the lid, a thick medicinal aroma filled the room. Just breathing in the pills' residue caused the barriers surrounding his five qi lakes to shudder slightly. Without any hesitation, he popped a pill into his mouth. It burned as it traveled down his throat and settled into his stomach. There, the pill separated into five streams of elemental energy, which impacted the barriers restraining his qi lakes.

Since the barriers had been weakened, he quickly took out a crystalized elemental essence stone and placed it on the portable energy-gathering plate. The rich qi assaulted the weakened membrane causing it to crack slightly.

Once more!

After a second assault, the cracks spread outward in the

shape of a spiderweb. A third rush of energy finally dissolved the weakened membrane. The borders of his qi lakes expanded, signifying that he had finally reached the sixth level of qi condensation.

Following his breakthrough, he instantly felt his soul being invigorated. It was time for the next step—earth body refining. He took the Clear Sky Brush out from his bag of holding and carefully started drawing out the next pattern.

Each pattern thus far had been created based on each elemental character. He only had a pitiful amount of information on each three-dimensional character and could only paint each one by trial and error. Fortunately, they seemed to follow three distinct rules: the base units were formed from the "essence" of the character, the connecting base was formed from the base character, and each "branch" in the character was formed by five subgroups of base units on each of twelve branches. In total, there were seventy-two key points to each character. Further, the character as a whole resembled the nature of the base character, such as flickering flames or growing trees.

This time, Cha Ming was going to attempt to build a character from jade bricks[5]. Earth was a stable element, and it was used to build foundations for roads and cities. As a result, Cha Ming guessed that the correct way to arrange it was in a similar fashion.

Whether he succeeded or not would depend on his luck and his efforts in the following week.

---

[5] The character for "jade tablet" (圭) is formed from stacked characters for earth or soil (土).

Nightfall.

An aged but muscular figure was seated in a plain brick room. He didn't like keeping any useless things around, as most would simply disintegrate when subjected to extreme temperatures. The only things that Bei Ling kept in the room was a stone bed made of obsidian and covered in a thick, fire-resistant cloth, as well as a large worktable forged with soul alloy and reinforced with trace amounts of star steel. Nothing short of a meteor crashing down on his dimensional abode stood a chance a damaging these prized possessions. Which, coincidentally, greatly resembled his own forging process.

He had stared at the pile of soul alloy for quite some time before finalizing the plan that had jumped in his mind when he watched the young whelp spar. Visions like this didn't come often. Inevitably, each weapon he forged after having a vision became a masterpiece. He couldn't let the opportunity go to waste.

His muscular figure inhaled deeply, imbuing the incoming air with burning hot foundation-establishment qi before breathing it out toward the materials. The pile of soul alloy didn't even react. He knew from experience, of course, that pure soul alloy would only melt at a temperature five times higher than necessary for steel. This was one of the reasons it was so difficult to work with and why so few craftsmen bothered working with this particular material.

After breathing fire on the soul alloy for the better part of an hour, the hundreds of stones quickly melted into a puddle, which he kept suspended in midair. The white-hot metal radiated with a soul-searing heat.

Not quite enough yet. He increased the temperature twice

more. At this point, the white-hot metal began bubbling as impure black smoke left it.

The process continued for twelve hours. Each time he increased the temperature, even more impurities were burned away. The resulting blob of soul alloy was seventy percent of the original mass. Without this extra purification process, soul-alloy weapons would never exhibit peak performance.

After exhausting himself thoroughly during the purification process, he rested while allowing the metal to cool naturally. Just before it solidified, he used his soul force to mold it into a rough cylindrical shape—seventy-two inches long and two inches thick as specified.

Now for the hard part. He gritted his teeth as he conjured a massive spiritual hammer, the same hammer that he had used while fighting Cha Ming.

He began pounding on the white cylinder as soon as the soul alloy solidified. Each strike released shockwaves due to his terrifying fleshly body power, which had reached the early stages of the Bone Forging realm. The pounding ensured that the very last impurities were expelled, all the while forming the material into its final shape. Keeping the temperature high was vital, since any significant drop in temperature would render the material too brittle to work with. Periodically, he let out a hot breath to increase the metal's temperature back to its melting point.

After pounding out impurities for a full day, he began the next step of the process—shaping. For this task, he split his hammer into two pieces. One piece resembled an extension of his hand, which he used to steady the hot, glowing metal. This hand was forged from pure soul force and was immune to the scalding temperatures. He could also control it with the same dexterity as his left hand—multiple tendrils connected his palms and fingers to the ethereal glove to enable such fine control.

The hammer in his right hand reduced to half its original size. In addition, the surface was concave. It was the perfect shape to slowly hammer the cylindrical weapon to perfection. He hammered at the rod of metal while holding it against his soul-alloy workbench, using a thin film of soul force to cushion the impact.

His brow was thick with sweat from the two days of heating and hammering. Fortunately the high temperature in the room evaporated any sweat before it had a chance to fall on and ruin the weapon he was creating. In fact, the heat would have also burned any normal possessions he was wearing. As a result, he only wore a pair of thick heat-resistant pants, goggles, and a simple hair tie.

The shaping work continued for two full days before he was satisfied with the initial state of the weapon.

Now, what runes to inscribe... This was what he had spent the initial day visualizing. His hammer quickly shrank in size until it was half a foot long with a chiseled end. This was the most precise part of the work, and the most mentally taxing. Any mistakes here would ultimately ruin the final product, and he would need to start over.

He started with the core of the design—five elemental patterns, which were carefully engraved onto the staff with extreme precision. He then started engraving supporting runes near the five patterns in a seemingly random order. As he inscribed, his demeanor turned feverish, and he soon abandoned his initial plan entirely. This was inspiration. It could never be sought, only found.

With every strike, a new runic line was formed. Had he been in his right mind, he could never have imagined making these lines—they just didn't make sense to him. They were far too mysterious and vastly exceeded his current realm of comprehension. With every strike, the pattern expanded from the center of the staff and proceeded to the edges. After reaching the edges, however, he did the unthinkable. Starting from five points, each five inches from the end of the staff, he carved out a spiral pattern that connected at the end of the staff. There, he inscribed a star.

This was something only weaponsmiths and talisman craftsmen knew—a star inscription or talisman would surely lead to the immediate destruction of the end product. However, this effect was delayed for a weapon inscription, as the inscription was only filled in at the end of the process.

He didn't stop there. He inscribed the other side of the staff in the same haphazard fashion, forging a mirror pattern at the end of the staff with an additional star. "Not strong enough," he muttered under his breath. "I need to strengthen the materials."

Without thinking much, he wandered over to a small cabinet on one side of the room. The cabinet was built out of the finest jade, the ideal material for preserving medicinal properties. He quickly grabbed eight small boxes from the cabinet, not bothering to close it afterward. The materials inside were priceless, but to the expert craftsman in an enlightened state, cost was irrelevant.

First, he crumbled a few jade leaves in his hands, sprinkling the crushed powder over the staff. The fine dust settled into a few of the inscriptions, after which he temporarily raised the temperature, allowing the material to infuse itself into the runes, which immediately shone with a green hue. He repeated the process four more times with crimson firestone, brown jadeite, cold iron, and eversnow. On a whim, he took out a glass vial from a special chest. After opening the stopper, a thick cloud wandered over to the staff and was quickly absorbed. This also caused the existing colors on the staff to smudge and merge.

Without waiting for the merging process to complete, he took out a second bottle and removed its stopper. A second cloud formed, but this one was dark and ominous. Nine fearsome strikes of lightning rained down on the merging colors, causing them to fragment and reassemble into new shapes. By the time the process was completed, the staff had become a translucent white color with shifting colored runes.

Finally, the man sprinkled the contents of the last box onto both ends. It was starsteel, the same material he had imbued into his workbench. This material was priceless, worth far more than the materials used in crafting the staff thus far. Nevertheless, he would *not* allow this to become a failed product. He couldn't stand to see such a masterpiece ruined!

Soon enough, the starsteel was absorbed into both ends, which would suffer the most intense destructive forces once the runes were activated. He nodded while admiring the nearly finished product. Who knew if his inspiration was going to pay off? He didn't understand half of what he had inscribed and had relied on pure instinct.

With a somber look on his face, he walked over to a nearby vat of glowing blue liquid. The liquid flew up at his command, forming a cylindrical pool. He threw the staff into said pool. Most products he normally forged were quenched in water, mercury, or oil. This time, however, he was quenching it in pure liquified elemental essence, which would conveniently activate the runes in the process.

The staff began to vibrate as it cooled. The runes on its body began to glow, starting with the five central runic patterns. They first glowed in five colors, after which the remaining runes followed them and flashed in five colors as well. The translucent body of the staff began to glow intensely. The original glow of the heated metal was like a candle compared to the shining sun!

Finally, the ends began glowing black as the final star-shaped runes lit up. An intense burst of energy made it difficult to approach the staff, but he gritted his teeth and continued observing the process. The tendrils of black snaked across the staff, threatening to destroy it. Fortunately, they seemed to be restrained by the glowing white energy in the staff.

They were neutralizing each other.

As he continued observing, however, he noticed that the balance was continuously being upset in favor of the destructive black energy.

Shit! He gritted his teeth as he poured his spiritual strength into the staff, attempting to fight back against the destructive energy. This did little to stop it, however.

Taking in a deep breath, he bit his tongue and spat out a globe of dark red blood onto the staff. This was his life's blood! Instantly, the man aged ten years.

This better work. This is all I can afford. As he observed closely, he noticed that the white strength in the staff finally balanced the black. They continuously faded until the ends of the staff resembled obsidian. The body had become a translucent white color. The runes, however, had faded. They were now nothing more than thin lines decorating the most beautiful weapon he had ever laid eyes on.

His lips formed a weak smile as he laid the finished product on his workbench. He was then overwhelmed with exhaustion and collapsed onto the hot brick floor.

The sound of bones cracking broke the silence in Cha Ming's room at dusk on the sixth day. After hundreds of attempts and repeated failures, his earth body refining had finally succeeded. Now he was at the seventh level of body refinement. As predicted, his fist strength had raised to 756 jin. As an added benefit, the earth body refining increased his defense by one level. With his defense, speed, and regenerative capabilities all being one level higher than normal, coupled with his cultivation at the sixth level of qi condensation, he could now match normal eighth-level cultivators in a head-on battle.

He let out a satisfied moan as he stretched his stiff limbs; sitting in a meditative posture for a full week was extremely uncomfortable. As he opened his eyes, he observed beautiful red-tinted clouds through an open window. They stretched across the horizon in a chaotic fashion, giving the rising half-moon a reddish hue.

This moment of calm was harshly interrupted by Huxian's whining and yipping. Cha Ming sighed. From the looks of the abnormally clean floor, the poor fellow had already run out of food. He did not know for how long he had gone hungry; all he knew was that every moment of hunger was a moment of agony for the rapidly growing fox.

Speaking of rapid growth, Cha Ming's eyes narrowed as he

noticed that the baby fox looked substantially stronger than before.

You broke through again? he asked Huxian mentally.

Yes, I broke through yesterday. I'm now a ninth-level spirit beast, Huxian replied with a worried voice. *I'm sorry, I can't help it. There's nothing I can do to stop myself. I even eat as little as possible!*

For the growing fox, Cha Ming understood that this was the biggest sacrifice possible.

There's nothing that can be done about it. At least both our strengths increased before this outing. I have a feeling that things won't be as simple as they seem. The effort surrounding this "mission" is too great given the information we have access to, Cha Ming said, patting Huxian on the head.

After exiting the quiet hotel room, they quickly paid a visit to a nearby restaurant. Cha Ming was hungry due to the rapid growth in his body. Huxian was just his normal hungry self. After consuming a full two tables of food, the young fox affirmed that while he was not yet full, he was no longer famished. They put in a large order for roast spirit beast meat for the next morning, which they would collect prior to leaving Fairweather City.

Huxian, lets go see if Master Bei has completed the weapon yet, Cha Ming said.

The man and the fox traveled at a leisurely pace to the rundown industrial district. After entering Bei Ling's small shack, they were directly teleported to the furnished living room. To their surprise, they were greeted by Hong Lai. The grim-faced man was serving a bowl of soup to Master Bei, who was resting in an armchair.

Cha Ming immediately noticed a conflicted mood in the

room. Master Bei, the vigorous older man who had undertaken the creation of his staff, was now pale and gaunt. The master weaponsmith seemed like half the man he was six days ago. His wiry frame had thinned significantly, and a bald patch had now appeared on his previously full head of white hair; it was as though the man had aged a full decade.

Despite this clear reduction in the man's physical prowess, an energetic glint could be seen in his eyes, a look of intense satisfaction. Hong Lai was at a loss on what to do for his master, so he poured them all a cup of tea and they sat in silence. Bei Ling was the first to speak.

"You're a lucky young lad, you know," he said. "Your staff is the finest weapon I've ever made. While crafting it, I was inspired to try things I'd never dreamed possible. I used countless treasures that I had been reserving to create my legacy weapon, my final work. Yet before I knew it, I had already created it.

"I will never make another weapon again. I don't have the heart to forge again. Spiritual blacksmiths are inspired by their pursuit of perfection. This staff is the final product in this journey. I call it the Clear Sky Staff." Bei Ling then withdrew the staff from the bag of holding at his waist.

Cha Ming shivered when he heard these words. He almost burst into tears when he saw the staff—his *staff*. The one he had seen plunged into the ground all those years ago on the planet Earth. The staff that had caused his rebirth.

It trembled as he slowly walked over. It sensed his presence as its owner. He could barely control his shaking hands as he grasped the Clear Sky Staff. As soon as his hands made contact, he felt a brief shock as it pulsed—the Clear Sky Brush, which was stored in his bag of holding, traveled through his body, into his hand, and finally, into the staff.

It was now the *true* Clear Sky Staff, soul and all.

The sickly man, who had spent ten years of his life completing the weapon, was carefully observing this process. When the staff gained life, he sensed it immediately. He could tell that the man and the staff were destined to be together. It would be nothing in the hands of anyone else.

"Thank you for finding it for me. I thought I'd lost it," Cha Ming whispered. Hong Lai's expression was puzzled, but Master Bei Ling's face was full of understanding.

"You're welcome. Seeing you hold it reminds me that making it was worth the effort. Although I still have a decade or so left in my life, I feel like I can finally die a happy man," Master Bei replied.

"Master Bei, would you like to accompany me to the arena to see it in action?" Cha Ming asked.

The man immediately got up to leave, his eyes gleaming with impatience.

"Master, it's cold out," Hong Lai said with a concerned voice. "Why don't we wait until morning?"

"No need! I've never felt better in my life!" The old smith quickly led them outside his shack toward the sparring arena.

Chapter 19:
The Wounded Soldier

The rhythmic beating of hooves on grassy soil broke the awkward silence in the hour just after sunset. This time was usually a lively one, where authority abruptly transferred from the day-roaming animals to the creatures of the night. Normally, travelers in these plains would be greeted with the chirping of thousands upon thousands of crickets and the occasional hoot of an owl. Now these creatures avoided the area. They specifically avoided the lone traveler slowly trotting forward on his lame horse.

Feng Ming was exhausted. The past week and a half of desperate fleeing had drained him in every way. Somehow he had managed to stick to his training and evade his pursuers. The gates of Fairweather were in his sights. They were closed, but that could be changed with a few convincing words. His only worry was that he had enemies *inside* the city. But there was nothing he could do about that.

The young man was covered in various wounds—knife wounds from a few close encounters with his pursuers, various rashes due to brushes with poisonous plants, and insect bites. He also had a single arrowhead stuck in his right arm. Luckily it had not struck a main artery. This stroke of luck had been his only respite during the entire chase. He was able to break away the main arrow shaft, leaving behind only a barbed metal head that could only be surgically removed.

Feng Ming's eyes carefully scanned the ground. He kept his eyes peeled for any pits or rocks. The past two days had proved especially challenging, and tripping and falling were not uncommon occurrences. Quite frankly, it was a miracle that his horse's leg wasn't broken after all these close encounters.

But speak of the devil, and he shall appear. After narrowly avoiding a gopher hole, the horse's hoof plunged into the tunnel network itself, which happened to be situated in unusually weak soil. His horse's screams echoed in the night, threatening to attract unwanted attention from the pursuers he assumed hadn't given up.

Feng Ming decisively cut the horse's throat, relieving it from its pain and exhaustion. They had been through much together, and under normal circumstances he would have sought out a healer. Unfortunately, he had to be careful. Who knew if his pursuers were nearby?

After accomplishing the grisly deed, he didn't have the strength to sheathe the bloodied sword. Instead, he opted to deposit it directly into his bag of holding, where it stained various other objects stowed there. There were far fewer objects than when he had set out from Crystal Meadows.

Any pills, food, and bandages had already been consumed or used. The few useful possessions he had remaining were a spare suit of armor, a couple of spare swords, and random tenting equipment—all standard issue in the army. He also had the remnants of an emergency kit, including a blanket and a flare. He had been hesitant to use it, fearing it would attract his pursuers.

The city wall was now two thousand feet away. He had no energy, but he forced his feet to keep moving forward.

Only two thousand steps. I can make it.

At least, that's what he thought before he realized that the wound on his abdomen had reopened during the fall from his horse. The wound had festered due to lack of treatment. The emergency ointment, which should have been able to ward off the usual infections, had failed to show any useful effects.

The sudden blood loss was the straw that broke the camel's back. Feng Ming collapsed to the ground, where an unfortunately placed sharp rock left a second deep gash in his side. He used his remaining moments of consciousness to take out the single precious flare from his storage. Most people would have struggled to light the flare—fortunately, Feng Ming dual cultivated fire and earth and quickly managed to light the fuse. The bright red flare flew into the air, where it quickly caught the attention of the guards on the city wall. Then, darkness took him.

Cha Ming, Bei Ling, Huxian, and Hong Lai arrived at the arena, where various adventurers in the city had been idle the entire week. These people liked fighting, whether to sharpen their skills or blow off steam. Watching exciting fights were a close second, since they could not get injured in the process.

The group of four bypassed the larger open-aired stadium where the masses gathered for entertainment. Instead, they proceeded to a brightly lit lounge where warriors were resting. As they walked, they heard enthusiastic voices praising the many prominent fighters that had appeared this past week.

"The Blood Queen is still my favorite," one man said. "Most people can't even look her straight in the eye without wetting themselves. The rest of them usually only last ten exchanges. Even then, it almost looks like she uses them for practice and toys around with them before finally putting them out of their misery. I hear that she defeated a seventh-level cultivator just two hours ago!"

Cha Ming had to admit that he was surprised at her rapid progress. To advance to his current realm, he had spent a small fortune on pills, consumed crystalized elemental essence through an expensive formation plate, and cultivated a variety of unusual techniques. Yet here she was, keeping up with his advancement step by step. Technically, Cha Ming's current talent level was a step higher than Gong Lan's, but this Blood World Scripture impacted more than just her combat prowess. It allowed her cultivation to progress rapidly despite the use of limited cultivation resources.

A beautiful woman dressed in a red leather outfit called out to him from the other side of the room. "Cha Ming, what brings you here?" Two large bloody sabers were strapped to her back. Gong Lan's greeting caused many people to glare at him enviously. If looks could kill, he would have died a dozen times right then.

Cha Ming chuckled as he and his three companions approached her. "A trial run," he said. "Master Bei has just completed my weapon, so I was looking for an opponent to test it out on. I heard your strength has increased once more. Care for a rematch?"

Gong Lan didn't need to be asked twice. She sped over to the registration desk and rented a private arena. This was disappointing for her growing fan group. Usually she opened a public arena, where people could watch from the sidelines after paying an admission fee. Every time she fought, they cheered for her while secretly hoping that she would be knocked into them, giving them an excuse to feel her tender skin under the guise of helping her up.

Before long, Cha Ming and Gong Lan were facing off against each other. They held their weapons out toward each other and saluted by touching weapons. Just like before, Gong Lan darted straight toward him. As a staff wielder, he needed distance from his opponents to properly execute his techniques. Infighting[6] against someone like Gong Lan was only the natural thing to do.

Cha Ming didn't choose to avoid her aggressive charge. Instead, he used it as an opportunity to try out some select techniques with his new staff. He started off with Sword Staff, carefully parrying every blow from the heavy sabers. Gong Lan's expression changed with each blow—a forceful recoil hit her every time she parried an attack. Unlike last time, the staff delivered sharp, forceful blows to counter her aggressive technique. Silver patterns appeared on the staff, slightly amplifying his metal-aligned staff arts as he executed them.

---

[6] Infighting and outfighting are common boxing terms. Infighters typically charge in, taking blows to close the distance and unleash powerful blows. They are typically shorter and stockier. Outfighters are typically thinner with long arms, and they use timing, technical skills, and counters to outmaneuver their often stronger opponents.

"Tch. Fine, let's see how you handle this style," she muttered as her aggressive blows became soft and subdued. Her movements became gentle, and her steps *flowed* as she walked in circles around Cha Ming, slashing gently instead of aggressively like before.

It took Cha Ming a few moments to adjust to this new rhythm. In the process of adjusting, he was nicked five times. Fortunately his skin was very tough, and these superficial cuts healed almost instantly. His movements and staff arts soon adjusted, fusing the Wading Through the Reeds and Trapping Staff Arts, and fusing White Willow Shade with the Skating in Paradise Movement Techniques.

In one incense time, the wood and water techniques slowly fused together until their battle resembled a gentle dance. Only Cha Ming and Gong Lan could feel the intensity of the battle. Light, fleeting steps eventually merged with circular and sliding steps, to the point that Cha Ming could no longer tell where one movement art ended and the other began. His staff techniques now combined redirection with constriction, pushing with pulling.

Bursts of wood qi occasionally manipulated the friction of the floor, which in turn affected both his and her movements. Sometimes he used his staff to redirect blows. At other times, he redirected *himself* by combining his staff and movement techniques. Two movement techniques and two staff techniques had now combined into a seamless whole.

I'll call this combined martial art Gentle Staff Art, he decided in his heart. He had finally developed the embryonic form of his *own* martial art, one that perfectly suited him.

In the Clear Sky World, the red-bearded man observed the fight closely. He nodded as his student finally transcended rote-learning and repetition, fusing them together with his own understanding. The boy had a long way to go, but it was a good start. This first transformation was very important. It would grow Cha Ming's confidence, enabling him to realize that he could create something new for himself if he set his mind to it.

Quite frankly, it would have been a miracle if something like this hadn't happened eventually. The man had stacked eleven techniques on the poor boy at once, which was overwhelming for any one person to use in battle. He would naturally realize which ones flowed together and which ones didn't and naturally discard the rest. The fusion of these techniques would come with time. It was why he'd picked those techniques in the first place.

It was a pity that his opponent, the pretty lass, wasn't learning this valuable lesson. Cha Ming was adapting his techniques to himself while the girl was instead losing herself to her techniques. Bit by bit, he saw her innocence consumed by killing intent. Like a pure white snowflake painted red with blood.

Such a pity.

They walked out of the arena complex one hour later. Bei Ling was all smiles after finally witnessing the opening performance of his masterpiece. Hong Lai relaxed visibly when he saw his master's face finally regain color and vitality. He took the opportunity to gift the two revised defensive brooches to both Cha Ming and Gong Lan. While they weren't much, they might be some help in their upcoming adventures.

As they were walking down the dark streets, a crimson light suddenly flashed across the sky.

"Is that a rescue flare?" Cha Ming asked.

The more experienced member of the group, Bei Ling, nodded gravely before replying. "Let's go to the front gate and check it out. The timing is too much of a coincidence."

Their group arrived at the front gates in one incense time. Just in time to see a bloodied figure being transported through the front gates on a stretcher. Cha Ming and Gong Lan recognized that figure.

"Feng Ming?" they cried out in unison and darted out toward their unconscious friend.

"Halt!" One of the guards stopped them from approaching Feng Ming's unconscious body.

"We know that man," Cha Ming replied. "He is our friend and is part of the Royal Army. He is Feng Ming, son of Feng Chuan."

The guard looked at him dubiously. "As per policy, we must bring him back to the army barracks, investigate his background, and question him. He must also receive immediate medical care. Please return to your accommodations for the night."

"We will accompany him to the army barracks, then," said Cha Ming. "I can't rest easy knowing that my friend is injured."

He also immediately released a spirit pearl manifestation—Healing Array—which quickly began mending Feng Ming's external wounds.

The guard's face flushed red. "What do you think you're doing? Stop it this instant! This is an important witness, and we can't have anyone poisoning him."

A few surrounding guards drew their swords as they approached Cha Ming. Cha Ming's expression became cold, and a clear staff suddenly materialized in his hands.

"How dare you accuse me of poisoning my friend and thinking you can do whatever you want with him. Who the hell do you think you are?" he shouted angrily at the guard. He did not retract the healing array. In response, the guards started closing in, prompting Gong Lan to draw her twin sabers.

The guard didn't back down. "I'm a captain of the guard in Fairweather City. I represent the lord here, and my word is law. Don't make me arrest you for disturbing the peace."

"Is there a problem here, gentlemen?" Bei Ling suddenly asked, causing the guard captain to freeze. The older man walked out from behind the others toward the soldiers, and his sudden appearance took the guards by surprise.

"Elder Bei," the lead soldier replied nervously, "the county lord instructed us to bring the one who shot the flare in for interrogation, as it might have a huge bearing on the local security of Fairweather City. We can't let anyone interfere in this matter."

"Well, these people aren't just anyone, and I will vouch for them. I also find it curious that the county lord has given such instructions, given his indifference to the security of Fairweather County recently," Bei Ling replied. Then, he turned to Hong Lai.

"Little Lai, kindly fetch Hai Tuo. This young man is badly wounded, and Hai Tuo is the best doctor in town. After that, please fetch Han Jinlong and Zhang Yifeng and bring them to the barracks. I'm sure they would be most interested in why a member of the Royal Army has been found just outside the city and badly wounded, especially since the rescue mission is heading out tomorrow. This man might have vital information for them."

Hong Lai quickly bowed before scampering off toward the center of town. Meanwhile, the guards had a sour expression on their faces. They quickly transported Feng Ming to the barracks under Cha Ming and company's close supervision.

A half dozen people were gathered around a bed in the barracks. They closely observed the gentle movements of an aged figure as he surveyed the unconscious young man on the bed. Occasionally, he prodded Feng Ming, prompting a soft groan from the unconscious patient.

After a half hour of observation, the man drew out a set of transparent needles. The 108 needles were clear and seemed to be crafted out of soul alloy. They quickly floated over Feng Ming's mostly naked body at the doctor's direction. The aged man then formed thirty-six hand seals, causing the 108 needles to gently stab into the wounded body at various key points.

Half of the needles glowed green, while the other half glowed blue. While this seemed like a simple process, beads of sweat had accumulated on the aged man's forehead. Yet he didn't let up his efforts. The needles continued to glow, and the man continued to concentrate.

After a half hour, the aged man suddenly grunted and stopped channeling his qi. Shaking his head, he looked back at the crowd of concerned people. "I'm sorry," he said. "I need to rest a short while before trying again. His wounds are very unfortunate. I have no idea how he survived so long given the circumstances."

"What exactly is wrong with him?" Cha Ming asked hurriedly.

"It's complicated, young man. Your friend has been poisoned with thirteen minor poisons, all of which are usually harmless. However, when combined in a very exact ratio, they produced a poison that rendered him comatose and began shutting down his organs.

"This normally wouldn't be problematic for me. However, using a treatment that should have a ninety-nine percent chance of success in normal cases didn't work. After probing his body once more, I observed that he has somehow awakened a special constitution. This would normally be a cause for great celebration, however it just happened to render the only method I had to counter it meaningless.

"Therefore, I tried to supplement his qi to take advantage of his awakened constitution's strength against poisons. To my surprise, the small amount of qi somehow caused him to reach a breakthrough in his cultivation. Which, in this *specific* situation, is disastrous! His body has entered a qi-deficient state, and due to some freak interaction, his body is rejecting any external qi.

"Simply put, this whole situation is a freakish accident. Your friend's heart could give out at any second."

Cha Ming and Gong Lan were devastated. How could such a thing happen to their friend? And who had pursued him so savagely, driving him into his current condition?

"That brown-haired kid probably made things worse with his 'healing,'" a hoarse voice said behind them. "Congratulations on killing your friend, kid. And who knows how many people." The man in question wore light-blue robes. The hem of his robes was embroidered with the characters for Fairweather. It was the county lord.

Cha Ming flushed red again. "Who the hell are you? You're not welcome here!" he snapped.

Hearing Cha Ming's words, the man's eyes narrowed, and a formless pressure suddenly weighed down on Cha Ming. It was the pressure of foundation establishment, which could cause any qi condensation cultivator's energy to lose control.

The pressure bearing down on him aimed to push him down to kneel. Since coming to this world, Cha Ming had never seen such an unreasonable and tyrannical person. Did he not see him as a person? Bei Ling frowned as he released his own power to counter the suppression. While the pressure eased up, Bei Ling was unable to completely remove the suppression.

Cha Ming gritted his teeth as he summoned forth his Clear Sky Staff and struggled to move forward. He was angry at being powerless, angry at the county lord's attitude, and more importantly, angry at his friend's treatment. He began to lose his usual clear-headedness, and his eyes turned red with rage. Huxian pounced forward to join Cha Ming, prompting Cha Ming to shout at him mentally.

Get back! I'll do it myself!

Huxian withdrew with a hurt look.

A little bit more, Cha Ming thought. He circulated his

cultivation a little faster, and the suppressive power shuddered, allowing him to take a step forward. He then used the momentum to bring out his staff and strike out at the county lord with Quake Staff. As he was a little too far away, he extended his staff to double its usual length and increased its weight to four times its original weight.

"Humph. Little ant. Know your place." The county lord lifted his hand to intercept the staff strike. It halted in midair before even reaching the man's palm, prompting Cha Ming to collapse and cough out blood. Bei Ling stood in front of him.

"That's enough," Bei Ling said coldly. The county lord snorted and kept advancing without withdrawing his power.

"Overbearing as usual, I see," a voice boomed. They looked to the back of the room, where two men were standing with an extremely displeased look on their faces. These men were Han Jinlong and Zhang Yifeng. With the combined presence of these three individuals, the county lord withdrew his foundation-establishment pressure, and Cha Ming was finally able to breathe properly. He was quickly supported by Gong Lan, who had been just outside the effective range of the county lord's pressure.

As the two walked over, they suddenly realized that the old doctor had walked over to Feng Ming and felt his pulse. "You bloody idiot!" he shouted at the county lord. "Your stupid peacock posturing stopped his heart!"

Chapter 20: Soldier of Fortune

Cha Ming's face paled, and he quickly ran to his friend's side. He was subsequently swatted away by the agitated doctor.

"Get back! All of you! I need as much space as possible to have any chance at saving the poor boy," the doctor exclaimed.

His fierce demeanor frightened everyone in the room. They quietly backed off to the side, vacating the side of the room that contained the bed. But that apparently wasn't enough.

"Get the hell back to the entrance, you little runts!" the doctor snapped. "And don't you dare step more than ten feet into this room without my permission!"

Everyone shuffled once more, at a loss for why the doctor needed so much space. Their confusion was soon cleared, however, when the old man manifested several strands of what appeared to be flat wet rope. The rope wrapped around Feng Ming, causing him to levitate off the bed and over the infirmary's floor. The makeshift ropes then disappeared without a trace. Without pausing, the doctor summoned his 108 needles once more, this time distributing them among various acupoints not located on his chest.

He followed up by manifesting a huge azure hand, which traveled to Feng Ming's chest. It pressed down on his chest thirty times at a moderate pace. With every compression, azure energy flowed into his chest, complementing the hand's motions.

After thirty compressions were completed, the man manifested another object, a small bellow, which he used to inject air into Feng Ming, causing his chest to rise and fall ever so slightly. At the doctor's instruction, the hand continued its compressions. He alternated thirty compressions to two breaths in a seamless fashion. Cha Ming recognized these motions—it was much like CPR in his previous life, though it was obviously an improved version that used qi to enhance the chances of resuscitation.

Three minutes later, the old man's robes were drenched in sweat. He was clearly exhausted. Cha Ming wasn't sure if it would help, but he tentatively extended two strands of qi, one for wood and one for water. The man looked toward him in surprise but didn't hesitate. He quickly made use of the qi that Cha Ming provided and continued for another minute.

Just as he was about to quit once more, Zhang Yifeng fed him another two strands of qi. He was clearly a triple cultivator in water, wood, and fire; only this combination would enable him to have water qi as an alchemist.

Unfortunately, transferring qi was not a highly efficient process. This was especially so for Zhang Yifeng, as his foundation establishment qi was too strong for Hai Tuo to handle. The doctor was only able to sustain his motions for another two minutes.

Seeing that no one was going to step up, Cha Ming created a white thread of creation qi. He was not experienced in converting his creation qi to water and wood, but he tried his best. The resulting qi enabled the man to last another thirty seconds, after which he collapsed to the floor, completely spent.

"This is all I can do. I'm sorry, everyone," the doctor said.

Cha Ming wasn't ready to give up on Feng Ming just yet. He quickly ran over to Feng Ming's side and started conducting manual CPR. While imperfect, the crude method might just give him a fighting chance. He completed thirty compressions and then tilted his friend's chin back and blew two breaths in through his mouth.

"Young man... it's admirable that you want to try saving him with this crude technique, but I'm sorry to say that your friend is dead." The old man shook his head. He got up and brushed his robes off. Cha Ming ignored him and continued compressing his friend's chest. He couldn't give up, no matter what!

If only Feng Ming had my last portion of luck, he thought. *I haven't prayed in this new life, but if there is a God, please help me save my friend. I beg you!*

As he thought this, he continued his compressions. The dozen people present were enthralled by his perseverance. Even the county lord, who had previously tried to trample him like the ant he thought he was, couldn't help but look at him in admiration.

Come on. Come on! I just need to get lucky!

Suddenly, Cha Ming felt a hot sensation travel from his upper back. It continued down his arms as he executed his compressions. He didn't dare stop now to give Feng Ming a breath. A miracle was about to occur.

The warmth continued to travel down his forearms and onto his hands, which were pressed on Feng Ming's chest. A bright white '幸运' character appeared, which could only be seen by Cha Ming. This encouraged him to continue his efforts.

As his compressions continued, the character flickered repeatedly. It followed a rhythm that Cha Ming couldn't understand, as though it was looking for the right moment to intervene. And intervene it did. After five minutes of compressions, the mark on Cha Ming's hands disappeared and flowed into Feng Ming's heart. He immediately removed his hands as Feng Ming gasped deeply for breath. Everyone in the room, including the old doctor, was shocked at this sudden miracle.

The doctor had wasted no time in recovering a small amount of his qi and spirit. "Be quiet and let me treat you, you lucky son of a goat," he said as he began healing Feng Ming, whose eyes were still wide with shock. The old man's eyes continued to light up as he checked one thing after another. He was unable to contain his shock.

"Incredible," he whispered. "When his heart stopped, the qi deficiency in his body was regulated by my original chest compressions. Since his blood had stopped flowing, the azure healing qi that I injected also neutralized the various poisons in his body. He is now recovering at an astonishing pace!"

Everyone in the room let out a sigh of relief, and they patiently waited for the doctor to complete his treatment. No one noticed the brooding expression in Feng Ming's eyes.

Previously

Feng Meng was delirious. He didn't know what was happening; he only knew that misfortune after misfortune happened to befall him. But he didn't give up. He continued to linger on the border of consciousness. After an indeterminate amount of time, he heard voices from the darkness.

"Holy hell, is this a sergeant from the royal army?" the voice said. "Quick, assemble the stretcher. Let's get him back to the city for treatment."

"We need to bring him back to the barracks directly first. County's lord's orders," a cold voice said.

"But he's dying!" another voice said.

"Don't forget your place," the cold voice replied. "We'll bring him back to the barracks and let the lord decide. Do I make myself clear?"

Feng Ming was now floating in a white space. It surrounded him, enveloped him, and embraced him. He felt comfortable in this space.

Am I going to the underworld now? Am I off to the Yellow River? He also noticed that his "body" was wreathed in a light layer of black flames. *Is this my sin? Why the hell am I carrying so much sin?*

"You idiot! Your stupid peacock posturing stopped his heart!" the voice of an old man yelled. The voice was faint, but it confirmed Feng Ming's guess. He was dying.

He sighed inwardly. *It's not so bad. I tried my best. Maybe my death will warn Fairweather City that something dangerous is out there. At least this time I made a difference,* he thought.

His mind drifted back to his reliance on Cha Ming and Wang Jun back in the spirit woods. He had gone to the army to make up for his failure. As far as *he* was concerned, he'd succeeded.

As he reflected on his waste of a life, the white light surrounding him began take on a grayish hue. It began shrinking, and soon Feng Ming could "see" darkness in the distance.

And here comes death. These past few weeks have left me with no regrets.

"How can you give up so easily?" a pleasant voice said from the darkness. "Your luck hasn't run out yet."

The darkness began to recede as a white glow spread out from Feng Ming's spiritual body. Before long, the black shadows that had previously overtaken him completely disappeared.

"This is…" Feng Ming said uncertainly.

"This is your spiritual sea. Myself, I'm nothing more than a remnant. It's a miracle that I survived for so long. Some people call me Good Fortune, but that was long in the past." An old man in a purple robe appeared in front of Feng Ming's spirit body.

"You don't have a lot of time. Only an hour in relative terms, since time passes by very quickly in this space. Use this time wisely and try to comprehend this inheritance, which I left behind just in case."

The man waved his hand, and glowing purple scripture appeared in front of Feng Ming. He couldn't understand the words, but as he concentrated on it, he felt like he was becoming aware of a universal truth, something that transcended language. The purple robed man didn't interrupt his concentration.

As Feng Ming's eyes wandered across the scripture in a haphazard manner, the characters he gained enlightenment on disappeared one by one, only to reappear on his spirit body. He felt a wonderful energy course into his soul with every character he gained. Accordingly, his speed at reading the characters increased drastically for each one absorbed. It was like a virtuous cycle.

Coincidentally, this was exactly what these characters were all about. Before long, he had completely absorbed the scripture. The old man dressed in purple had disappeared, and in the man's place, he found a poem.

Good fortune.
A virtuous cycle that is never ending.
Selfless deeds lead to true happiness.
A pure heart never dies.

Before awakening, he noticed that his spirit body was no longer wreathed in black flames. He had also gained an initial understanding of the vast amount of information branded into his soul. Inside his mind, he found a book. It read: *Good Fortune Scripture Volume One: Soldier of Fortune*[7].

---

[7] A soldier of fortune can also translate to a mercenary. A mercenary is a man that braves dangers to seek monetary fortune. The type of fortune referred to here transcends monetary wealth.

Under Hai Tuo's intensive care, Feng Ming soon recovered his presence of mind and managed to muster up enough energy to speak.

"Who is everyone? Is this Fairweather City?" he asked, then looked toward Cha Ming for answers. He had known for some time that Cha Ming was still alive; Wang Jun's messengers had somehow found him in the middle of a field operation. The man's efficiency frightened him.

"Feng Ming, you are currently inside Fairweather City's guard barracks. Aside from Gong Lan and Huxian, whom you already know, the spirit doctor who treated you is named Hai Tuo. These men are Bei Ling, Han Jinlong, Zhang Yifeng, and the county lord. They are all foundation establishment elders. Wait, I never got the county lord's name." Cha Ming looked toward the county lord with a cold expression. "What's your name again?"

The county lord snorted. "You may call me Lord Sun Chuan. Now then, care to explain how you arrived in front of my city in such a miserable shape?"

A displeased expression appeared on Feng Ming's face, but he steeled his heart and began his tale.

"It all began when we were scouting Crystal Meadows…"

Feng Ming described the murder of his captain and companions, his escape, and his journey to Fairweather City without any interruption. As he spoke, Han Jinlong and Zhang Yifeng's eyes reddened and tears ran down their face. Cha

Ming and Gong Lan were shocked by the revelations, and at his description of those evil beings that ate steel and were immune to pain.

Han Jinlong sighed. "It is as Yifeng and I suspected. We had tried to investigate the area previously, but these rebels possessed sufficient strength to repel us. However, no one would believe us, and we were forced to recruit mercenaries for this rescue mission. Unfortunately, we haven't been able to reveal these details to the mercenaries because they might refuse to participate.

"While we were out scouting, we noticed a thick stench of blood and several sites where devilish rituals had been conducted. However, these aberrations you described didn't make any appearances; we only had our suspicions. Now, however, we can strongly assert that these 'rebels' are in fact a devil-worshiping cult. Are you happy now, Sun Chuan? Will you send out your troops to support us now?"

"Based on a lone sergeant's words?" Sun Chuan retorted. "I am responsible for maintaining peace in this county, not fighting a war. This is clearly beyond the scope of my responsibilities. If I lend my troops to help you, the city will remain undefended. I can only stand by and send this sergeant and one of my trusted messengers to Green Leaf City, where they can inform the General. Only *he* can make a decision like this, and I stand by all my previous decisions on this matter."

"Have you lost your mind?" Han Jinlong yelled. "The evidence is right here, and the people out there can't wait for someone else to make a decision. We need to act *now*!"

"My word is final until it is overturned by someone with greater authority. You may do as you wish," Sun Chuan replied and walked out of the room toward the exit. Han Jinlong and

Zhang Yifeng were seething with rage. Then they looked at Cha Ming and Gong Lan.

"I'm sorry for not telling you the truth, my young friends. You don't have to participate in this matter, and I will relieve you of your contractual obligations," said Zhang Yifeng.

Cha Ming shook his head. His blood was boiling after everything he had heard. There was no way he could back out now, not without getting revenge for his friend's injuries! Gong Lan seemed to share the same opinion. Her killing intent had peaked in the middle of Feng Ming's explanation, frightening their old friend. Feng Ming might have stopped speaking if not for the fact that he had just escaped these devilish cultivators, experienced extreme hardship, and briefly come into contact with death's door.

"There's no need, Elder Zhang," said Cha Ming. "It wouldn't feel right leaving *any* of these rebels alive. They can't even be considered as people anymore, only devils."

Han Jinlong and Zhang Yifeng both looked at him gratefully and bowed in thanks. They then left the room, leaving only Feng Ming, Cha Ming, Gong Lan, and Hai Tuo. The latter was currently meditating, recovering his energy for the next round of treatment.

"What are your plans now?" asked Cha Ming. While he wanted his friend to tag along on the rescue mission, he knew that he had other obligations.

Feng Ming shook his head. "I need to recover quickly and set out to deliver a message to my father as soon as possible. Normally, I would need to report in to my commander. However, the situation is very urgent, and the closest general is in Green Leaf City. Besides, my father and my current commander are good friends, so this move won't ruffle any feathers and will allow the king's army to react as efficiently as possible."

They sat quietly for a few moments, not sure what to say. Finally, it was Feng Ming who broke the awkward silence. "Cha Ming, Gong Lan, there's more to this than meets the eye. Aside from those devilish cultivators that ate metal and ignored pain, I'm even more concerned about that Li Piao. Why was she able to bewitch my captain so easily? It's easy to brush it off, but the captain *definitely* wasn't acting like himself. Further, most of our men were assassinated in the same manner without putting up a fight. I can't help but think that the enemy has the ability to bewitch people, making them experts at assassination and espionage.

"If that's the case, then what other devilish abilities are they hiding? And are they limited to this immediate area? Also, there is something else that I didn't tell the others. When I finally felt that I had escaped my pursuers, my luck suddenly turned for the worse. I tripped where I shouldn't have. I was poisoned accidentally by countless plants. My wounds worsened instead of healing. Further, when I was at death's door, I managed to see my spiritual body. It was lightly covered by black flames. They felt despicable, *evil*. Where did these flames come from, and how did they affect my soul?"

Cha Ming and Gong Lan were at a loss.

Hey, Exalted Teacher, do you know what could have caused this? Cha Ming asked mentally to the bearded man.

After a few breaths, the bearded man replied. *It seems to me like your friend was cursed when he escaped. Those flames sound like the flames of sin. It is very difficult to curse your friend with sin, and unless he has a dark past he didn't mention, it should be impossible for him to have accumulated enough sin to lightly coat his soul in black flames.*

Unfortunately, Cha Ming didn't know how to explain this concept to his friends. He could only remain silent. It was then that the spirit doctor opened his eyes.

"Young man, if I've guessed correctly, you were cursed in some fashion. With misfortune. This is why the freakish series of events made it so difficult for me to heal you and revive you. It is a miracle that you survived, and that your friend Cha Ming was able to revitalize you with his crude technique."

"Crude technique? What crude technique did he use?" Feng Ming asked curiously. He also wondered how he had acquired the Good Fortune Scripture.

"Well, you see…" When the old doctor finished describing the sequence of events, Gong Lan blushed furiously, while Cha Ming considered himself fortunate that his friend was injured and in no shape to fight. He had a feeling that this inside joke would never die, and that he would always be remembered as the man who stole Feng Ming's first kiss.

Chapter 21: Setting Out

A shade of red appeared on the skyline as the first light of the sun descended on the tranquil landscape near Fairweather. It was a beautiful scene, like a fresh panting that would only last a few moments. Many of the artisans in Fairweather City had risen with the sun, hoping to find inspiration in the dawn's natural beauty.

Lin Fan was one such person, a painter. He was seated in front of a large canvas, with a brush in one hand and a paint palette in the other. Off to the side, a rag and an assortment of brushes laid in wait for their turn to shine. They were separated by color, as the oily medium he used could only be wiped off but not rinsed.

After firmly visualizing the scenery within his mind, he started his painting with the sky. It was a peculiar shade of blue, one that only lasted a quarter hour each morning. He didn't stop there—after finishing the initial shade, a light red flame appeared before the painting to accelerate the drying process.

Next, he painted the red sun. It was currently one-fifth exposed on the horizon.

Before long the canvas was filled with red-tinted clouds, hills, and conifers. Next came a deer, which just happened to cross his line of sight. The painting was like a half-hour recording, all captured as a single moment. Lin Fan wasn't satisfied with his latest work. He wiped sweat from his brow. This work had required much more effort than usual. It wasn't easy attempting to paint a masterpiece when three hundred rowdy mercenaries were assembled just a hundred paces away.

Unfortunately, there was little he could do. He recognized many of the people assembled. Some were even his neighbors. More importantly, he recognized Han Jinlong and Zhang Yifeng. It wasn't worth offending them over such a trifling matter. After all, the perfect sunset he had waited twelve years for *could* come by once again in his lifetime.

"You would think that a group of mercenaries would be much more energetic, even if it *is* early in the morning," Cha Ming said between mouthfuls of his breakfast. He had managed, with great difficulty, to locate a bakery that made steamed red-bean buns. It was one of his favorite breakfasts, though he still preferred rice porridge and pickles. Alas, such a meal could not be eaten while walking.

Gong Lan, on the other hand, was snacking on a strip of beef jerky. "Only half of these people are *actual* mercenaries. The rest are local recruits from Fairweather. Many of them are only coming along because they have family in the surrounding villages that were attacked. These people know nothing of living out in the wilderness or getting by without sleep."

Huxian was having the time of his life. While contract beasts were rare, there were seven of them in this small group of mercenaries. Whenever he encountered one, he made sure to thoroughly oppress it and gloat to Cha Ming about his superiority over his lesser brethren. One of the contract beasts was a rarely seen bobcat. In its pride, it refused to yield to the younger fox—for about fifteen seconds. Huxian forced it to kowtow for its defiance. The large feline's master could only suffer in silence, as she herself was no stronger than her companion beast.

Their small group wandered toward the front, where many of the stronger individuals were located. This included Master Han and Master Zhang. The mercenaries had been instructed to gather one hour before dawn, and only a quarter hour remained. At the front, they met Sima Qian and Wu Jin, whom they had met at the auction house a week ago. They spoke for a short while before a booming voice resounded across the large crowd of cultivators.

"On behalf of everyone with relatives near Fairweather, I thank you all for accepting this mission," said Han Jinlong. "I won't lie to you, the information we've received indicates that this will be a dangerous outing. But I'm sure most of you have guessed this, given the ample rewards for successfully completing the mission. Rest assured—if you fall in battle, we are contractually obligated to pay the full amount for the mission to your designated beneficiary. However, I would like each one of you to know that we want you to return home safely.

"Master Zhang has prepared a welcome gift for everyone." Several green specks flew out toward the various cultivators. Each of them caught a clear crystal bottle containing three green pills. "These green pills are emerald healing pills concocted by Master Zhang and his apprentices. These pills will heal many grievous injuries within minutes. This way, you can all rest assured as we venture forward to rescue our relatives and friends.

"Now, I will split everyone into three groups. I will lead the first group, Master Zhang will lead the second group, and the Ling brothers—three experts at the peak of qi condensation—will lead the third group.

"First group, Jin Lihai.

"Second group, Bai Liangtao.

"Third..."

Han Jinlong continued to list off names one by one until everyone was sorted. Cha Ming and Huxian were in Group Two, while Gong Lan was in Group One. Wu Jin and Sima Qian were both in Group Three.

"Each of the three groups will head out in separate directions toward the three nearest villages, where we will begin our investigation. We will then proceed through several checkpoints before finally meeting at a town called Jade Spring, where we suspect that rebels are keeping nearby residents as prisoners.

"Everyone... stay strong."

With that, Han Jinlong set out toward the northwest. He ran at a moderate pace easily achievable by the various cultivators. Zhang Yifeng ran toward the south, while the Ling brothers led their group toward the southwest. Cha Ming gave Gong Lan,

Wu Jin, and Sima Qian a wave before following along.

Everyone... stay strong.

Crackle. Crackle.

The sounds of breaking ice could barely be heard amongst the dull footsteps of the hundred cultivators in Zhang Yifeng's group. They were walking along a clay road just outside Crystal Meadows, their first stop on this journey.

Cha Ming was fiddling with a pine cone he had picked from a nearby tree. There weren't many trees in this barren land, which was barely suitable for pasture. Though, judging by the length of the grass, the land had not been used for this purpose recently. Cha Ming didn't think too much on this point and tossed the pine cone to Huxian, who quickly bounced it off his nose back to Cha Ming in an improvised game of catch.

Before long, the group arrived at the entrance to Crystal Meadows. The first sight that greeted them was a broken-down pen. It didn't contain any livestock, however, as they had all been removed in a very violent manner. Here and there, they saw clumps of wool coated in blood. The ground was covered in small pools of putrid, rotting blood, a sign of a rough and hurried slaughter.

They didn't dwell too long on this sight but turned their attention toward the village itself. Cha Ming and Huxian were near the front of the group, along with some stronger mercenaries. Together with Zhang Yifeng, they were the vanguard of this expeditionary force.

Under Master Zhang's guidance, they first headed toward the inn, which according to Feng Ming had doubled up as a mayoral office for Li Piao. They found nothing but a smoldering wreck. The building had clearly been burned down to destroy all evidence of the scuffle with the royal army. This result was disappointing, but not unexpected.

Not wanting to waste any time, Zhang Yifeng had the group of one hundred people split up into pairs. The weaker ones were paired with the stronger ones. Of course, Cha Ming and Huxian counted as one person. They were accompanied by a lucky female cultivator at the third level of qi condensation. Unlike most cultivators, her looks were only average. She kept short hair, and her left shoulder bore the insignia of the Black Eagle Mercenary Company.

On a whim, Cha Ming led his group to a nearby workshop. The outside of the large building was in good repair. He opened the door slowly, and Huxian and the female mercenary stood ready in case of an attack. Only a light creak sounded out, indicating that the door had been oiled on a regular basis.

The inside of the building was dark, as few windows had been built into the building in the first place. Perhaps this had something to do with the crystal glass artisans' preferences. Cha Ming knew that if he tried working with glass, he would want as little external light as possible. Glass was prone to refracting and reflecting light, potentially leading to errors in the crafting process.

"Huxian, light, please," Cha Ming said softly to his companion. At Cha Ming's instruction, Huxian's fur started to shimmer. The shimmering grew brighter and brighter, until finally all the specks of light that had accumulated on his fur gathered up into a small globe, which floated in front of them.

It cast light in all directions in a thirty-foot radius. Yet the light did not seem to follow the normal rules. Within those thirty feet, everything was bright as day. Outside of that distance, everything abruptly reverted to the original darkness in the room.

"Good Huxian," Cha Ming said while petting his ears. Their third wheel didn't say much, though her gaze softened whenever she looked at the playful little fox. "Stay within ten feet of the light, Xiaobei. Huxian and I will stay on the periphery in case anything unexpected comes out from the darkness. Keep your eyes peeled for anything unusual, especially any writing or runes."

The girl was used to taking instruction from superior cultivators and did as she was told. They slowly but surely observed every nook and cranny. Unfortunately, the building was unusually barren. It seemed like all the crafting equipment except for the large furnaces had been removed from the building.

Maybe they also took the craftsmen away? After all, this equipment is useless without craftsmen.

Soon their group stumbled upon a desk in the workshop. The desk seemed to have been carved out of a single piece of stone and was covered in exquisite designs. Cha Ming let his hand wander along the cool surface of the desk, looking for any clues or hidden compartments. It was then that he noticed a rune cleverly disguised as another decoration. Upon further observation, he noticed that it was paired with another rune. These were characters for "open" and "conceal."

He activated the "open" rune by pouring in some of his qi. A drawer opened on a previously flush surface, revealing a notebook, a pen, a picture, some jewelry, and some spirit stones. He quickly scooped up the contents into his bag of holding. Surely Master Zhang would want to see these items. After carefully inspecting the rest of the desk, he found nothing else of importance and proceeded to inspect the chair.

"Cha Ming, come see this," Xiaobei said. She was crouched down on the floor looking at a strange symbol. Cha Ming walked over and saw a rune painted on the floor with black and green ink. He frowned when he saw this character, however. "Tinder" wasn't a character that could be utilized on its own. However, it was surrounded by geometric shapes, as well as slightly curved and straight lines that headed outward from the symbol. One such line headed toward the center of town.

I should go there as soon as possible. It looks like a talisman, but it's not painted on paper. Perhaps it's part of a formation?

Just as he was about to pull their trio out of the building, Huxian started whining softly. *Big Brother, I hear someone crying and whimpering. And I smell fear. Quick, follow me!* The little fox darted off to a far corner of the workshop. The floor there was covered in stone slates. Cha Ming instantly recognized the same pattern he had just seen on the desk. He quickly poured qi into the "open" character, which opened a three-foot-by-three-foot entrance.

Huxian, being the most durable member of their group, darted in first. *Come in, brother. You need to see this.*

As Cha Ming climbed down, the light source followed him at Huxian's command. The small room appeared to be a cellar, and it reeked of alcohol. In a corner of the room, a little girl was trembling, trying to remain as quiet as possible.

"You need to be quiet, Mimi, you need to be quiet. If you're not quiet, those monsters will take you and eat you. You need to be quiet, Mimi…" she mumbled repeatedly.

Cha Ming approached her quietly and crouched down in front of her. "Hello, little one. It's going to be okay."

Her eyes quickly shot upward toward his voice, and she immediately started backing away on her hands and feet. "Monster, you're a monster! Get away from me!" she yelled.

Her voice was hoarse, as though she hadn't had any water in days. This caused Cha Ming to look toward the opened barrels and bottles of alcohol. Clearly she had been drinking it to stay hydrated, which may or may not have been a wise decision, depending on the contents of the barrels.

"It's going to be okay, little one," Cha Ming said, crouching down in front of her once more. "Do you know Master Zhang Yifeng or Han Jinlong?" At the mention of these two names, her eyes became a little more focused.

"You know Uncle Zhang?" she said nervously.

Cha Ming nodded. "Yes, your Uncle Zhang has come here to save you. He is outside looking for others right now. Do you want to come with me to come see him?"

She nodded slowly and tried to get up, only to stumble. Her frame was extremely skinny, and he suspected that she was starved, dehydrated, *and* drunk from living down here.

"Can you take little brothers Tao and Yong too?" she mumbled.

Cha Ming looked toward Huxian, who had been exploring another corner. The little fox shook his head. The two little boys who were down here with her had died a few days ago.

"They are sleeping, little one. We'll come get them when they wake up, okay?" he said reassuringly. He then put away his staff and picked her up in his arms, then carried her up the stairs.

Xiaobei was very surprised to see a living girl come out

from the cellar but took it in stride. They soon exited the workshop and headed toward the center of the town.

There were only a dozen or so people out on the streets, as the mercenaries were busy searching for clues. They shot Cha Ming a surprised look as they saw the little girl in his arms.

Soon enough, Cha Ming arrived at the center of the town, where a statue had been erected. He was mesmerized by its beauty and soon realized that it was a decorative spirit treasure. Here and there, he could see some lightly engraved runes, some for strengthening, and some for beauty and charm. He continued observing these runes, starting from the face of the statue and working his way downward. He frowned once he got to the base of the twenty-foot statue.

There he saw some dark runes engraved on a plaque. There was one large rune surrounded by twenty smaller ones. Twelve of these runes were lit with a dull red light. Unfortunately, Cha Ming had never studied formations. He did, however, know that the smaller runic characters meant "trigger." These twenty runes were surrounded by an outer circle and an inner circle. Twenty lines came out from the outer circle and left the statue, while thirteen lines led toward the inner rune.

Twelve of them are lit, he thought, frowning. *Does this mean thirteen runes must be lit to trigger the central rune?*

His face turned pale when he saw the central rune, "Inferno."

"Master Zhang!" he yelled out with all his might. "We need to get out *now*!"

Suddenly a hole blew out from a nearby building, and Master Zhang ran out toward him at a speed not possible for qi condensation cultivators.

"What's the matter, Cha Ming?" Master Zhang asked.

"It's a trap, Master Zhang. If one more trigger is activated—"

Cha Ming's explanation was interrupted as a light hum sounded out. Thirteen lines were now lit, and the central rune was glowing bright red. "No time now. We triggered a trap, and this whole town is going to burn. Get everyone out of here *immediately*."

With that, he held the little girl tightly with his right arm and, using a movement technique and his high physical strength, he grabbed Xiaobei with his left. She tried to free herself from his grip, only to realize that her struggles meant nothing to Cha Ming. As soon as he grabbed the two, seventy-two pearls burst out from his wrist, and he was surrounded with a blue snowflake. Mere moments after he reacted, the entire town burst into flames.

It wasn't just the buildings that caught fire; even the air began burning violently. Fortunately, Cha Ming was able to shield the ones near him. Zhang Yifeng wasted no time and darted out toward other nearby mercenaries. He used his precise control over flames to disperse the inferno near them, and these adventurers gathered around him to save others.

Cha Ming immediately followed his example and began gathering nearby mercenaries. Fortunately, some of them cultivated water and earth arts and were able to protect themselves independently. Cha Ming ignored these people and let them flee alone.

After running for a dozen breaths, he found three cultivators who were huddled together around a single water element cultivator, who was using her qi to protect them. Her qi was wavering, and it was clear that she wouldn't be able to hold out for long. Cha Ming quickly expanded the scope of his frozen domain and signaled for them to follow him. They all looked at him gratefully and accompanied him to collect other such groups.

Unfortunately, he couldn't save everyone. Several times, he saw screaming cultivators that had been lit up like torches. They ran for a few brief moments before collapsing to the ground. He didn't have time to save these people. Other times they encountered badly burned individuals that couldn't walk anymore. These cultivators were carried off by those in the group that still had a bit of strength remaining.

Finally, they managed to escape the formation, which was a large circle that completely encapsulated the town. Their group was soon joined by Zhang Yifeng, who had rescued thirty-five cultivators. With Cha Ming's twenty-four cultivators and the few odd people who had managed to escape on their own, a total of seventy-three cultivators had survived the trap.

The survivors looked at the burning town in silence while nursing their wounds, hoping that even one more of their companions would escape. No one did.

Chapter 22: The Girl's Story

The flames died down the next morning. Though the air was still hot and smoky, at least it was bearable. Several dozen mercenaries set out to find if there were any lucky survivors. In the end, all they could do was bury partially burned corpses.

Meanwhile, Cha Ming assisted Master Zhang in his treatment of the little girl from the workshop cellar. Because of Cha Ming's protection, she had not suffered any burns. However, she was severely malnourished, dehydrated, and dependent on alcohol. The last issue was not overly concerning, as Zhang Yifeng happened to have some detoxifying pills. He also fed her some nutrition pills, which quickly satiated her hunger and thirst.

"What's your name, little girl? And why do you look so familiar? Have we met before?" the kindly man asked. The little girl was currently hugging a gourd of water. As soon as she had taken the detoxifying pill, she began crying as she recalled recent events.

"My name is Meng Xiaomei, Mimi for short. We met when I was very little. You came to visit Aunty Zhang, my father's sister," she replied.

The older man looked both surprised at the coincidence but glad that he had finally found one of his relatives.

"I'm sorry I couldn't come earlier," Zhang Yifeng said, his voice laced with regret. Han Jinlong and I have gathered a small army to rescue everyone. Can you tell me what happened?"

The little girl's eyes were downcast as she recalled what had happened. "It all started with the bandit leader. One day, a group of twenty bandits appeared in our village without warning. Normally, in such a situation, we would hand over all of our wealth. Papa told me that it would be fine if we gave them everything, and that the lord of Fairweather County would compensate us, like always.

"Just to be safe, two other boys and I headed down to an emergency cellar. It wasn't long before we heard screams outside. I… I don't know what happened to them," the little girl said while doing her best to hold back her tears.

Master Zhang wiped the tears off her cheeks and reassured her. She continued talking after taking a small gulp of water.

"We were underground for who knows how long. There was food and water there in case of an emergency, but there was only so much. We lost track of time. All I know is that the work upstairs never stopped.

"Usually my father and the other uncles in the workshop would only work ten hours a day, and they would never work at night. But while we were in the cellar, the roaring of the furnace never stopped. Every once in a while, an argument would break out.

"One day, one of the uncles had enough and started arguing

and yelling. Some unfamiliar voices yelled back, and I heard a crash and the sound of breaking glass upstairs." The little girl shivered a little before continuing. "'*You monster!*', Uncle said. And then I heard his screams. Then the man told my father and the other uncles to get back to work.

"Some time later, I woke up and heard some shouting. There were sounds of furniture, equipment, and crates being moved. The sounds lasted for what I think was a half day, and then everything was quiet. After waiting for a long time, we tried to get out, but we couldn't figure out how to open the cellar. We had already run out of food. Soon, we ran out of water. That's when we started drinking the alcohol in the cellar. I don't remember much after that..." By the time she had finished recounting the story, her eyes were red, and her face was covered in tears.

"It's going to be all right, Mimi. We're going to save your parents," Master Zhang said. He then turned around and addressed the female mercenary. "Xiaobei, can you please take Mimi to get cleaned up? Take her back to my tent afterward so she can get some rest." She nodded and led Mimi away.

After the little girl left, the older man sighed and looked over to Cha Ming. "Are you a formation master?" he asked Cha Ming, his eyes full of expectation.

The younger man shook his head. "Sadly, I know nothing about formations. This is my first time seeing one. I was only able to guess what was going to happen because I recognized some runic characters that are often used when making talismans. There was a "tinder" character connected with lines in the building that I was exploring, and a line that led to the center of town. When I looked at the statue, I recognized twenty "trigger" characters and a large "inferno" character. It wasn't difficult to guess what was going to happen," Cha Ming finished.

The older man nodded. "A reasonable deduction. Unfortunately, alchemy is not one of the runic arts, like weaponsmithing, talisman artistry, or formation masters. I am useless in this regard, and it seems like the enemy has laid down several traps for us. Please keep your eyes peeled for any runic characters as we continue onward.

"Further, this behavior makes me uneasy. The trap killed thirty weaker cultivators and injured twenty other low-level cultivators. Why go through all this trouble only to kill a few lesser cultivators? It would have been much more effective to set a trap that could injure higher-level cultivators, or even Han Jinlong or myself. All they did was delay us while we bury people and recuperate."

Cha Ming shook his head. "I don't know, either. However, perhaps this book will give us some clues on what they did while they were here?" Cha Ming pulled out the items that he had collected earlier—the notebook, the pen, the picture, the spirit stones, and some jewelry.

The older man accepted it and opened the front cover. He then sighed. "As I suspected. This is that girl's father's notebook. My brother-in-law's. Let's read through this together and see what we can find out."

Fairweather City

It didn't take long for Feng Ming to get fed up with his accommodations in the barracks. By the end of the first day, he had already taken the initiative and asked Master Bei if he could stay with him. Bei Ling was happy to receive him, so he continued his medical treatments under his and Hong Lai's care.

The physician was astounded by Feng Ming's rate of recovery; every medicinal supplement he fed him performed to more than full effect. This was especially surprising considering the repeated failures beforehand. If it weren't for Master Bei's presence, Feng Ming was sure the physician would have detained him as a medical research subject.

"One more day and you'll be fully healed," the doctor Hai Tuo said after his latest visit. Feng Ming was ecstatic. While staying at Master Bei's residence was much better than staying at the city guard's barracks, it wasn't any less awkward. He couldn't complain too much, though. He kept getting the willies whenever he turned his back to anyone. Here, he just existed in perpetual boredom.

Feng Ming had been mentored from a young age and was an expert in holding conversations and socializing. However, all this training meant nothing to Bei Ling and Hong Lai, who were both helpless crafting addicts. Even meaningless conversations about the newly budding spring flowers would somehow become a discussion about crafting a brooch.

After a few hours of meandering conversations, he asked the two weaponsmiths for permission to wander around the very spacious abode. They granted him permission immediately but barred him from the workshop.

As if I'd want to wander around a stinking workshop, he thought.

Before long, he discovered that describing the abode as very spacious was an understatement. The main hallway he was currently exploring was a great example. It was long and wide and contained several dozen doors. By trial and error, he discovered that these doors often led to other hallways, which were also full of other doors. It was like a maze. Regrettably, he had always hated mazes as a child. Therefore, instead of figuring out the maze by brute force, he decided to test out his newly found strength—luck.

That was how he found himself in the middle of the hallway playing *Spin the Dagger,* which was not to be confused with a popular game amongst youngsters, *Spin the Flask,* where the one spinning the flask would need to kiss the one it pointed to. In this game, Feng Ming spun a dagger to discover which door he should open. He figured the maze was a defense mechanism inherent to this mysterious abode, which was likely the reason why he was allowed to wander around in the first place.

After three consecutive doors, he began to doubt the effectiveness of his method. The ornate dagger, an old heirloom he had taken from home before leaving, gradually came to a stop after his latest spin.

Last try, he thought. *After this one, I'm just going back to the living room and resting.* This time he didn't find a hallway on the other side. Instead he found what looked a lot like a cross between a museum and a storage room.

In this room, weapons of all kinds were strewn about on display racks. Most of the weapons were swords, sabers, and daggers. There were also a few suits of ornate armor. He disdained these, however. They seemed bulky and clumsy, and he would never allow armor to interfere with his swift and graceful fighting style. Light armor was best.

He was very interested when it came to the weapons. He picked them up one by one, testing their balance and compatibility with his fighting style. One of them was a greatsword that looked like it weighed twice as much as him. To his surprise, it was light as a feather in his hands. "Overlord Sword, Grade Eight Spirit Weapon, Lightness in Heaviness Runic Ability" was written on its display case.

Well, that explains it. After a few more swings, he placed the weapon back on its shelf—greatswords just didn't suit his style.

He'd already made up his mind to shamelessly request one of the weapons. He no longer had a suitable weapon after his last battle, and he really didn't feel comfortable at the thought of being accompanied home by the county lord's men. Money wasn't an issue for him—it was whether or not the picky spiritual blacksmiths would be willing to sell.

After searching for the better part of an hour, he shook his head in disappointment. Alas, none of the weapons truly suited him. This made him doubt his good fortune. Wasn't he supposed to find good things everywhere now that he was cultivating the Good Fortune Scripture? Or did he still need to accumulate a lot more merit to make this luck materialize?

Sighing, he picked up one of the plain swords on a shelf. It wasn't a special weapon, but it was a fifth-grade sword that was suited to his fighting style. Before making his decision, he ran a few tests, expertly using his sword to execute one of his various sword techniques. Unfortunately, the storage room was not very suitable for practicing. He soon tripped backward on a crate and bumped into a shelf. A rolling sound alerted him, prompting him to roll away from the shelf. He looked back just in time to see a black spear falling down tip-first where he had previously been.

Spear, huh? I've never tried a spear before. Feng Ming picked it up and tried swinging it around. He had always liked the thought of wielding a spear, but his father had always said that a general's weapon was a sword. Spears were for *soldiers*. But wasn't he supposed to be a *Soldier* of Fortune? Trying never hurt anyone.

But how do I even use a spear? I wish I had some basic technique. Shrugging, he continued his footwork drills and decided to infuse some qi into the newfound weapon to see if he might gain any inspiration. To his surprise, the black spear began glowing with white runes, and information instantly rushed into his mind.

Nine Lives Lucky Spear. Magic weapon. Can only be wielded by the fated, ignores cultivation realm restrictions.

Lucky Spear Art. A spear and footwork art specifically designed for reckless, lucky individuals.

The weapon and spear art seemed tailor-made for him.

I'll be damned, this whole Soldier of Fortune thing is legitimate, he thought. To his surprise, the spear art didn't even need to be learned. It had imbued itself into his muscles and nerves, granting him muscle memory and reflexes consistent with the spear art!

He practiced for a short while before taking the spear out of storage and meeting with Bei Ling and Hong Lai. He gave them a short demonstration of his skills with the spear and requested the spear, since they were clearly fated.

"Take it. It's yours," Bei Ling said. "Take the second left, third right, and second left again to get to the training room."

Feng Ming was surprised at Bei Ling's easygoing nature. He quickly excused himself before the master smith changed his mind.

Hong Lai had observed the whole process in a daze. He came back to his senses and asked, "Master Bei, isn't that the cursed spear that the supposed 'Lucky General' used in the past? The one that caused the death of twelve cultivators before someone finally gave us the spear for safekeeping?"

"Yep, that's the one," Bei Ling replied dryly.

"Is it… appropriate to gift it to this little friend?"

"Yep, totally appropriate. Like the man said, he's fated with it," Bei Ling replied without any hesitation.

"How do you know he's fated with it?" Hong Lai asked.

"Well, for starters, he actually found the room it was stored in. Then he somehow found it despite it being hidden on the top shelf. Meanwhile, he hasn't stabbed himself in the foot yet, nor has he broken any of my furniture. I'd say that's a good start," Bei Ling concluded. Hong Lai couldn't refute him.

After a good night's sleep, Feng Ming was declared fully recovered by the doctor. He bade farewell to Bei Ling and Hong Lai before finally heading out to the barracks. There, he met his road companion, Sergeant Gou Dan. The man had brought four horses with him, so that they had two each to maximize their speed. Feng Ming approved, and they set off immediately. Getting the message to his father was of paramount importance. His friends' lives were at stake.

Wang Jun was sitting at his desk in front of a mountain of paperwork. Despite the enormous workload, he remained unphased. His exquisite penmanship was utilized for signatures when needed, and he quickly memorized every document he read.

Elder Bai entered the room just as Wang Jun finished reading a thick dossier titled "Politics, Law, and Trade in the Song Kingdom." The information had been compiled by the best intelligence agents in the dynasty for his perusal.

"Young Master, we've received the reply from the Song Kingdom's medical association. The election for a new chairman has been triggered and will take place in four days. Our candidate will be promoting free trade in alchemical products, for the betterment of the Song Kingdom's health and the goodwill of the people.

"Meanwhile, the propaganda campaign vilifying the Alchemists Association is fully underway. We've added inflammatory remarks and directed mudslinging to Zhou Li's uncle, the prominent alchemist in Green Leaf City," Elder Bai said, concluding his report. Dark circles could be seen around his eyes, an unusual phenomenon for foundation establishment elders.

"Very good, Elder Bai. Let's start the second phase of the plan. Please have Elder Chong sue the Alchemists Association for illegal trade infringement. Simultaneously, have him sue Zhou Li's uncle for contract infringement and conflict of interest, effectively resulting in price fixing. We also need to begin slinging some mud at Zhou Jia, Zhou Li's sister. Please skew the mudslinging toward her personally, making the crown prince a victim. Actually…"

A devilish grin suddenly appeared on the young man's face. "Have the rumors discuss Zhou Jia's illicit relations with her brother Zhou Li. Make sure it is heavily publicized. Concurrently promote the opinion that the crown prince is much too noble to be interacting with scum like her, and that she should be set out onto the streets. Meanwhile, coordinate with the others in his harem to try shaking up her position."

Wang Jun always treated his friends with utmost kindness. But he would never show a shred of mercy to his enemies. Nor to himself. He didn't pause to rest after the conversation and continued poring over the documents on his desk. As he was reading one of the documents, Wang Jun lifted his eyes to Elder Bai and asked, "By the way, how is the other matter coming along?"

A twinkle appeared in Elder Bai's eye. "Swimmingly," he replied.

Chapter 23: Unforgiveable

It was one of the last remaining days of winter, and the smell of fresh grass and budding leaves permeated the air. Birds and squirrels who had remained hidden all winter peeked their small heads out, chirping to announce their imminent return. In the distance, a "V" of ducks was flying at a steady pace, returning to the lush lands it remembered.

A younger, curious duck decided to split off from the flock, landing in a small pond near the side of the road. A poor decision, to be sure, as it was instantly pierced in the neck by an arrow. The flock scattered as the duck squawked just prior to its untimely demise. Its corpse was retrieved by an enthusiastic man in his early twenties, who brought it back to a group of one hundred mercenaries plodding along at a steady pace.

"Look, Sister Gong. I caught us supper!" the young man exclaimed enthusiastically, causing Gong Lan to massage her temple for the sixth time that day. While she found the man insufferable, she couldn't fault his honesty and kind demeanor. She just preferred cold men. Manly men like her brother.

Regrettably, he didn't have any good mercenary friends, so she had to find someone the hard way.

She had originally thought Cha Ming would be a good guy to chase, but it turned out that he was too nice. Manly, but nice. *Definitely* friend-zone material. She didn't need to be babied or pampered; she just need someone with a sultry sense of humor, veins of steel, and chiseled features. Someone who looked like he was sculpted out of granite, inside and out. She didn't think this was asking for too much.

The young man continued talking, so she tuned him out, occasionally smiling at something he said just to be polite. Fortunately, this was only a temporary arrangement. He had been pestering her ever since Han Jinlong's group set out. She figured he took her to be a weak and lone adventurer, one who should be protected. Little did he know that *he* was the one who needed protecting.

Occasionally, she pictured herself decapitating the man for his annoying behavior, only to remind herself that decapitating friends was not very polite. A strange thought, certainly, but not uncommon. Over the past two months, thoughts like these had often visited her dreams both in the day and at night. It was much worse when she saw blood. Even more so under the full moon.

Their group continued marching until they arrived at the entrance of a small village. Hundreds of crows surrounded the village; it was clear that Brother Death had paid a visit recently. Gong Lan looked toward Han Jinlong, who dismounted his flying sword. The ugly expression on his face became extremely apparent when he looked toward the hundred mercenaries and motioned for them to quiet down.

"Everyone, separate into pairs and look around. See what

you can find. Also, keep your eyes peeled for runic symbols. Zhang Yifeng's group recently encountered a trap array formation in Crystal Meadows, so we need to be extremely cautious," Han Jinlong said.

This caused much discussion among the many mercenaries, which was likely why he had waited until now to share the news.

How does he know this happened? Does he have some sort of tool that he can use to communicate with the squad leaders? Gong Lan wondered. Like clockwork, her annoying "friend" chimed in with words of reassurance.

"Luckily, I'm a third-grade spiritual blacksmith," he said. "While I'm not very gifted in runes, I should at least be able to spot unusual ones if I get close to them. Don't worry, Sister Gong, you're safe with Brother An Hao." The man beat his chest, and Gong Lan had to resist rolling her eyes. Clearly this man overestimated himself. Cha Ming was a seventh-grade talisman artist, and even he wasn't able to stop them from triggering the trap. An Hao didn't stand a chance.

Hopefully he's okay, she thought. *And Huxian, too, that cute little fox. That cute but freakishly strong fox.* She still hadn't gotten over the consecutive defeats she had suffered at the baby spirit beast's hands, especially the ones where she had teamed up with Cha Ming for good measure.

Since they had to pair up, she decided to team up with An Hao. She couldn't let such a nice guy die young. Besides, she could use it as an opportunity to give him a sober awakening and show him that she really didn't need to be taken care of.

She had prepared herself mentally before entering the village, but nothing could have prepared her for the sight that greeted her. Hundreds of crows flew away as they walked in, revealing a sight that caused the entire group to hesitate. Even Han Jinlong could barely maintain his composure. Over three quarters of the mercenaries gagged and threw up, including the experienced ones.

Corpses littered the ground as far as the eyes could see. Most of them were either dismembered, partially eaten, or both. If Gong Lan had not experienced these past two months of merciless slaughter, she too would have vomited at such a sight, like her friend An Hao. Now, she did not feel any revulsion, only *anger*.

She took a few moments to calm down, then gritted her teeth before heading toward the front, where Han Jinlong was standing. She saw that his eyes were red and moist. She was sure he only held back his tears for the sake of the men behind him.

"Spread out and search for survivors," he said amidst the sounds of retching men. Gong Lan dutifully walked toward one of the houses.

An Hao, who was still feeling queasy, dutifully stayed beside her. In fact, he still remembered to try opening the door for her, only to jump back in surprise as she kicked it open to vent her temper.

"Light a torch," she grunted as she pulled out her twin sabers. Her intimidating demeanor prompted immediate compliance. The man quickly produced a spirit lamp, which could burn for hours without being extinguished. He also held a three-foot sword in his right hand, ready to fend off any potential assailants.

The inside of the house was no different than the outside. The walls were painted in blood, and the putrid stench of rotting flesh nauseated them as they made their way through.

They found nothing of importance. There were no records of the incident, indicating that it was likely a sudden invasion.

The duo continued looking through several more houses, finding roughly eight bodies in the process. It was only an estimate, however, as very few of the bodies were intact. In the fourth house they looked through, they found a secret compartment behind a bookshelf. The books had all been cleared and were spread out across the floor. Only now did Gong Lan realize that she hadn't found a single valuable thing, which was common behavior for bandits. Yet she knew in her heart that these were not mere bandits; slaves were worth money, and they would never allow such wanton slaughter.

Her feeling was confirmed as she opened the hidden compartment behind the bookcase. There she found four whole corpses huddling together. They had clearly been trapped there for at least a few days.

Why would bandits spend several days in a village? The thought quickly sparked her temper once more as she recalled the corpses of naked women and prepubescent girls, women and girls who had clearly been disrespected thoroughly before their death. The thought caused her to lash out with one of her sabers, taking out a chunk from a nearby wall. An Hao quickly jumped back in fright, thanking his lucky stars that he hadn't been standing beside her.

Putting away her sabers, she quickly patted down the rotting bodies, looking for any signs of identification. She soon found a notebook inside a man's bag of holding. After flipping through this booklet, she concluded that the man's name was Han Wenqing.

"Is he related to Han Jinlong?" she wondered aloud.

Just as she was about to leave the hidden compartment, she

spotted some unusual red characters. These characters weren't runic characters, but ordinary writing. They were written in blood, likely from the man's bloody finger. The message was clear: "Beware the Blood Moon." Gong Lan shivered involuntarily before making her way back to the center of town.

Han Jinlong nodded as he heard her findings and accepted the small notebook solemnly. He then took out a black notebook and jotted down some details. Seeing that most mercenaries had returned, he yelled out in a booming voice, "Everyone, we'll stay a day here and bury the dead. We owe them that much."

With these words, a large shovel quickly materialized in his hands. He dug the shovel into the ground, setting the example for the rest of the mercenary team.

At least when he worked, the sweat would hide his tears.

Gong Lan was running. It was a dream, the same dream that she'd had for the past month. She was running because she had slaughtered someone influential. He had committed atrocious deeds, and she had punished him for them. Yet to her surprise, dozens of cultivators chased her down to bring her to justice. Why was the world so unfair?

A soldier jumped out at her as she rounded a corner. She quickly dispatched him with one of her twin sabers. His blood splashed onto her, adding to the bloody film on her skin. In the dream, she always smelled blood. She always felt anger. *Why? Why? Why?*

The dream was always the same. She always killed someone with just cause, yet the world punished her for it. It made her angry, and it made her curse the world.

She continued to run about in the dream for what seemed like an eternity. Finally, she saw the familiar apparition of her twin sabers. They were red and pulsating with blood.

Why don't you just give in to your anger? they asked. *Why do you run away? Things will be so much better if you just give in and kill them all. It doesn't matter if they condemn you, because dead men can't judge.* She ignored the tempting voices in her head. She was afraid that if she gave in, she would lose herself.

The sabers continued asking over and over, nearly driving her to madness. Finally, after they saw that she would not submit, they flew up in the air and put her out of her misery. They *allowed* her to leave the terrible dream.

Gong Lan gasped as she woke up with a start. She was holding one of her sabers, and that saber had just torn a hole in her tent. She thanked the heavens that she had a tent to herself, as her slashing motion would likely have decapitating anyone sleeping beside her.

These dreams came to her every night, and she knew instinctively that no matter what, she couldn't give in to those bloody sabers. She wished she could throw them away, but she relied on them. How many of her friends would die if she didn't? Everything good thing in the world had a price.

After getting up, she showered with water qi. The filth and

sweat left her body, but she could never wash away the smell of blood, which seeped into her very core. One day she would throw away these wretched sabers. But not today.

Her brother had once told her to see him if she ever felt strange, like all the killing was too much for her. He had succumbed to bloodlust in the past, and it had taken him a year to recover. However, that was after he had bathed in the blood of his enemies for half a decade. She had only started two months ago. How could she face her brother when she was so weak? She needed to be strong. For her brother and her friends, personal safety be damned.

As she walked out of her tent, she was greeted by the smell of roasting meat. An Hao was cooking the duck he'd caught yesterday.

"Breakfast is almost ready, Sister Gong."

She wasn't in the mood to complain now and thanked him gently for the breakfast. He then joyfully rambled on for a good half hour. She didn't interrupt him and gracefully nibbled on her half of the duck.

There was one more stop before Jade Spring—the nearby spirit woods. Normally, these woods were off-limits to cultivators. However, the brutality in the village reminded them that people could be even more vicious than animals, and what better place for them to hide than the spirit woods?

This time they fanned out within earshot of each other. Han Jinlong had specially prepared some whistles for the excursion. They had two settings—five-hundred-foot routine whistle, and ten-thousand-foot emergency whistle. Anyone with a matching whistle would be able to hear them, as well as the general direction it came from.

Gong Lan and An Hao paired up once more. After walking

a hundred paces forward, she blew a short-range whistle, confirming that everything was safe. They continued for four hours before finally taking a break.

Their lunch consisted of rations of dried meat, stale bread, and dried fruit. It was during their quiet lunch that Gong Lan noticed something strange.

"An Hao, have you heard any birds or squirrels since we came into the woods?" she asked.

The man paused and listened. He then frowned and shook his head. "I can't say I remember hearing them." He looked more than a little worried. Yesterday's events had been traumatizing.

After completing their break, they continued their exploration, and the sounds of whistles continued. This time they tried to keep as quiet as possible, to make out the sounds of local wildlife. All they heard was the gentle rustling of tree branches and some overgrown grass.

What they saw wasn't any more reassuring. The trees here were strange. Red sap leaked from their thin bark, making it seem like the trees were crying tears of blood.

"Is it just me, or does it smell like blood?" An Hao said softly.

Gong Lan looked at him helplessly. She *always* smelled blood. She put her hand to her lips, indicating that he should be quiet. She then held the whistle to her lips and drew out her saber.

Gong Lan's group wasn't the only suspicious one. Han Jinlong was on high alert. Since the warning from Brother Zhang, he was constantly probing outward with his spiritual force, looking for any arrays that might potentially detonate or trap them.

The sudden smell of blood worried him. *Is it the trees?* he thought. No, he was familiar with the red sap from these trees. The smell wasn't coming from them. Four hours later, they still hadn't found any sign of anyone. They were now in the middle of the woods. The smell of blood intensified with every step, and he hoped they wouldn't find them remnants of yet another massacre.

After all, he hadn't had time to properly grieve for his nieces and nephews, whose corpses he'd found in the village. He still held on to some faint hope that his eldest niece and sister were still alive. Their corpses hadn't been found in the village, but he wasn't sure whether this was a fortune or a curse. However, hope was all he had. His own wife had passed away long ago, and he had no children of his own.

His thoughts were interrupted by a loud whistle coming from the west. He dashed in the direction of the whistling without any hesitation, only to find a large pool of blood. It was fresh human blood, spilled less than a half day ago, judging by the smell of it.

Han Jinlong saw Gong Lan out of the corner of his eyes. She was clearly seething with rage.

I need to keep an eye on that firecracker. Who knows when she'll lose it.

Only one thought ran through Gong Lan's mind. *Just how many innocent people died to fill such a large pool of blood?*

Her hands gripped her sabers tightly as her blood boiled. She slashed her arm out of reflex with one of her sabers. The pain brought her back to her senses, and she started assessing the situation.

They were situated in a circular clearing surrounded by pine trees. The various holes in the ground indicated that the clearing had been prepared specially for the occasion. But why would the rebels go through all that effort?

It was then that she noticed several trails of blood that ran from the central pool. She traced the lines to smaller pools, where stones could barely be seen on the surface. The strange markings on these stones that caught her attention. Were those... runes?

"Master Han!" she yelled out hurriedly. The man jumped over to her in an instant.

"What is it, little one?" he asked.

She answered by pointing to a small pool right beside them. His eyes narrowed as he realized what was happening. Just as he was about to give the order to evacuate everyone from the vicinity, the eerie quietness was interrupted by vicious howls and growls. The man's keen eyesight focused toward the outside of the clearing, where he saw hundreds of shaded figures in every direction.

"Shit. Everyone, group together and prepare to defend our position!"

Chaos ensued as the hundred mercenaries scrambled toward him. They were so scared that he had to physically push himself out toward the edge of the group. "We need to make a circle! I want half of all able-bodied cultivators on the outside, and half on the inside. This is going to be a long fight, and we need to preserve as much energy as possible. When you get tired, step back inside the circle, and someone will relieve you. Be strong, and we'll somehow survive!"

Within a few breaths, their hastily assembled formation was attacked from all sides by hundreds of weak first-level spirit wolves.

Chapter 24: Breaking the Formation

S *lash. Hack. Slash.*

Gong Lan was numb to killing, and she used the rhythm of slaughter to keep focused on the task at hand. With every beast she decapitated, her bloody aura grew stronger and stronger. It had been a few hours since they had started fighting, and only three quarters of their group remained. Yet the tide of beasts seemed endless. She wanted nothing more than to jump out and kill every single beast out there, but she forced herself to keep in formation.

Just a little more. She continued hacking away, her killing intent growing stronger and stronger. *Break!* A sudden surge of energy flooded her meridians as her bloody qi forced open the barrier in her dantian, expanding her qi lake into an ocean. The bloody water qi seethed in excitement as she advanced to the seventh level of qi condensation. She began slashing even more wildly, occasionally throwing out blades of bloody saber qi toward ferocious spirit swine.

The wolves had died long ago thanks to their firm combat

formation. The normally docile spirit deer had attacked after them, attempting to pierce them with their antlers and trample them with their hooves. Countless demonic birds followed, and finally, the spirit swine.

She let out a shout as she spotted one of their leaders, quickly darting out of the protective formation and closing in for a kill. The leader swine had eight horns instead of four. She heard Han Jinlong curse as she left the formation, but she knew that he was too preoccupied with protecting the weaker cultivators huddled behind him.

Her blades danced and drew blood with every swing. The spirit swine tore open her tender skin with its tusks several times, yet she was unconcerned. She felt boundless strength flow through her each time her blades drew blood. This was one of the many advantages of the Blood World Scripture. Every time she drew blood, her wounds would heal. Yet forsaking her defenses meant that if she didn't kill, she wouldn't survive.

Many of the swine retreated in fear as they saw her approaching. That was fine by her. She simply dispatched a few unfortunate swine in passing and continued to head toward her main objective—the leader. The dire swine was a sixth-level spirit beast, yet it trembled in fear as she approached it. It fought back tooth and nail, deflecting one blow after another with its tough skin and sharp horns. Eventually it succumbed to exhaustion. Its fall weakened the other nearby spirit swine, relieving the pressure on the remainder of the group.

How in the heavens are we going to survive this? she thought as she danced about and decapitated a few more swine, moving back to the group. She wasn't silly enough to stay exposed on the outside now that the leader was gone. After all, the next wave of spirit beasts was coming soon.

We can't keep going on like this.

Han Jinlong hadn't been relaxing this whole time. Given the situation, he truly wished that he hadn't cheated to pass formation array class. Despite his numerous attempts at damaging the formation that seemed to be summoning the unreasonable amount of spirit beasts, he hadn't managed to dent it. Each character on the stones bathed in blood appeared to be indestructible, despite his foundation-establishment cultivation base.

He could easily escape by himself, but that would mean abandoning everyone else. He would have ordered them to flee, but the repeated waves showed no openings. He would rather die than abandon his comrades. His hammer flew out once more toward a nearby rune, just in case the formation had weakened over time. This was wishful thinking—he could tell that the formation had only strengthened due to the accumulation of blood in the clearing.

We need to do something soon. Before it's too late.

Gong Lan was now at peak exhaustion. Even her Blood World Scripture could no longer support her consumption of qi and vitality. The tenth wave consisted of spirit snakes. These beasts were tricky to handle, since their small forms were difficult to target without area of effect techniques. *If I had enough blood, I would bathe the battlefield in a thousand sabers.*

She cleaved two snakes in half before they had a chance to bite her pretty face. Their blood splashed into her eyes, painting her field of vision in red. As she looked up in the sky, she saw a moon that was almost full. The moon was red because of the film of blood in her eyes.

Is this the blood moon? She laughed wildly at the sudden enlightenment. *Why does it need to be my own blood? I have tons right here!*

With that thought, she became a maelstrom of death. With each strike, she whipped up a huge amount of blood that was pooled at their heels, forming vicious red saber light in the process. It swept outward and hacked fifty spirit snakes apart.

She laughed wildly at the revelation and ran toward the center of the lake of blood, which went halfway up her thighs. "Take this, you bloody snakes!"

She continued sweeping out her sabers, throwing larger and larger blades of blood into the distance. Each blade sliced dozens of snakes into ribbons. After all the snakes around her were cleared, she didn't stop. She kept sweeping out larger and larger blades, until a literal storm of bloody blades rained down on the army of countless snakes outside the clearing.

Each wave Gong Lan dispatched held only one one-thousandth of the total count, but the defenders noticed a substantial decrease in the pressure they were withstanding.

"Get out of the way, quickly!" Han Jinlong shouted. The cultivators realized that the only snakes remaining were behind Gong Lan, who was madly swinging away with her eyes closed. They ran away just in time, dodging one of her many attacks that tore apart the remaining legion.

Han Jinlong was sweating profusely. He was tired. Most of the men and women had taken rests, but he hadn't dared to. Any sign of weakness might cause their formation to collapse. Off in the distance, he finally saw a ray of hope.

Is the formation weakening? Is the pool's volume going down because she's throwing the blood out from the clearing?

At first, he was very enthusiastic. Until he realized that their enemies had thinned considerably. He quickly made the decision to relocate their squad, lest they be caught in the crossfire. Soon enough, the snakes were gone. But Gong Lan didn't stop. She turned her dreadful gaze toward the remaining cultivators with a cruel smile on her face.

Shit, has she gone crazy now? Just like my old friend...

But he didn't want to her to stop just yet. He was more than capable of knocking her out, but he could feel the formation weakening with every swing.

What to do. He made the decision to use himself as bait. "Everyone, run south three hundred paces! I'll hold her back!"

At this point, the entire group was filled with dread. Their goddess of battle had turned against them! At Han Jinlong's instruction, they darted south. Han Jinlong kept fifty paces away, ducking and weaving to avoid her bloody saber light. He didn't deflect them; he expertly maneuvered between them.

"Why doesn't he knock her out?" one cultivator asked. "He's a foundation establishment elder, so he has to be able to do it."

"Just trust Master Han. He knows what he's doing," a

nearby cultivator rebuked. The dissidents went quiet, and the remaining half of the mercenaries just stood there and enjoyed the show.

Just a little more, thought Han Jinlong. Fortunately, he had cultivated both his body and qi. His endurance was unmatched, and he could simply shrug off the few hits that struck him.

Before long, the last of the blood left the pool, causing the formation to dim and lose its power. Han Jinlong immediately darted out and hit each point of the formation with his spirit hammer. The rocks used as formation points crumbled to dust within a dozen breaths.

Gong Lan, as though realizing that no more blood was available, let out a fierce yell and darted toward Han Jinlong. Fortunately, he was experienced in this type of thing. He darted behind her and quickly chopped at a pressure point on her neck, causing her to crumple to the bloody forest floor.

Hong Xin was lying in her bed, flipping through one of her favorite books. It was a book about romance, where a rich man found a poor girl and showered her with love and affection. His family, upset at the disruption to their plans, threatened to kill the girl's family unless she left him voluntarily. After agonizing over her choice, she decided to do what was best for her family and cut off all contact with him.

Yet she soon discovered that she had a secret admirer. He sent her flowers and love letters, and she finally decided that maybe life isn't so unfair, and that there was someone out there for her after all. She secretly met with the man under cover of darkness, only to discover the rich man. He had stolen his family fortune and ran away with her and her family. They lived happily ever after.

I wish I was in that fairy tale. I wish Wang Jun would run away with me. She'd thought this every day for the past few days, but reality was cold and cruel. After he cut off relations with her, she had never heard from him again. Whenever she asked her brother, Hong Ling, he simply shook his head and said she shouldn't ask such questions. *When did my own brother become so cruel to me?*

She heard creaking downstairs, indicating that someone had just arrived. Likely Hong Ling, given the sounds of his footsteps. She imagined him moving through the living room to the kitchen. Judging by the sounds of cutlery and the warm welcome, dinner was about to begin.

Soon she heard footsteps heading up the stairs. Three soft knocks were followed by the sweet sound of her mother's voice. "May I come in?" she said.

"Fine," Hong Xin replied. Her mother came in with a bowl of food.

"Why don't you come downstairs for supper?" she asked sweetly. "Your father misses you terribly."

"I don't want to go. *He's* downstairs." She ignored her mother and continued reading her book. Her mother shook her head and walked back downstairs, where the rest of the family continued their meal. After some time, she heard her father's voice.

"You're heading out for weeks? Why the hell do you work yourself to the bone for this *young master*? He was so cruel to your sister!" Hong Jin was clearly upset. She heard the sound of utensils being set down, after which she heard her brother's faint voice. To better hear the conversation, she gently opened her door and tiptoed out of her room toward the flight of stairs.

"It's a lot more complicated than you can imagine. Do you have any idea what's going on?" he said coldly to his father.

"Do I need to know what's going on? He hurt my daughter, and I don't want you working for him!" he retorted.

"Did he really hurt her?" Hong Ling replied. "Well, let me tell you a little bit about my upcoming business trip, and maybe you'll change your mind. This time, we're going to the capital to pursue two people in court. The first one is Zhou Li, the oracle's apprentice, and his uncle, the head of the Song Kingdom Alchemists Association. We'll be accompanied by three foundation-establishment elders in case the Zhou family attempts to assassinate us.

"Meanwhile, we'll also be facing off against the crown prince and his chief consort, Zhou Jia. This will be extremely dangerous, and I'm frightened at the potential repercussions. Yet the young master needs me and every able-bodied assistant he has. It's a good opportunity for promotion, and I'm going to take it.

"Now, given the danger, do you think he's being considerate or inconsiderate to Xin Er? Can she even defend herself? She knows nothing about politics, nothing about intrigue. Her cultivation is worthless in the capital. Meanwhile, he'll be fighting with his life on the line, to the point where he needs three elders to defend him. Have you thought that maybe he is distancing himself to protect her?"

She heard the sounds of a chair being pulled out, and her brother's footsteps heading toward the front entrance. "I'm sorry for yelling, Father," said Hong Ling. "I'll ask him to personally come here and apologize after this matter is over. That, or he can take my resignation."

The door closed. She now realized where the problem lay. She just wasn't good enough for him. It wasn't that she was poor, but that she was weak. She couldn't defend herself, and she knew nothing of politics and finance. In short, she was useless to him. This harsh revelation caused her to burst into tears.

That night, she cried herself to sleep. Only this time it was for a different reason.

Gong Lan woke to the sound of running water. The smell of blood hadn't faded, but she could tell from the absence of sticky blood on her skin that someone had washed her. She winced as she finally sat herself up and looked around. It was just as she imagined—she had been laid down on the rocky shore by a creek in the forest. Someone had left a blanket on her as she slept.

"How are you feeling, little girl?" a deep voice sounded out from above. She looked up to see Han Jinlong sitting leisurely on a tree branch. It was one of the few deciduous trees in the forest, as only the rich soil and ample water in the area could support them over conifers.

Gong Lan struggled to stand up and stretch her lithe waist. She felt stinging pain all over her body, likely from the cuts that covered her fair skin from the neck down. Shaking her head, she popped one of the three healing pills that Zhang Yifeng had given them at the start of their journey. A warm current of energy suffused her body, and the cuts on her arms, legs, and torso began healing rapidly.

Good pill.

After her quick stretch, she looked back up to the fatherly figure in the tree. "I've felt worse. What happened in the fight? I must have passed out from blood loss." Her cheeks flushed red with embarrassment as she imagined her moment of weakness.

"I didn't figure you'd remember," Han Jinlong said wryly. "After the swine and just as the snakes began attacking, you started laughing madly. You rushed out toward the pool of blood and began unleashing a blood-related technique. It was extremely powerful and dispatched countless low-level enemies. You seemed to have limitless energy as you drew from the blood in the pool.

"It was *very* effective, in fact, that you single-handedly dispatched all of the snakes. Then I evacuated everyone just in time for them to dodge your blood technique and avoid any fatalities. Afterward, I had to dance around you for a quarter hour until you fully depleted the blood pool.

"Coincidentally, this was the weakness of the formation. Once you depleted the blood, I was able to destroy the formation eyes and deactivate the formation. In the eyes of many, you're a hero," the man concluded gravely.

Gong Lan's face flushed again. This time, it was due to shame. *What if Han Jinlong hadn't been there? Would I have killed everyone in the group? I don't remember anything past those spirit swine.*

Seeing that she was deep in thought, Han Jinlong didn't say anything. He continued to look at the river, watching it flow by. Every so often, the current carried a small piece of wood, which eventually got trapped by a beaver dam downstream.

"I'm a monster," she whispered. Tears streaked down face, because she knew that she had done this to herself. *She* had been the one who asked her brother for help, and then followed his advice. Han Jinlong's hard expression softened as he observed her self-deprecating behavior.

"You're not a monster. Yet," he said. "But you can't keep treading down this path. Let me tell you a story. I once had a good friend, you see. He was just like you—someone who followed an unconventional path. His path was one of slaughter, and he lived to drink the blood of his enemies. He began following that path because when he was young, his village was attacked by bandits. They killed his parents and the other villagers, and he was only able to escape with a girl his age. After that, he dreamed of vengeance every night.

"He eventually married the girl, and for decades, she kept urging him to reconsider the path he'd chosen. However, I need to give credit where it's due—his path was effective. He saved me three times, and many of my close friends owe their lives to him. He was able to continue this way for three decades."

"And then he died," Han Jinlong whispered softly.

Gong Lan had stopped crying and was paying close attention. "How did he die?" she asked.

Han Jinlong paused for a few moments before continuing. "He died in my arms. We were on a mission together, and this one was his breaking point. His wife was with us as well. She was a healer, you see, because she was always concerned for his safety. First, he hacked down his best friend. Then he hacked down another, and finally, he killed his wife as she jumped on him to stop him from hurting anyone else. I was left with no other choice. I killed him.

"As he laid in my arms, he regained a brief moment of clarity. He confessed that he always regretted taking that road. But the further he went, the harder it was to stop." After finishing, Han Jinlong hopped down from the tree and began walking toward the village.

"It's not too late for you," he said while walking. "You're not suited for this path. If you already can't take it at your age, it's time you stop. For the sake of everyone you hold dear. And especially for yourself."

Chapter 25: Caravan

Noon.

Cha Ming's group, under the direction of Zhang Yifeng, was currently stationed behind a grassy hill. The few stronger individuals, Cha Ming included, were crouched down at the top of the hill. They were observing a peculiar situation. A caravan full of prisoners was currently headed toward Jade Spring. The large carts laden with cages were being escorted by dozens of burly men bearing leather armor and cruel-looking sabers.

The situation wasn't peculiar because of the caravan—human trafficking was the least of the rebels' crimes. Rather, it was the timing of the caravan that had them on edge. What were the odds that a caravan happened to be waiting for them so close to Jade Spring, given their recent activities and the meticulous traps they had encountered?

It was clearly a trap, no one disputed this. Yet Zhang Yifeng and half of the stronger individuals looked torn about the situation. The other half were mercenaries who did not have strong attachments to any potential prisoners.

"To attack or not to attack…" Master Zhang muttered. His words made the mercenaries ashamed, because he was clearly considering their welfare. Cha Ming could understand their uneasiness, but the events of the past few days had left his heart seething with rage. He couldn't stop himself from speaking out.

"Master Zhang, even though this is clearly a trap, I believe that your participation assures success," Cha Ming said. "What I'm worried about is that all the traps we've collectively encountered have something in common—they are delaying us. However, there are some traps that a cultivator must walk into knowingly, lest they regret it for the rest of their lives.

"Why don't we try this? Our small group of elite cultivators could rush out to fight them, while the rest of the cultivators wait behind this hill. That way we wouldn't expose those with lower cultivation bases to the trap. In addition, I am willing to supply these eight Cloud Step talismans to those of us who haven't reached foundation establishment. I have specially prepared them during our downtime, and these sixth-grade talismans offer a sharp increase in speed for a short time. They are ideal single-use items for fleeing if we encounter danger. In the event that nothing happens, you can all return these to me."

Zhang Yifeng shot Cha Ming a grateful look and then looked at the wider group. "Very well. I will compensate our young friend for his efforts. Additionally, I will also supply you with a seventh-grade healing pill, which you can use to restore yourself from serious injuries, including some internal organ damage. They will even allow a severed limb to be reattached if the limb is still intact. If you don't need to use them, you can keep them as additional compensation."

With these words, ten bottles of pills flew out toward them. Three of them went to Cha Ming. Two of the bottles were clearly meant as compensation for his talismans. None of the cultivators shot him any jealous looks, however, as his actions had just increased their chances of survival and had netted them a tidy profit. He even suspected that, before this moment, many of the mercenaries had considered cancelling their contract and forfeiting 75% of the compensation.

After a few quick instructions, the small group of nine cultivators broke off from the main group and stealthily approached the caravan.

"Number Three, why did we suddenly need to move the merchandise today? And in broad daylight, at that? Don't you know that we are on high alert against potential intruders?" one large man asked another.

"You'd best learn to shut up, Number Six," Number Three said, berating his slightly smaller companion. "The master's orders are never to be questioned. If he wants us to move merchandise in the desert and wearing nothing but our underwear, that's what we'll do."

A small child began crying in the back of one of the cages. "Mommy, what's going to happen to us? I don't want to stay in this cage. I want to run around and play. And I'm soooo thirsty." A woman quickly reached out to him and covered his mouth.

"Stop complaining, Xiaohong, or they'll beat you too," she whispered. "You saw what happened to the little girl yesterday, right? They kicked her until she stopped moving. You need to be a good boy and behave."

But the feared beating didn't come. Instead, they heard breaking bones and clashing blades.

After days of traps and no enemies to speak of, the elite cultivators were finally able to let loose and blow off some steam. Cha Ming was like a god of war, breaking several bones with each strike of his staff. He used Mountain Stance to root himself to the ground and increased the weight of his staff by fivefold. Each strike took a life.

As expected, roars of rage thundered as a hundred figures rushed out from the woods in ambush. Seeing this, Zhang Yifeng took the initiative and broke away from the remainder of the group to stop the assault. Cha Ming and Huxian followed suit while the others continued clearing away the caravan guards.

While Cha Ming and Huxian were good in one-on-one combat, their supplemental skills made them extremely effective in dealing with large groups of enemies. The former surrounded himself in a snowflake formation, slowing down his opponent's responses while he beat away at them with his heavy, elongated staff. Sometimes he was even able to mow down several enemies with a single blow.

Meanwhile, Huxian showed off his abilities by activating his purification skill. The light emanating from him was particularly effective against this group of bloodthirsty individuals. In fact, several bandits roared and transformed in response. Their figures grew, and an evil aura shot out of one in ten bandits. They let out howls of rage, cursing Huxian as though he was their natural enemy.

Huxian seemed unconcerned with their reaction. For each monstrosity that came, he struck one down. Missing limbs were not enough to deter their assault, and some even went so far as to self-detonate to eliminate Huxian. These explosions barely scratched him, as his aura of light was able to restrain the savage qi that burst out from each figure.

The battle ended after an incense time. There was no suspense, and they had not lost any of their cultivators. Had they overestimated these enemies due to the multiple traps they had encountered? Or was there more to this ambush than met the eye?

The eight cultivators circled the area before confirming that there were indeed no enemy cultivators present in the vicinity. Only then did they join Zhang Yifeng and unlock the prisoners. They ushered them back to the hill where the other troops were stationed, because they feared that their most vulnerable members might have been attacked from the rear while they were preoccupied. These worries were unfounded, however. Everyone was safe.

Yet Cha Ming could not shake an uneasy feeling in the back of his mind. Something is wrong. Is it the prisoners? The prisoners were currently surrounded by the weaker mercenaries, their wounds were being tended, and they were being given hot meals. Each of the freed prisoners looked extremely grateful, and he could see no menacing expressions on any of them.

"Could it really be so simple?" Cha Ming asked Zhang Yifeng.

"That seems to be the case," Zhang Yifeng replied. "However, I can't help but feel uneasy. If the enemy set a trap for us, they should have prepared better. Are they just trying to buy time by slowing us down with all of these prisoners?"

Cha Ming wasn't sure, so he went back to talk with the various prisoners. A grateful little boy was running around without a shirt. He was clearly injured, as his chest was fully bandaged. Another young man was seated at the fire and eating stew. His abdomen was also freshly bandaged, which made him applaud the efforts of the healers in the group.

"I didn't realize that we'd brought so many fresh bandages with us on this expedition," he said to a nearby spirit doctor. "The healers were quite thoughtful." The man shook his head self-deprecatingly.

"Actually, we forgot to bring any at all. Most wounds can be cured with potions and pills, so we didn't think to bring anything for so many injured people. Thankfully, their jailors were not as cruel as we had imagined. They made sure to bandage their prisoners' wounds for fear of losing any of their 'merchandise,'" the man elaborated with disgust.

Cha Ming frowned. "Did you remove the bandages to inspect and treat their injuries?" he said.

"No need. We just gave them some healing pills, which is enough to heal any of their wounds within the hour. They'll naturally take them off themselves," the spirit doctor said. He sounded as if this was common sense, and the look he gave Cha Ming said he was puzzled at Cha Ming's concern.

Nearby, the young boy was scratching at his chest. "Momma, it itches so much. Can I take them off?" the boy said.

The lady, presumably his mother, reprimanded him. "You can take them off after one hour. The doctor said that the wound will heal faster if you don't take them off. You need to be a good boy and not cause any trouble."

Cha Ming approached the little boy, and his mother and greeted them with a smile. They recognized him as one of their nine saviors, so they quickly bowed in thanks. "Do you mind if I look at your boy's wound? I happen to be a healer, so I might be able to help him get better quicker. Besides, it's safest to look if the bandages are uncomfortable. The woman begrudgingly nodded and gave Cha Ming permission to peel the bandage off the little boy's chest.

As he unwrapped the bandage, a cruel, blood-red cut was revealed on his chest.

What kind of monsters are these bandits to scar a little child like this? It was apparent that the healing potion was having little effect, as the skin hadn't even started closing over. Instead, it continuously poured out small amounts of fresh blood.

It was only after unwrapping the fifth pass of bandages that Cha Ming's heart skipped a beat. The cut looked familiar. He hastened the process of removing the bandages. His expression turned ugly as he saw a blood-red runic character beginning to glow. There were four characters on his chest that said: "flesh" and "explosion." It was surrounded by an array containing four bloody runes representing "healing trigger." The healing medicines had been effective, but they also meant they'd killed these poor people. The pills had activated the runes on the little boy's chest.

"Everyone, it's a trap! Get out now! Leave the prisoners!" Cha Ming yelled and darted away with Huxian. Everyone was confused, as he had been the greatest advocate for rescuing the imprisoned villagers. They hesitated, but not for long. The strongest among them were overcome with a feeling of crisis, a sixth sense accumulated over multiple life and death experiences. Zhang Yifeng never felt any such crisis, however. This trap was no threat to him, after all.

Less than half of the cultivators managed to escape before multiple prisoners exploded. Their bodies burst into pieces like cheap pottery. Limbs and blood sprayed everywhere, and the weaker cultivators who were a tad too slow were caught up in the deadly blast.

The sudden impact caused Cha Ming to close his eyes and cover his ears. He came to his senses just in time to hear the wailing of injured and dying mercenaries, many of whom were missing limbs. The lucky ones had been killed in the blast.

It was a trap after all, a trap that they couldn't help but walk into. It had been perfectly planned, and perfectly executed. If not for Cha Ming's last-minute warning, most of the remaining group would have perished in the explosion. Instead, a quarter of them had died and a quarter had been wounded beyond recognition. None of the prisoners survived.

"I can't stand any of those pompous asses in the city," Gou Dan complained for the twentieth time. "They always say they're pursuing the pinnacle of their craft. Meanwhile, they sell off their 'exquisite goods' for one and a half times the market price in other cities. It's just a scheme for making money. It's a conspiracy, and they're all behind it."

Feng Ming massaged his temple as he fought back the urge to beat some sense into his annoying road companion. "Why don't you just go to another city and buy weapons there?" he asked. He immediately regretted speaking, as these words only served to agitate the ugly man.

"That's what I'm talking about. It's extortion! The nearest city is three days away, and *no one* can get that much time off. They're taking advantage of their location, which is unethical. Further, everyone looks down on you in town if you have an ugly weapon. I was forced to fork over a fortune for this high-grade longsword," Gou Dan said as he unsheathed his blade. He looked at it in disgust.

Feng Ming shook his head. "Just keep your complaints to yourself. The horses are traveling slowly because of the bad atmosphere." He nudged his horse forward in response.

"Wait up!" the man called out from behind him. Feng Ming heard his horse trotting to catch up. Just as he was about to look over, however, his horse caught its foot in a gopher hole. He heard a sickening crack as he started falling with the horse.

I thought I was only supposed to have good *luck now,* he thought. That is, until he felt a small chunk of his hair go missing as Gou Dan's longsword missed his neck.

Feng Ming reacted quickly. He pounced off the back of the falling horse and landed on his feet. He then took out his spear, which he held out menacingly to face off against his mounted opponent.

"You lucky sonofabitch. You'd be dead if it wasn't for that gopher hole. Oh well, I can always kill you the old-fashioned way. Lord's orders, after all." With that, the man wasted no time and charged toward Feng Ming. Feng Ming couldn't find any openings, so he dodged to the side, barely avoiding the horse's hooves.

Gou Dan snorted and readied his mount for another charge. Just as the horse approached, Feng Ming decided to change tactics. A hot sandstorm surrounded him, causing the horse to suddenly raise its front hooves and neigh. Gou Dan barely managed to hold on.

This was the opening Feng Ming needed. His lightly armored figure suddenly emerged from the cloud of sand, his spear sweeping out in a wide arc. It gracefully avoided the man's shoulder armor and helmet, slashing the man's tender neck. The horse ran away in a panic. It was then that Feng Ming realized that all the remaining horses had either been killed or had run away. Gou Dan had left nothing to chance.

What shitty luck, Feng Ming thought. *What am I supposed to do now?* Then he saw a small farm in the distance. It was a typical farm with pigs, chickens, and a few cows. And horses.

"I guess I *am* lucky," he thought out loud. He strapped his spear to his back and started running toward the little farm. In no time at all, he explained the situation and quickly bought the man's fastest horse at ten times the market price. Now he had a choice to make.

The county lord clearly doesn't want me to deliver this news to my father. It's like he's trying to buy time. Will it be too late if I head over to Green Leaf City now? Is Fairweather in danger?

He pondered this for a quarter hour before deciding to flip a coin. "I'll just trust my luck," he mumbled. With that thought, he flipped a golden coin in the air.

The result caused him to question whether he was lucky or cursed.

Chapter 26: Jade Spring

It took the better part of a day to clean up the aftermath of the exploding slaves. The mercenaries who'd survived consumed healing pills, and Zhang Yifeng treated as many as he could. Even though Cha Ming expected to be blamed for the incident, no one dared say a single word. After all, who among them could have imagined that the enemy was so heartless?

After tending to the wounded, they gathered what remained of their companions and the innocent slaves and buried them all communally in a pit, as it was impossible to match the pieces together for a proper burial. It was all they could do to prevent wild beasts from defiling their bodies.

That evening, no one was in the mood to eat anything. They set up camp near the location of the explosion. Fortunately, a geomancer had joined their group, and they were able to set up crude earthen barriers to strengthen their camp's defenses. Twenty percent of the group was out on patrol, and the rest hovered around a crackling fire. Even the most helpless souls could find comfort in flickering flames.

Cha Ming returned to his camp early after obtaining an exemption from Master Zhang. Instead of keeping watch, he spent all his remaining time crafting low-level talismans, which might come in handy in the upcoming battle. He had until the remaining troops arrived from their patrol to complete his work.

He exhausted himself after only three hours of crafting. Fortunately, he had obtained pills from Master Zhang to replenish his spiritual strength. Recovering qi was much easier, especially when he had the assistance of his formation plate. The night passed by uneventfully. He continued throughout the morning and was only interrupted when Gong Lan's group and the Ling brothers arrived. At noon, one of the mercenaries came to summon Cha Ming to Master Zhang's tent to discuss tactics for storming Jade Spring.

Only fourteen people were present in the meeting room, including Cha Ming, Gong Lan, Master Zhang, Master Han, two of the Ling brothers, and eight others. Huxian wasn't included in the count. Not that he had anything to contribute besides guarding the entrance to the tent.

"It's got to be a trap. Given everything that we've seen, how can it not be?" Han Jinlong said in a loud voice. He was very imposing, and none of the qi-condensation cultivators dared speak up.

"What if they're just on their last legs with no remaining options? None of the traps they laid before managed to completely stop us. This could just be their last-ditch effort to frighten us off," Zhang Yifeng said.

"And why would they keep all of the captured civilians in a pen in the middle of town? Have you forgotten the exploding slaves already?" Han Jinlong pressed on.

"How dare you?" Zhang Yifeng exploded in rage. The argument continued, and Cha Ming had no choice but to find Gong Lan to fill him in on the details.

Apparently a scouting party had investigated Jade Spring, and they discovered the city wide open, with the prisoners in plain sight. No guards could be seen on the walls; it was as though the city was declaring their surrender. The situation reminded Cha Ming of Zhuge Liang's empty city[8] ploy, which allowed him to hold off Sima Yi's advance.

Still, he couldn't argue against the effectiveness of such a tactic. There were many traps that could be used after baiting an enemy behind a city's walls. While Jade Spring's walls were made of wood, scaling them was no easy task for lesser cultivators. If they encountered something like the inferno trap in Crystal Meadows, most of their members and the prisoners would be roasted alive.

"How about destroying the possibility of a trap?" Cha

---

[8] The empty city stratagem was used by Zhuge Liang when he was faced with a sudden assault by Sima Yi on a city he was defending. His troops were too far away to assist, so he ordered his men to open the city gates as the enemy advanced while he sat calmly in the palace and played his zither in plain sight of the enemy. Sima Yi, knowing that Zhuge Liang was a master strategist like himself, could not help but think it was a trap. After much hesitation, he ultimately left the city and did not attack. It could also be argued that this was a self-serving move as well—with Zhuge Liang still alive, the king that Sima Yi served would still have a use for him. This eventually gave Sima Yi enough time to organize his rebellion.

Ming said suddenly. His weak voice attracted the attention of the nearby cultivators, who felt oppressed by the might of two foundation-establishment cultivators.

"Can you please elaborate, young friend Cha Ming?" Zhou Yifeng asked. Cha Ming figured that his contributions earlier in their adventure had earned their admiration, despite the setback with the exploding prisoners.

"Well, it's clearly easier to defend a city while taking advantage of the walls. This tactic is effective even against cultivators. Even foundation-establishment cultivators like Master Zhang and Master Han cannot fly; they can only rely on magic swords to hover up to ten feet above the ground. Meanwhile, any archers or cultivators with long-distance techniques could attack us with impunity as we gradually scale the walls.

"Now, it's tempting to directly enter the city since the gate is open—after all, it would save us a lot of trouble. However, if the gates shut after we enter, or if they want to forcibly hold us inside, we will be surrounded, and it will be difficult for us to escape. That is why I propose that we... break down the walls!"

Everyone nodded as they heard the suggestion. Cha Ming continued, seeing the acknowledgment from the group.

"Completely destroying the walls is difficult. In addition, giving them too much time to respond may endanger the prisoners. However, destroying three sections of the wall to simplify escape is quite feasible. Instead of charging through the gates, we could have Master Zhang and Master Yifeng burst in through the walls on the sides," he explained. "After all, they are experts in playing with fire, and their foundation-establishment experts would not have time to react to the sudden assault from two sides. Meanwhile, I could also create another hole in the back of the city."

The two Ling brothers frowned before the eldest asked, "How exactly are you going to create a hole in those wooden walls? They may be made of wood, but they are quite thick."

In response to this question, Cha Ming smiled and took out a thick wad of talismans.

The Ling brothers looked confused, but Zhang Yifeng and Han Jinlong were experienced and recognized them in an instant. Zhang Yifeng nodded and said, "You do indeed possess that ability. I am in support of this plan. What do you think, Brother Han?"

Han Jinlong looked a little reluctant. He looked toward Cha Ming and asked, "What if this is what they expect, and they ambush a single group with their full force?" he asked.

"That isn't a problem," Cha Ming said. "Regardless of our success, we will retreat immediately after damaging the walls, and we will enter together through the entrance at the back of the city. This way, they will be unable to divide and conquer our forces."

Han Jinlong accepted this explanation.

The following discussion proceeded smoothly, and the forces were divided according to their remaining composition. Cha Ming and Gong Lan ended up in the same group as the Ling brothers this time. Due to the absence of a foundation-establishment elder, their team was stacked with many high-level qi condensation experts.

Did you find anything? Cha Ming asked Huxian mentally. The little fox shook his head as he exited the shadows. They had chosen nighttime to invade to avoid detection near the city walls.

I didn't see anyone on top of the walls, and I didn't find anyone outside the buildings, either. Except for those prisoners. It's much too quiet. Is there really no one in this city?

We can't relax, Cha Ming replied. *Each group has been ambushed twice, and the Ling brothers suffered the greatest loss. Only two of the three brothers survived, and they only managed to come back with three other cultivators, one of whom was crippled. Both Wu Jin and Sima Qian are dead. Now, are you sure you didn't see any symbols, flags, or impressions in the ground? Anything that feels or smells like a talisman, formation, or trap?*

I'm sure I didn't see anything like that. The one who made the formation would need to be much stronger than me if I can't detect anything, Huxian replied smugly.

That's exactly what I'm afraid of, Cha Ming replied.

After finishing their conversation, Cha Ming walked up to the two remaining Ling brothers. "Huxian didn't seen anything suspicious, which worries me. But it doesn't look like there are guards outside the buildings or on the wall. Still, it's best to be cautious and follow the plan."

The Ling brothers nodded. The older one motioned for everyone to come together. "All right everyone, just follow the plan. Everyone needs to stay beside Cha Ming and cover him until we get to the wall. Scatter when he says scatter, or else I won't give a rat's ass if anyone's ears are blown off. Move!"

They arrived beside the wall without any problems. Cha Ming withdrew the wad of talismans from his bag of holding and started slapping them onto the wall one by one. Each of these talismans was a third-level Lesser Fire Blast talisman that Cha Ming had prepared in case anything needed to be demolished, or if many weaker assailants became a problem. Soon over fifty talismans covered a ten-foot-by-ten-foot square on the wall. Not a single square inch remained uncovered.

"All right, only one incense time, and we can blow this wall up." Their group waited, worrying, hoping that the enemy wouldn't spot them. No one came, and to everyone's relief, the eldest Ling brother, whose name was Ling Tong, nodded to Cha Ming.

"Scatter!" Cha Ming shouted before slapping another talisman on the wall. This was a time-delayed talisman. When he'd originally made the blast talismans, he hadn't expected to detonate fifty at once. The time-delayed activation talisman was effectively a three-second timer that he'd made immediately after the meeting.

Not wanting to get caught up in the blast, the group of thirty cultivators quickly retreated toward the back of the wall, where Han Jinlong would blast open a hole. They would all charge into the city as one group, lest the enemy attempt to divide and conquer them. Only Huxian stayed behind, hiding in the shadows.

Boom!

A large explosion sounded by the retreating group. Cha Ming and the rest ran toward another similar blast, and they were quickly joined by Huxian. Huxian seemed extremely excited as he reported the blast to Cha Ming.

Brother Cha Ming, that was amazing! There's like a twenty-foot piece of wall missing now, and some of the houses inside the city even collapsed because of the explosion!

"No need to worry, there's a twenty-foot gap in the wall.

Things went as planned," Cha Ming relayed to the Ling brothers. The eldest brother let out a sigh of relief as he led the cultivators to join Han Jinlong's group. The three groups met without any suspense. What surprised everyone was the total lack of response from the city, except for crying children and wailing mothers from the pen of prisoners in the middle of town.

Though everything had gone according to plan, Cha Ming once again felt a sense of foreboding. Instinctively, he looked up at the moon in the sky. It was only missing a sliver. Tomorrow, a full moon would appear to bid farewell to the winter. He pushed the thought out of his mind just in time to hear Han Jinlong's booming voice.

"Charge inside, everyone. First we'll secure the prisoners. We'll retreat immediately after checking their bodies for traps." He was the first to run toward the center of town. There, one hundred prisoners were huddled in a cramped cage.

One man in the cage looked at the approaching group. "What are you doing? Get away! You shouldn't have come here," the man said in a panic.

"Is that you, Uncle?" Han Jinlong asked in a quivering voice.

"Little dragon[9], you need to get back to Fairweather right away! The higher-ups in the village all left at noon, but that doesn't mean the guys left behind are weak. They're literally monsters!"

Before the rescue party had any time to react, the ground beneath the cage suddenly began to glow red.

---

[9] Jinlong is a name composed of two characters. "Jin" means gold, while "Long" means dragon. Therefore, "little dragon" is a very suitable term of endearment.

"No. It's too late! Run aw—" His voice was abruptly cut off as he burst into a bloody mess. The blood didn't burst outward, but instead gathered toward the center of the pen, where it was absorbed by a bloody rune floating in the air. Cha Ming had never seen such a rune before.

Instead of remaining, the bloody rune shattered into three pieces and darted out toward Han Jinlong, Zhang Yifeng, and Huxian! The three strongest individuals on their team were suddenly surrounded by a transparent crystal enclosure. Each of them tried to strike at the crystal from the inside, but to no avail.

Brother Cha Ming, I can't escape this! It's such a strong spatial isolation that I'm helpless. There's no way something like this can exist without external support. You've got to break us out!

Cha Ming's face paled as he heard this. If Huxian couldn't escape a spatial constraint, the two masters didn't stand a chance. Just to be sure, he struck Huxian's prison with his strongest staff blow, but nothing happened.

"Someone's coming!" Gong Lan suddenly yelled, drawing her sabers. As Cha Ming moved to join up with her, he felt a sharp stabbing sensation in his shoulder blade. He jumped away from his current position and saw the eldest Ling brother holding a bloody dagger.

"Why?" he said as he fell to one knee. "You're from Fairweather. You should care about this rescue." Cha Ming coughed out a mouthful of blood as he said these words. Fortunately, his strong physical body enabled him to endure and not immediately collapse. The dagger had barely missed his lung and heart, but his left arm was now hanging limply by his side.

"Yes, I care about them deeply. But I care about my brothers more! My brother was captured on our way here, so we have no choice but to join them." His young brother nodded and unsheathed his sword. While their words were harsh, Cha Ming could tell that betraying their comrades was a heart-wrenching experience for them. The hands of both Ling brothers were shaking, and they could barely hold their swords.

"You guys are scum," Cha Ming said. "We all have choices to make, but you chose to betray. The deepest hells are reserved for traitors." He then withdrew three bottles from his bag of holding. They were the three pills that he had received from Zhang Yifeng earlier. He removed their lids and gulped all three pills without any hesitation. Such a bad injury would be difficult to recover from.

The rosary on his right arm then glowed green, and seventy-two pearls floated out around him, forming a green formation in the shape of a flower. Coupled with the medicinal pills, his wounds began recovering at a visible pace. After only a few breaths, he was able to use the strength of his muscles to hold his staff despite the injury to his ligaments.

"Let's take these guys down," he called out to Gong Lan and the other mercenaries. If looks could kill, they would have already torn these superior cultivators at the great circle of qi condensation to pieces.

But before they could do anything, the air around them shimmered. Suddenly the square in the center of town wasn't so empty. Three women and thirteen men appeared, each with vicious glints in their eyes. Eight of the men wielded large axes and were twice the size of regular men. The five other men wielded cruel sabers, and their eyes glowed red with rage. The group of newcomers didn't stand on ceremony and immediately charged at them. The square was suddenly plunged into chaos, leaving only Gong Lan, Cha Ming, and three other eighth-level cultivators to take care of the Ling brothers.

Using the support of his Healing Flower manifestation, Cha Ming charged up to the Ling brothers with Gong Lan. Gong Lan's battle proficiency was extremely high, enabling her to expertly dodge their sword strikes despite the difference in their cultivation levels.

Cha Ming wasn't as proficient, but he made up for his lack of agility by taking hits with his durable body. Thanks to the earth body refining and the wood body refining, his defensive and regenerative abilities were very impressive. Every few breaths, he got slashed by one of the brothers' swords, only to have the shallow wound rapidly heal again. He relied on his Gentle Staff Art to avoid as many blows as possible, but the brothers were very coordinated, using their cultivation bases to their fullest. If not for the support of the three eighth-level cultivators, Cha Ming and Gong Lan would already be dead.

This can't keep going on.

While Cha Ming knew that it was unwise to get distracted in such a heated battle, he glanced over to the other mercenaries to evaluate their condition. The battle between the mercenaries and the devilish cultivators was not going favorably for the mercenaries. Over ten cultivators had already been killed, while one of the red-eyed devils, despite being pierced through the torso with five different weapons, continued to fight on.

"Try cutting off their heads and see what happens!" he shouted. Unfortunately, when he did this, he revealed an opening and was quickly punished for his mistake. He retreated backward and held his chest, where a sword had slashed a deep wound.

"We need to finish these two off as soon as possible. You two, use your talismans. Gong Lan, retreat to me, quickly!" Fortunately, two of the fighters happened to be part of Cha Ming's original group. They nodded and pulled out their Cloud Step talismans, which led to a sharp increase in their movement speed.

Cha Ming plastered two other talismans on himself. One of them was a Cloud Step talisman, while the other one was an Iron Skin talisman, which would greatly increase his defense. He threw two similar talismans to the retreating Gong Lan and yelled, "Don't defend, just attack with me!"

She nodded and charged with Cha Ming. Her attacks became violent and overbearing, a maelstrom of bloody sabers.

Chapter 27: Escaping the Trap

To complement Gong Lan's offensive, Cha Ming abandoned his Gentle Staff Art. Instead, he took advantage of his increased speed to outmaneuver his opponents using Ghost Steps and strike them fiercely with Sword Staff. Every few exchanges, he increased the weight of his staff by several times and used Quake Staff to disrupt their rhythm. His Mountain Stance Technique enabled him to fully concentrate his weight during these important strikes.

He took several strikes to his torso in exchange for his offensive. They whittled away at his Iron Skin, and it ultimately resulted in a deep gash across his leg. He ignored the pain, however, and yelled out toward his allies as his opponents reeled under the aggressive blows of his Quake Staff. "Now!"

Despite being injured, he changed the healing formation into a snowflake formation, which suddenly restricted the Ling brothers' ability to dodge. The two mercenaries with enhanced speed took this opportunity and slashed at the younger brother's legs. He couldn't block because he was busy defending against Gong Lan, who had leapt up into the air and executed Blood Saber Art—Twin Decapitation. The younger brother was forced to his knees, and Cha Ming struck once more with Quake Staff, smashing his skull.

"Brother!" The elder brother's eyes became bloodshot, and he withdrew a black pill from his bag of holding and swallowed it. Cha Ming's eyes narrowed as he saw the eldest Ling brother's aura increase sharply, reaching a level that caused their group to tremble—half-step foundation establishment! Evidently, the man had used a forbidden medicine to force up his strength, just like Zhou Xian had in the past. He followed up by immediately lashing out at Gong Lan with his most powerful blow yet. A crimson light flashed as she was pushed back without injury, and Cha Ming saw the crimson lotus brooch she had been wearing crumble into dust.

Only desperate cultivators used such medicines, as the side effects included prolonged weakness and sometimes crippled a cultivator's foundation. Cha Ming could understand this act of madness. He'd betrayed his companions to save his brother, only to lose another. He had nowhere to run, and he could only try his best to kill Cha Ming and his companions. Although Cha Ming understood him, he still couldn't forgive the man. Betrayal was unforgiveable.

Meanwhile, the battle between the weaker mercenaries and the devil cultivators had taken a turn for the worse. Another ten had fallen, giving them the opportunity to surround their targets.

"Zen, Xiong, go help them. Leave him to the three of us!" Cha Ming yelled. The two nodded and filled in the gaps, preventing the devil cultivators from flanking the weaker mercenaries. The presence of the two greater cultivators reversed the tide, instantly leading to the decapitation of one of the wounded devil cultivators and the suppression of another.

Just as things seemed to be improving, however, the three women who had been resting nearby suddenly opened their eyes. They began singing a macabre tune, which caused the mercenaries to turn sluggish. Even the two stronger cultivators were affected, albeit to a lesser extent.

"Fan, quickly. Go kill those three and come back!"

Their last helper, who was still under the effect of the Cloud Step talisman, quickly darted out toward the trio. Two devil cultivators broke off from the main group to intercept him, but Cha Ming had anticipated this. He threw out three Stone Wall talismans, which instantly blocked off their path and gave Fan a straight line to the three women.

He was unable to keep paying attention to Fan's actions, however, as the eldest Ling brother's aggression skyrocketed.

"I'll kill you!" he said and started attacking Cha Ming without reservation.

Cha Ming could only grit his teeth and increase the weight of his staff to minimize the recoil from each blow he defended against. He used his most skillful technique, Sword Staff, to repeatedly parry the other man's blows. Unfortunately, the difference between half-step foundation establishment and qi condensation was substantial. Each strike blocked caused Cha Ming to cough up blood.

Gong Lan didn't give up, however. The bloody tempest, which Ling Tong had been able to keep at bay with his superior qi, weapon, and techniques, suddenly erupted with furious killing intent. This caused him to back up, granting Cha Ming a breath of respite. He used this opportunity to pop another lesser healing pill from his bag of holding. He also slapped out two healing talismans for good measure, one for himself and one for Gong Lan. He then charged to support her offensive, manifesting a lethal sword with his spirit pearls and slashing at Ling Tong from behind.

The man snorted and activated a movement technique, which brought him right beside Gong Lan. She let out a vicious yell, causing her killing intent to skyrocket once more. She deflected three consecutive blows, and on the third, her baleful aura increased once more, followed by a familiar crack. It was a sound that all qi condensation cultivators would recognize: Gong Lan had broken through to the eighth level of qi condensation!

Cha Ming finally caught up to them using Burst Steps and began assisting Gong Lan once more. Yet despite their progress, the eldest Ling Brother's defense was ironclad. It was time for desperate measures.

"Gong Lan, get ready!" he yelled, activating the Healing Flower manifestation once more. He gave up on parrying and instead struck out with one Quake Staff after another.

He was full of openings, which his opponent took advantage of immediately. Cha Ming cringed as the expected counterattack came slashing toward his arm. But instead of blocking, he jumped into the blow, using his Gentle Staff Art to offset the blow slightly and avoid damage to his internal organs. The sword bit down hard into his left bicep, almost shearing his arm in half. He ignored the pain and held on to the sword with all his might, causing it to dig deeper into his bloodied arm. Fortunately, the flow of blood had been slightly stemmed by the residual medicinal strength in his body and the Healing Flower manifestation.

Gong Lan didn't need to be told twice. She sidestepped the

man, first cleaving off his trapped arm and following up with a lethal strike to his neck. He didn't have time to scream before she unceremoniously lopped off his head, showering both Cha Ming and herself in blood. She didn't pause to help Cha Ming after their hard-earned victory. Instead, she plunged into the nearby carnage and began dispatching the remaining devils. They weren't faring so well after the three bewitching women had been slain by Fan and their mental effects were removed.

As the battle raged on, Cha Ming kneeled and struggled to stay conscious despite the pain and the blood loss. He didn't dare remove the sword from his bleeding bicep without any assistance, so he simply endured the pain and sat cross-legged in meditation. He kept himself conscious by mumbling to himself over and over, "I need to free Huxian, and we need to save Fairweather City."

The battle was over after roughly an incense time. Only half of the original mercenaries that charged in remained, though this time, the casualties affected the weak and the strong alike. Everyone was exhausted and collapsed, popping healing pills and circulating their cultivation bases to recover. Several people were missing limbs—without any precious medicines, they would never be able to fight at the same level ever again.

Fortunately for Cha Ming, his arm was only *mostly* severed. After taking two minutes to recover her state of mind, Gong Lan and Fan wandered over. Fan had not been gravely injured in the battle, so he pulled out the healing pill that Zhang Yifeng had given him and handed it to Cha Ming.

Cha Ming didn't stand on ceremony and nodded to Gong Lan. She swiftly pulled out the saber lodged in his bicep, almost causing Cha Ming to pass out from the pain and immediate blood loss. He popped the pill in his mouth and continued pouring qi into his Healing Flower manifestation. After a half hour of recovery, his arm was whole and functional once more. All that remained was a thin scar where the saber had been lodged.

The aftermath of the carnage was no laughing matter. Several people had been crippled, but most of the remaining mercenaries had used spirit medicines to fully recover. Seeing that the situation was under control, Cha Ming walked over to Huxian's crystal prison to inspect it. Huxian looked at Cha Ming with a worried expression. After all, he had seen everything that had transpired. He had kept silent throughout the battle to avoid breaking Cha Ming's concentration.

As Cha Ming's hands ran over the crystal surface, he heard the voice of the red-bearded man from inside the Clear Sky world.

That's a type of stasis formation, and the one who set it was at least a foundation establishment expert. This formation should have six "formation eyes" set up inside the village. That's why the formation isn't inscribed into the ground, like the ones in the last village. Find them, then follow my instructions. A strong lock is worthless when someone has the key.

Cha Ming gave the man a mental nod, then quickly gathered Gong Lan and the four strongest remaining mercenaries. Soon enough, they found a glowing red rune in one of the shacks in the village. From what they could tell, there were no remaining rebels or devil cultivators in the village. The rest had evacuated prior to their attack, if Han Jinlong's uncle's words were to be believed.

What do I do now? Cha Ming asked the man mentally.

Paint this pattern on the floor with the Clear Sky Brush, surrounding the rune. Use earth qi, as it's the antithesis of blood and water. Cha Ming instantly became aware of a runic pattern. It wasn't like any talisman he'd painted before. It consisted of four runic symbols, joined together by geometric shapes and lines.

Is this a formation? Cha Ming asked.

Yes, dummy, it's a formation. Just paint it the same way you would a talisman. Talismans and formations come from the same source, after all.

Cha Ming followed his instruction and took out the Clear Sky Brush and a pot of liquified earth essence, absorbing some of it into the brush. He then began carefully tracing out the pattern in his mind. The process was ten times slower than if he needed to draw a talisman of the same grade. He might be great at painting runic characters, but drawing straight and circular lines was a skill that had always eluded him. After a quarter hour, the last line was drawn, and the blood-red rune suddenly sank into the floor and was absorbed into the counter rune. One formation eye down, five to go.

After two hours, Cha Ming returned to the center of the square and laid down the last counter rune, dissipating the stasis trap. Huxian jumped out while yipping, and Han Jinlong and Zhang Yifeng stood from their meditative postures. While they appeared calm on the outside, Cha Ming could sense they were boiling over with murderous intent.

"I think it's clear to everyone that their plan was to kill the weakest of us and stall the strongest of us," Han Jinlong said. "They even dared to turn the Ling brothers against us. That means that their strongest members are on their way to Fairweather now. We will take the strongest four with us and set out on flying swords immediately. Everyone else, please follow at your own pace. I only pray we'll make it there on time."

With these words, Cha Ming hopped onto Zhang Yifeng's sword, while Gong Lan jumped on Han Jinlong's sword. Two other cultivators accompanied them, and Huxian simply hitched a ride on Cha Ming's shoulders. Fortunately, the little fox was still a baby.

They left the remaining forty-odd mercenaries in Jade Spring and vanished into the night.

A flock of geese took flight as the sounds of crashing hooves interrupted their mid-morning bath. These were some of the first geese of spring. They migrated as soon as ponds no longer froze over in the Song Kingdom. A carriage rolled past them as they flew away to another nearby pond. It was pulled by a dozen fierce-looking horses. Their red manes were draped across large black bodies, a testament to their demonic heritage.

The carriage plowed through what most would consider obstacles in the road, like puddles and rocks. It didn't slow down in the slightest. If one looked closely, they would see that the wheels skimmed the water and shattered stones in such a way that the carriage's motion remained undisturbed.

Inside the carriage, Wang Jun and Elder Bai sat in meditation while Hong Lin and two others sifted through a large pile of documents, taking advantage of every waking moment to submerge themselves in vital information. Unlike Wang Jun and Elder Bai, these three were not cultivators. They had no natural advantage in absorbing information, making perseverance and hard work even more important.

Wang Jun slowly opened his eyes to the sight of these three hardworking individuals. He secretly praised them inwardly. He didn't require mediocre cultivators who happened to be business people; rather, he required only the best business minds. Cultivators were usually too preoccupied with meditation or fighting, not bothering themselves with what they saw as trifling activities like business and law. For a clan to survive, both supreme experts and sharp business minds were necessary.

As per his usual custom on this three-day trek, he wandered over to the front of the carriage, where the coachman Ren Wufa was seated. The middle-aged man had his eyes closed, but Wang Jun knew that he was fully aware of his surroundings. Wang Jun respectfully sat beside him and waited for him to speak.

"It seems like this latest session was very productive for you. You've improved once more, and your cultivation is at the peak of qi condensation," the man said as he opened his eyes. "When will you stop supressing your advancement and make your breakthrough?"

Wang Jun smiled and replied politely. "Protector Ren, I can't hide anything from you. I intend to break through in a few days. However, I have something very important to accomplish in the capital, and my breakthrough will have to wait until the matter is finished."

His reply prompted a snort from his protector. "I can only see your cultivation if you let me. Anyhow, what could be so important as to delay your cultivation? Strength is everything in the cultivation world."

"A few days won't matter much," Wang Jun replied. "However, the events in the next few days will affect the whole

Song Kingdom. Trifling as it is, the Song Kingdom is critical to my plans. You wouldn't understand. Besides which, this task will also help a very important friend."

The man shrugged and handed a bag of holding to Wang Jun, who peeked inside before asking, "How many last night?"

"Just seven," Wufa replied casually. "Five feelers at peak qi condensation, one distraction at early foundation establishment, and an actual assassin at mid-foundation establishment. I just can't understand why you would leak your involvement in the rumors behind the princess and subsequently announce your intent to personally attend the trial. It's obvious that they would send assassins after you, but killing these small fries isn't worth giving up the element of surprise."

Wang Jun shrugged. "You're right, they aren't worth it. But the resulting chaos *is* worth it. I am also baiting an opponent to remain in the city for the next few days. I'm naturally not concerned about these minions while you're around."

The man sighed. "But I won't always be around..." They both sat in silence as they approached the gates of the Song Kingdom's capital, Songjing City. Their demonic horses neighed loudly as they came to a sudden halt before the city's drawbridge. The guards at the gate were not accustomed to such mounts, and they quickly made arrangements for them to enter the city, lest they provoke some unreasonable young master by delaying him.

Soon, they arrived at the Songjing Jade Bamboo Auction House. The familiar décor incorporating carefully cultivated bamboo was a sight for sore eyes for those who had been trapped in the carriage these last three days. The carriage was naturally taken care of by a group of attendants, and the six of them walked into the building.

After walking for only a few breaths, they were greeted by a squeaky voice. "Young Master Wang, welcome to the Songjing branch. Everyone and everything here is at your disposal." A five-foot-tall man in purple robes trotted hurriedly toward them and bowed slightly. Wang Jun nodded slightly in response to the bow.

"Elder Jin, you know I hate all the pomp and fanfare." Wang Jun said. "Please take us to the meeting room to review the situation. Also, I'm parched. Please arrange for snacks and tea for me and my companions. White Celadon tea is well suited to the local cuisine's flavor, am I right?"

"Of course, Young Master. We bought several limited-edition packages specifically for your arrival. If this tea was ranked second in the dynasty, no one would dare claim first," he said in a humble tone.

After a quarter hour, the tea and refreshments had been delivered to the meeting room, and everyone took a moment to relax. Everyone except Wang Jun, who reviewed the latest information at lightning speed. Their future plans would be determined by this carefully collected information.

As he reviewed the information, a smirk appeared on Wang Jun's handsome face. The smirk soon turned into a chuckle once he reached the last page.

"Elder Jin, please go ahead and send out the messenger falcon, instructing our partners outside the city to proceed as planned. Meanwhile, everyone else should review the case once more and see if they can determine any additional variables. Meanwhile… Xiao Li?"

"Yes, Young Master?" Xiao Li was one of the young attendants who had accompanied them on the journey. Besides her sharp, business-oriented mind, her looks were also top notch.

"You and I are going on a date tonight. I hear the Radiant Dynasty Pavilion's pheasant dish is to die for."

Chapter 28: The End Goal

The sound of clinking dishes could barely be heard amidst the murmuring and gentle zither music in the Radiant Dynasty Pavilion. She was the best zither player in the entire kingdom, and this famous restaurant had spared no expense in roping her in. Her music ran like water and soothed the soul, calming even the most agitated and stressed individuals. As such, the people that came to this pavilion invariably came out with straightened backs and lightened shoulders.

The seating arrangement in this establishment was quite peculiar. There were no such thing as private booths. Instead, there was only a single floor with no differentiation in status. Attendance was a clear indication of social class, as both status and wealth were required to enter in the first place. Any attendants, Dao protectors, or chaperones were strictly prohibited. They were hosted in an adjacent building, where they waited for their charges to leave the premises.

Wang Jun and Xiao Li were seated at a table for two, one of twelve such tables surrounding three larger tables in the center.

All tables were occupied, as this restaurant never lacked a waiting list. In fact, Elder Jin had pulled several dozen strings to arrange for this "date." Xiao Li clearly relished the opportunity, and she had spent the whole afternoon dressing up for the occasion. She wore a slim green dress covered in vines and beautiful mauve blossoms. Unfortunately, she lacked matching earrings, but settled for a mauve hairclip that fastened her long jet-black hair.

Wang Jun was dazzled for a moment when he first saw the dress. It made him recall his first date with Hong Xin. After the pain in his heart subsided, he brought her over to the restaurant with a fake smile plastered on his face.

"The Song Kingdom boasts some of the best spiritual blacksmiths. It's a pity that their alchemists are so lacking," Wang Jun said casually to Xiao Li, who agreed with him profusely. They both ignored cold stares from multiple directions.

"Of course, dearest," Xiao Li said. "Everyone outside the kingdom knows the alchemists here are garbage. They even have to hide behind trade barriers to make a living. You'll teach them a lesson in court tomorrow though, won't you?" Wang Jun was amazed to hear such vicious words coming from the sweet woman's mouth. *Should I get her a raise?* he wondered.

"Of course I will. I just hope that Zhou Li is man enough to attend. Maybe he'll be too busy making love to his sister. Have you heard the latest rumor?" Wang Jun's latest comment was followed by a loud crash. Several attendants rushed over to another table in a panic, picking up pieces of broken glass and sweeping away spilled wine with their qi.

Wang Jun continued as though nothing had happened. "I heard that he and his sister make love every three nights, the same schedule as she's together with the crown prince.

It's amazing that he hasn't clued in yet. I guess that makes it exciting. The mere thought of getting caught in the—"

"You *dare*?" an angry voice shouted. A man and a woman, both with long black hair and dressed in purple robes, walked out from the rubble that was once their table. The scent of fire and sulfur was thick in the air as the man walked toward them with a murderous aura.

"How dare you slander me in this city. You might talk big to impress women, but I *dare* you to leave your name." As the man spoke, the woman beside him gave both Wang Jun and Xiao Li a blood-chilling glare.

Wang Jun finished eating a few bites before looking up, unperturbed. "And who might you be?" he said nonchalantly. "Oh, you said I was slandering *you*. Well, I didn't slander anyone that I know of; I just stated facts. Speaking lies and deceit is morally reprehensible. In fact, we were only discussing the cuckold crown prince and his incestuous consort. Now, where was I?"

The young man, who was clearly Zhou Li, couldn't take it anymore, and black flames began to accumulate in his open palm. The woman beside him glanced at the fistful of flames nervously and whispered to him, "Brother dearest, you know we can't act as we wish here. Just let it go, and we'll keep tabs on him later."

"You should listen to your sister. She clearly cares a lot about you. If my eyes don't deceive me, she might just be willing to bear your children. Now, I'm not one to stand against forbidden love, but the citizens in the Song Kingdom—"

Crash.

The table in front of Wang Jun was smashed to bits. None of the food flew out, however, as it was instantly incinerated by the strange black flames. The pale-faced Xiao Li was breathing quickly, while Wang Jun was still holding a cup full of tea. He drank a few sips, then looked up to a set of stairs leading to the establishment's second level.

"Manager," Wang Jun said, "is this how you allow guests to treat each other in your establishment?"

A cold voice snorted, and a blur of a figure shot out, placing himself between Wang Jun and Zhou Li. The black flame summoned by Zhou Li was quickly extinguished by a mysterious force.

"Of course not. I'll be seeing these two out shortly," said an aged man with short-cropped hair. Many of the people in the group gasped audibly when they saw the figure. Few people dared to disturb the peace in this restaurant, as it was backed by a higher power than the Song Kingdom's royal family.

"That's quite all right. We were just leaving anyway. I'm not sure if this guest can afford it, so here is a little extra for the damages."

A small bright crystal shot out from his hand, and the old man pocketed it before anyone could see it. Wang Jun was sure the man knew what exactly had transpired and didn't want to leave a bad impression. Problems that money could solve weren't *real* problems.

As Wang Jun and Xiao Li were leaving the establishment, Wang Jun turned around and looked Zhou Li straight in the eyes. "You have such a childish temper. You really need to learn to control it, or you'll never be worthy to touch the hems of my robes. By the way, my name is Wang Jun. I'll see you in court tomorrow, if you dare."

Crash.

Zhou Li smashed a piece of furniture to vent his frustration at his failed divination. His divinations should yield information on anyone below core formation. Yet here he was, surrounded by broken chairs and shattered pottery. He could not help but think of the shadowy figure in the painting.

Is there really such a coincidence? The Wang family is reputed to be very rich and overbearing. However, they wouldn't send anyone important to this backwater kingdom. No, they must have just supplied Wang Jun with a shielding treasure, one that can protect him from my immature seer's eyes.

His red pupils glowed slightly as he changed his focus. He needed to monitor a key operation tonight, and it would begin any moment. He took out an ornate mirror from his bag of holding and muttered an incantation that caused it to darken. In that darkness, figures in white began to materialize, followed by the contours of a city. It soon revealed a perfect aerial picture of Fairweather City.

"Good," he muttered. "At least *some* plans are going well. Mirror, please focus on my brother." At his command, the mirror shimmered, revealing a hooded figure. Zhou Xian was currently busy painting an elaborate, blood-red rune on a stone floor. He wasn't painting the full rune, of course. Such a rune was beyond him—he was simply performing some finishing touches on a product at 90% completion.

It was then that he noticed an inky substance seeping from the side of the mirror. Zhou Li frowned and tried to dispel it, but to no avail. "Mirror, show me the Merchant," he said. By the time the image changed, half the mirror was covered by darkness, but he could barely make out the contours of a golden formation, which was almost complete. This was the last thing he saw in the mirror before it became completely coated in what seemed like black ink.

Zhou Li cautiously touched the surface of the mirror and pulled away his finger. It was coated in a thick, shadowy layer, which attempted to dive into his skin. He quickly burnt it away with his qi, and seeing that fire was effective on the ink covering his finger, he tried the same on the mirror without any results. He massaged his temples in frustration, taking a deep breath before realizing that he had another means of communication.

He picked up his black notebook to write a message. Magical treasures were very difficult to tamper with, after all. When he opened it, however, he saw that the pages were illegible. They were similarly coated in black. Seeing this, he tossed the small black book against a far wall, causing a precious painting to fall to the floor.

Could it really be him? Is Wang Jun the shadow? he pondered. Since he couldn't scry and couldn't communicate, he sat down in meditation. *I'll try again in an hour. Let's see if whoever is blocking me is willing to do it all night.*

Feng Ming arrived at Fairweather City just in time to see the sun setting beyond the horizon. His pace had been agonizingly slow, but he could hardly blame the horse. It was born and bred for the plow, and a full day's trot had completely exhausted it. He shook his head as he realized that he could now *walk* faster than the horse could move, so he found a lone tree and tied it off. The horse didn't eat the nearby grass or drink from the nearby puddle. Instead, it collapsed from fatigue.

Feng Ming wasted no time and ran toward Fairweather on foot. As he approached the city, he noticed that the gates were closed.

Strange, he thought, *the gates don't usually close until one hour after sundown.* Fortunately, he hadn't planned to waltz through the front gate in the first place. He approached the city from the river, which ran right through the city wall. The setting sun screened him as he darted out from the trees and plunged into the cold river near the wall. He swam underwater for twenty meters before surfacing just before the grate, where water passed into the city.

After observing the thick grate for a while, he retrieved his lucky spear from his back of holding. He used it to cut away at the pieces of metal holding the grate to the city wall. He replaced the grate after pulling himself through. The process was very loud, so he thanked his luck there were no guards on patrol nearby.

Quick as a viper, he snuck through the various alleyways, past beggars and orphans. He followed the winding alleys to the workshop district, where he had no choice but to run out in the open toward Bei Ling's rundown shack. He was surprised to see that there was no one walking on the empty streets, and there were no guards patrolling either. This was uncharacteristic for such a busy town.

Regardless, he let himself into the shack, lest he be discovered. A pleasant smell made his mouth water as he walked through the door to the dimensional abode. After all, he hadn't had a proper meal in two days. He walked into the dining room, where four dishes and two sets of cutlery had been laid out. Hong Lai and Bei Ling were just about to eat supper when Feng Ming appeared out of nowhere.

"Didn't you set out toward Green Leaf City two days ago?" Bei Ling asked, frowning. The younger man nodded his head in response.

"Yes, I did. I didn't make it, unfortunately. After a day's travel, I was attacked from behind by the man the county lord sent to accompany me. The horses were all killed or escaped, so I came back as fast as I could with a farmer's plow horse. Something fishy is going on with the county lord, and I had a hunch that I didn't have time to ride for reinforcements."

"Hong Lai, have you noticed anything unusual lately?" asked Bei Ling.

"Well," Hong Lai replied, "the guards have been very active lately. However, everything calmed down today. For some reason, the gate closed early, and they called a curfew. I didn't know what was going on, but it didn't seem like something worth fighting over. Maybe they just have something to do tonight, and they don't want to deal with manning the gate for the extra hour or two."

Bei Ling pondered for a moment before grabbing his coat off a rack. "I have a bad feeling. I'm going to go pay a visit to the county lord. You guys stay put."

Hong Lai looked at the abandoned supper and back to Feng Ming, who seemed positively exhausted. "Well, are you hungry?" he asked.

"Starving," Feng Ming replied.

A half hour later, a soldier and a blacksmith were sneaking through the alleys toward a nearby guard house. Because of the curfew, no one was walking on the open streets. Instead, the undesirables in the city had all huddled into the concealed alleys, where the guards wouldn't cause them any grief.

"Master Bei said to stay out of trouble," the blacksmith whispered angrily to his lightly armored companion.

Feng Ming chuckled and said, "I wanted to, but I got an itch. I want to go check out what those guards are so busy with. Don't worry, we'll be back in a jiffy. Besides, I can hardly cause trouble with you around, right?"

He ignored Hong Lai's whining and darted into another alley. They arrived at a dead end. Ignoring Hong Lai's puzzled expression, Feng Ming used his Burst Steps Technique to scale a small wall, propelling himself to the roof of a secluded shop. "Are you coming?" he whispered. Hong Lai sighed as he also executed a movement technique and landed beside Feng Ming.

"Do you do this a lot where you come from?" Hong Lai whispered as they walked on the rooftops while crouching.

"Not really. Only when I go peek at the bathhouse. I'm a master at sneaking and hiding, you know. I never get caught," Feng Ming replied, silencing the curious Hong Lai.

Soon they reached the other side of the rooftop adjacent to the guard shack. Feng Ming looked down and saw multiple guards stationed at the entrance, looking out at the street vigilantly. Of course, they never thought to look at the rooftops.

Feng Ming took advantage of this blind spot and leapt across the gap. Hong Lai shook his head and followed, but his less than nimble movements caused a tile to fall from the roof and onto the street near the guard shack.

One of the guards walked to check the source of the ruckus, only to find a few broken tiles. "I told them to fix the roof last summer," he muttered. He looked up, barely missing Feng Ming and Hong Lai's shadows as they ducked into a half-open window.

"I really wonder who hired these guards," Feng Ming whispered. "They left a window open in an empty room. It doesn't get any more unprofessional than this."

Hong Lai glared at him, but just as he was about to speak, Feng Ming held up his hand to silence him.

"What's the lord thinking with this sudden curfew? And what's with those people downstairs? They give me the creeps," they heard a muffled voice say from behind the wooden wall.

"I heard that it's some kind of auspicious ceremony. That's why they're painting runes down there," another voice said.

"But those runes give me the creeps. And so do those people. I don't trust them one bit," a third voice said. He didn't continue speaking, however, as a man with a heavy set of footsteps walked down the hallway and opened the door.

"Ceremony's almost done," a grating voice said. "This day will be a turning point for Fairweather City." The voice then continued to elaborate in a loud voice. Feng Ming had heard enough. This distraction was a golden opportunity, and he signaled Hong Lai to follow him as he stepped out toward the hallway.

The wooden floor didn't creak as they walked, despite its aged condition. And neither did the stairs as they walked to the halfway point, where they crouched down to observe what was happening on the first floor. There, a few robed figures were busy chanting in the center of the room. They were surrounded by blood-red runes, which pulsed with light as the chanting progressed. The chanting and the bloody runes gave Feng Ming the willies. It was like a voice inside his head was yelling at him to immediately charge down there and stop them, yet he held himself back and continued to observe.

Right beside the chanting figures, a glowing golden rune hovered in midair, and many golden lines intersected that same rune. The runic characters were all gibberish to Feng Ming, so he focused on the other figures in the room. There were no guards here, only five men. Three of them were large men, while the others were lanky. His eyes narrowed as he focused on one man whom he'd seen before. He'd caught a glimpse of his face just before he cut down his fellow soldier as they tried to escape Crystal Meadows.

Hong Lai tensed as he saw Feng Ming's grip tighten on his spear. "Are you going to start a fight with those people?" he whispered.

"Those aren't people," Feng Ming replied, then he darted out with his spear and slashed the lanky man in half. He had avenged his friend, but it was far from enough. As this thought ran through his head, he felt a tingling sensation and decided to lean backward, causing a heavy blade to barely miss him. The blade came from one of the larger men, who had now doubled in girth.

"Complete the ceremony, quickly!" one of the lanky men with red eyes yelled angrily. In response, the hooded figure's chanting sped up. Feng Ming tried to break away toward the hooded figures, only to be intercepted by yet another large figure, who tried to grab him with his meaty hands.

"Tch." Feng Ming darted between them quickly and slashed at the large man's stomach. It felt like he was cutting through mud, and he realized immediately that the abomination was unharmed. They surrounded him once again, attacking him from three sides. He deflected some blows with his spear, dodging others. He followed his heart as he slashed out at random, and his spear always seemed to hit its mark. Before long, he had decapitated another two of the creatures.

"Hong Lai, stop them!" Feng Ming bellowed. Hong Lai, who hadn't moved since the fight started, suddenly pulled out his own weapon, an intricate longsword. He darted toward the three figures, two of which continued chanting as he hacked down one of them. Seeing that this hadn't stopped them, Hong Lai decapitated a second hooded figure, then stabbed the last one through the heart. This last figure chuckled as blood oozed out of his mouth.

"You're too late," the figure said hoarsely as he coughed out blood. "This town is *ours* now." With these words, he muttered one last syllable, and the red array lit up, concentrating its light into a glowing red rune that floated out from the floor.

The entire room was bathed in an eerie red light. Feng Ming, who had just decapitated the last creature, suddenly saw Hong Lai collapse to the floor. As he ran up to support him, he saw the strong man was resisting something with all his might. His eyes were bloodshot.

Just beneath Hong Lai, Feng Ming saw a slender red thread connecting him to the nearby rune. There were countless red threads leading out from blood red rune at the center of the room. With every breath that passed by, the rune pulsed. And with every pulse, it grew a little bit brighter.

Chapter 29: Blood and Gold

Several deer darted to the side, barely avoiding a group of six cultivators balancing themselves on flying swords. They flew a few feet off the ground, avoiding obstacles that mere mortals would have to bypass or trod through with great frustration. The six cultivators were clearly separated into two groups of three. They were each led by older men, whose intimidating presence had caused the deer to flee in the first place.

Three of the four other cultivators were trembling. Balancing on a flying sword was very tiring for a qi-condensation cultivator since the sword itself was controlled by the foundation establishment elders nearby. The lack of synchronization caused balancing on the sword to be taxing on both the mind and body.

Only Cha Ming seemed immune, as his strong body and spiritual force kept him perfectly balanced. There was no way to shield himself from the strong winds that buffeted their group, however. Therefore, he occasionally circulated his fire qi to fight the cold, bringing warmth to the tips of his fingers and toes. Spring had barely started, and the winter chill still hung thick in the air.

Their group had been traveling since well before sunrise, not wasting a single moment in the hopes of overtaking the masterminds from Jade Spring. Every time they felt tired, the fresh memories of what had transpired over the past few days forced them to press on despite their fatigue.

Cha Ming flexed his bicep and rotated his arm as he continued balancing on the flying sword. Master Zhang had passed him a strong healing medicine, which ensured that his arm had healed with few side effects. He thanked his lucky stars that he had trained both his body and mind. His body cultivation had increased his defense and regenerative abilities, while the Creation Qi Manipulation Technique had tempered his tolerance to pain. Compared to the searing pain required to establish new qi pathways, having one's arm almost completely severed was nothing.

"We're only a half hour away," Zhang Yifeng mumbled. "I hope we're not too late. Given what we've experienced thus far, there will definitely be formations in Fairweather. That means that the enemy could have been in Fairweather even before we departed." Cha Ming nodded in response.

Soon enough, Fairweather City appeared on the horizon. Many lights were lit, hinting that things were not so bad as they imagined. Yet as they sighed in relief, an ominous red light appeared near the city gate. It was soon accompanied by three others, casting the entire city in an eerie red fog.

"What sorcery is this…" Master Zhang whispered. Yet the spectacle didn't finish there. Soon, a golden spot lit up near the city gate and was accompanied by three others. A gold mist spread out over the whole city and melded with the red. It resembled an unholy medley of blood and gold.

"We're a hair too late. Hold on, everyone, we need to speed up," Han Jinlong said. Both masters circulated their cultivation bases, causing the swords that supported their group to speed up threefold. They dashed toward the city from the side while leaving behind a trail of stars.

They didn't slow down as they approached the thick stone walls. Instead, Han Jinlong drew out a one-handed hammer, concentrating his qi onto its flat head. Meanwhile, Zhang Yifeng held a spear in both hands. A tricolored glow appeared on the tip of the spear. The blue, green, and red lights resonated with a runic pattern on the sphere, causing it to give off a dreadful pressure.

"Hang on, kids!" Han Jinlong shouted. Both his and Yifeng's swords continued while the four other swords stopped abruptly midflight. The four cultivators landed fifty feet away from the wall, and the two foundation establishment elders flew forward, each striking the city wall with a vicious blow.

Their strikes instantly pierced two significant holes through five meters of stone. Cha Ming and company didn't hesitate to jump through and join their two elders on the other side. The instant Cha Ming stepped through to the other side, he felt his blood reel, almost causing him to lose consciousness. After stabilizing his breathing, he realized that he was weakening; his blood vitality seeming to seep out into four different directions, the ones where the red lights had originated from.

"We need to head to the center of the city. Once we find out what kind of formation this is, we'll act accordingly," Master Zhang instructed. The others nodded and followed his lead.

While Cha Ming felt a little weaker, he noticed that two individuals in their group seemed unaffected. The first was

Gong Lan, which was unsurprising given her cultivation method. Huxian also seemed unaffected.

Let me guess. You ate it? Cha Ming asked mentally.

That's right. I'm eating it as we speak! Huxian replied cheerfully.

Cha Ming could only shake his head in response. *Oh well, it's a good thing.*

They soon arrived at the center of town. The square at the center of the city had been razed; the statues and the fountain, renowned works of art and the symbol of Fairweather, had been reduced to rubble. In their place stood two glowing formations, one gold and one red. The gold formation was occupied by a skinny man with golden skin. He sat there cross-legged in meditation, and golden energy flowed through the formation and directly into his body with every passing second.

The second figure in the blood-red formation was Cha Ming's old friend.

"Zhou Xian!" he yelled. The younger man didn't react. Instead, he sat cross-legged in meditation while he focused on absorbing the incoming bloody energy.

Han Jinlong held his hand up, preventing them from approaching the two solitary figures at the center of Fairweather. His eyes narrowed as he observed the runes one by one. "Everyone, it seems that there are two energy gathering formations at the center of town. One gathers the energy of blood, while the other gathers the energy of gold.

"With every second that passes, these two will grow increasingly powerful. This will continue until the formation depletes... all the blood and all the wealth in the city!"

Cha Ming trembled involuntarily before asking, "Do you mean... the red formation is absorbing power from the blood of the citizens of Fairweather, and it will only stop after killing every single person here?"

"I'm afraid so. Not just that, the process is occurring extremely quickly. Yifeng!" Han Jinlong shouted. Master Zhang nodded and they both attacked the two meditating figures with their full strength. Their attacks stopped abruptly at the contours of the formation. Despite their inability to penetrate the formation, the younger man's eyes opened. He frowned as he looked out at the group of cultivators outside the formation.

"Your turn will come. Why must you rush me?" he asked in a sinister voice.

Master Zhang and Master Han attacked once more in response. This caused the man to flinch slightly, and the bloody glow, which had been flowing toward him, was briefly interrupted. The two men nodded to each other and stood on opposite sides of Zhou Xian. They began pressing down against the bloody formation, supressing it.

"Cha Ming, Gong Lan, Xing Tong, Liu Fei," Han Jinlong barked. "Each of you must set out to the north, south, east, and west sides of the city and find a formation eye. I don't know if it's possible, but you *must* try to stop it by any means possible. Don't bother with the gold formation—you *must* stop the blood formation. If you don't, the fifty thousand people in the city will all die. Yifeng and I will try to disrupt the formation as much as possible."

The four of them nodded and headed out separately.

Huxian, can you head out with Xing Tong and see if you can help him disrupt his formation eye? The small fox nodded obediently and began tailing the female cultivator.

Would their abilities be enough to stop the formation? Cha Ming wasn't sure. He had the bearded man's instructions, and

Huxian would likely figure out a way to eat his. Would Gong Lan, who seemed immune to the formation's draining power, be able to stop a formation eye with her limited power?

"What have you done, you bastard son of a goat!" Bei Ling said as he recovered from the shock caused to his aging body. The blood red mist that had sprung up suddenly in the county lord's residence immediately took its toll on the master smith. Several maids and guards collapsed to the floor, yet the county lord and two of his guards remained unaffected. The mist avoided them, preferring to direct its attention to juicier targets like Bei Ling and the others.

Bei Ling clutched his arm as a sharp pain ran through his chest.

My heart. I can't take much more of this godforsaken mist. Just what evil thing has he done? The curfew, the way his guard had attacked Feng Ming, and the county lord's recent behavior—Bei Ling no longer had any doubts. They had been betrayed.

"I'm just looking out for the country's best interests. We can't fight them, so why not join them?" Sun Chuan smirked as he confessed.

He's just trying to stall for time. He can see how badly this mist is affecting me.

"There's no use talking, then. I could beat your late father with one hand tied behind my back. I don't know what you've done, but it's about time you got the beating your father should have given you all those years ago." Bei Ling breathed in deeply, circulating his early foundation-establishment qi and his four-thousand-jin fist strength. As a spiritual blacksmith, his body forging had attained an impressive boundary. His many years of training had brought him to early-stage bone forging. He condensed his soul force into a massive warhammer, which materialized in his hands.

"Tch. So troublesome. You two, stall for time as I activate my secret art," Sun Chuan instructed. The two to his side nodded obediently and advanced. They both roared as they let loose their power. Surprisingly, they were both half-step foundation establishment.

"I'll polish you whelps off in less than ten breaths. One!" Bei Ling charged toward the one on the right, swinging out fiercely with his hammer. The guard quickly crossed his hands in front of himself, and a brown Earthen Tower Shield instantly materialized in front of him. It broke apart as Bei Ling's hammer smashed against it, forcing the man back with the residual fiery shockwave from his martial technique.

Bei Ling was not a fool. He took advantage of the opening to charge toward Sun Chuan, who had his eyes closed while rapidly forming hand seals. The cultivator he had just smashed away coughed out blood and formed hand seals as well. The earth in front of Sun Chuan suddenly trembled, and five sharp spikes shot out toward the charging Bei Ling, forcing him to change directions toward the cultivator on the left.

This cultivator had anticipated Bei Ling's movement, and his hands shot out toward the charging Bei Ling and unleashed a frozen dragon from his open palms. The dragon roared, causing Bei Ling to pause for a fraction of a breath before charging onward. This time, he used a clever movement technique and appeared right beside the ice cultivator. He didn't get a chance to scream before his head was blown off by Bei Ling.

Bei Ling then followed by breathing in deeply and exhaling toward his two remaining opponents. Like a dragon, flames rolled out of his mouth and enveloped them. He heard only one scream before the flames faded away, revealing the charred corpse of a guard and Sun Chuan holding out a saber. Sun Chuan was surrounded by an eerie black-and-red glow. His aura had improved significantly and broken into mid-foundation establishment.

"I may have executed a forbidden technique, but it's more than enough to handle an old geezer like you!" Sun Chuan yelled and darted out toward Bei Ling. He didn't let the older man breathe as he relentlessly attacked him with his magic saber, which was fueled by the power of his mid-level foundation establishment.

Bei Ling grunted as he received each blow, quickly maneuvering himself to avoid critical damage. Thankfully, he cultivated both body and qi, and while he might be at a disadvantage against mid-level foundation establishment, it wasn't an insurmountable gap. However, he was aware of his body's limitations. With each blow he took, he felt his heart shudder.

He had heard once that each heart only had a finite number of beats. An increase in cultivation realm reforged the heart, increasing the cultivator's lifespan in the process. He wasn't sure if he believed this, but one thing was certain—he didn't have much time left. Now it was time to make a choice. Should he take the gamble?

"It's only a matter of time before you die. How about you

surrender, and I'll grant you death with an intact corpse?"[10] Sun Chuan said between attacks. His saber was covered in a metallic sheen, greatly increasing its sharpness and range. Simultaneously, forty-eight daggers flew up from various positions in his body, attacking Bei Ling in tandem.

"Dream on," Bei Ling shouted as he fended off the daggers with an equal number of golden ball bearings. They clashed in the air as Bei Ling continued to fend off each saber strike, calming his mind in preparation for his last-ditch effort. An intact corpse was the least of his problems.

First Rune. He gathered qi and spiritual force to a tattoo on his chest over his heart. It was an intricate rune, and its activation caused Bei Ling's power to surge. He took advantage of the increased power and started mounting his own offensive. Both his warhammer and the golden ball bearings surrounding him increased in power. For good measure, he also added a fifty-foot-wide inferno, forcing Sun Chuan to divert his attention.

"So what if you also have a forbidden technique? How long can you possibly last?" the county lord yelled. Yet he was now in a passive position, and he could only deflect the incoming hammer blows. He summoned a cloud of mist to surround himself, countering the flames attacking him.

"Longer than you," Bei Ling said in response. *Second Rune.* An intricate silver pattern appeared on Bei Ling's exposed left arm, causing his power to surge once more. The first rune overdrew on Bei Ling's vitality while the second overdrew on his left arm. This meant that regardless of success or failure, his left arm would be crippled and unusable for the rest of his life.

---

[10] In the Confucian tradition, the body is a sacred gift from one's parents. Therefore, death by dismemberment is considered an insult to one's ancestors. The more pieces, the worse the insult.

However, Bei Ling didn't care. He coughed out blood and felt his old wounds opening within his body.

Sun Chuan desperately defended each blow with great difficulty. It was impossible to block them all, and a few hammer strikes smashed against his qi armor, severely depleting his remaining power. Things didn't stop there.

Third Rune. Fourth Rune. Fifth Rune! This was Bei Ling's last-ditch effort. He would likely die today, no matter the outcome. If he somehow survived, he would be a useless cripple for the rest of his life. Blood began to drip out of his pores as his arms and legs inflated. His skin turned red and his veins turned purple as he gripped his warhammer in two meaty fists.

Now I only have three breaths. One!

He struck out with his hammer, crushing downward and forcing Sun Chuan to block. Sun Chuan sent out his forty-eight daggers first, but they were instantly reduced in power by Bei Ling's overwhelming strength. He then took out his magic saber and deflected three times before it too crumbled to pieces. *Two.*

As he smashed downward, Sun Chuan threw out three talismans, which transformed into a bright blue shield of qi. But these three shields lasted only one strike each before collapsing. *Three.*

Bei Ling took what remained of his strength, infusing it in his hammer. First he struck Sun Chuan's chest. The blow made his armor creak, and it finally gave way, causing blood to spurt out of his mouth and onto Bei Ling. But the older man didn't care. He swiftly rotated his hammer, bringing it up while smacking Sun Chuan's chin with the handle, knocking him to the floor.

Finally, he poured in the last of his power, the last of his strength, and the last of his life, into the last strike he would ever make. A sickening thud brought complete silence to what remained of the county lord's manor.

Chapter 30: Coordinated Strike

It was dark out. Strangely, all the lights in Fairweather had been extinguished. The only source of illumination in the empty city streets was the full moon shining in all its glory. Its white light was filtered through the red mist covering the entire city, making it appear like a giant bloody moon. But the darkness didn't bother Huxian. The darkness was his home.

He expertly darted between buildings, hiding in one alley after another. Occasionally, he encountered people who had not been lucky enough to find shelter for the night. They sat outside, weakly clinging to their remaining vitality. Some of the older homeless individuals had collapsed after losing consciousness. The unhealthy ones had already moved on.

To Huxian, life and death were both necessary. There couldn't be life without death, just like there couldn't be good without evil. The death of these poor people meant nothing to him—what bothered him was that they were hurting those select few that he considered friends: the restaurant owner, the cook, and the little girl who petted him every time he walked by. Those who dared hurt them deserved to die, plain and simple. He was only too happy to assist Cha Ming.

He wasn't overly worried about *breaking* the formation—that much was simple. The only thing that concerned him was the questioned that had haunted generations of his ancestors: Are formations tasty? His inherited memories were vague on the subject. Many formations were edible, but whether they were *tasty* was a controversial subject. His ancestors had deemed the topic worthy enough to pass on to their progeny, so the least he could do was to contribute empirical evidence.

She's so slow. Is she really an eighth-level cultivator? he asked himself as he stalked Xing Tong from the darkness. Unfortunately, he didn't know the way to the guard house and could only follow her helplessly. To kill time, he ducked into a nearby residence. There he found a small family with two children sitting at a kitchen table. His beady eyes narrowed as he realized that one of the children was the little girl who always fed him scraps whenever he brushed past her legs. Rage bubbled up in him when he saw her vitality getting syphoned away.

These beasts have gone too far!

While he didn't have time to stay here and help her weather the crisis, he could help her in passing. Huxian's small figure blurred as his shadow darted out and expanded itself tenfold. He activated a technique, and the few lights in the room were swallowed by the shadow, plunging it into darkness. The red mist in the room was sucked up along with the light, as were the red threads that connected the two children and their parents to the formation.

As he prepared to leave, he shot a worried look at the table full of food. What would happen to the poor family if they woke up and ate the food that had been out all night? Would they become sick or get food poisoning? He wasn't sure, but it would be unethical to allow them to take that risk, so he walked up to the table and ate everything in a single gulp. His duty accomplished, he darted out of the house and caught up to Xing Tong.

It took them an incense time to arrive at a small stone building that protruded from the city wall.

This must be the guard house they spoke of. Well, I shouldn't let such a pretty lady face danger on her own.

Huxian jumped into a nearby shadow. His immaterial form passed through the barred windows and into a dimly lit room. There he saw five individuals. Two skinny men were sitting down, sharpening deadly spirit sabers. One larger man was chewing on a large haunch of meat, his large truncheon leaning against the table.

How impolite. They clearly aren't ready for company. The two other individuals were cloaked men. They were chanting, and with each syllable, the two runes in the room glowed brighter.

Huxian took advantage of his shadow form and edged along the wall toward one of the bite-sized figures. His shadow expanded, but this time its gaping maw protruded from the wall and bit down viciously. The skinny man didn't have time to scream before half his body disappeared. The other half tumbled on the floor, spurting blood. The other two guards swiftly grabbed their weapons and faced the wall. Uncertainty flashed in their eyes as the shadow disappeared and a small figure walked out of the darkness.

"Yip!"

Huxian darted at the larger one, who had his mouth wide open. The mouth was like a dark abyss, and it quickly expanded to two three times the size of the small fox. Several rows of dagger-like teeth lined the horrendous mouth.

Playing with a knife in front of an expert swordsman?[11] Huxian thought. The mark on his forehead began glowing, and his shadow, which had disappeared previously, turned into the vivid projection of large black fox.

One of the saber wielders reacted quickly and attempted to attack the shadowy projection. His spirit saber bounced off the lifelike projection with no noticeable effect. The massive fox bit down on the large man, devouring him in a single gulp. The remaining saber wielder didn't hesitate and attempted to escape the building. He only made it three steps before being eaten just like his comrade.

As Huxian approached the glowing formations, he noticed a few red threads separating from the formation and attempting to latch on to him. A bright white glow appeared around him, and the bloody threads evaporated into thin air. With a thought, Huxian expanded the white glow, encompassing the chanting figures. They howled in agony as the purifying white aura ate away at the unholy power they controlled. Soon, only their cloaks remained.

Now to answer the question—for posterity. Huxian glowed once more, but this time two projections appeared behind him. One was a large black fox, and the other was a large white fox. The moment the white fox appeared, both formation eyes and their supporting formations creaked under the strain and began crumbling bit by bit. The large black fox ate each piece as it broke away. It took less than ten breaths before the two

---

[11] The full Chinese idiom is 班门弄斧, which means showing off one's meager skill in front of an expert.

formation eyes were fully dismantled.

His two projections disappeared just before Xing Tong walked in. She found the cute baby fox sitting among the remnants of the ruined formation. The only evidence that people were once present was the half-eaten corpse of a devilish cultivator and two empty cloaks. Huxian involuntarily let out a cute, satisfied burp. Huxian had determined that formations *were* tasty. But he was in no hurry to submit his verdict, as there would be many more to sample in the future. Meanwhile, he felt the blood and gold energy he gathered strengthen his body and toughen his skin.

"What are you doing here? Cha Ming will be upset if he knows you ran away," she said cheerfully while petting him. Huxian indulged her for a few moments before letting out a shrill wail of agony. The sudden shriek forced Xing Tong to the floor with blood seeping out of her ears.

Uh oh. He felt a sharp, burning sensation as an object sprouted from his backside. It was a second tail. Huxian was now halfway to becoming a demon beast. He then became instantly aware of a frightening fact: His tribulation would arrive in three days.

Cha Ming's footsteps echoed through a lonely street near the eastern guard house. He was distracted by what he had just witnessed in a nearby shop. He hadn't intended to step into the shop, but a large crashing sound changed his mind. It was caused by the owner of the shop, who had collapsed on a display case. The room was covered in shattered glass splattered with blood.

As he rushed over to help the man, he quickly discovered that he wasn't simply unconscious. The elderly man's fires of life had been burning low even before tonight's events. The blood-gathering formation was just the last nail in his coffin. The cruel reality of the situation pressed the urgency of the situation: Many young children and the elderly would be the first to die if the blood formation wasn't stopped.

He glanced over the empty shelves in the shop before leaving. What should have been a thriving jewelry shop full of expensive merchandise had been thoroughly looted. He would have suspected looters if not for his timely arrival. The store's owner had just died, and he watched as the golden watch on the old man's wrist suddenly evaporated into a gold mist and wandered toward the nearby guard house.

Cha Ming understood that the priority was to stop the blood formation. But what if all the wealth in this rich city was used to strengthen the second individual? He resolved to destroy the gold formation eye after the blood formation eye.

He readied the Clear Sky Staff in his hands as he approached the guard house. Using his Mountain Stance, he rooted himself to the stone pavement as he heaved the elongated and weight-enhanced staff. It was now eighteen feet long and weighed 200 jin.

His bones creaked as he used the entire strength of his physical body while simultaneously channeling earth qi into the staff. The staff bent as he wielded it and performed a pure vertical strike toward the center of the guard house. The vibrations Cha Ming had imbued ensured that any stone encountered would crumble to dust.

A deafening boom broke the silence in the empty city streets. Without any warning, two saber-wielding individuals burst out from the newly formed entrance and lunged at Cha Ming, who wasted no time and counter-charged them. He put down each one with a single strike of his Sword Staff Art, and his precise blows crushed their necks and smashed their spinal cords. He felt no pity for them, however. These devil cultivators couldn't be considered human.

Cha Ming jumped over the rubble and noticed that a large figure had been crushed to a pulp, then saw two hooded figures at the back of the room, dead. Seemingly, the impact of the blow had thrown them into the wall and killed them. He left nothing to chance as he approached the formation, sending out a Flame Manifestation with his rosary. The two figures were reduced to ashes in mere moments.

"So, what next, great teacher?" he asked. His dependence on the red-bearded man grew more obvious with each passing day. *I should really learn formation arts once everything is said and done.*

A surge of information rushed to Cha Ming's head. *For the blood formation, paint these seven formations at these key points and then connect them accordingly.*

Cha Ming asked in an embarrassed voice, "The formation is a bit large. How am I supposed to paint it with this tiny brush?"

You have rocks for brains, the man replied. *Can't you see that the Clear Sky Brush and Clear Sky Staff are one and the same? Just get the brush to grow bigger and you won't have a problem!*

Cha Ming blushed as he realized his mistake. The Clear Sky Brush appeared in his hand at his command. With but a thought, it grew to the size of the Clear Sky Staff.

Don't waste time. Every second you waste means one more soul sent to Diyu. Cha Ming nodded and willed earth qi and liquified earth essence to the tip of his brush, which he used to draw a complex symbol he had never seen before. He then drew a symbol with water-aligned material, then earth again, then fire. As he continued to paint everything, Cha Ming shook his head self deprecatingly. He was like a fake artist, copying original works for a living.

After a half incense time, the formation he drew on the ground lit up, causing the bloody mist in the vicinity to halt all movement. The bloody mist flowed back from where it had come, unravelling the bloody formation eye in the process.

This will send as much blood energy as possible to the remaining victims. I can't do anything for the dead, the red-bearded man said with regret.

They wasted no time and proceeded to the gold formation. The formation for this one took much less time, as they were unconcerned with sending the residual energy back where it came from. Once the formation eye was destroyed, the gold mist in the room converged together to form three golden crystals, which Cha Ming collected. But the instant he collected them, he heard a deep voice resounding in his mind.

Bagua Huxian will be undergoing heavenly tribulation in three days' time. As per the Contract of Equals, you are obligated to share all trials and tribulations.

Cha Ming massaged his brow once he heard this piece of information, wondering why his advancement had happened so soon. Then it dawned on him. The glutton had probably eaten the formation eyes.

Gong Lan was vigilant as she walked down the cobblestone street toward the third guard house, her twin sabers ready in case of an ambush. A blood-red moon was shining in the sky, illuminating the city with its eerie light. It reminded Gong Lan of the writing she'd found in the village which read "Beware the Blood Moon."

Were they warning us about this? Did they know what would happen? She shuddered at the revelation.

She waltzed into the guard house, decapitating five figures with a few swift strikes. She knew from experience that the most effective way to deal with them was to lop off their heads. Hacking away a limb meant nothing to those crazed devil cultivators. It made her wonder if they were still human.

Unlike the others, she had no way to deal with formations. Therefore, she decided to try doing things the good old-fashioned way—by smashing and cutting them to tiny bits. It only took her a few strikes to notice that striking the formation eye was completely ineffective, so she turned her attention to the wooden planks below. Her heavy sabers smashed the wooden planks, destroying the runic patterns below the floating runes. Unfortunately, the formation eyes didn't weaken, and she could only sigh in dejection.

As she continued observing the formation eyes, she realized the red rune felt familiar. She reached out and traced the runic patterns on the formation eye in the hopes of gleaning some insight. After an incense time, she noticed that the aura of the bloody formation matched her cultivation technique, the Blood World Scripture.

Time was of the essence, so she didn't hesitate to drive her cultivation base and begin absorbing ambient qi. As predicted, the bloody rune shook, and the red mist in the room wandered toward Gong Lan. But in the midst of absorbing the blood energy, her heart began to pound uncontrollably. Tears welled in her eyes as she suffered the resentment of those who were harmed or killed by the formation.

I'm not the one who did this, she pleaded. But no one could hear her.

Despite being heavily affected, she didn't stop absorbing. Rather, seeing that her rate of absorption was having little or no effect, she increased the absorption rate tenfold. The frequency of voices she heard and resentment she felt increased proportionately, yet she gritted her teeth and cried as she continued the forceful absorption. Within sixty breaths, she noticed that she'd broken through to the ninth level of qi condensation. With her breakthrough, she was able to increase the rate of absorption to thirty times. This caused the formation eye to shudder and crack, breaking off pieces to be absorbed by the Blood World Scripture.

It cracked little by little, until finally, several large pieces broke off together, and the formation eye was destroyed. Only Gong Lan and the golden formation eye remained in the room. The golden formation eye continued humming as though nothing had happened, leaving Gong Lan kneeling with her hands on the floor. She cried tears of blood, and her arms shook as she supressed the aura of resentment that came with the blood energy. A powerful aura surrounded her as she wept. It was the aura of half-step foundation establishment.

Meanwhile, Feng Ming and Hong Lai were wracking their brains trying to figure out how to break the formation in the remaining guard house. If Feng Ming had his way, he would just keep hitting it with his spear. Unfortunately, Hong Lai pointed out that there might be grave repercussions if they didn't break the formation properly. So Feng Ming waited as Hong Lai weakened with every passing moment. It was only a matter of time before he lost consciousness, as the blood red thread was continually sapping away his vitality.

While Hong Lai was busy studying the formation, Feng Ming noticed a distortion in the formation.

"Did you see that?" he asked Hong Lai.

"See what? Quit distracting me while I'm breaking the formation." Hong Lai was currently crouched down, weakly using his spiritual hammer to attack key points near the formation eye.

Feng Ming shook his head and continued observing. A half incense time passed before he saw another two consecutive flickers. To Feng Ming, who was completely untrained in formations, the rune seemed dull and lifeless compared to its original state. He glanced down at Hong Lai, who was completely focused on his work.

"I've had enough of this," Feng Ming said, brandishing his spear. "I'm going to try breaking it."

"You can't do that!" Hong Lai yelled. His warning fell on deaf ears. Feng Ming stabbed the formation eye where he'd observed a slight distortion. His spear glowed red as he poured all his strength into that single strike, digging his feet into the ground with earthen power. A small crack appeared in the formation eye. Retracting his spear, he struck again and again.

Soon enough, the rune crumbled away, and the bloody mist in the room dissipated. Hong Lai, who had previously been struggling to remain conscious, looked at the spear in Feng Ming's hand in awe. Feng Ming wasn't paying attention, however. As soon as the rune crumbled, he was enveloped with a mysterious golden glow. It wasn't the same ominous glow that came from the gold formation; rather, it was the light of providence. He had performed great merit by destroying the formation and saving many lives, and that merit was being channeled through Feng Ming's soul through the Good Fortune Scripture.

"Yep," Feng Ming said. "With a single strike of my lucky spear, I send formations crumbling into dust." He didn't wait for Hong Lai's reply. The key to acting cool was to know when to leave.

Chapter 31: Fated Battle

The Fairweather Auction House was a shadow of its former glory. Its intricately carved walls, gildings, and decorations had lost their luster or had disappeared under the gold-plundering formation. Entire rooms had crumbled due to structural weakening.

While most of the employees in the auction house had returned to their dwellings, there was one man who remained in the building every night. The auction house was his home, and he viewed the wealth it generated as his personal collection. He wore an unsightly expression as he struggled to use his aura to save his most valuable treasures. However, there was only so much the power of Foundation Establishment could do to stave away the plundering gold mist. Even bags of holding couldn't stop the elusive thief. Little by little, his treasures crumbled to dust and evaporated before his very eyes. The only ones that didn't disappear were those that were bonded to him, like his flying sword and a few life-saving treasures.

"You all may as well come out," he said with a grunt. A

few short moments of silence were broken by the sounds of swishing blades as three cultivators flew in on magic swords. Each of them radiated the power of foundation establishment.

"Your senses are still sharp for such an old man," a masked figure commented as he jumped off his flying perch. The flying sword began spinning around him in a haphazard fashion when he landed. The other two masked men beside him followed suit, surrounding the white-haired auctioneer.

"I see that the three of you have come to court death," he said while brushing off his blue robes. Three silver-blue lights flashed as they darted out from the man's mouth and flew toward the three assailants. The three masked men deflected them with great difficulty. Surprisingly, the auctioneer could control three flying swords at once.

"Very impressive," the lead masked man said. "Flying swords are much harder to control than small daggers, pins, pearls, and other such objects. Moreover, these are high-level flying swords. It's no wonder that our master sent three of us to deal with you."

"You think you three alone are enough? Naïve." The three swords hummed, and an icy pattern resembling a snowflake spread out from each of them. The three patterns continued expanding and connected, forming a much larger pattern that surrounded him.

"No, you misunderstand. Our job is simply to stall you, so why don't you make this easy for yourself and stay put?" the masked man said while forming hand seals. His sword began to burn with a red flame. Meanwhile, his two assistants performed similar actions. Their swords turned green and yellow-brown respectively.

"The Earth, Wind, and Fire formation, how amusing."

The auctioneer formed a dozen hand seals and threw a bag of silver dust in the air. It absorbed into his skin, giving him the appearance of a man made of pure quicksilver. "Let us fight!"

Cha Ming felt the pressure on his vital force ease up with the disappearance of the red mist. Looking outside the guard shack, he realized that somehow, all four formation eyes had been destroyed.

I wonder who handled the fourth eye? he thought. He wasted no time and ran back toward the center of town, where he met Gong Lan and Huxian.

The blood moon in the sky had faded, and it now resembled a moon made of pure gold. The whole city became a dazzling sight to behold. He followed a yellow brick road to the city center, where both a red and gold formation still glowed brightly. The scope of the red formation was much smaller than before, however. Both Han Jinlong and Zhang Yifeng were using their power to supress Zhou Xian. He grimaced as he was forced to stand up from his meditative posture.

Zhou Xian looked at his skinny companion. "How much time do you need so you can supress these two, Merchant?"

The skinny man's eyes opened, and he looked at the two

master artisans with disinterest. "I still require an incense time to obtain seventy percent assurance. I'd ask for more time, but it seems you'll have your hands full."

Zhou Xian took a deep breath before withdrawing two scrolls from his bag of holding. The residual blood formation prevented Han Jinlong and Zhang Yifeng from interfering.

He flung the two scrolls into the air, where they unfurled into two golden contracts. He bit his thumb and swiped it across the first scroll. The golden contract's black writing glowed red before falling to the ground. The writing separated itself from the parchment and spread out in a circular formation while Zhou Xian signed the second contract in blood.

This time, the writing peeled off from the contract midair and created a formation in the shape of a gate. Within a few breaths' time, two powerful creatures emerged from their respective portals. One was a black hound with a sickly green mane while the other was a lithe beauty wearing barely anything. She appeared human, yet her entire form was red like blood.

"According to the contract, you may command us for half an incense time. What do you require, master?" the red creature inquired.

"Delay these two men for the duration of the contract," he instructed.

"Understood," the succubus responded. Both her and the hellhound darted out from the blood-red formation, shattering it. They immediately engaged Han Jinlong and Zhang Yifeng, leaving Zhou Xian to face Cha Ming, Gong Lan, and Huxian. The presence of foundation establishment oozed out from him.

Zhou Xian looked at Cha Ming and Huxian with a friendly smile. "My dear friends, it been so long. It's so nice to see you both. Alive." He glanced at Cha Ming with these words, and Zhou Xian's presence transformed.

Cha Ming had never fought against anyone at Foundation Establishment, so the initial aura was already imposing. Now that it had transformed, it no longer felt like suppression from a higher power. Rather, it was now a filthy feeling that aimed to corrupt his flesh, essence, and soul. The sickening feeling made it impossible for him to display his full strength.

Seeing Cha Ming's predicament, Huxian's figure blurred as he split into a black and a white fox, both with two tails. The white fox emanated a purifying aura, which neutralized part of Zhou Xian's evil presence. However, the disparity between realms was apparent. Huxian was only a half step into foundation establishment, after all.

Zhou Xiang clicked his tongue derisively at the expected intrusion. "So predictable, little fox. You stay put for a while." He formed a dozen hand seals and lifted his right hand up to the sky. A dark statuette appeared and subsequently scattered into thousands of black particles.

"Poison Suppression Idol!" he yelled. The figurine suddenly materialized above Huxian's white clone, and four characters surrounded him. They began emitting a frightening pressure that ate away at the purifying aura until it receded to one foot around the white Huxian.

Cha Ming and Gong Lan didn't waste any time, and neither

did the black Huxian, who turned into a black pool of shadows at the base of Zhou Xian's feet. Hundreds of mouths rushed out from the pool, threatening to devour Zhou Xian, starting with his legs.

Cha Ming knew that his power was much weaker than everyone else's, but he could still play a significant assisting role. He launched seventy-two pearls toward Zhou Xian, and they formed a Snowflake Manifestation, plunging the temperature well below freezing. He then rushed out toward the white Huxian and began analyzing the supressing runes.

Gong Lan used both Huxian's devouring pool and Cha Ming's freezing manifestation to full effect, slashing at Zhou Xian with seven blades of blood. They froze as they entered the snowflake formation, becoming physical blades of bloody ice that threatened to eviscerate him. Zhou Xian grunted and spit out a dark-green flying sword. It zipped around him and parried each of the bloody blades in succession. Only bits and pieces of sharp ice hit him, leaving shallow flesh wounds on his arms and chest.

After dispatching the blades, Zhou Xian ignored both Cha Ming and Gong Lan, directing his attention to the ground below. He paused for a few moments before sending his flying sword plunging down into the dark abyss beneath him. It didn't shatter the black pool, rather, it dove down inside it and began dispatching many of the toothy maws that threatened to devour him. He was not wounded thus far, but the devouring power beneath him was sapping away at his qi reserves.

As Gong Lan continued to launch more blades from a distance, Cha Ming transformed his Clear Sky Staff into a large Clear Sky Brush. He quickly painted a character in the air, which then shot out toward one of the characters supressing

Huxian. Zhou Xian's eyes narrowed when saw this, and he chose to send his flying sword out from the darkness to finish off Cha Ming, whom he saw as a weak fly.

Cha Ming was forced to retreat from the sudden assault, barely deflecting the sword with the Clear Sky Brush. He instantly changed his tactics to defense, using his Seven Cloud Steps to dart away and his Shearing Staff Art to deflect the incoming sword. It continued to harass him, and occasionally, it found openings in his imperfect defense. Fortunately, his earth and wood body refining had improved his defense and regeneration. However, with every shallow slash he took, he noticed an inky black substance seeping into his veins. It was clearly poison.

Seeing that Zhou Xian was focusing on Cha Ming, Gong Lan erupted with killing intent and charged at the restrained Zhou Xian. Zhou Xian drew another sword from his bag of holding, which he used to parry Gong Lan's dual saber assault. He confidently deflected her first few attacks, but she was building momentum. Soon, each blow made Zhou Xian's blood roil, and he was forced to divert attention from his flying sword to take care of the immediate threat. Meanwhile, Huxian's black clone continued assaulting Zhou Xian, devouring the power of his shield.

The lack of finely tuned control of the flying sword became quickly apparent to Cha Ming, who began using Burst Steps to instantaneously change directions and throw off the flying sword. After throwing it off for the fraction of a breath, he used Seven Cloud Steps to quickly move toward the white Huxian, using the opening to paint a single line in the air.

He didn't stop there, however. He made use of his extreme speed to slowly accumulate several lines in succession while simultaneously dodging the flying sword. After fifteen strokes, a character took shape and instantly flew out toward the second restraining character. The white Huxian roared and began assaulting the statuette with waves of purifying power.

As Cha Ming continued his combined evasion and painting motions, he felt something click. His darting motions, his instantaneous shifting, his quick parrying blows, and his quick brushing motions fused together. Before he knew it, the embryonic form of his second staff art took shape.

I'll call it the Swift Staff Art.

He immediately used his newly minted technique to good effect, completing a third rune in a few breaths' time. Zhou Xian, despite having broken through to early foundation establishment, was unable to endure and shouted, "Merchant, you need to come out *now!*"

"Useless," the Merchant said coldly. However, he followed Zhou Xian's request, and the golden formation around the merchant was quickly absorbed through his skin. He now looked like a man made of pure gold. The golden mist above the city disappeared with the formation, revealing a starry sky and a full moon.

Since the Merchant was no longer retracting his aura, the restraining effect of his qi on Cha Ming and the others was much higher than Zhou Xian's. Moreover, Cha Ming felt an additional form of suppression. His body trembled, and he felt as though his bones desired to prostrate themselves in worship.

Is this the power of Bone Forging, the equivalent of the Foundation Establishment Realm in body cultivation? He gulped at this revelation.

Fortunately, Han Jinlong and Zhang Yifeng appeared between them and the Merchant. They were panting heavily, and it was clear that the battle against the summoned devils had been extremely taxing. However, the summoned creatures had suddenly disappeared, and they were now available to face the Merchant with them.

The Merchant had no chance to prepare himself before Han Jinlong threw his hammer. The Merchant received it with his body, sliding back fifty feet before finally stopping. He remained unwounded and casually tossed the hammer aside. Han Jinlong grunted, and the hammer rematerialized in his hands.

"This is going to be a tough fight, kids," Han Jinlong said. "You need to hold back the small fry until we finish with this 'Merchant.' Neither myself nor Yifeng can hold him back by ourselves." Both he and Master Zhang darted out and began to attack the golden man with full force.

Zhou Xian's expression darkened when he saw he would be getting no reprieve. "You leave me no choice!" he bellowed. A dark green pill appeared in his hand. He crushed it in his hand and inhaled the resulting green dust. His aura soared instantly. Although this forbidden medicine didn't increase his strength by a full level, both Cha Ming and Gong Lan were now firmly supressed, and Cha Ming could no longer continue freeing the white Huxian as he was now busy avoiding the flying sword's skewering flight pattern. Without a turning point, it would be impossible to reverse the situation.

Han Jinlong deflected a punch from the golden man with his

hammer. Despite being forced back three feet, he barely left a mark on the man's fist. It was tougher than any metal he had forged to date. In addition to the Merchant's mid-level bone-forging body, he had also cultivated his skin, rendering it difficult to pierce or dent with metallic weapons.

Just how did he do it? Han Jinlong wondered. *His skin should not be so tough at his realm.*

The golden man was overthrowing everything Han Jinlong knew about body cultivation. He himself was a low-level bone-forging cultivator. He had been taught that body cultivators first strengthened and purified their bodies, bringing it to its most natural base state. Then came the forging of the bones and the strengthening of the tendons. This was the basis for bone-forging cultivators, and only those who completed these steps could begin cultivating their skin.

Still, the heavens were fair. Everything under the heavens had a weakness, and Han Jinlong and Zhang Yifeng only needed to find it. What worried him most was that, while the Merchant had a cultivation base at mid-level foundation establishment, he had yet to use any qi techniques. Just what kind of trump cards did he have? And was his whole body really like a human weapon?

Wait, a weapon! His skin is golden. Does this mean his body is like metal? To test his theory, he breathed out a plume of blue and bathed the golden man's body in flames. This time, he didn't shrug off the blow. A shield of qi materialized around him, resisting the scorching flames in his body's stead.

Yifeng, use your alchemist's flames to attack him. He's susceptible to fire, and he's been reserving his qi to counter it! Han Jinlong said mentally. His partner nodded and formed many intricate hand seals. Two red flame dragons shot out from his hands and began attacking the skinny man in tandem with Zhang Yifeng and his spear.

Zhang Yifeng's arms tingled with every strike of his spear. The spear was an unusual weapon choice for an alchemist, and he usually used the spear defensively to keep his opponent at bay.

Only when you keep your opponent away will your techniques truly shine. Instead of relying on the raw strength of his body, Zhang Yifeng imbued his weapon with qi. This made the long-ranged weapon a deadly threat to just about anyone. However, the golden man was an exception.

They were evenly matched in qi cultivation, but the Merchant had an equivalent body cultivation to complement it. His spear strikes had little to no effect. Zhang Yifeng wondered why the man kept defending instead of attacking. With such a strong defense, he could afford to ignore whatever they threw at him. Yet, the Merchant continued to defend against the alchemist's spear, his two meticulously controlled fire dragons, and Han Jinlong's relentless assault with both hammer and flames.

This really isn't easy. I feel like my weapon is about to break from all the strain, he thought. That was when he noticed the first crack on his weapon. It had grown dull compared to its usual magnificence. This treasured spear, a precious gift from Han Jinlong, was now on the verge of shattering.

So that's his game, he thought. After communicating his

findings to Han Jinlong, he gritted his teeth and continued attacking. Regrettably, he had expended all his wealth on the expedition and no longer had any major life-saving treasures or extra weapons. He could only endure and continue attacking the Merchant, hoping that his spear would last until the end of the battle.

Chapter 32: Mutual Destruction

Cha Ming was in dire straits. The sharp increase in Zhou Xian's power had forced him to devote all his power to fleeing. Not only was he using his newly created Swift Staff Art to constantly evade and deflect the dark-green flying sword, he had also been forced to withdraw the Snowflake Manifestation for personal protection.

He darted to the side, only to find a flying sword charging toward him. Seeing that his speed was insufficient to avoid it at close range, he conjured a Sword Manifestation to deflect it before fleeing once more.

At this rate, I'll never be able to free Huxian. And now that my Snowflake Manifestation is absent, Gong Lan can no longer fight toe-to-toe with Zhou Xian.

All he needed was a few breaths to add the finishing touches to the counter-formation, then White Huxian would be free to continue his assault. Then he was caught mid-thought by a familiar green glimmer. *Shit, I can't take much more of this,* he thought. Yet, to his surprise, the sword was deflected by a metallic weapon. It was a long black spear wielded by a familiar figure.

"Feng Ming!" Cha Ming shouted. His friend didn't answer but coughed up blood instead. Cha Ming didn't hesitate to send his Healing Flower Manifestation to Feng Ming before darting off toward White Huxian. "Buy me three breaths," he shouted to Feng Ming.

The sword tried to evade Feng Ming, but the latter's spear technique was unfathomable and unpredictable. He moved between Cha Ming and the sword, using his spear's reach to smash it away. While his cultivation base was much lower than Cha Ming's, his weapon was much stronger than Zhou Xian's.

Cha Ming wasted no time and arrived beside Huxian to paint the remaining lines. The flying sword tried to fly around Feng Ming, but to no avail. It started attacking Feng Ming directly.

Clang. Clang. Clang. Every strike from the sword knocked Feng Ming back a few feet. The first few times caused him to cough up blood. This was due to a disparity between realms, and it was a miracle that he wasn't instantly killed. The fourth strike caused his hands to bleed. Finally, the sword knocked his spear two dozen feet away. But it did not kill Feng Ming. Instead, it slashed his arm in passing and traveled at lightning speed toward its true goal: Cha Ming.

However, the flying sword was too late. Cha Ming finished the last stroke of his brush when the sword was merely three feet away. Huxian, who had been attentive this entire time, jumped out in front of the flying sword, shielding Cha Ming with his body. The sword bounced off his fur with a loud *clang*, and Huxian's aura of purification burst out, relieving everyone from the weakening effects of Zhou Xian's aura.

Feng Ming was kneeling on the floor, shaking. He had taken far too much damage in the exchange and couldn't even stand properly, much less retrieve his spear. Furthermore, the poison had begun spreading from the wound on his arm, forcing him to circulate his cultivation base to keep it at bay. He had a satisfied smile on his face. After all, they had lost his support in exchange for Huxian's—a worthy trade!

Huxian's aura continued to soar as he joined his black clone in attacking Zhou Xian. Unfortunately, he was a tad too late, and Gong Lan was struck by a poison dragon. She was forced to kneel as she grasped the right side of her chest where the poison dragon had struck her. Black lines were snaking up her right arm and neck from the exposed region. Seeing that support had arrived, she sat down in meditation and began expelling the poison from her blood with the Blood World Scripture.

Huxian howled as he attacked Zhou Xian with both clones simultaneously. Brother, he sent mentally, *I can't defeat him, he's much too strong. I need your help.*

How? Cha Ming responded while rushing toward him. He had absolute trust in his brother. Fortunately, Zhou Xian's attention had been diverted and he could no longer control the flying sword.

Stand beside my white clone and put your arm on it.

Cha Ming complied, only to see the pool of darkness below Zhou Xian travel back toward the white clone. The two clones were superimposed momentarily, and Cha Ming felt a surge of energy pass through his hand and into his body and dantian.

What's this? he asked in amazement.

That is the qi that I've been plundering from Zhou Xian since the beginning of the fight, Huxian replied. *I absorbed it with my black clone and purified it with my white clone. You can temporarily use it as qi or to enhance your physical prowess. It will only last for the next thirty breaths. Let's use it to gain the advantage!*

Cha Ming didn't need to be told twice—he quickly used a Flame Manifestation, enhancing it with both wood and water qi. He needed to use these thirty seconds to deal as much damage as possible. He didn't have time to defend.

Blood gushed out of a wound on Zhang Yifeng's chest as the Merchant tore through his qi defense with his bare hands. The man's hands resembled golden claws more than anything else. They had ignored Yifeng's defensive magic robes, which hadn't been breached in a full decade. The older man gnashed his teeth and continued dousing the Merchant in his alchemist flames.

The flames an alchemist could conjure far exceeded those of normal cultivators. They could achieve much higher temperatures than even blacksmiths, fueling their fires with wood qi. Further, Zhang Yifeng didn't hesitate to use various medicinal powders, all of which enhanced the already elevated temperature of his crimson flames.

The Merchant shrieked as a powder-enhanced burst singed his arm. For the first time in the battle, the alchemist's flames had bypassed the golden man's qi barrier. A thin layer of his skin melted, but it recovered soon after.

"I hate spending more than anything else in the world, but

you've forced me to do this!" The Merchant was livid, his face rife with madness. He brought his left hand to his mouth and bit down on his little finger. He didn't wail as the finger was removed, and no blood leaked out from the fresh wound. It was as though the finger was never flesh to begin with, and no bone could be seen where it had previously been connected to his hand.

The Merchant chewed loudly, and his mastication sounded like metal on metal. He quickly followed up with an incantation in a dark language. Despite not speaking the language, everyone nearby could hear the meaning in their hearts.

"The price is paid. Almighty Greed, lend me your strength!" With these words, the Merchant's aura soared a small step higher.

With his newfound strength, he charged toward Zhang Yifeng and slashed at him with his right claw. The claw no longer resembled anything like a human hand. Instead, two-inch-long silvery nails now tipped each finger.

No! I won't be able to avoid this! Yifeng closed his eyes and gritted his teeth in preparation for the incoming blow, which would likely kill him. However, it never came. He opened his eyes slightly, only to see Han Jinlong standing in front of him. A golden hand protruded from his back.

Han Jinlong coughed weakly. "You need to finish him after this, Yifeng. Save this town. Save our people." Each word was uttered with great difficulty, and Zhang Yifeng couldn't stop tears from streaming down his cheeks.

"Jinlong, you fool!" he whispered. The Merchant grunted in response to the interference and flung his arm out to throw away the smith's corpse. But the smith remained firmly attached. A panicked expression covered the Merchant's face as

Zhang Yifeng noticed a frightening energy quickly rising. Han Jinlong had chosen to sacrifice himself via self-detonation!

Yifeng was able to retreat fifty feet before a massive explosion buffeted him. His qi shield soaked up the shock wave. He had no attention to spare for the fighting children and could only wish them the best. The only thought on his mind was to avenge his dear friend, to avenge his friends and family and the countless villagers who had perished at the Merchant's hands.

No pieces of Han Jinlong could be found amid the wreckage near the middle of the explosion. Only the Merchant stood there, or what was left of him. Half his torso and a full arm were missing. Yifeng no longer wondered how that *thing* was still standing. He could see no organs, or bones, or blood. The Merchant was only bleeding one thing, and that was gold.

Yifeng didn't hesitate to swallow a magic qi recovery pill and throw out a large packet of green powder. He channeled his wood-fueled fire qi to ignite the powder, which created a vivid green flame. This flame was double the temperature of anything he had used previously. The Merchant shrieked as his skin and extremities melted. The alchemist wasn't sure if it was due to pain or due to the realization that its demise was imminent.

He didn't let up the attack and continued pressing on. He used priceless pills and reagents to continuously boost the temperature of his flame. It might be overkill, but he knew one thing for certain: The least he owed his friend was the best funeral pyre Fairweather had ever seen.

Earlier

Cha Ming focused his newfound strength, channeling it to temporarily strengthen his body. His qi techniques were lackluster compared to his physical strength and combat techniques, after all. To complement his fist strength of 1,080 jin, he increased the weight of his staff to 200 jin.

He used Burst Steps to charge at Zhou Xian while Huxian flanked him on two other sides. White Huxian's purifying power was used at full force, negating Zhou Xian's poisonous aura while forcing him to maintain it, lest the purifying aura suppress him. Black Huxian gave up his previous trick of attacking Zhou Xian's body from the shadows. Instead, he turned his sights to Zhou Xian's shadow. Thus, Zhou Xian was forced to defend on three fronts. Meanwhile, the Flame Manifestation grinded away at his armor of qi, depleting it bit by bit.

Cha Ming focused his weight by using Mountain Stance and struck out using combinations of Sword Staff and Quake Staff. Horizontal, vertical, and diagonal strikes combined into a seamless whole, while his weight control and Burst Steps combined into a whole new form of movement. He varied the weight and length of his staff in an unpredictable but aggressive fashion. With each passing moment, he became aware that he'd created the embryonic form of his third combat style—Hard Staff Art.

While he was hardly Zhou Xian's match one-on-one, that didn't matter. After all, he wasn't alone. With Huxian's help, they began beating Zhou Xian into submission. Yet Cha Ming knew that time was limited. He only had ten seconds left with this borrowed strength.

Huxian, lend me a hand and pin him down, Cha Ming sent mentally.

Huxian's two clones ran around Zhou Xian with lightning speed. Everywhere they passed, they left a ribbon of light and darkness. These ribbons seemed like solidified light and shadow. Zhou Xian was unable to react before the two clones darted in opposite directions, tightening the ribbons around the dark-robed man. Although the ribbons didn't make contact, Zhou Xian was immobile.

Cha Ming didn't require a prompt. He swiftly increased the weight of his staff once more to 500 jin and rooted himself to the ground. He pounded at Zhou Xian's head with one strike after another. Each strike threatened the integrity of his qi shield, yet nothing managed to damage the foundation-establishment cultivator. With every strike, he felt a vicious counter-force that made his blood roil.

Three seconds left. He hacked away with strike after strike, using his Hard Staff Art. After two more seconds, he was rewarded for his efforts when a trickle of blood appeared on Zhou Xian's face. But blood was rushing out of Cha Ming's mouth ten times as fast.

This is my last strike, Huxian! Cha Ming jumped back and pulled his staff all the way behind him. He used every last bit of his strength to both elongate the staff to triple its length, smashing downward at ten times the speed originally possible with a regular six-foot staff. In addition, he used Quake Staff, imbuing it with the power of vibration!

This last strike completely depleted Cha Ming's energy. A look of horror appeared on Zhou Xian's face as he realized he couldn't defend against it. He tried once more to free himself, but to no avail. Finally, he let out an angry shriek as a frightening fluctuation emitted from his body, engulfing both Cha Ming and the two Huxians in a dreadful explosion. After the first explosion, Cha Ming heard a second explosion from a hundred feet away.

Who self-detonated? Are both Master Zhang and Master Han all right? This was the last thought that flashed through his mind before he lost consciousness.

Two consecutive blasts made the windows and doors of the auction house shudder. The auctioneer was breathing deeply, and he was bleeding from several deep cuts. His opponents weren't faring any better. They were littered with cuts, and one of the men's arms was hanging limp by his side.

"Would you care to find out who those people were?" he asked.

The three men and the auctioneer rushed out of the building in tacit agreement. Soon, they witnessed a horrifying sight. The crumbling remnants of what used to be opulent buildings littered the streets. Yet the buildings with the simplest construction remained untouched. It was a very bizarre sight.

Two large craters occupied a large area at the center of town. Three cultivators and a spirit beast were still standing, while one cultivator was passed out. It was clear who the two craters belonged to.

"Flee!" yelled the three cultivators. The auctioneer snorted and sent all three swords at one of the cultivators. He tumbled to the ground with three swords lodged in his back. The other two managed to escape. It wasn't possible for all three of them to retreat against such a superior cultivator.

The auctioneer flew over to Zhang Yifeng, who stood near a puddle of gold, mourning. "Did Jinlong…" he started. Zhang Yifeng nodded his head in sorrow. The auctioneer shook his head and flew over to the three youngsters and the fox. Three of them were in bad condition, and one of them had already passed out. The auctioneer tossed two pellets to Gong Lan and Feng Ming, who swallowed them without hesitation. Their wounds began healing at a rate visible to the naked eye.

He then tossed another bottle to Gong Lan. "Feed this to that kid. He'll recover soon. I'm going to the county lord's manor to investigate the situation," he said before flying off.

When he arrived, he found a house full of fainted maids, two dead guards, one dead county lord, and Bei Ling.

"Oh, my dear old friend…" the auctioneer muttered softly. "At least you died with a smile on your face. Not many people in this city can say the same." With these words, he flew off to find several trusted individuals, waking them one by one.

There was much work to be done.

Zhou Li suddenly awoke from his cultivation session. It was the middle of the night, and he hadn't heard any word from Fairweather. Despite his multiple attempts, he had not managed to divine the situation. Therefore, he could only hope for the best and make the meddler pay the highest price possible for his actions.

"Protector Song, did you find the rat yet?" Zhou Li asked the empty room. A golden-armored figure appeared in front of him, kneeling.

"Young Master, my apologies for my incompetence. I still can't find any trace of anyone. Are you sure this isn't a long-distance curse?" he asked doubtfully.

"Yes, I'm sure," Zhou Li responded. "It's not possible for someone to interfere at a long range, not unless the one interfering is a Transcendent. However, the price a Transcendent would pay is much too large for this trifling matter. He *must* be nearby."

The armored man nodded slowly.

Suddenly, Zhou Li grimaced as he realized a very important thread of karma had been severed. Another even more important thread was severed shortly after. There was only one explanation for this—both his brother and the Merchant had fallen.

"Who dares!" he yelled out. Seething with rage, he withdrew a small black pouch from his belt and took out six crystals. They emanated a sensation of pure evil, as though they were sin incarnate. Zhou Li slammed his chest with his fist and spat a mouthful of heart blood on the crystals, then immediately burned away the offering with obsidian flames. His aura surged as he yelled, "You will *not* hamper me. Not this time!"

The man in the golden armor stood by with a serious expression as Zhou Li took out a small mirror from his pouch. The mirror was covered with an inky film. He expanded it to ten times its size in the span of a few breaths. Then he flung out his hands, incinerating the black film with his obsidian flames. Unlike the previous times, the black film melted away with no resistance.

The mirror quickly portrayed a bird's-eye view of Fairweather City. There, he saw several symbols. There were two bloodied sabers, a black armor with white runes, and an alchemist's flame. Two other symbols were there, but their symbols were blurred.

"You *will* show me!" he yelled fiercely, coughing up blood in the process. The fog obscuring one of the symbols was lifted, showing a coin engraved with a white circle and a black star, as well as five colored points. A golden tether connected it to the other blurred figure.

It's you! he thought. He knew that this figure had killed his brother—they were connected by a blood-red thread of karma, a blood debt. A sinister grin appeared on Zhou Li's face as he withdrew six more crystals.

Anything I do to you will affect the other. You've both been a thorn in my side—that will end today. All for the small price of twelve Sin Crystals.

He coughed up his heart blood once more, using his blood and the six crystals to fuel the obsidian flame again. The flame traveled along the blood-red karma thread at a slow pace. Once the last bit of black flame was sent down, he grasped the red thread and gathered a portion of it into a small pearl in his hand. He then flicked the pearl into a fengxue compass[12], which immediately began pointing in Fairweather's direction.

"Protector Song," he said, "take this compass and hunt down the man named Du Cha Ming. Kill both him and the fox. This compass will point to him until he dies. I won't be able to accompany you—I have a troublesome opponent to meet in

---

[12] Also known as a Luo Pan, uses a moving needle and an external plate full of information that is adjusted manually.

court in a few hours. Return to me once the task is completed."

The man bowed and immediately flew out of the room. He didn't use a flying sword. No, he flew unassisted! He passed over the guards and the city's people without being noticed. Except by one man. The man had been sitting cross-legged beneath the window Protector Song had just left from. He was wreathed in shadows and couldn't be discovered by anyone.

A smile appeared on Wang Jun's face as he saw the man fly off. He formed several dozen hand seals, which manifested a needle that flew out toward Protector Song. It completely avoided him but settled down on the Fengxue compass he was carrying. Wang Jun let out a sigh as he felt another ten years of his life flow out from between his fingers. Cha Ming was the biggest bet in his life, and his only friend.

In for a penny, in for a pound.

Chapter 33: Calamity

Cha Ming awoke to the scent of jasmine and a soft pillow. It took him a few moments to realize that the "pillow" was a human one, and the jasmine he smelled was Gong Lan's perfume. He looked up to see her smiling face. Yet he could see grief behind her imperfect façade. That was when he smelled ashes and molten metal.

He sat up quickly, only to discover that he was perfectly fine. The internal injuries he had sustained from the fight had healed, and the poison had subsided. "Did we win?" he asked.

"At a cost," she explained while nodding. "Han Jinlong sacrificed himself, and the so-called Merchant was killed by Zhang Yifeng. The auction master was attacked by three foundation-establishment cultivators. He killed one, the other two escaped. Finally..."

She hesitated to finish.

"Who else died?" Cha Ming asked.

She sighed. "Bei Ling died while killing the county lord. It seems he was involved in the entire plot. Feng Ming and Hong

Lai managed to destroy one of the formation eyes, so they were lucky to avoid the bulk of the effects. They are currently out searching for survivors and finding who needs immediate treatment. So many babies and children, so many elderly..." She burst into tears as she finished.

Cha Ming understood that the blood formation had drained vital energy from the whole city. Those with the least vitality, children and the elderly, would be the most heavily affected. Even if they hadn't died, the effect of losing so much vitality would likely cripple their growth and greatly shorten their lifespan. Such was the cruelty of these devil cultivators.

I should go help them, he thought helplessly.

You will do no such thing! yelled an angry voice inside his head. It was the red-bearded man, and the tone of his voice was particularly grave. *While you were asleep, someone cast a terrible curse on you from afar. Not only will it give you terrible luck, but it shows that whoever did this knew where you were at the time of casting. While I can no longer sense the thread of karma, someone is bound to come here soon. You need to flee as far as possible, lest you burden everyone around you with this curse.*

In addition, you and your fox friend must undergo a Heavenly Tribulation in less than three days. We need to be far away from anyone, and we need ample time to prepare. Otherwise, both you and the fox will become piles of smoldering meat!

Just how bad is this tribulation? Cha Ming asked Huxian.

Brother, it's worse than you could ever imagine. Normally it wouldn't be a problem for me. However, I sense that the tribulation this time will be much worse than normal. You need to remember, you're not even at half-step foundation establishment. You're at best a seventh-level cultivator with a few fortunate encounters.

Even foundation-establishment experts would need to be wary of this tribulation.

Although the fox didn't say it directly, Cha Ming could tell from his body movements that he was eager to leave.

Cha Ming sighed. *So much effort, so much fighting, just to run away.* Cha Ming shook his head. "Gong Lan, I need to leave now."

She looked confused and bewildered at his sudden change in demeanor. "What you do you mean *leave?*"

"I mean that me and Huxian need to go. A disaster is about to strike us, and if we stay, it will involve the whole city. Stay in Fairweather for a few days. We're leaving now." With these words, Cha Ming began running toward the hole in the city wall where they had entered. Huxian thought this was too slow, so he grew a few sizes larger, and Cha Ming jumped on his back.

The painter and the fox ran off toward the north. They did not turn back, so they never saw the beautiful girl with short-cropped hair crying as she stared out at the skyline.

Protector Song heaved a sigh of relief as he flew toward Fairweather. Accompanying the Young Master always gave him the creeps. Not that he had much of a choice in the matter. He had sold his life the moment he'd set foot in the castle. He'd soon found out that he was worth nothing to them. Someone to be trampled on and ridiculed. It wasn't until he was accepted into the Old Master's service that he gained great power. But was it worth it? The price was his soul.

Still, there was no arguing that he felt great satisfaction when he trampled all those who had put him down over the years. Sure, he had to follow orders. But when he was unoccupied, he could do whatever he liked. The young and old masters thought he was stupid, and he didn't try to correct them, lest they get him to take on additional responsibilities. At least this way he could get a game or two in every week.

The breeze this morning was quite refreshing, and the dawn was one of the most beautiful he'd seen in many years. The feeling of flying without a sword was exhilarating, and he took advantage of it whenever he could.

Out in the distance, he saw what remained of Fairweather. Several ant-like figures scurried about, bringing people out of houses on stretchers. Healers were administrating medicine, and doctors were curing the more difficult cases. At the same time, he saw a much larger pile of corpses. They were being collected onto funeral pyres, as there were too many to bury outside the city.

He sat above the city, floating while meditating. His senses reached out, and he picked up pieces of information.

"Why did Cha Ming leave suddenly? That isn't like him," a young man said.

"I don't know," a sobbing voice replied. "All he said was that a disaster was about to strike him and Huxian, so they left. They rode off to the north."

The man listened for a few more moments before heading north, toward the mountains. He wasn't concerned with these small fries. He had things to do, people to kill. Unfortunately, the fengxue compass he had been given to track said people was defective. No matter how hard he tried, the needle refused to budge.

He sped off into the distance, passing by meadows, forests, and all sorts of wonderful land features. There were mountains up ahead. And beneath him, he saw the most beautiful lake he had ever laid eyes on. He tried to ignore it, yet he was attracted to a beautiful weeping willow.

The tree was covered in small buds, which was surprising given how spring had only just started. Despite his urgency, he felt compelled to walk beneath it and appreciate the scenery. The water beside the tree was calm, and the grass was emerald green. If he were a painter, he would have tried to capture the moment.

Suddenly he heard the familiar sound of shaking stones behind him. He was surprised to see that an old man with unruly short hair was sitting beneath a tree in meditation. The white-haired man was sitting down in front of an *Angels and Devils* board. He was holding a cat, who was sleeping on his lap, purring. Normally, he would have asked the man to play a game. He had a mission to complete, however, so he turned around to leave.

"Just where do you think you're going, Song Qing Rou?"

Protector Song was startled. *How does he know my name?* he wondered. He turned around and noticed that the man was smiling. He didn't sense a wisp of cultivation from him. That meant one of two things: Either the man was not a cultivator, or he was a supreme cultivator. However, it was very difficult for an ordinary man to appear so far out in the wilderness. He decided to play it safe and replied, "Does Senior require something?"

"Yes, I just happen to need your help with something," the

man replied. "I'll be going away for a long time, and I've long wanted to challenge the regional *Angels and Devils* champion. I would be extremely honored to play a game with you before I leave."

Protector Song faltered when he heard the man's request. *How in the world did he know I would come here, and how the hell does he know I'm the regional champion? Even my mother doesn't know!* He composed himself before answering, "My apologies, Senior, but I'm off to accomplish an important mission. Could you perhaps wait for half a day before I return? I would be willing to play to your heart's content."

The older man frowned. "I'm afraid I can't wait that long. How about we play a game, and then I'll let you go?"

Suddenly Protector Song felt a stifling pressure bearing down on him. It was complete suppression, and he felt that he barely had the strength to kill a chicken. Meanwhile, the cat sitting on the man's lap got up and stretched. It walked out, step by step, growing with each passing breath. It grew until it became one hundred feet long. It no longer resembled a housecat—rather, it now looked like an impressive demon bobcat.

Protector Song shivered when he saw this and breathed out a sigh of relief when the "cat" stretched out and laid down lazily. "Now, now, Mr. Mao Mao, no need to act so intimidating," the older man said, his eyes shining mischievously. "I'm sure that this man will be very reasonable and play a game with me. Besides, we can't slaughter mere mortals without incurring great karma. That is, unless they insult us. But I'm sure that 'Protector Song' wouldn't be so foolish as to insult us by refusing a game, right?"

The armored man gulped as he heard their conversation.

He wasn't sure exactly how the Heavenly Dao operated, but he wasn't about to gamble with his life. *I've heard that it's forbidden for Transcendents to murder mortals. But what* are *their limitations? What rotten luck.* He sat down in front of the elder with great humility and placed the first black stone. The devils had made their move, and it was the angels' turn to play.

"I object, Your Honor," Wang Jun said, his voice full of confidence. He was standing amidst a dozen seated people, a combination of the best minds available to him and a few select guardians. Protector Ren Wufa was seated near the rear of their group. He appeared to be on full alert, but in reality, he was napping. His alert disposition was just a cheap illusion, barely enough to fool the judge and supervising guards. After all, only a madman would attack them within the courthouse.

"Based on what grounds, Mr. Wang?" the judge asked while calmly adjusting his spectacles.

"On the grounds that this is no longer a matter of private contracts," Wang Jun replied. "Zhou Li and Zhou Jia's manipulation of the country's officials have restricted access to alchemical products from other countries. As a result, they have created a monopoly that greatly inflates prices for the common people. Their breaking of the contract prematurely is not just an inter-company dispute, but rather a precursor to a larger merger, a conspiracy to line their pockets at the expense of the kingdom's welfare. This even extends to the spirit-doctor community, who only has the best interests of the people in mind.

"While this does not infringe on current trade laws, I argue that it will affect the trade relationship between countries and infringes upon the kingdom's Declaration on the Welfare of Citizens, which states that monopolies that threaten the welfare of the people are prohibited.

"There are notable exceptions that have proven a monopoly to be beneficial—both Sijun Iron Refining and Wailin Coal Corporation have proven beyond a shadow of a doubt that their monopoly of the market reduced costs to their end consumers. They continue filing reports to prove things as such. However, what we have seen from the Alchemist's Association is a steep inflation in pricing. Therefore, I ask the court to either break up this newly formed monopoly, heavily regulate it, or open the border to free trade."

The judge massaged his brow as he sat, deep in thought. Then, looking to Zhou Li, he asked, "Does the defendant have a statement before we adjourn for the day?

"Yes, your honor," Zhou Li replied. "This decision to cancel the trade agreement is well within our rights. This is clearly stated in the contract. As for the other considerations, I ask that these be dismissed by the court, as they are superfluous to the current case."

The judge nodded. "Very well, we will reconvene again tomorrow morning. Please stay posted for the exact time. You will be notified one hour prior to court convening." With this, the judge hammered the desk with his wooden mallet.

Zhou Li and Wang Jun met outside the courtroom. "You must be kidding with this joke of a lawsuit," said Zhou Li. "You don't have a case to make. Give it a few days, and it will be thrown out of court. I'll make sure to send you our bill for legal services."

Wang Jun shrugged. "We will see. The Wang family never gives up without a fight. You think you can take our share of the pie without getting your wrist slapped? By the way, you look awfully tired and pale. Have you been sick lately? Or perhaps you haven't been getting enough sleep? No, wait, you were with your sister last night—it all makes sense now!"

He walked away nonchalantly, his entourage in tow. Zhou Li was left seething with rage.

Two days passed by in a flash. Huxian and Cha Ming hadn't stopped to rest on their trek toward the mountains. They ignored all sorts of spirit beasts on their way, only stopping when Huxian needed to eat to replenish his energy stores. Neither did they bother to stop for the medicinal ingredients they encountered on the way. Every second counted.

At last, they arrived on a flat surface at the top of a mountain. The sun was just setting in the distance. He could see the wilderness stretching out in each of the four cardinal directions. There were plains to the north, a forest to the south, and a mountain chain to the east and the west. The mountain chain was a natural border to the north of the Song Kingdom. Numerous armies had attempted to flood through its passes over the years, though few had succeeded in the end.

It's time, Cha Ming, said the red-bearded man. *I can help you with this tribulation, but it will take a lot out of me. You'll be on your own for the next long while. Remember, though, due to the curse on your body, this tribulation will be much stronger than usual. On the plus side, the curse will not survive the tribulation. Lightning is the nemesis of curses, the enemy of evil.*

The last glimmer of sunshine disappeared on the horizon as he finished these words. Cha Ming became solemn but didn't speak. A sigh traveled outward from the Clear Sky Staff in Cha Ming's hands. He was alarmed when he realized that another hand was also gripping it beside him. It was the red-bearded man. He was much taller in reality than inside the Clear Sky World. He wasn't wearing a shirt, only red pants that matched his impressive beard and unruly red hair.

He looked toward Cha Ming with his crimson irises and put out his hand. "I need the Clear Sky Staff and your bag of holding. Then get to the edge of the mountain."

Cha Ming bowed deeply and gave him both items. His bag of holding held all his life savings, and the Clear Sky Staff was his fated treasure. Yet he trusted the mysterious man with his life.

Cha Ming and Huxian sat near the side of the flat mountaintop as they observed the red-bearded man. He clasped his hands in meditation and sat still for a half hour before finally opening his eyes. His aura surged as he lifted the Clear Sky Staff. It transformed into the Clear Sky Brush, its tip glowing with pure white light.

He jumped up in the air and hovered there as he slashed outward with the brush. Wherever he slashed, white ink splashed out and formed rune marks on the mountaintop. There were all sorts of complicated runes and geometric symbols. This continued for two hours, and during this time, Cha Ming saw over ten thousand perfect white runes get laid down one after another, yet he could barely understand one percent of them. They formed a large white circle, which encompassed most of the mountaintop.

"Get in, kids," the man said. Cha Ming and Huxian immediately complied and traveled to the center of the circle. The man flung out his hand, and dozens of purple stones traveled from his hand to various points in the formation. These were all bits of crystalized elemental essence from Cha Ming's bag of holding. His heart ached, yet he didn't speak out. After all, his life was much more important than his wealth.

The red-bearded man formed a thousand hand seals before yelling out, "Circle of Protection—Lightning!" The white formation began to glow even more intensely. The night was now pitch black, and the circle stood out like a beacon.

Following this, he pulled out the bundle of metal stakes tied with a chain. He held them out before his face and breathed into them. As he breathed, the stakes began to glow. Several white runes lit up on each dagger-like object, as well as the chain itself. As they began to glow, he began to fade. He was now a transparent version of his former self. Then, using the last of his strength, he threw the daggers into the air.

They traveled upward for a few dozen feet before finally setting themselves in place. They didn't stop—no, they *pierced* the sky. The chains connecting all the spikes had formed a complex formation above them.

Cha Ming looked at the red-bearded man worriedly. "You're fading... What's going on?"

"This is all I can do for you kids," said the red-bearded man. "I won't be able to help you with the next one. Now I'll fall into a deep sleep. Make sure you find something to bring me back in the future, okay? I have something important I want you to do."

Cha Ming, who wasn't sure how to react, bowed deeply in thanks.

He hesitated before finally asking a question that had lingered on his mind since they first met. "What's your name?"

The fading man looked reluctant to share this information. After all, he was in such an embarrassing situation, and the loss of face wasn't small.

"My name is Sun Wukong. Remember it well!" With these words, the man faded into mist and traveled back inside the Clear Sky Brush. It was as Cha Ming thought. The red-bearded man was the legendary Monkey King.

"We'll get you back. Don't you worry," Cha Ming whispered. Yet he didn't have time to relax. The moment Sun Wukong vanished, dark clouds began to gather above them and obscure the starry sky. Thunder roared in the skies as these clouds prepared to unleash Heaven's wrath on them.

Brother, let's split up on each side of the circle. Although we are undergoing a split tribulation, we still need to fight it alone. It will be divided into nine strikes of lightning, each one stronger than the last. Fortunately, this is only the first tribulation. Only white lightning will rain down from the sky. You can resist with your weapons and techniques, but items like talismans and formations are forbidden unless they were personally created. I have no idea where Sun Wukong discovered this heaven-defying formation.

The lightning crackled in a threatening manner, warning them that it was about to begin. Cha Ming readied his staff and his rosary. He knew running wouldn't help. Only when he withstood the full might of Heaven's punishment would he be allowed to continue living. Huxian howled at the stormy sky in defiance.

Begin!

Chapter 34: Survival

Protector Song sweated profusely as he made a move. It was the most difficult game he had ever played in his life and made him wonder if Transcendents had an unfair advantage in the game.

Can he read my mind? he wondered. No, that's impossible. There's no way a Transcendent who can read minds would be stuck in a backwater place like this.

Mind reading or not, the entire game hinged on this final point. It was a Ko fight[13], a stage of the game where they sought out each other's weaknesses. Protector Song wasn't bothered by such a close game. After all, he had gone through many grueling games such as this in the past. What bothered him was that he had precisely thirteen weaknesses left while his opponent had forty-seven. He was clearly slow rolling him! Yet the man was

---

[13] As mentioned in the previous book, Ko is a special situation in Go where a board position can't be repeated. A back-and-forth exchange ensues. However, it takes many steps to return to the original position. Each back-and-forth exploration for weakness takes about six moves.

unfathomably powerful, and he could only play along.

Truth be told, the endgame had been ongoing for the past twelve hours. With every move, his frightening opponent took an unreasonable amount of time.

Is he trying to delay me? No, that can't be. How would that whelp know someone so unreasonably powerful? The only reasonable explanation is that he's an eccentric master that passionately loves this game.

Despite the eighty or so remaining moves, the game continued until well after sunset. Protector Song wore a long face as he made each of his moves with lightning speed, only to be chastised by the older man for being too impatient. Impatient, my ass! You're just making this difficult for no reason. Resign![14]

Finally, only three moves were left. The older man finally let out a long sigh and voiced a silent resignation. Tears were practically streaming down Protector Song's cheeks. He swiftly got up and bowed to the superior cultivator. "Thank you for the game!" he shouted.

"Off you go, you little runt." Protector Song darted off, flying toward the nearby mountain range, where ominous clouds were gathering. "The younger generation is so impolite nowadays," the older man muttered.

---

[14] Western culture romanticizes never giving up no matter what. However, in Go and chess, not giving up when the result is guaranteed is considered rude. In fact, professional-level players in Go can "calculate" the end score with extreme precision. The higher the skill level, the higher awareness they have, and the ruder it is not to resign when there is a clear difference.

Elder Ling let out a long sigh as he looked toward the weeping willow behind him. "You may as well come out. I know you're here." A few breaths of silence followed. Elder Ling grunted and threw a talisman toward the tree. The projection of massive fangs appeared in front of the tree and bit down on the tough bark. Splinters flew out everywhere until the tree completely disappeared. A beautiful woman with long black hair and black robes now stood in its place.

"If you can hide for fifty years, why can't I hide for a few moments?" the woman spat back, her voice full of venom.

"My dear wife, you sure know how to jest. It's so boring in the sect, and I knew that it was fine in your perfectly capable hands," Elder Ling said with a smile on his face.

"Shameless!" she yelled. Thousands of pitch black chains appeared in front of her. They darted out and surrounded Elder Ling, who didn't resist in the slightest. Mr. Mao Mao got up and howled in rage at the treatment. The woman frowned.

She snorted. "The third wheel. Well, I have an old friend here to keep you company." A tiny little white kitten stepped out from behind the woman. While it looked defenseless, Mao Mao's pupils narrowed as he backed away shivering.

"Damn you, you vicious witch!" Mao Mao roared. "How dare you bring that thing here?" Mao Mao's intimidating aura faded little by little as he gradually shrunk in size. Yet he still stood in front of Elder Ling, protecting him.

"Get him, Miu Miu!" she said. The baby kitten nodded and disappeared before suddenly reappearing beside Mao Mao.

She extended her baby kitten claws and shot out a white web, trapping Mao Mao. He was now a little helpless cat ball, and Miu Miu began playing him with an expression of pure joy.

"I'm taking you back to the sect," she said. "You're grounded for a hundred years."

Elder Ling teared up when he heard this. "Can I just do one small thing before going? I only need a couple of hours. It's very important this time, I swear!"

"What could possibly be important in this backwater place?" She sniffed before flying out into the sky at ten times the speed of lightning. Both the frightening Elder Ling and the imposing Mr. Mao Mao were nothing in front of that woman and the kitten. This wasn't the first time they'd escaped, however. They knew resistance was futile.

Protector Song kept his perception expanded in every direction, searching for signs of the two convicts. They weren't even at foundation establishment, so he figured there was only so far they could travel. Meanwhile, the ominous black cloud had precipitated its first bolt of lightning. It would shoot out any minute.

Calamity Lightning? There shouldn't be anyone transcending here in the middle of nowhere. Just what is going on? Of course, it wasn't possible for him to interfere with Heaven's judgment. As long as he didn't enter the lightning's deadly range, no harm would come to him.

His eyes narrowed when he finally saw the area where the

lightning would strike. A young man and his pet fox where sitting in the middle of a strange formation. A white circle surrounded them, and a web protected them from above.

How is this possible? he thought. *Even a Godbeast wouldn't have to overcome a Calamity Lightning to enter Foundation Establishment.*

Still, he had found his quarry. He sat cross-legged in midair just outside the range of the Heavenly Tribulation, waiting for it to end. When he noticed the lightning splitting into two portions, he shook his head derisively.

Alas, I might not even need to act. They'll need a miracle to survive.

Cha Ming gripped his staff tightly as he gazed up at the sinister clouds. They crackled in rage as they prepared to smite down those who dared defy the heavens. The first bolt struck down suddenly, giving Cha Ming barely any time to react before striking the shield of knives. Much of its power dissipated, and the remaining strength of the bolt, which was as thick as a needle, dissipated as soon as it struck the white bubble generated by the circle of protection. He still felt his skin tingle as some residual lightning bathed his body and soul.

He had overcome the first strike without needing to lift a finger, but he knew it wouldn't be so easy from now on. A second bolt of lightning flew down from the heavens. This time, it was two fingers thick. It weakened considerably as it crossed both shields. Cha Ming was ready for this one and struck out at the bolt with his staff. It was an ordinary strike with his Hard Staff Art, but it dissipated a good deal of the lightning's energy. Cha Ming lost all feeling in his body as the lightning traveled through his head and down to his toes. He felt great exhaustion from the bolt, both physically and spiritually.

Still, he readied himself to receive the third bolt. This time, he didn't fool around and increased the weight of his staff to 100 jin. The first part of the test was a battle of endurance, and he needed to waste as little energy as possible. The heavens rumbled for an incense time before accumulating into a lightning bolt as thick as a fist. It was weakened two times consecutively, and Cha Ming used a Quake Staff strike to dissipate the majority of it. This time, however, it took him several breaths to recover his motor functions.

How frightening, he thought. *And Huxian and I will have to fight nine of these?* This part could be considered a warmup. He looked over at Huxian curiously, only to see him yawn as he waited for the next bolt. *Alas, not everyone is created equal.*

The next bolt gathered for a quarter hour before crashing down. It was as thick as a leg, and it caused the formations to tremble as it traveled through them. Cha Ming increased the weight of his staff to 500 jin. He coughed out blood as the bolt struck him, searing several portions of his flesh. He instantly activated Healing Flower Manifestation with his rosary, recovering from the serious wounds. Unfortunately, there was nothing he could do about the charred flesh.

However, he didn't have as much time to recover as he expected. The next bolt came down after a single incense time. This one was as thick as a human body. The air screamed as the lightning passed and struck the shield with full force. Cha Ming manifested a fiery shield atop of himself before barely defending with his staff. The might of the impact finally made him realize the severity of the situation. If the red-bearded man hadn't made these formations, he would have died by now.

One incense time later, the sixth bolt rushed down from the heavens. It roared as it descended, taking the shape of a flood dragon. The lightning flood dragon's power and speed were frighteningly stronger than the last two bolts, and Cha Ming was forced to defend once more. This time, he felt his insides sear as the lightning traveled through him. The formation above them cracked slightly with the latest blow.

Brother, this is bad, Huxian warned. *This was as strong as the final bolt of a Calamity Lightning, and this is only the sixth bolt! I don't think the formations will be able to last for very long. Use everything you have and hang in there.*

Cha Ming focused his eyes on the sky above. His pupils contracted when he saw that the lightning in the sky was no longer white, but red instead. The sky rumbled for three quarters of an hour before a single, finger-thick peal of red lightning struck down four times as fast as the previous one. Cha Ming felt death approach with this bolt of lightning. He didn't hesitate to pour wood qi and fire qi into an Earth Shield Manifestation above him. He increased the weight of his staff to 756 jin and increased the length to double its original. This small bolt of red lightning shattered the top formation as it passed through. It weakened while passing through the circle of protection, but it took Cha Ming's full strength to ward it off. Despite this, he suffered grievous injuries in the process.

Cha Ming gritted his teeth as he noticed that a second peal of red lightning rained down on them half an incense time later. He didn't hesitate to send out 36 pearls in advance as a giant sword. The lightning impacted the circle of protection, shattering it. The sword slightly weakened the lightning before it hit on Cha Ming's earth shield once more, breaking it apart like crumbly bread. Cha Ming used his strongest physical strike to resist once more. He felt his heart stop for a full three breaths before starting up again.

How on earth am I going to resist it? He looked over to Huxian, whose fur was singed. The fox was otherwise all right. He looked toward Cha Ming worriedly.

Don't worry about me, brother, Huxian said. *This last lightning bolt is the least threatening for me. I'll use my powers as a Bagua Fox to first purify then swallow the bolt of lightning. The energy will form the basis of my advancement as a demon beast. Just focus on yourself, and don't hold anything back!*

The last bolt of lightning accumulated for a full hour before coming down. It was a red bolt as thick as a fist. Cha Ming gulped as he saw it rushing down. He was practically helpless without the aid of the formations. Yet he didn't give up. First, he imbued twelve pearls with all five types of qi. They glowed with a white light as they flew into the sky. As the bolt of lightning flew toward him, Cha Ming decisively clenched his fist and detonated the pearls, slightly weakening the bolt in the process. He then threw up thirty-six pearls. They hovered together in a circular formation. As the bolt approached it, he detonated them as well.

Finally, he threw up the last seventy-two pearls. They flew to the sky in a formation that looked very similar to the circle Sun Wukong had drawn. This was a last-ditch effort by Cha Ming, an imitation of the Circle of Protection formation. He had no idea if it would work, but it was worth trying!

The seventy-two pearls glowed brightly as they came together, forming an intricate circle with complex geometric symbols. Cha Ming had imbued them with all his remaining five-element qi, in addition to all of his creation qi. They shuddered as the lightning tore through them, though it had clearly weakened in the process. It only took an instant for them to crack and finally shatter from the power of the red lightning bolt.

Cha Ming looked at the bolt with determination as it came down. He took his 756 jin, 18-foot-long staff and swung it out with perfect timing. The staff struck the bolt with the most power Cha Ming had ever imbued in it. It shook slightly but did not shatter. Instead, it winked out of existence and flew into Cha Ming's body.

Cha Ming stayed calm as the lightning approached. A red lotus brooch on his shirt glowed slightly as it activated its one-time defensive function. This was the brooch that Hong Lai had crafted for Cha Ming as compensation for pointing out a flaw in his craftmanship. It didn't do much to weaken the lightning, but mosquito meat is still meat[15]. The lightning struck Cha Ming square in the chest. He felt intense pain as the lightning devastated his body. His internal organs cooked, and his meridians began burning and tearing.

Blood burst out of his mouth, and he was forced to kneel and catch his breath. Simply existing at this point was pure agony. By his side, he saw Huxian turn into two gigantic foxes, one black and one white. They calmly swallowed the lightning just as he had said. The calamity was now over. The clouds quickly dispersed, and Huxian trotted over to Cha Ming and began licking his wounds. His brother had survived. Barely.

Then there was the sound of clapping.

---

[15] A Chinese saying that means something is better than nothing.

Both Cha Ming and Huxian looked up to see a floating armored figure.

"Congratulations, my friends," the figure said. It's not every day you see someone passing a tribulation prior to entering Foundation Establishment." The figure floated down to the top of the mountain. Cha Ming forced himself to stand up, despite his grievous wounds.

"Does Senior require anything from us?" Cha Ming asked. He understood that people could barely manage to fly at the foundation-establishment realm. But even then they had to use flying swords. This figure didn't use any such treasure.

"Ah, thank you for asking, young friend," the man replied amicably. "You see, Cha Ming, I am here for your life."

Cha Ming paled when he heard this. They were clearly not this man's match, so he struggled to find an answer that could buy them time. It was so unfair. They had survived Heaven's wrath only to be killed by a cultivator.

"Why might you be needing my life, sir? I can't say that I'm acquainted with you," Cha Ming said.

"No, you aren't. But you see, my Young Master Zhou Li's older brother perished recently. The Young Master has determined that you are the culprit. So guilty or not, I must kill you. Any last words?" The armored man drew his sword as he spoke and pointed it toward Cha Ming.

Cha Ming held out his injured left hand and put it on Huxian's head. Then he reached inside his bag of holding and retrieved a badly damaged piece of paper. It was the ruined talisman that he had purchased at the trade meet. After Sun Wukong had laid out the protection formation, Cha Ming was destitute. All his spirit stones, crystalized elemental essence, and ink had been utilized. After using the brooch to defend against the Calamity Lightning, all he had left was this worn-out piece of paper.

Where's all my good luck when I need it? he said to Huxian mentally. *I gave the last of it to Feng Ming, so I can only trust fate will get us through this. Get ready. I'm going to use the talisman. We have a ninety-eight percent chance it's a dud, and a one percent chance of success. If it's the other one percent... at least we'll have a great way to commit suicide.*

The armored man frowned when he saw the talisman but didn't stop them once he saw it in its wretched state. "Are you sure you want to risk using such a wasted object? How about you just give up, and I'll leave you a complete corpse?"

Cha Ming smiled at the man before pouring what remained of his qi and spiritual force into the talisman. "Tell Zhou Li I'll come back to collect our debts."

Protector Song grunted and sent his sword flying toward Cha Ming, aiming to impale him.

Cha Ming felt a small prick on his chest as the sword stabbed into him. But it didn't continue. It was as though time and space had frozen. He tried to communicate with Huxian, but to no avail. Then he noticed the space around him breaking up, piece by piece. A storm of mysterious black energy was heading toward them like a whirlwind.

Cha Ming looked down toward Huxian, who now had an expression of fear in his eyes. The storm of black energy blew them apart, and they flew off into the distance. Cha Ming felt his body being torn apart by the strain. His damaged meridians were being chopped into tiny pieces. He felt his bones shatter and his skin break.

And then his mind went blank.

Epilogue

Zhou Li frowned as he saw the latest note in his little black book. Many messages had popped up over the last few hours since morning. They arrived once the ink on his notebook had faded. He saw many notes about updates to the plan, warnings about potential intruders, and finally, some notes about the failure of the operation in Fairweather.

The latest note he received was the most infuriating. Protector Song had located Du Cha Ming and the little fox. They had just survived a calamity, but they somehow escaped using a heavily damaged spatial-transmission talisman. Who knew if they were dead or alive? Unfortunately, he discovered a few short minutes later that the thread of karma between him and Cha Ming had vanished.

Lightning, the nemesis of karma and evil. What rotten luck I have. What's worse, this confirms my guess. That the little fox is a Godbeast descendent. It now has a second tail, and its growth rate is astonishing. Well, on the bright side, this court case is going well.

Zhou Li continued his plotting and planning as he waited for the court procedures to wrap up.

"Wang Jun, I regret to inform you that your case has been rejected from the highest court with no chance for appeal. The trade laws and regulations in the Song Kingdom are not for you to question, and the termination of the contract was perfectly legitimate." The old judge's announcement didn't surprise Wang Jun.

He calmly looked over to the other side of the room with a pleasant smile on his face. Zhou Li was smirking while engaging in what Wang Jun could only assume was congratulatory small talk.

Smug bastard. He doesn't even know he lost yet.

"However," continued the judge, "I advise the plaintiff and the defendant to note the recent trade agreement and its impacts on matters discussed in court these past few days. Of course, this has no bearing on the current case, as the case was filed before the agreement was made. Court is adjourned."

Wang Jun and his group calmly walked out of the courthouse, past the frowning Zhou Li and his entourage.

"Congratulations on your monumental victory, Zhou Li," Wang Jun said before exiting. He didn't walk for long before he heard a yell from the courthouse.

"Why do you look so happy, Wang Jun? You just lost. Do you know something I don't?" Zhou Li had walked ahead of his entourage and stopped only a few feet from Wang Jun.

Protector Ren began stepping up, but Wang Jun held him back.

"Of course I do," Wang Jun said, still smiling. "You didn't really think I cared about this court case, did you? It was all just a smokescreen to eat up your time. A black cover on a window, or ink on a notebook. Whatever way you want to put it. But since I'm in a charitable mood today, I'll share a bit of information.

"A trilateral trade agreement was just ratified last night by the Song Kingdom's ambassador between the Song Kingdom, the Xia Empire, and the Ming Empire. The Song Kingdom has just agreed to eliminate trade barriers for alchemical products in exchange for the unrestricted trade access to products containing significant portions of soul alloy, blue gold, cold iron, and elemental dust. Therefore, the court results were meaningless. The Song Kingdom Alchemist's Association is now a sinking ship, and you're the captain. Congratulations!"

"Bullshit," Zhou Li spat. "There isn't a vein for any of these products in the kingdom, and these are all highly restricted trade products. The Song Kingdom might have the skill to forge these, but we have no access to raw materials. I refuse to believe that the king would authorize this. I'll make sure the Crown Prince tears this agreement apart."

"Go ahead," Wang Jun said. "Coincidentally, it's no great secret that the Wang family has begun developing a mine for these very products in conjunction with the third prince. We're very happy to be conducting business jointly with the royal family. The mine is located near Greatwood Bridge. But you should already be *very* familiar with that area, shouldn't you?"

Wang Jun walked away calmly after saying these words. He was in a very good mood. His obstruction had been successful, his trade deals had been established, and Zhou Li was now extremely upset. This was all small news, of course. After all, he had just divined the fate of his dear friend before arriving at court.

Cha Ming was alive.

Gong Lan dragged her feet as she hopped off a wagon and entered Green Leaf City. She felt so tired, so empty. Something was missing from her life, but she just couldn't put her finger on it.

Oh well, she thought. *I'll go see Brother. He always knows how to cheer me up.*

Feng Ming had entered the city at the same time. Apparently, he needed to report to his father as quickly as possible. It was understandable but tedious. She sighed as she realized that there were many tedious things she should do soon. Like eating and showering. She didn't like showering. It washed away her natural fragrance, covering it with smelly perfumes and herbs.

She continued walking lifelessly down the street. A few blocks down the road, she bumped into a young street urchin, who was sent flying a few feet backward as a result of their collision.

Whatever, that's his problem. He should look where he's going.

Suddenly she realized that her belt pouch was missing. In a flash, she appeared beside the young street urchin and pressed her saber to his cheek. A dribble of blood leaked out from the small cut.

"You should watch where you're going!" she said in a

heated manner. The street urchin gulped and kowtowed in apology. "All right, all right. Leave the belt pouch, stop robbing, and scram!" she said. After dropping the pouch, the little boy scampered off in the distance and didn't look back.

All of a sudden, she felt refreshed. She began running off toward her brother's place. Several people on the streets gave her a quick nod as she flashed past. Life was wonderful. Or was it?

Fatigue hit her once again like a sack of bricks. *Is it excitement that's missing from my life?* She limped a few more blocks before sitting down on a bench to rest. Just in front of her, she saw several people moving barrels of wine into a bar nearby.

"Liu Bai, make sure you get me the thirty-year barrel next. I need to stick it in the back of the cellar," an older man said from behind a large cart.

"Are you sure? It's a little awkward to get to you. How about you wait until we get a few barrels out?" a younger man asked.

"No need. Just pass it over the rest. I'll catch it," the old man replied. The younger man complied and began rolling the barrel.

Gong Lan rolled her eyes as she saw the scene. They were practically begging to get hurt.

Predictably, the young man tumbled as he struggled to push the barrel over a few others. The barrel clanked down the ramp, and the old man screamed as he was pinned between the barrel of wine and the earth. The momentum ensured that it rolled over his face, leaving him with a crushed, bloody nose.

Gong Lan's heart thumped when she saw the scene. She felt her emotions stirring, like life was worth living. She looked at the scene painted in red. It was *beautiful.*

That was when she realized why she was down. *It's not excitement I'm missing,* she thought. *It's blood.* She had chased after power and lost herself in the process.

Feng Ming was standing at attention in front of his father. The latter was massaging his temples as he read the report. It only took him an incense time to finish.

"In short, you discovered a sinister plot and escaped miraculously. Then, instead of reporting to your commanding officer, you ignored the chain of command and fled to Green Leaf City to report to me, your father. *Then*, when you were ambushed halfway, you didn't even bother to finish your report and rushed back to the city. According to the report, you saved the situation. You even brought a letter of recommendation from Zhang Yifeng, the master alchemist in Fairweather, or what's left of it." Feng Ming's father paused for a moment before affirming the obvious.

"You're a terrible scout," he concluded.

"I realize that, but—" Feng Ming started, only to be interrupted by his father.

"No buts! You should have done your duty. It's not like you're a commando or anything. You're just a soldier, and soldiers follow orders. Now, how to deal with reporting this to your commander..."

Feng Ming sweated while he waited for his father's decision. By all rights, he should be court martialed for his insubordination. However, he had performed great merit and should be rewarded. All he could hope for was that these canceled each other out.

"I've got it!" his father suddenly exclaimed. "The perfect reward, and the perfect punishment. I'm going to recommend to your commander that, in light of the circumstances, you decided to do what's best for the kingdom. However, since you did break military protocol, the merit for this will cancel itself out. Now, the problem is that the general is a stickler for order in his army. You can't stay there. So I'll request that you be transferred to a good friend of mine. He loves crazy people like you."

Feng Ming trembled when he heard this. "Which good friend might you be talking about?" he asked.

"Colonel Long Ping," he replied. "Commanding officer of the Special Forces."

A young girl wearing a large cloak was trotting down the road at night on an old brown horse. It was exhausted, but so was she. Besides, where would they stop to rest if they had no money? Running away was hardly the smartest thing Hong Xin had ever done. However, *anything* was better than facing her friends and family.

"Little brown," she whispered, "it looks like I'm going to have to sell you. Otherwise we'll both starve." The horse couldn't understand, of course. It was just a regular farm horse.

"I wish I wasn't so useless," she said aloud. "I wish I was brave like Gong Lan, smart like Wang Jun, and strong like

Cha Ming." Unfortunately, this didn't seem to be her lot in life. Being abandoned by Wang Jun had been a crushing blow to her self esteem.

She looked into her purse and noted the contents: twenty pieces of silver, her purple hair clip, and a few days' worth of dried rations. A night's stay at an inn would cost her five pieces of silver, but then she wouldn't be able to keep running for very long.

Perhaps I'll find a stack of hay we can rest on. She didn't know where she was going, but one thing was certain: She would find her place in life or die trying.

Dawn.

A small fox licked his lips as he saw a nearby spirit wolf walking toward his small cave dwelling with a dead spirit rabbit in its jaws. It was Huxian's first day in the area, and he had luckily stumbled upon the perfect temporary dwelling as he recovered from his wounds. Heck, it even came with servants!

The wolf placed the fresh prey in front of Huxian and then backed away with his head down. It didn't turn around until it left Huxian's line of sight.

The nice thing about these servants is that I only had to beat up one of them and they all came begging to serve. So what if that wolf was a little bigger than the rest? He sighed and shook his head in contempt. *Spirit beasts nowadays have no self respect.*

He bit down on the chunk of raw meat while wagging his two tails. It wasn't very filling, but it was better than nothing.

Besides, he wasn't in peak shape. The space storm had broken several of his bones and cut up his flesh quite badly. He figured it would take a few months until he fully recovered.

I wonder how Cha Ming is doing? he wondered. *I know he's still alive, but he was almost dead even before he used the talisman. The transmission function didn't even activate. Rather, the talisman created a spatial storm and sent us both god knows where. If only I wasn't so weak.*

Unfortunately, there was nothing that could be done besides recovering and finding out where he was. And what that dreadful presence was at the peak of the mountain.

Yep, it's better to lay low for now.

It was a beautiful, sunny day in the Ming Empire. The fertile plains at the base of the mountains were filled with droves of farmers and oxen. It was the fourth day of spring, and according to local tradition, this was the best time to plant crops. The poor farmers would spend the next week planting like their lives depended on it. Farming had always been an unforgiving occupation, and everyone whose livelihood depended on it scrambled to obtain all the luck they could get.

The children were tasked with drawing water from the village, loading it onto oxen so that it could be delivered and poured on the freshly planted seeds. Hundreds of children traveled to and from the nearby river. This large river came from a nearby mountain chain. It passed by the smaller mountains and gathered water from tributary rivers. Given it massive size, it was no wonder that they didn't see the figure of a naked man as he was washed downstream.

The young man was somehow holding onto a large log, despite being unconscious. He was riddled with cuts and covered in black burns. It was a miracle he was still alive. Despite his injuries, he continued floating past one village after another. Every so often, his eye would twitch.

Like this, Cha Ming continued to flow downstream toward an unknown destination. As he traveled, he dreamed of friendship and adventure, of a journey in the spirit woods. He dreamed of finding the Clear Sky Brush and sparring with the Monkey King.

Eventually he fell down a steep waterfall. He surfaced soon after, somehow having survived the fall and the rocks below. He washed up on shore where he was discovered by a few young children. They tried to wake him, but they couldn't. He was having a nightmare, one that wouldn't let him escape. In the nightmare, there were devils and angels. There was a final battle, and jade eyes with orange pupils.

There were mountains of jade and a throne of bones, and finally, a blood-red moon.

— End Book 2 —

Acknowledgments

As I continue to write, I find that this list of acknowledgments grows. There are far too many people to thank— if I missed you, I'm sorry. It wasn't intentional. Just like before, I would like to acknowledge my wife and parents, who continue to encourage me on my journey in writing this novel series.

Likewise, thanks go to my two brothers and my sister. More specifically, thank you to Denis, who has finally started reading the series after much persuasion. Levi will fall in line eventually.

Thank you to all my friends once again. I recently took some time off work to focus on writing, and after talking to them, I'm convinced that I've made the right decision. Thank you to Dave for once again beta reading Book 2. And once again, thank you to my friend Usama, who is now a recurring character in my prologues.

Many thanks to Crystal Watanabe for her excellent support while editing my novel. My writing continues to improve with her help, so I'm glad to have her on board. Thank you Samuel Alves for the excellent cover remake.

Thank you, Tinalyngue, author of Blue Phoenix, for your continued coaching. I've avoided many pitfalls due to your help. I would also like to thank Deathblade (currently translating A Will Eternal by Er Gen) and Tinalynge from wuxiaworld.com for their shout-outs. Thank you to my patrons, who fund me and believe in me. They are a great encouragement as I continue writing. Finally, thank you to my readers. I write to tell stories to people, and a story is worth nothing if it isn't shared.

About the Author

Patrick Georges Laplante was born in a small town in the Canadian prairies in 1987. He began publishing *Painting the Mists* online under the pseudonym RedMirage in January 2018.

An engineer by trade, he graduated from the University of Alberta in 2009 and completed his master's degree in 2011. While writing and engineering have little in common, he actively utilizes his experiences and attention to detail in fleshing out a vivid world and answering the "whys," which are often left unanswered in Xianxia fiction.

As an avid vegan, he aims to prompt internal reflection in his readers through various themes like non-violence, choice, and begging the question: Is personhood restricted to humanity? And what is proper conduct, morality, and love?

His work is inspired by a combination of Western fiction, *Dungeons and Dragons*, Chinese web novels, and various Japanese, Korean, and Chinese comics and illustrated novels.

A Note to Readers

If you've enjoyed this book, I would greatly appreciate it if you left a rating on the site where you purchased it. Ratings lead to credibility in this competitive marketplace, and by leaving one, you signal to the world that this book is worth reading.

As some of you might know, I release each book as I write it. It wasn't necessary for you to buy this book, but your support is greatly appreciated. If you are so inclined, you can continue reading as I write at:

https://royalroadl.com/fiction/16320/painting-the-mists.

I can't promise fully edited or proofread content, but I will do my best to continue maintaining frequent and high-quality releases.

If you would like to be notified of any book releases, please follow me on Facebook or Twitter.

Facebook: https://www.facebook.com/RedMiragePtM/
Twitter: @RedMirage_PtM